Dragon Sect

Book 2 of the Highcliff Guardians

A Soul Forge Universe Story

Dragon Sect is dedicated to Extend-a-Family Kingston. Thank you for the difference you make in the lives of so many.

I wish to personally thank Extend-a-Family Kingston participant, Ben Myers. Ben named the dragon, Keaf—an acronym for: Kingston Extend-a-Family.

As a side note: because of Ben's dragon name, a second dragon name was born. Keaf's father became Kingstone.

Artwork in the Highcliff Guardians

I include pieces of artwork in all my books as I believe the images provide the reader with a more intimate connection to the characters in my stories.

Interior Art in Order of Appearance

1. Miragan and Ouderling by Richard H. Stephens: www.richardhstephens.com

2. Ouderling, Miragan, Jyllana, and Dagomar by Richard H. Stephens: www.richardhstephens.com

3. Scale and Zorain by Richard H. Stephens: www.richardhstephens.com

4. Braen Wys

5. Ouderling and Keaf by Aklat Cover Design: www.facebook.com/aklatcovers

6. Cassava by Covered by Nicole

Acknowledgements

Dragon Sect is book 2 in the Highcliff Guardians Series. This book would not be possible without the invaluable input of my editors, Caroline Davidson and Joshua Stephens. Your attention to detail refines the magic in my stories.

I would like to give credit to Aklat Covers, and Melony Paradise for giving *Dragon Sect* such a beautiful cover.

A special note of gratitude goes out to Stan White, whose poem, Ars Poetica, has given a magical touch to the storyline. (stanjwhite.com)

As in most of my books, I appreciate the people who name dragons and characters in my books. Thank you for enhancing the story with a touch of you.

Aaron's Opinion Podcast, for naming the dwarf, Ohz
Allyson VanDellen, for naming the dragon, Atsila
Ben Myers, for naming the dragon, Keaf
Brenda Allen, for naming the dragon, Unniass
Jennifer Schlag, for naming the dragon, Danzinnia
Lambert Cook, for naming the dragons, Qinora, and Dagomar
Melissa Sharp, for naming the dragon, Zorain
Mikhail Roberts, for naming the dragon, Athgaan
Misty Cummings, for naming the wyvern, Miragan, and the dragon, Hyperion
Victoria Jadrych, for naming the dragon, Dawnbreaker

And finally, a heartfelt thank you to **Mike MacCumber**, for naming the wyvern, Sarafinious. I met Mike while signing books at a local market. Here's to Sara, whose spirit left our world to fly with the faeries much too soon.

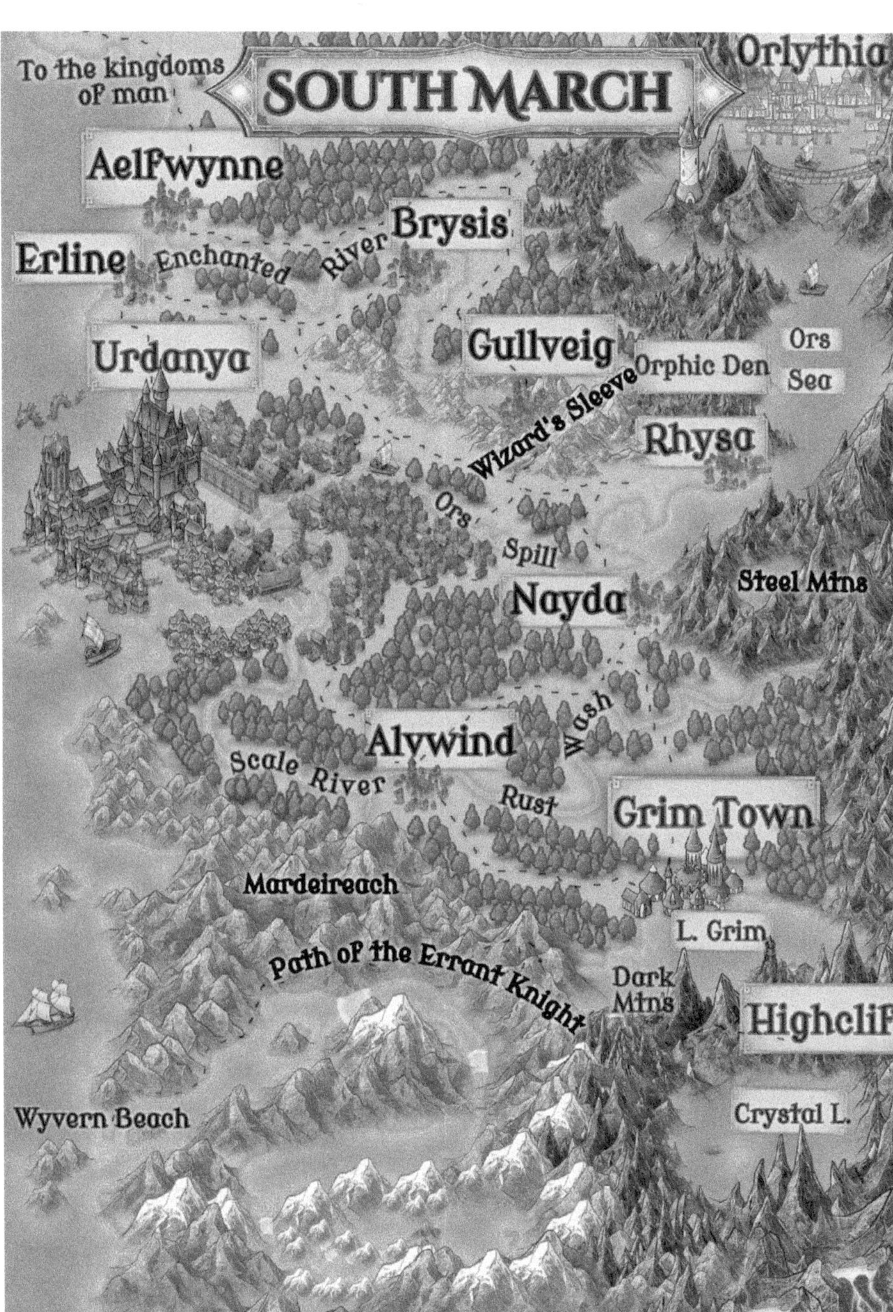

To the kingdoms of man
SOUTH MARCH
Orlythia
Aelfwynne
Brysis
Erline
Enchanted
River
Gullveig
Ors Sea
Orphic Den
Urdanya
Wizard's Sleeve
Rhysa
Ors
Spill
Nayda
Steel Mtns
Wash
Alywind
Scale River
Rust
Grim Town
Mardeireach
L. Grim
Path of the Errant Knight
Dark Mtns
Highcliff
Wyvern Beach
Crystal L.

Table of Contents

Ars Poetica

I write of stars,
and of the infinity behind mirrors,
and of the inconsequence of trifles.

I write in the sound of the sea in shells,
and of the crescendo of silence
in the light of an eye in the deep of sleep.

I write between a memory and a forget,
in the fading half-light at the end of days,
and upon the eve of every eve.

I write in the epilogues of myths,
of where the seaward runes once told
of when a never is born and a forever ends.

I write of where an echo fades,
in the touch of a lover's hand,
and of where a rainbow strays.

I write in the idiom of daydreamed days,
and in the sounds of tip toes in the night,
and wake to a chorister of birds singing.

I write in the loneliness of distant mountains,
and in the thirsts of desert sands
craving the tranquility of still waters.

I write in the confusion of happening
that the startled pheasant takes into the air.

I write of a shoe that has never stepped,
and of the hem of the emperor's clothes,
and the weight of a sadness and a regret.

I write in the feeling of falling fast,
and in the sea-saw of the tides.

I write in the crevices of dawns,
and in the drone of the mumble bees,
and of where a fall of wood smoke goes.

I write in the synonym of time,
and of the night side of the moon,
and in the breath of fairy kneeling flowers.

I write of stars.

~Sir Stanley White, Zephyr Knight~

Dragon Sect

Braen Wys looked up from where he read under the flickering glow of a solitary candle. Something wasn't right.

He gazed around his spacious sleeping quarters in search of the cause of the disturbance. Other than the storm raging outside the bay window beside him, he was met with tomb-like silence. As was to be expected. High in the western wing of Urdanya Castle, he wasn't likely to hear anything in the middle of the night, besides the movement of the Sea Guard patrolling the grand hallways outside his royal chambers.

The only thing he could attribute to the unmistakable sense of foreboding gripping him was that his mother, Princess Odyne, was probably dabbling with her dark magic again.

He shook his head. Returning his attention to the old tome in his lap, he found he couldn't concentrate on the text. His mother would never change. What she thought to gain by disturbing forces she had no business delving into, he had no idea.

Unlike her discontented brother in the south, Odyne no longer cared for her place in the succession to the Willow Throne. By happenstance, her twin sister had been born a few moments before her, but ever since Odyne had discovered her gift for summoning things that were better left alone, she no longer desired that seat.

Odyne occupied the Sea Throne, presiding primarily over Urdanya—a great coastal city harbouring half the elven population of South March in and around its sprawling borders. That was good enough for her. Should banners ever be called, those loyal to Odyne's benevolent, if somewhat bizarre, rule would outnumber the troops of Khae and Orlythe combined.

Fortunately, Braen mused, his mother preferred to be left to her own devices. To pursue her own interests. *Unfortunately*, her activities left him feeling extremely uncomfortable more often than not. Someday, she would go too far. Cross one line too many. When that happened, he didn't want to be anywhere near her. Or Urdanya Castle for that matter. Though he would never wish her harm, he secretly hoped that someday soon one of her spells would backfire badly enough to scare her away from unsettling dark things that should not be disturbed. Knowing she preferred to practice these rituals at night, often made sleep difficult to come by.

Tonight was one of those nights. Accompanying the slashing rain battering the multi-paned bay window, a cold draft whistled through the imperfect molding, threatening to extinguish his candle yet again. He doubted sleep would come until the morn.

He sighed and opened the tome to where the frayed, golden ribbon marked his page. Allowing himself to be soothed by the lovely verse, thoughts of his mother eased from the forefront of his mind as the written words flowed softly past his lips,

Dragon Sect

He blinked and looked up, marvelling at the imagery the verse evoked. Always the dreamer, he frequently wondered of foreign lands and the adventures awaiting anyone brave enough to put aside the notion that the elven kingdom of South March was superior to other realms. Oh, what wonders were there to be had in the infinity beyond the mirrors of society's reproach?

If only he had the fortitude to stand up to his mother and demand she reconsider the vow she had made him swear. A promise reluctantly entered into out of fear of reprisal should he not bow to her overbearing perception of the greater world.

Considering the text his pointer finger traced across the yellowed page, he found it hard to imagine that the kingdom of man was as callous as the elven people were led to believe.

Dragon Sect

How could anyone capable of inking such thought-provoking words be as barbaric as he had been taught?

He closed the tome and ran a finger over the flaking, golden letters of the author's name carved into the leather cover. A *man's* name, no less!

Sir Stanley White, Zephyr Knight

Why, even the name was poetic.

He swallowed despite the fact he was alone. He would be well-advised not to let anyone know he possessed such a book.

The dark wood cabinetry in the bed chamber lit up as the lignite sky flashed several times in a row; the brilliance too bright to have been lightning unless it had struck the castle somewhere near by. He cringed in anticipation of the thunder that never came.

Almost afraid to get closer to the window, Braen put the tome on a table beside his chair and worked up the courage. Swallowing his unease, he leaned into the space provided by the bay window, searching the sullen night. Grey silhouettes of Urdanya Castle's ramparts were visible through the downpour far below the level of his quarters. Though unable to see them, he knew the Witch Watch would be huddled around braziers inside the many wall towers carved into the natural stone of the keep.

A sudden flash made him jump. Even before he looked north to the pinnacle of a lone tower that rose stark against the sky in defiance of the storm, his worst fear was realized. It hadn't been lightning.

Partially obscured by a roiling mass of storm clouds, Sea Witch's Sceptre rose from the dark rock along the jagged shoreline to penetrate the sky's low ceiling.

Only visible when illuminated by unnatural bursts of light, the octagonal top of the highest tower of Urdanya Castle rested upon a spire of grey rock. Legend claimed the Sea

Dragon Sect

Witch Sceptre had been carved out of the mountain peak that had once dominated the shoreline north of the Ors Spill. The daunting pillar connected to Urdanya Castle by an open-air, arched causeway, a few hundred feet above the crashing surf unseen below the sweep of the castle's thick ramparts.

Braen covered his face with an upraised arm as another series of flashes reflected off various, slick rock faces. He leaned back into the room—an eerie sensation turning his skin cold. His mother was conjuring something big. And that likely meant something dangerous.

Though he had no idea how he knew, know he did. If he didn't get up there fast and intervene, he had a sixth sense that she was about to summon her own demise. Grabbing his grease-smeared, leather slicker, he threw open the outer door of his chamber and charged through the labyrinth of granite-walled corridors. Several Witch Watch stationed along the hallways of the vast royal wing gave chase.

Not encumbered by the heavy armour of the Watch, Braen outdistanced the elven guard appointed with his well-being. He rolled his eyes at the thought. More likely they were assigned to ensure he didn't do anything without his mother's consent.

The arched causeway to Sea Witch Sceptre was accessed by a set of massive iron doors designed to be barred from the outside. As high up the castle walls as the causeway stood, Braen had to descend several flights of steps hewn out of bedrock to access it from the royal wing.

Built from a lone mountain, Urdanya Castle was a marvel of dwarven ingenuity. Aside from decorative fountains and several walkways added after the fact, the colossal edifice had been sculpted out of the living rock—hammered, chiselled, and shaped by master craftsmen long before the seeds had been sewn to establish the sovereign realm of South March.

Luckily, Princess Odyne hadn't seen fit to bar the causeway doors—something she had been known to do in the past. That simple fact niggled at Braen as he took the full brunt of the storm ravaging the west coast full in the face. Perhaps tonight would be the night his mother went too far.

Soaked in an instant, despite the protection offered by his outer garments, he staggered against the eastern edge of the causeway—its stone bed arched over a seething torrent of water spilling around the castle's northern flank. He had to bend low to grab the knee-high bulwark lining the span to keep from being thrown over the brink and dashed against the rocks far below.

In a fit of stops and starts, Braen dashed across the causeway, fearing his next step might be his last. Upon reaching the wet stone pillar that comprised the Sea Witch Sceptre, he glanced back the way he had come. If the Witch Watch followed, there was no evidence of their presence.

Another metal door barred his passage, this one a singular entranceway, smaller than those exiting the castle. It resisted his push.

Worried he might inadvertently set off wards his mother was known to employ, he took several calming breaths to settle his hammering heart. Tapping into his elven magic, he examined the steel barrier and surrounding stone but found no such hindrances. With any luck, she had simply locked it. A means to keep out most anyone but those possessing a magical aptitude.

He looked skyward, squinting against the persistent drizzle lashing sideways in the wind. It was hard to make out anything in the misty darkness, but as he stared, the clouds around the spire's summit flashed three times, illuminated by whatever magical forces were being unleashed up there.

Guided by an extension of his magic, he reached through the metal slab and manipulated the mechanism on the opposite side of the door. The lock opened without incident. A cursory glance across the causeway, its peaked midsection obscured by a sudden increase in the rainfall, informed him he was alone.

Dragon Sect

Faint light flicked from somewhere beyond the first bend in the steep steps ascending through the otherwise solid stone interior of the tower. A tunnel-like stairwell climbed in no apparent semblance of uniformity—as if following the path of a drunken artisan through the rock. Limited by the tight confines to only take one step at a time, he didn't relish a large person having to ascend the Sea Witch Sceptre.

The climb tonight took longer than usual. Whether due to his tiredness, or the fear of what he was about to walk in on, Braen couldn't say. His thighs screamed long before he reached what he had always referred to as 'cloud level.'

Rounding the last bend, the dark stairwell flickered. The door to the octagonal chamber he had visited many times before stood ajar. Another peculiarity when it came to dealing with the summoning of whatever his mother was up to. If she *were* conjuring spirits from another plane, be they Fae or darker still, she would never have been so careless. The chamber walls acted as a containment field. According to Odyne's teachings, a breach of any kind could result in an unenviable creature escaping into the real world.

He slowed his advance, listening carefully as he snuck up to the door, hugging the inside curvature of the tunnel. Standing on the last two steps, he became aware of a deep cold that wafted through the gap between the metal door and the granite doorjamb. It was like his mother had summoned an ice demon.

Braen swallowed. What if she had? And if so, why had she left the door open?

Beside him, a small, wooden door led off the tight landing—barring access to a storage closet carved into the centre of the pillar. He had often retrieved items for his mother in there. Barely big enough to stand upright inside, the storage area held tallow, parchment, unguents, and other supplies used in the casting of spells. Witch's spells! Elven magic didn't require the aid of earthly materials.

Leaning forward he tried to see into the chamber, but aside from a tall window facing him from the other side of the room, nothing appeared to be out of the ordinary.

The room beyond the door flashed again. Once. Twice. Three times.

Unsure how to proceed, Braen covered his eyes and hesitated. To disturb her once she had begun a ritual was a dangerous proposition. If he threw off her concentration at a critical juncture in the spellcasting, there was a very real possibility that she would lose control of whatever she had summoned—not to mention the punishment he would receive as a result.

He had half a mind to ease the door closed, slink back down the steps, and leave well enough alone, but a deep-throated laugh stopped him. One that couldn't have originated from his mother.

The ensuing shriek, however, did.

"Who are you?" Odyne Wys' raspy voice inquired. "How did you get up here?"

Braen swallowed. Someone had snuck into the chamber with his mother. Someone she didn't know.

He eased the door open a little further, absently berating himself for not bringing a weapon. Not the most physical of elves, without his rapier, he would be useless if he had to defend her. He raised his eyebrows at that. He'd likely have to defend the intruder from her.

"You're ruining everything!" Odyne lamented from where she stood beside a slab of granite in the middle of the room; a large tome open between two thick candles on its surface. She raised sticklike arms; nondescript, red robes hanging from her slight form. "Stay away from me!"

Movement beyond his mother drew Braen's attention. Clad in long, black robes that appeared to hover just off the floor, a figure moved toward Odyne, seemingly unconcerned by her warning shout.

Energy crackled along Odyne's fingers and leapt across the space between them.

The figure hidden beneath a ratty cowl met Odyne's attack with raised fingers of his own—the skeletal hands making Braen shudder.

A voice sounding of metal grating on metal cackled back at her, "Or what, princess? You're but a puppet in the grand scheme of things. A means to an end."

Braen cowered on the threshold, crouching so as not to be seen. Had his mother summoned this…this creature? For surely it could not be an elf. At least not one that was alive.

Red pin pricks of light intensified from within the shadows of its cowl. "Your death will set into motion the downfall of South March and give rise to a power the world has never known."

Odyne's magical attack crackled and sparked as it crept up the intruder's sleeves, its effectiveness fizzling out before it reached the creature's shoulders.

Braen searched the room, looking for a weapon of opportunity, but other than books and small candleholders, there were none to be had. An odd tingling crept along his skin. A sensation he had fought against for as long as he could remember. He shook his head, struggling to subdue the curse of his birthright.

Odyne stepped around the stone table, putting it between herself and the creature—its back to the only door in the chamber.

Braen stepped into the room. Left with no other choice, he was going to have to physically subdue the creature.

His mother's eyes widened as they found his. She shook her head, warning him not to interfere. Emitting a loud shriek, she spoke words unintelligible to him and loosed another volley of energy, the blast so intense that blue arcs sizzled errantly around the chamber, striking tomes, and impacting the ground and stone ceiling.

Dragon Sect

Braen backstepped onto the landing, covering his head with his arms, afraid he was about to be hit by his mother's discharge. He stumbled onto his backside and tumbled a few steps before he arrested a potentially fatal fall down the steep flight.

"Your witchery is useless against me, Odyne," the intruder growled. "You should never have forsaken your brother. Together you two could have rid the realm of Nyxa's spawn corrupting the Willow Throne. Prepare to face the consequences of your short-sightedness."

Braen fought to right himself in the tight stairwell, his tangled limbs making it difficult to keep from falling farther.

"Your death is but the second of three. Soon, your brother will ascend the Willow Throne. When that happens, South March will fall into a chaos it hasn't known since the arrival of the great wyrm."

A high-pitched scream pierced Braen's skull and then everything went quiet.

"Give my regards to your niece," the creature rasped after a few moments of eerie silence.

A dull thud came from the chamber. Wild with fear and disbelief, Braen pulled himself upright. He wasn't a seasoned elf, but neither was he naïve. The significance of the thud could only mean one thing. The tingling beneath his skin intensified.

A soft chuckle emanated from beyond the doorway. "Now to deal with your sister."

Too afraid to fight or run, Braen slipped into the storage cubby and pulled the door closed, trying hard to keep his limbs from trembling and his heavy breathing from giving him away. He examined his fingers, fearful that his latent magic might stir. Afraid it would give him away.

A waft of cold air slipped under the door. He shivered. Though not certain, he imagined his heart had stopped momentarily during the agonizing moments it took him to realize the creature had passed his hiding spot and departed the Sea Witch Sceptre.

A long while elapsed before he could gather the courage to leave the sanctuary the closet offered.

It was nearly dawn when he reached the bottom of the mystic tower—the body of his mother draped over his shoulder. He had to pause several times on the way down to step over corpses of the Witch Watch who had tried to come to their aid.

Dragon Sect

Consequential Decisions of State

Borreraig Palace was a beautiful place to behold during the rebirth brought on by the late winter thaw. Though not known for its appreciable snowfall, the northern regions of South March had suffered an extended period of extreme cold—conditions usually unheard of above the Rust Wash.

Amongst the many inconveniences precipitated by the unprecedented weather, the royal gardens at Borreraig Palace had been devastated, rendering Khae's ritual of enjoying an early morning reprieve from the pressures of state with her husband almost obsolete.

After last year's tragic incidents in the south, spurred on by her brother's blatant flaunting of his relentless desire to expand the elven borders into the barbaric lands of man and who knew what else thrived beyond the kingdoms north of the natural divide known as the Undying Wall, Khae had been kept busy mending the crown's tenuous relations with the southern duchy, and indeed that of Orphic Den.

Backed by High Wizard Aelfwynne and a dozen dragons, Khae had accepted Sagora's apology for his attitude with regard to her request for aid from the wizards' guild. Though she knew the headmaster of Gullveig did so under duress, Khae had left the Wizard's Sleeve content in the knowledge that she hadn't allowed the arrogant wizard's slight from last year to go unanswered. She had made it clear to the headmaster that the 'Queen's Law,' took precedence over any pact signed by her dearly departed mother or that of the deceased warlock, Gullveig.

And yet, Khae wasn't naïve. She knew full well that for as long as Aelfwynne occupied the highest magic office in the land, Orphic Den would never willingly assist the crown without the added encouragement of the few remaining majestic creatures watching over the Crystal Cavern.

After the Battle at the Gate, half of the dragon population had flown north, following the young upstart, Demonic. Rumours pointed to the rogue dragons flying well beyond the Undying Wall to an unknown destination. Certainly not in search of Grimclaw—unless they had gone to do battle with the self-proclaimed leader of dragonkind.

Khae fingered the buds of regrowth, trying hard to still her rambling thoughts—thinking not for the first time how she wished fate hadn't determined that she was Nyxa's firstborn daughter.

She took a quick intake of breath, recalling the horrific news she had received on her way back to Gullveig after the trouble with her brother's human wizard. Her sister had been murdered. In her own castle! Odyne's life taken by what her son, Braen, had described as a wraith.

Khae shuddered. Her sister had fallen victim to the very same phantasm who had visited her all those months ago beneath the palace. The creature that, according to Orlythe, had subverted his human wizard and had tried to kill Ouderling. Would have succeeded, in fact, if not for High Wizard Aelfwynne's intervention—not once, but twice.

Since then, there had been no news of the dreadful creature. She clung to the futile hope that the Dragon Witch Wraith, for that was who Aelfwynne had claimed it was all those months ago in his warning letter, had returned to wherever it had hidden since the formation of South March. She would worry about its imminent return until the day the high wizard found a way to retrieve his talisman from wherever it had been hidden away. Until the Staff of Reckoning could be located, Highcliff would be no match for the wraith should it ever find a way to overcome the bane the Crystal Cavern had over it.

"There you are."

Khae stiffened but smiled at the king's approach.

"Why didn't you wake me?"

Khae shrugged. "You were snoring comfortably, and I knew it would be cold out. I didn't want to disturb you."

"Don't be silly. I'm only disturbed when you're not with me." Hammas kissed her on the lips and moved in behind to hold her in his arms and lean his chin on her shoulder, examining the lilac bush before them. "Looks like it survived."

She leaned her head against his and covered his clasped hands where they rested just below her stomach. "They're hardy plants. Take more than cold to keep them from coming back."

"You ready for another interesting day?"

She laughed and broke free of his hold to face him, not wishing to dwell on the drudgery of petitions. "Yay. I wonder what they'll complain about today?"

Visibly shivering in the lightening hours of dawn, Hammas replied, "Probably going to ask when we're going to bring the heat back."

Khae rolled her eyes but couldn't forget the sense of foreboding that had kept her awake for most of the night. "No doubt."

"What's the matter?"

She had to hand it to him. Though usually uninterested in most things that went on around him, she knew Hammas was intuitively aware of her feelings. Not wanting to bother him this early in the day, she said, "Nothing."

Hammas' knowing grin spoke volumes. "Come on. I know you better than that."

"The crops," she lied.

He mulled that over.

Judging by his look, he didn't believe her. Whatever had taken hold of the farmlands had been every bit as devastating as the farmer had feared that fateful day a raven had flown into Orlythia with news of the attempt on Ouderling's life.

He tilted his head. "I'm thinking that's not what's troubling you."

Sensing her discomfort, she knew he wouldn't let it go. Grasping his hands, she kept her eyes lowered, unsure of how to begin. It was a conversation she had been meaning to have with him for a while now, but had been loath to bring it up. Not sure how to say it without provoking his ire, she decided it best to just blurt it out. "I must go to Urdanya."

Hammas blinked several times, a frown accentuating the lines on his face. "Urdanya? What would make you want to go there?"

"Braen."

"Braen? Why? What's happened? Is he alright?"

She smiled sadly. "Oh, he's fine as far as I know."

"Then why go?"

She sighed, attempting to find a way to put words to how she felt. She raised an eyebrow. "Can you imagine Ouderling assuming the Willow Throne if something were to happen to us today?"

His frown deepened as he attempted to respond but nothing escaped his hanging jaw. A deep shudder wracked his body.

"Exactly!" Khae squeezed his hands. "Braen's not much older than Ouderling. I can't imagine what he's going through."

Hammas thought about it. After a while he nodded. "Yes, I'm sure it's not easy for him, but it's his responsibility. Besides, he's only looking after a city. It's not like—"

"A city with a population that equals the rest of the land!" Khae interrupted more emphatically than she meant to. She released his hands and sighed. "This business with the wraith isn't over. I'm not sure where it went, but my communion with nature's essence tells me something dark is coming again. Sooner than we think if I have the right of it."

"Then why go to Urdanya? If what you fear is true, you'll be in danger travelling halfway across the realm." His face ashen, he added under his breath, "Especially in that forsaken den of lawlessness."

Khae didn't know how to sum up the insecurity she had experienced ever since the day the dragons had turned on her host and slain several hundred elves upon the Bascule Plains. For months, her thoughts had swirled with what-ifs about how she could have dealt with the situation in a more efficient manner. Scenario after unsatisfactory scenario had assailed her, plaguing her thoughts during the deepest part of most every night afterward, disturbing her sleep—many times causing her to jerk awake in a cold sweat.

So preoccupied by how badly the turn of events had gone, she had even braved the perils of Grim Watch Tower on a weekly basis whenever the weather permitted—escorted by

Home Guard handpicked by her ever-vigilant husband, of course.

Her sojourn to the dark tower had provided glimpses of what was to come if the wraith were to return, but after dispatching Odyne last year, it had simply disappeared. That, in and of itself, was bad enough—leaving her looking over her shoulder at the strangest of times. But it was her fear for Ouderling living so far away from Borreraig Palace that had sapped the shrinking amount of fortitude she desperately tried to cling to. Should something happen to the heir to the Willow Throne, Khae didn't think she could carry on living.

She swallowed, her eyes on the verge of spilling tears. "I can't explain it in a way that you would understand."

Hammas' face darkened.

"Hear me out," she pleaded with a breaking voice. "My communion with the Fae is never straightforward. I honestly think they're trying to warn me that not everything is right in Urdanya. Something sinister conspires to usurp the Sea Throne, and that we cannot allow. Should someone gain control of the city's population and turn it against us, our rule will be sorely tested. If Urdanya's numbers are mobilized, we'll be hard put to defend ourselves." She sniffed and wiped at her eyes, lowering her voice, and looking away. "We certainly won't receive support from Grim Town." *Nor from Gullveig,* she thought, but kept that to herself.

"Then I'm coming with you."

"No!"

"What do you mean, no? I'm coming. End of discussion."

Khae sighed. "No. You are not."

Hammas opened his mouth to launch into one of his rare tirades, but she held a warning finger between them. "If something happens while I'm away, I need you here to make sure the proper action is taken." She raised her eyebrows.

"You're the ultimate head of the army. Should it require mobilization, it'll happen quicker under your command."

Hammas' chest heaved several times, a storm swirling behind his deep green eyes. "I don't like it."

She put on a brave smile and grabbed his hands again. "Neither do I, my love. Believe me, if I thought there was any other way, I would gladly do it, but there isn't. I need to witness with my own eyes what is going on in Urdanya. And, with the magic contained in the Sea Witch Sceptre, I'll be able to continue my dialogue with the Fae. Perhaps glean a different perspective."

Hammas bit back whatever he was going to say and whispered, "How long will you be?"

"As long as it takes."

His eyes narrowed.

"I don't know. Hopefully no more than a fortnight or two."

"Or two?" Hammas sounded incredulous.

"It's seven days there, in good weather, and seven back. If I'm wrong about the danger threatening Braen's hold on the Sea Throne, I promise I'll have Captain Kall force march us home again."

Hammas pulled free of her grasp. He turned to stare into the distance. His chest heaved once in a great sigh, and he turned back. "I expect you to run the entire way."

"Hold me, you silly elf." Khae spit out a wet laugh and embraced him. Her head pressed against the top of his chest, she said, "A day without you by my side will feel like an eternity."

Taking in his smell, she rubbed her face against his tunic to hide the tears she unsuccessfully kept from falling. Perhaps Hammas had been right all along. Orlythe's head should have entertained the tip of pike long ago.

Dragon Sect

Wyvern Beach

"**Wouldn't** Aelfy cringe if he could see me now?" Ouderling said to a dirty white mare beneath her as they stopped on the edge of a bluff overlooking a long strip of sandy beach abutting the Niad Ocean. The great body of water, calmer than she had ever seen it before, rolling onto the shore with the slightest of whitecaps.

Given a rare day off by all three of her mentors at Highcliff, she had seized the opportunity to fly to the oceanside and spend a day of quiet reflection without the incessant cares of being a princess or a Highcliff Guardian in training. Though she had managed over the winter months to convince everyone to treat her as an equal, their best intentions were tempered by the underlying knowledge of who she was. The future Queen of the Elves.

She adjusted her fancy bow, brought for protection against the wild creatures inhabiting the rugged terrain of the Mardeireach, though she didn't expect to be troubled by them during the day. Pecklyn had brought her out here on several occasions—calling the endless stretch of sand, Wyvern Beach. The ever-smiling Highcliff Guardian claimed that Wyvern Beach was his favourite place in all the world to visit whenever he needed a break from the trials of everyday life. Admiring the tranquil beauty of the vista below, she understood why.

The bareback horse snorted, not wishing to remain stationary.

Ouderling laughed and patted the side of its neck, surprised she had been able to get close to the wild animal, let alone mount it and ride across the foothills of the Mardeireach. She could only assume the solitary animal had sought company in the dangerous wilderness south of the mighty waterway paralleling the Path of the Errant Knight. Whatever had prompted the mare to approach, she had been more than happy to oblige.

Bittersweet memories of life with her old horse, Buddy, assailed her as she carefully walked the mare down the steep embankment, conscious of how awkward and uncomfortable it must be for the horse to carry not just *someone*, but an elf in heavy armour plate.

Stepping onto the sand, Ouderling carefully slid from the horse and strolled along beside it as they made their way down the beach—talking to the animal as if they were old friends.

The sweltering heat of the late afternoon tempted her to remove her armour and go for a swim, but Pecklyn's voice sounded in her head as if he stood next to her—admonishing her not to risk exposing herself in what could quickly become a hostile environment. Her armour meant the difference between life and death. Instead, she pulled the cowl of her surcoat over her head to ward against the worst of the sun's rays.

Dragon Sect

Her hand against the mare's rippling flank, she praised it for being such a beautiful creature and thanked it profusely for making her day special.

It was a rare day when none of her trainers had time for her. Something big was brewing at Highcliff, but no one had bothered mentioning anything to her. Not even her personal protector Jyllana.

The red-headed Home Guard, who had become more of a friend than a guard to her, hadn't had time for her today either, claiming she had business with Eolande in the Crystal Cavern, whatever that meant. Ouderling had wanted to visit the old goblin caretaker and see what was going on, but as she had combed out her hair earlier in the day, another idea had come to mind.

It was times like these that being a princess had its benefits. She seized the opportunity to seek out a dragon to fly her to the coast. Not quite expecting to be taken seriously, the white dragon, Zorain, happened to be sitting on the promontory fronting Highcliff, preparing to set out on his coastal watch.

Waiting until Scale and the head Watchman, Kingstone, had finished speaking with Zorain, Ouderling caught the dragon alone and persuaded him to fly her to Wyvern Beach. Had she been anyone else other than a princess, she doubted Zorain would have agreed. Besides, the white dragon liked her. They had shared a special bond since that fateful day the human wizard had attacked Highcliff.

So engrossed in her thoughts, she was caught off guard when a shadow passed overhead, announcing the arrival of a black and brown wyvern who landed before her with a skull-shattering shriek.

The mare whinnied and reared beside her.

Startled, Ouderling pulled her bow free. The grueling training sessions with Balewynd prevalent in her instinctive reaction to defend herself. Bringing her bow to bear she was about to pull an arrow free of the quiver hanging from her hip like a sword, but stopped short, blue eyes intense.

"Ouderling Wys! Thank the Fae, I've found you," the female voice of Miragan the wyvern sounded in her head.

"Mir. What're you doing here?" Ouderling asked, her attention divided between the wyvern and the white mare galloping up the beach away from danger, idly musing how big the wyvern had grown.

"Kingstone's worried sick over you."

"Me? Why? I'm fine."

"You won't be when Master Aelfwynne learns that you left Highcliff without an escort. None of us will." Miragan scanned the beach and the hills beyond. *"Where's Zorain?"*

Ouderling shrugged. "He said he'd return before sunset."

"Sunset?" Miragan's usual calm voice thundered. *"That crazy dragon sure is a fitting life mate for the wizard's apprentice. Neither one is blessed with half a wit."*

Dragon Sect

A sudden pang of guilt assailed Ouderling. What she had thought of as a harmless excursion to the seaside had upset the head of the dragons of Highcliff. She never thought Kingstone might become involved.

A shriek echoed off the peaks to the east. Looking up, it took Ouderling a few moments to spot the white dragon against the sky. Zorain crested the high bluff at the north end of the beach, his low approach provoking the quickly disappearing mare to alter her course and head inland.

Zorain hit the beach hard. Great claws gouged the beach and back-flapping wings stirred up a cloud of sand.

Ouderling covered her face until the worst of it settled.

"Miragan. What're you doing here?" Zorain asked, a hint of shock in his deep voice.

Miragan glared. *"You should worry more about what she's doing here. Kingstone's looking for the princess north of the Path of the Errant Knight as we speak."*

"Kingstone?" Zorain's orange eyes widened. He looked up the coast as if expecting to see the head dragon. *"How'd he find out?"*

"Apparently Pecklyn finished whatever he was doing early and went looking for Ouderling."

Zorain's thick neck convulsed in a swallow. *"If Pecklyn knows, he'll tell Master Aelfwynne."*

"If you get Ouderling back before Pecklyn returns, you might be able to call him off."

"Why? Where's Pecklyn?"

"Out searching, like the rest of us."

"How many are searching?" Zorain's voice cracked.

"Just Kingstone, Dawnbreaker and Pecklyn, and myself as far as I know."

Zorain's wild eyes turned on Ouderling. He dropped to the sand beside her. *"Quick. Get on."*

Dragon Sect

Ouderling approached Zorain. *"I guess I've done it this time. Old Aelfy will never trust me again."*

"Fear not, pretty lady. I'll see what I can do to keep everyone quiet." Miragan sighed, glaring at Zorain. *"If you've any sense, you'll get Ouderling back and then beg for Kingstone's forgiveness."*

Zorain nodded with a grimace.

Ouderling shouldered her bow and climbed into place, patting Zorain's neck to let him know she was ready. "Sorry, Zorain. I've really fixed us this time."

Flying swiftly into the Mardeireach, the mountain peaks soared past them on either side.

Dragon Sect

Dragon Dance

Being a Guardian was much tougher than Ouderling ever envisioned. If she had any delusions that the no-nonsense elf, Balewynd, would ease the rigours of her training regimen, especially after being gravely injured at the Battle at the Gate, she was sadly mistaken.

On a positive note, the long, winter months had done wonders for not only Ouderling's physical stamina but her mental fortitude as well. Gone were the lingering doubts about her right to be included in the elite group of Crystal Cavern caretakers. But she didn't fool herself. She had much to learn before coming close to attaining the prowess of her trainers. On the days she wasn't with Balewynd, Aelfwynne, and Pecklyn worked her equally as hard.

Thinking of Pecklyn, she couldn't recall a time the blonde-haired rider of the purple dragon, Dawnbreaker, had been anything but outwardly happy—other than that horrific day her uncle's dragons had attacked her mother's forces. The same day Pecklyn had recovered Balewynd's broken body and flown the dying Guardian back to Highcliff with the belief of easing her passing into the next world.

Dragon Sect

A knock on the door of her quarters startled her out of her reverie. Though not unexpected, she cringed. Another day of being thrown around mercilessly and then berated for her short-comings as she stared down the scarred visage of Balewynd—the warrior elf unemotional as ever.

"Come in," Ouderling called out, placing her breakfast platter on the marred surface of a cabinet at the foot of her straw pallet.

The door opened, revealing the impatient brunette; her nose bent to the right, between bright, blue eyes—the result of an injury sustained during her involvement in an ill-fated rescue attempt of the high wizard beneath Grim Keep. Curiously, the Guardian wasn't dressed in her usual training gear.

A rare smile illuminated Balewynd's face, lifting another scar she had picked up when she had fallen from the sky at the Battle at the Gate. The grisly reminder ran from her high cheekbone to below the lobe of her left ear. As startling as the mark appeared, Ouderling thought it gave Balewynd a rugged beauty—one she imagined the elder Guardian, Xantha, had exuded for centuries.

Ouderling wiped her mouth. "What gives?"

Balewynd remained at the door. "Forget your weapons. Today is the day of the dragon dance."

Ouderling's eyes changed colour from brown to blue. "They're hatching?"

Balewynd nodded. "If we don't hurry, we're going to miss it."

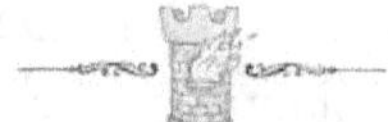

Even at a headlong run, it took Ouderling and Balewynd a while to reach the largest cave in the Highcliff complex. Deeper into the mountain than the Crystal Cavern, the Hatching Warren was surprisingly warm.

Dragon Sect

Bathed in a sheen of sweat, Ouderling found she had no trouble matching Balewynd's headlong run, something inconceivable a month ago. Her arduous training had finally generated noticeable results.

They slowed at the end of a tunnel large enough to allow the biggest of the dragons access to the mammoth cave. Leaving the flickering rushlight of the passageway, mesmerizing faerie light greeted them—the air shimmering with thousands of pinpricks of white light.

Too small to be observed for what they actually were, Ouderling knew from experience while travelling the servant tunnel beneath Borreraig Palace that faerie light consisted of miniscule, butterfly-shaped creatures flitting about. The most incredible aspect of the magical glow was that the Fae were only capable of burning brightly for short periods of time before having to return to wherever faeries existed, but there were always more to take their place.

As wondrous an experience as the artificial light presented on a normal day, it was the sight of half a dozen full-sized dragons lying beside their clutch of eggs that took her breath away.

Shells larger than her head quivered sporadically throughout the cavern, drawing the eyes of all those assembled from one dragon to another. Between each dragon stood two Highcliff Guardians bearing long polearms with barbed tips.

Movement from a small crowd of Guardians gathered on the right side of the cavern caught Ouderling's attention. Jyllana Ordalf's beaming smile met hers over the shoulders of her Guardian cohorts.

An orange dragon, larger than Balewynd's blue, licked at the mucus coating the cutest sight Ouderling had ever laid eyes on. A pale orange, baby dragon staggered about, its footing unsure. A faint squeak escaped the dragonling's fang infested mouth as it attempted to lift its wings and fell to its side, eliciting a series of 'oohs' and 'ahs' from the crowd.

"Here!" a polearm bearing Guardian with a peculiar shade of grey hair called from across the cavern. It was obvious by his face that the grey hair was a peculiar colour for one so young.

"Come on!" Jyllana grabbed Ouderling's elbow and dragged her across the Hatching Warren—a bold act the redhead would never have considered before they had arrived at Highcliff.

Ouderling fell into step without argument. Not due to Jyllana's position as her personal protector, but because of the close bond they had forged. A friendship that left Ouderling anxious if a day went by without sharing in Jyllana's fervor for life. The Home Guard's presence had been the tonic Ouderling had needed to get her through the early, dark days of their arrival at the dragon colony.

A pang of sad remembrance tempered Ouderling's enthusiasm. Highcliff was also home to wyverns. Two-legged dragons entrusted with the maintenance of the Crystal Cavern. A collection of brown-scaled caretakers whose population had been cut in half the day the human wizard, Afara Maral, had subverted the red dragon, Demonic, and attacked Highcliff.

The human wizard had come calling while the Highcliff dragons had flown off to fight in the Battle at the Gate. Fond memories of the ancient wyvern, Perch, were never far from her thoughts. She had made it a point to visit the slain wyvern's granddaughter at least once a week since then to ensure the wyvernling was okay.

Ouderling smiled ruefully. She really needn't have bothered. The way the old caretaker goblin, Eolande, doted on Miragan, even as big as she had become, it was a wonder the wyvern was allowed to do anything on her own on the off chance she came to harm.

A dark green dragon growled as the Guardians approached where she lay beside a solitary egg; her black horns and dark edged wings highlighted with golden accents.

Ashe, the grey-haired elf with the polearm, put his hands up to keep the gathering crowd from getting too close as he spoke over his shoulder to the mother dragon, "Easy, Hyperion. No one's going to interfere."

If dragons had the capacity to discharge fire with their eyes, Ouderling was sure Hyperion's forest green orbs would have incinerated the entire group of onlookers.

A large crack drew Hyperion's concerned gaze to the egg quivering by her head. Without opening her mouth, she expelled a small swath of fire through her nostrils, the flames licking at the ground around the base of the cream-coloured shell.

Ouderling felt Jyllana tense beside her, when Balewynd stuck her head between them. With a hand on each of their shoulders, the rugged Guardian whispered, "It's okay. Dragons can withstand a great deal of heat."

Ouderling frowned. Whatever was responsible for warming the Hatching Warren had her sweating. Could it simply be the result of the mother dragons heating the stone around them? She peered at the intent faces close by, their damp complexions matching her own.

"Look!" Draakyr, a middle-aged Guardian with a polearm in one hand, squeezed Ouderling's forearm to gain her attention—the black-haired elf's mustachioed face alight with excitement.

It was as if he had never witnessed such an event before, but Ouderling knew he must have. She didn't know a lot about Draakyr other than he had been with Highcliff for more than two centuries. As the elf in charge of the Watchmen dragons, Draakyr had surely witnessed many of these wondrous events.

The egg rocked so hard that it rolled against its mother's outstretched, front paw and came to rest in an upright position. It fell still for a moment—all sound in the cavern falling away in anticipation.

The egg trembled and rolled onto its side, but before it came to a stop, a pale green horn no longer than Ouderling's pointer finger pierced the tip of the shell.

Wedged in place, the little horn tilted one way and then another. A jagged line extended along the egg's surface from where the horn struggled, lengthening around the circumference of the egg's narrow end.

The sound of the eggshell cracking was immediately followed by a tiny dragon head popping free of its prison with a piece of shell anchored on the end of the horn protruding from the tip of its triangular snout.

It wasn't until a faint squeak escaped the dragonling that Ouderling remembered to breathe.

The egg rolled sideways, spilling the cat-sized baby onto its side. It emitted another cute sound, clearly agitated as it struggled to free itself. A blunt horn pushed free of the egg beside its head, and with a mighty crack, the rest of the egg opened, its halves forced aside by the press of the dragonling's wings.

Hyperion's great sigh of contentment precipitated a round of applause for Highcliff's newest resident.

"That has to be the cutest thing I've ever seen." Jyllana beamed at Ouderling across a stone tabletop in the Highcliff mess hall. Her gaze flicked to Pecklyn who had recently joined them for a midday meal.

"It truly is a wondrous spectacle to behold," Pecklyn agreed around a mouthful of food. "Too bad it was my turn to stand watch."

"Ain't missed much," Balewynd grunted beside Jyllana. "Just the usual cracking and stress."

"Any trouble with the dragons?" Pecklyn asked.

"Nah, Draakyr and the others kept them well enough apart.

Pecklyn explained for Jyllana and Ouderling's benefit, "Dragons are known to eat each other's eggs."

He smiled at the shock on their face, raising an eyebrow in confirmation. Turning back to Balewynd, his laden spoon stopped before it entered his mouth. "How many made it?"

Without missing a chew, Balewynd muttered, "Four."

"Weren't there eight eggs?" Pecklyn frowned.

"Aye," Balewynd said as if half the eggs not hatching wasn't a big deal.

Pecklyn's gaze flicked between Balewynd and Jyllana. "Whose eggs didn't make it?"

Jyllana shrugged but Balewynd said, "Danzinnia lost one of her two, Unniass lost her only one, and Atsila lost both of hers."

Pecklyn winced at the mention of Atsila's plight. "That's a shame. Been a hard year on her. I'm sure her fight with Eldron hurt her more than she let on. Draakyr was surprised she took part in the mating festival this year."

"As if Athgaan would have given her much choice," Balewynd grunted, flashing Pecklyn a sour look.

"True." Pecklyn smiled. He looked around, as if making sure no one was close by. "Was Aelfy there?"

"Ya right," Balewynd scoffed. "Ever since that Home Guard magician showed up, he hasn't had time for anyone else except Ouderling."

Pecklyn nodded. "What about Xantha?"

Balewynd rolled her eyes as if he were daft. "You expect her to nurse little Dithreab alongside the dragons?"

Pecklyn shrugged, a smirk lifting one side of his face. "That'd be fitting, wouldn't it?"

Balewynd gaped.

"I don't mean Xantha's a dragon." Pecklyn almost spit out what was in his mouth. "Though she is as powerful as one. Likely stronger, years ago. Being the son of Aelfwynne *and* Xantha, I think I'd rather wrestle a dragon than tangle with Dithreab when he grows up."

Balewynd shoved her bowl aside, wiped her mouth on the cuff of her tunic, and stood.

"Where are you off to?" Pecklyn lowered his spoon.

"I promised to relieve Fanyr so he could watch the dance," Balewynd grunted. She grabbed her bowl, deposited it on a stone shelf before a large opening in the back wall that led to the kitchen, and exited the mess hall without looking back.

Jyllana paused in midchew to watch the morose Guardian depart. She raised her eyebrows at Pecklyn.

"Ya. She's a real pip," Pecklyn said. "Like I said before, don't let her gruffness fool you. She really enjoys things like the dragon dance. So much so, in fact, that it bothers her to distraction if someone has to miss it."

"That makes no sense. Why would she take Fanyr's place then?" Ouderling asked.

"So Fanyr can take part."

"But…?" Ouderling shook her head.

"I know." Pecklyn shrugged. "In her head it's the right thing to do. Sacrifice her own needs for the sake of others.

Her heart's in the right place, even if her demeanour is colder than an ice dragon's breath."

Jyllana frowned. "Ice dragons are just a myth, aren't they? I thought all dragons breathed fire."

Pecklyn scooped the last of his gruel with a finger as he stood. "Who knows? Finish up. It should be an interesting afternoon."

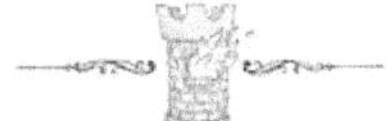

If anything, the temperature in the Hatching Warren had risen since the morning. Pecklyn stood between Ouderling and Jyllana, quietly informing them what to expect as they gathered in a large semi-circle in the cavern's centre.

He scanned the cave floor and said quietly so that only Ouderling and Jyllana could hear. "Atsila and Unniass have left to grieve their loss on their own."

Jyllana appeared on the verge of tears. "That's so sad."

Pecklyn wrapped an arm around her shoulder, pulling her close. "That's the life of a dragon for ya."

"Why's it so hot in here?" Ouderling asked.

Pecklyn placed his other arm over Ouderling's shoulder. "Aren't we the curious one today?" He gave her a playful hug. "Weren't you listening to Balewynd's teachings?"

Ouderling answered sarcastically, "She never got into temperature fluctuations inherent to the inner warrens of the Highcliff complex."

"Ha!" Pecklyn squeezed tighter and let go. "Allow me to be your Chronicler. In an effort to keep the dragonlings warm, their mothers continually heat the stone around them."

"Interesting." Ouderling's tone indicated that Pecklyn's comment was anything but. "So, what happens now?"

"You'll see."

Dragon Sect

Pecklyn had no sooner answered than eight elves who had recently arrived at Highcliff entered the cavern, adorned in simple white robes—five males and three females.

He whispered to the princess and Jyllana, "Those are the Initiates. They have been selected from across South March to partake in what is known as the Dragon Dance. A competition to be chosen by one of the dragonlings."

Eolande followed on the Initiate's heels and waited until they positioned themselves in the centre of the cavern, their backs to the dragons resting along the back wall.

To an elf, the newcomers' faces were filled with a mixture of awe and trepidation.

Ouderling leaned into Pecklyn. "What happens to the four who aren't chosen?"

Pecklyn shrugged. "That'll be up to Master Aelfwynne. He usually interrogates the unsuccessful ones."

"I don't envy them that," Ouderling muttered.

Pecklyn frowned, his voice dropping lower; barely audible. "True. An audience with Master Aelfwynne usually doesn't turn out well for the hopefuls. Most are escorted back to Grim Town and sent home. Now, watch."

An expectant hush fell over the Hatching Warren as Eolande walked in front of the Initiates and turned to face them. He looked each participant in the eye until they nodded. Pulling a small, bone flute from his belt, the old goblin began to play a song consisting of high-pitched notes.

The mournful lilt reverberated hauntingly off the walls, bathing the cavern in a surreal atmosphere as the elves vying for the attention of the four dragonlings began to dance. Each Initiate gyrated in a unique sequence of empty-handed battle stances and mesmerizing feats of flexibility—all in sync with the tremolo of Eolande's long, drawn-out notes.

Dragon Sect

Captivated by the music, the dragonlings left their mother's sides. As if possessed by a hypnotic trance, their unsure legs carried them toward the whirling Initiates twirling in front of Eolande.

Eolande stepped to the side, his music never missing a beat.

At once, the amber dragonling belonging to the dragon known as Danzinnia, walked straight up to the tallest male elf dancing in the middle and let out a screech surprisingly loud for one so little.

The elf dropped to his knees and held out a tentative hand.

"This is where it gets interesting," Pecklyn whispered, his eyes rivetted on the unfolding scene.

The dragonling leaned backward as if unsure it wanted anything more to do with the tall elf and emitted another loud screech.

The elf's hand shook in the air between them.

Little as they were, Pecklyn knew from experience that dragonlings were capable of incredible violence—their razor-sharp teeth enough to sever a hand. He draped his arms over Jyllana and Ouderling's shoulders and held them tight, unaware he was doing so as he watched. It was up to the Initiate to prove their bravery in the face of their impending peril.

Eolande's tune played on, encouraging the other Initiates to ignore what was going on with the amber dragonling, and maintain their own dragon dance.

Through it all, the tall elf never balked, even though his hand visibly trembled. Leaning forward, he held his fingers close to the dragonling's nostrils.

The dragonling's bright red eyes glared at the elf. Without warning, its mouth opened wide, but the Initiate held as steady as his shaking arm allowed. The frightened elf winced as an ear-piercing screech resounded throughout the cavern—longer than the dragonling's previous shriek.

When the dragonling finally ceased its disconcerting roar and closed its mouth, the elf turned his palm upward with outstretched fingers and accepted the creature's scaly chin in his hand.

Pecklyn squeezed Jyllana and Ouderling tighter, bobbing up and down in excitement. "It chose him! It chose him!"

Ouderling cast him a curious look. "You act like you've never seen a dragon dance before."

He hugged them both closer. "Oh, but it's so exciting!"

An older, female Guardian separated from the crowd and knelt beside the tall Initiate, placing a hand on his shoulder. She whispered something into his ear before they both stood and left the Hatching Warren—the Initiate unable to stop looking over his shoulder at the dragonling who had chosen him.

Pecklyn diverted his attention to the remaining participants, enthralled by their exuberance as they vied for the attention of one of the three remaining baby dragonlings—his smile no less big than it had been upon entering the cavern.

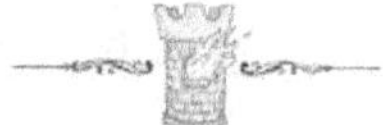

"So that's it?" Ouderling watched as five dejected Initiates were escorted from the Hatching Warren. Her gaze returned to the green dragonling who had put on an entertaining show earlier when he had emerged from his egg. Throughout the Dragon Dance, he had strutted defiantly in a circle near his mother, uninterested in the ceremony. "What happens to that one?"

"It's not unusual for a dragonling to refuse a rider," Pecklyn answered. "When that happens, their future is entrusted to Draakyr. He trains them to become Watchmen. A solitary position more suited to their temperament."

"Are all Watchmen that angry?" Ouderling mused.

Pecklyn smiled as the green baby emitted a cringe-worthy shriek and clawed at the cave floor, its amber eyes watching them. "Ha ha. Not usually. Ferocious little beast that one. Probably a good thing he didn't participate in the dragon dance. I'm thinking he would've torn the arm off whoever he selected."

"How old do they have to be before they can be ridden?"

Pecklyn shrugged. "Depends on the colour, mostly. Reds are generally the strongest and biggest by nature, but not always. That one being a green, I would hazard to guess in half a year's time or so, but judging by his temperament, I'd pity anyone riding him at any age."

Jyllana stepped into view from Pecklyn's other side. "Zorain is a Watchman, and he chose a rider later on."

"True. Dragons are unpredictable at the best of times, but it's usually apparent from birth where a dragon's disposition places them. There must be something special about Scale that prompted Zorain to alter his solitary lifestyle. As far as I know, occurrences like that rarely happen." He stared at the green dragonling a moment longer before turning to follow the rest of the departing crowd—Jyllana close behind. "Come. We should go. No sense aggravating the little guy further."

Ouderling was about to join them but something about the baby dragon made her pause. It was as if the dragonling watched *her*. He certainly followed her movements.

Hyperion raised her large head off the floor to stare at Ouderling. Smoke puffed from her nostrils—a low rumble escaping her closed mouth.

Ouderling stiffened, but it was the soft female whisper inside her head that shocked her the most.

"He likes you. Why didn't you participate in the dragon dance?"

Despite the fact she knew at once where the foreign voice originated, Ouderling searched the cavern in case she was mistaken.

Pecklyn and Jyllana had stopped at the exit, regarding her with puzzled expressions. Ouderling ignored them and turned her attention back to Hyperion. Pointing a finger at herself she asked, "Me?"

"Don't see anyone else around."

"W-why, I w-wasn't invited. I'm—"

"I know who you are," Hyperion interrupted, her voice deepening. *"Do you think that because you're royalty you're too good for dragons?"*

The question slapped her in the face. "Of course not. Quite the opposite, in fact. I'm not worthy of a dragon's attention."

"You're the princess of South March. Your word is law."

Ouderling spat a skeptical laugh. "Ha! I doubt that very much. Especially now that I'm under Master Aelfwynne's protection. Even if I were queen, I'd never think to demand a dragon's fealty. Heck, I wouldn't demand the fealty of anyone. I'm no more important than the next elf."

"A noble sentiment, but you belittle your station. You represent what the future has in store for all of us. Through you we will discover if everything your mother and grandmother fought for was toward a greater ideal or just another empty promise to those who have lain down their lives for a cause they believed in."

Ouderling swallowed, unsure of what Hyperion was getting at. Heavy matters of state were not her strength.

Dragon Sect

"Regardless how you view your importance, it's ultimately what the realm believes that'll win the day. Like it or not, your future word will become the law. The laws you impose will determine whether the kingdom remains united under your banner or is torn asunder by you sowing the seeds of discontent. Choose your path wisely, Your Majesty, and dragonkind will forever be by your side."

Hyperion's dragonling screeched, sending jolts of trepidation shooting along Ouderling's nerves. Hyperion spoke of grave matters Ouderling knew she had yet to appreciate. She swallowed her rising dread of what the dragon's words entailed, wondering for the life of her how to respond in a way that didn't make her sound like an elfling, but the erratic movements of the dragonling diverted her attention.

The baby dragon slunk toward Ouderling; his head low as if searching for an opening in which to spring.

"Ouderling!" Jyllana cried out, attempting to come to her rescue, but Pecklyn grabbed the redhead by the arm and held her back.

"Watch," was all he said as they observed the unfolding scene.

Ouderling glanced at her companions, beseeching their help, but the dragonling commanded her attention.

He strutted up to her, seemingly more surefooted than the previous dragonlings—his head no higher than her knee. Rearing, he brought his head level with her waist. A deafening screech belched forth from his razor-fanged maw as he leaned forward, placing his front feet on her thighs. Sharp claws bit through her breeks.

Afraid to move, Ouderling worried the dragonling was preparing to leap at her face, but he simply stared her in the eye, his head tilting one way and then another.

"Don't fret, Your Majesty. If he meant you harm, you would already be dead. He's different than the others."

Great, Ouderling thought. Hyperion's reassurance doing little to ease her terror.

"Though not in accordance with the ritual, it appears my son has chosen you as his rider."

"Me? I'm not even a Guardian. I'm here because my mother fears for my life. I'll be returning to Borreraig Palace when this business is done with my uncle and the demon he keeps."

"It's high time the palace was graced with a resident dragon, don't you think?"

If not for the dragonling's excruciating hold on her thighs, Ouderling was sure she would have fallen over backward, overwhelmed by disbelief.

Not really aware of what she was about, she cupped the dragonling's rough cheeks in her hands and smiled into the most beautiful gaze she had ever experienced in her life.

Dragon Sect

From Unhappy Endings

"**Dithreab** wouldn't want us fussing over him like this," Aelfwynne grumbled.

Scale looked up from where he had dug the headstone into the ground in the space that the entrance stump had sat rotting until earlier in the day. It had taken a lot of backbreaking work to remove the remains of the old tree fronting the entrance tunnel to the wood sprite's lair and fill in the gaping hole left behind to prevent anyone else from finding it.

Scale's hands and face matched his dirt-smeared clothing. Glad he had chosen not to wear the usual black leather armour he had pilfered from Castle Grim last year, he looked up from where he mucked about in the dirt to espy the clean countenance of the high wizard of South March. "Don't worry, Master Aelfwynne. There's no *us* fussing over the poor little guy. More like, just me."

"Bah!" Aelfwynne waved a claw-tipped hand in dismissal. "The old knot head wouldn't be any the wiser if we never bothered."

Dragon Sect

Scale rolled his eyes, ignoring the cantankerous, old goblin, and patted at the dirt surrounding the magically inscribed lava stone grave marker. One that had been designed meticulously by Aelfwynne himself. The high wizard had spent weeks crafting it, destroying several earlier renditions before this one—stating they hadn't been good enough. Dithreab had meant more to Aelfwynne than the grumpy, old wizard let on.

Wiping filthy hands on the thighs of his breeks, Scale sat back against a wall of rock shooting up from the rear of the ledge he and Aelfwynne attended and grabbed the waterskin from the ground beside the goblin. He frowned at how much Aelfwynne had consumed already, but the high wizard didn't appear bothered by the scrutiny.

Scale sighed. Some things never changed. He had trained under High Wizard Aelfwynne ever since he had saved the goblin from certain death at the hands of Afara Maral. At first, he had believed that Aelfwynne tutored him out of a sense of obligation for Scale's role in Afara Maral's death, but as the winter months had passed into spring, Aelfwynne still insisted on training him between Aelfwynne's other duties and the attention the high wizard spent on Princess Ouderling—all undertaken with the same crotchety enthusiasm the persnickety goblin was renowned for.

For the first time in his life, Scale was able to put aside the self-doubt instilled by his father with regard to his gift—something the hard-nosed captain of the Queen's Guard had tried to break him of before his heroic death in the Passage of Dolor. According to Aelfwynne, if Captain Gerrant hadn't sacrificed himself to save Princess Ouderling, the future of South March would have been bleak indeed.

As it was, the high wizard had made it obvious that he wasn't overly optimistic about the realm's future—asserting on more than one occasion during their training sessions that if South March was to survive the coming decades, the mystical princess was the only one who stood between them and imminent death at the hands of the soulless one.

Aelfwynne snatched the unattended waterskin from Scale's hand and drank deeply, his shrewd gaze taking in Scale's appearance. "You'll be lucky if Zorain will fly you looking like that."

"Ya? Well, it would've been nice if I had help."

"Help? How do you expect to learn anything if I do all the work?"

"*All* the work? You've done nothing since we came here except drink our water."

"Someone has to be in charge."

Scale bit his tongue and looked out over the forest. New spring growth tipped the branches, and green shoots fought their way clear of the last year's detritus to welcome the new season. If not for the many ridges lining the foothills of Faelyn's Nest, Scale believed he would be able to see the dark mass of Castle Grim through the leafless trees. A sight he was happy not to witness.

A large branch snapped somewhere in the quiet woodland. He smiled. His white dragon, Zorain, was somewhere close by, rooting through the undergrowth—flushing out unsuspecting animals to satisfy his voracious appetite.

Despite the chill on the breeze, a warm sensation flushed him. As recently as last summer, he would never have dreamt that not only would he be the recipient of private lessons from the highest wizard in the land, but that he would become a dragon rider as well. One of a select few who soared across the sky on the shoulders of a wondrous beast. Something he did now on a regular basis without thinking about it.

Dragon Sect

He glanced at the beautiful headstone, a fitting tribute to such a magical creature, marvelling at the greenish glint Aelfwynne had imbued along the edges of the intricately cut stone, and thought of the event happening back at Highcliff. With the work done here, they might be able to witness the hatching. He picked up the waterskin, realized Aelfwynne had finished it, and dropped it again.

Aelfwynne's look dared him to complain.

The wizard was such a rascal. Biting back how he felt about the empty waterskin, he forced himself to say casually, "Zorain said the dragonlings will hatch today. He mentioned something about a dragon dance, whatever that is."

"I'm not deaf. I heard him."

"Be kind of nice to watch."

"You don't need to see it. You already got a dragon."

"But I've never been to a hatching."

"Of course you haven't, ya big galoop. You've never been to Highcliff before I brought you here."

"It would be a great experience."

"Bah! I've seen enough of them for both of us."

Scale frowned at the selfish response. He looked away, afraid of saying something he might regret. Although he appreciated Aelfwynne's lessons—his magic had come a long way from the day he had tried to unlock the magical binding restraining Aelfwynne in Crag's Forge—he wasn't sure he could continue to refrain from lashing out at the old goblin's snarly attitude.

"Be too late now, anyway," Aelfwynne broke the uncomfortable silence, his tone bearing the slightest hint of reconciliation.

Scale didn't trust himself to speak until he inhaled and exhaled deeply three times—an exercise Aelfwynne had taught him to control his excitement and anxiety should he ever have to cast a spell under pressure.

Not happy with his mentor, he said with hopeful promise, "It's been half a year since you started training me. How am I doing?"

"Alright, for someone so old."

"Old?" Scale choked.

"To become a master magician, you started late in life. So yes. Old."

"I just turned fifty-six less than a month ago. I'm barely out of my elfling years."

"Fifty-six years late, then. I'm surprised at how well you *are* doing, but don't get too excited. Your best learning years were wasted chasing menial pursuits."

Scale glowered. Just once it would be nice if the high wizard threw him the odd compliment or word of encouragement. It wasn't his fault he hadn't been singled out for arcane training earlier. His father had scoffed at the notion.

Holding the wizard's gaze, Scale wondered how he kept from biting his tongue off putting up with Aelfwynne. "And how old were you when you started your training?"

Aelfwynne opened his mouth to speak, but stopped, his eyes widening. A quick grin flashed across his face but disappeared when he said, "That's different."

Of course, it's different. Scale rolled his eyes. *Why wouldn't it be?* He kept his thoughts to himself but decided it might be fun to exploit Aelfwynne's slip. "Ah, so you weren't young either."

Aelfwynne's eyes narrowed. His rough-skinned throat contracted in a swallow as he looked away.

"Hah! I'm right," Scale persisted but thought better of his short-lived exuberance as Aelfwynne's evil glare threatened to consume him.

"I'm a goblin. We don't have the benefit of tolerance in most societies. Not even in the civilized realm of South March am I accepted for who I am with the exception of a few elves. If not for Gullveig's intervention, I would've been killed along with the rest of my clan centuries ago."

Gullveig? Gullveig? Scale had heard that name before—besides knowing it as the name of the mountain village that supplied the wizards' guild in Orphic Den. Recognition dawned on him. "You mean, Grimlock?"

"No, you witless northerner, I mean Gullveig."

"But wasn't he—"

"Yes! To the uncouth rabble, he was known as the Warlock of Grim Watch Tower. Thus, he earned the nickname, Grimlock. He took me and the Dragon Witch under his wing and sheltered us until Rhysa found a way to deal with Urdanya."

Scale nodded, recalling the legends. "The sorceress Urdanya."

Aelfwynne's eyes narrowed further, his voice dropping to a dangerous growl. "Aye, ya imbecile. Who else do you know is called Urdanya?"

Scale almost laughed at that. Aelfwynne did have a point. Knowing what little he did of the high wizard, he wondered, "Given the fact that you are but a goblin who isn't liked by the elven masses, have you ever been entrusted to train *anyone* before me? I'm guessing the queen knows of our arrangement?"

Aelfwynne cast him a withering glare. When Scale flinched, the wizard looked away, a profound sadness in his beady, red eyes.

Dragon Sect

Scale sighed. He had upset the high wizard. Again. "Look, I'm sorry. I didn't mean that the way it sounded."

A long silence settled between them. The wooded slopes of Faelyn's Nest darkened as the sun dropped below the peaks of the Mardeireach—a damp cold settled across the forest floor. Branches snapped, the noise growing in volume. Zorain had returned to take them home.

"I have trained two others."

Scale barely heard Aelfwynne's soft words. He swallowed and waited for him to continue.

"Once, long ago, I trained a talented young wizard in the hopes that someday his prowess would rival that of the Dragon Witch. From his humble beginnings as a scout in young Nyxa's army, he became a formidable practitioner. It was my belief that if Islen Ors combined his magic with Rhysa's, they would be strong enough to crush Urdanya and end her evil reign. I had hoped to prevent the needless hardship and death that ensued as a result of Urdanya's rise to power. Alas, Islen was betrayed by someone he had taken into his confidence and was sacrificed in one of the sorceress' demonic rituals."

Scale thought hard on the name. "Islen Ors?"

"Aye. Pecklyn's grandfather."

Scale nodded, goosebumps flushing his skin.

"The other was Queen Khae's only son." Aelfwynne lowered his chin to his chest, dejected. "I failed them both."

A cold wind whistled through the dense branches overhead, swirling the clouds eastward. The iron-grey sky foretold of nasty weather sweeping in from the Niad Ocean.

Scale wiped the worst of the twigs and dried dirt from his clothing and placed a thumb and finger to his lips, emitting a shrill whistle to summon Zorain.

Zorain's answering screech echoed off the hills.

Dragon Sect

Scale held out a hand. "We'd best get back to Highcliff before we're caught in the storm."

Aelfwynne didn't acknowledge him at first, but as the tell-tale sounds of Zorain crashing through the undergrowth grew in volume, he allowed himself to be helped up.

Standing side-by-side, looking out over the forest floor at the white dragon's approach, Scale put a comforting hand on Aelfwynne's shoulder. "From unhappy endings, new beginnings are forged, Master Aelfwynne. Show me the way and I'll make you proud."

Dragon Sect

Scheming Wizard

Orlythe Wys stormed along the southern ramparts of Castle Grim, something he had taken to doing quite regularly since the humiliating defeat at the Battle at the Gate. The ultimate betrayal of Afara Maral had left him reeling in the face of a concerted response of the dragons loyal to Highcliff. The human scum's failure to secure the Crystal Cavern had resulted in the wizard's death, but it was the subsequent abandonment of the dragons that Orlythe had believed were loyal to him that had ultimately undermined his position with his sister, the Queen of the Elves.

If he chose to entertain the obnoxious reports, Khae had garnered a new sense of respect from the general population south of the Ors Spill as a result of the unprovoked attack on her troops. He would have to do something about that.

To make matters worse, Princess Ouderling had survived the ambush in the Passage of Dolor and the blame had landed on his doorstep. A claim he refuted, of course, but as much as he despised his sister, he had to admit she wasn't naïve.

Even the death of his other sister, Odyne, hadn't gone the way it had been foretold by that rapscallion wraith. Where the vile creature had gone since that stormy night was anyone's guess. With any luck, it had fled back across the ocean. Or better yet, it had drowned along the way.

He stopped to stare out over the choppy waves battering the dark stone base of Castle Grim's bulwarks far below—the constant ebb and flow of Lake Grim obscuring the daily noise of the keep and the incessant din of Grim Town beyond the northeastern wall.

The Dark Mountains, as black as his mood, lined the vast southern shoreline—their peaks perpetually enshrouded in mist generated by the warmth of the large body of water nestled high in the embrace of a ring of active volcanoes. Somewhere within the veil, on the southern face of the mountains, the protected catacombs of Highcliff carried on its activities with impunity to the Duchy of Grim's governance—another slight he had had to endure as the overlord of the southlands.

A commotion to his right drew his anger. The Grim Guard, entrusted to ensure he wasn't disturbed, parted, admitting a pale-skinned, young elf—immaculate red robes flowing about his wiry frame.

A lone Grim Guard started after the wizard and tried to grab onto him, but stepped back with his hands in the air. "Alright. Alright."

Orlythe shook his head. Incompetent fools. What good were they if they couldn't prevent a simple magic-user from passing by them without opposition. He'd have to speak to Captain Drake about this. Perhaps it was time for new blood in the elite ranks of the Grim Guard.

The exasperated Grim Guard followed on Ryedyn's heels, staring past the gangly wizard at Orlythe, his face apologetic.

Orlythe didn't bother responding to the inept buffoon. He would deal with him later. Instead, he leaned his elbows on the waist-high wall and stared out over the lake, feigning indifference to the wizard's presence.

"M'lord?" Ryedyn stopped behind him. "If I may?"

Orlythe chewed his hairy, lower lip. "Don't see as I have much choice." With a twitch of his head, he motioned for Ryedyn to join him against the stone barrier.

The defeated Grim Guard's boot steps receded toward the corner tower.

"No, m'lord. I mean, yes, m'lord, but this is important."

Important or not, Orlythe fought the urge to grab the insolent wizard and toss him to the surf-pounded rocks at the base of the wall. Instead, he continued to stare over the lake, absently hoping Ryedyn would take the hint and toss himself.

If the whelp hadn't been his only arcane defense on the day Afara had shown his true colours, he would have beheaded him long ago. Unless Ryedyn bore news of Khae's sudden demise, he had better hope he could justify the interruption.

"Urdanya is the way to the Willow Throne, m'lord."

Ryedyn's simple but prophetic words washed over Orlythe—absorbing into his psyche and startling his senses to the core. His eyes opened wide—the panorama before him lost to the whirling images that assailed him as a result of Ryedyn's simple statement. It was as if the wizard had cast a spell over him, stirring up the deepest wells of his demented mind—his darkest desires irrational by his own admission. He turned slowly to regard the sticklike elf—the wizard's head too big for his gangly frame.

"What do you know?"

"The son of Odyne is weak. Not fit to rule. The people of Urdanya grow restless."

Orlythe's eyes narrowed. "What's that got to do with me?"

"Nothing and everything, m'lord. The Sea Throne sits vacant. Braen Wys refuses its embrace."

"I fail to see how that's got anything to do with me. I don't covet the sorceress' Sea Throne. Odyne's death, though convenient, still leaves two insurmountable obstacles in my path."

"True, m'lord. For now. But, with the proper nurturing, perhaps you might find a way to bring the populous of Urdanya into your fold." Ryedyn raised his eyebrows twice in quick succession.

Orlythe considered that proposition, nodding slightly. "Mmm. There's merit in that scenario, but it's flawed. Have you not warned me on more than one occasion over the last few months of the peril we face?"

"Oh, aye, m'lord. And it's true. It is as the wraith foretold. The dragonborn has come. We must strike while a weakness still presents itself."

Chin in hand, Orlythe considered Ryedyn's words, a troubled expression twisting his mien. The scheming wizard was up to something. Magic-users always were. "You know as well as I do, with the rise of Aelfwynne's apparent successor, Ouderling is untouchable as long as she shelters at Highcliff."

A sly smirk crossed Ryedyn's pasty face. "Precisely why we must draw her away from her sanctuary."

Dragon Sect

Keaf

Volcanic activity on the distant, southern shores of Crystal Lake captivated Ouderling, easing her mind of the lingering doubts her future had in store. As much as she had come to feel at home at Highcliff, if not for Jyllana, she doubted she would have mentally survived this long.

She placed her hand on top of Jyllana's, who sat beside her, as they dangled their legs over the fatal drop on the edge of the black rock promontory fronting the main entrance into Highcliff.

Faithful Jyllana smiled, the redhead lost in her own thoughts.

Ouderling wondered what her appointed protector dreamed about. Judging by how well they got along, she imagined Jyllana thought often of Pecklyn. In fact, Ouderling was surprised nothing had come of the amicable friendship her protector and the Guardian shared. Perhaps it was time to take it upon herself to encourage the ever-smiling Guardian to take the next step.

A quick intake of breath covered the conflicting emotions assailing her as she attempted to shift her focus to the orangey-red glow of several streams of lava sliding down distant slopes across the lake—the run-off creating plumes of vapour above the water.

Thinking about Pecklyn, she found it hard to concentrate. Her mind reeled with the sheer amount of knowledge her trainers expected her to absorb. From Balewynd's physical training to Pecklyn's dragon instruction to Aelfwynne's mind bending exercises, she felt like she was being suffocated by the constant information they fed her.

A loud snort from somewhere along the platform reminded her they weren't alone. There hadn't been a day since Afara Maral had attacked Highcliff that she had found herself alone—well, except that day she had convinced Zorain to fly her to Wyvern Beach, and that hadn't ended well for either of them.

Aelfwynne insisted she be watched day and night—her only respite coming while in the sparse surroundings of her sleeping quarters. The same, cramped space she had lived in from the start of her stay in Highcliff. At least they had given Jyllana her own quarters, albeit next door.

"What do you sense, Kingstone?" Ouderling asked without looking back.

"I cannot put a name to it, my child," the large green dragon, his scales highlighted with shiny bronze edges, responded from where he patrolled the rock ledge on foot.

"Are we in danger out here?"

A long pause ensued, the sound of Kingstone's claws clacking on the rock informed Ouderling where he was without having to look. She glanced over her shoulder, watching him sniff at the air; the pale moonlight glinting off his shiny scales.

Dragon Sect

"Not at the moment, but I sense a foul taint in the air. A change in the winds of fate if you will. Something dark lingers close by but I cannot put a name to it."

Jyllana stiffened and rose to her feet, twin daggers at the ready as she searched the deep shadows around the base of the cliff.

"It's okay, red midge. Our ward won't come to harm this night."

Ouderling smiled at Kingstone's pet name for Jyllana. Aelfwynne entrusted Jyllana and Kingstone with her safety whenever she wasn't with Balewynd, Pecklyn, or himself. Not that she minded the ministrations of Highcliff's largest dragon. During the intervening winter months, he had proven to be as fierce as he was kind. As Hyperion's mate, Kingstone struck Ouderling as the unofficial leader of the Highcliff dragons. "Where do you think it's originating from?"

Kingstone's great head swivelled to stare at the cliff face, but Ouderling knew he didn't mean Highcliff. "My uncle again?"

"Always the duke, my child, but there's something else. Something sinister."

Ouderling chuckled nervously. "Sounds like my uncle, alright."

"He's involved, of that there's no doubt, but to what extent I cannot ascertain as of yet." Kingstone's heavy footfalls shook the shelf. *"The winds speak of an upheaval in nature's alignment."*

"You really need to meet my mother. You two would love each other."

"So you've said."

"Well, it's true. You're so much alike, I fear she'd never leave you alone."

Dragon Sect

"You're not any different from Her Majesty."

It was all Ouderling could do not to gape, but Kingstone wasn't looking her way. Something had caught his attention beyond the western edge of the platform.

"That's hardly a nice thing to say."

"Whether you deem it good or ill is something only you can reconcile. The queen is a great elf. You'd be well-advised to follow in her footsteps and nurture the gift you've been given."

Ouderling considered his words. He sounded uncannily like Aelfwynne and Balewynd. In fact, everyone at Highcliff seemed to know what was best for her. Everyone except her. Unsure how to respond without sounding petty, she remained quiet.

"Red midge. Watch her. I'm going for a fly about to ensure all is as it should be," Kingstone said, the moonlight glinting in his golden eyes as he stared across the shelf at Ouderling. *"When I come back, my child, I would like you to enrich me with the name you have chosen for my son."*

Ouderling cared less that her jaw hung low. Conscious of the rumours circulating around Highcliff, she had been afraid to pay Hyperion a visit after the dragon dance. Though never spoken to her face, she had overheard hushed conversations. Someone would have to be insane to entertain the idea of flying the dragonling fiend one day.

Hyperion and Kingstone's dragonling had been so unruly and out of control since he had chosen Ouderling as a life companion that he had to be moved into a private cave lest he tear apart the other hatchlings.

Not knowing what to do, Ouderling hadn't dared to contemplate the baby demon's selection of her as his life companion, and yet, the dragonling had never been far from her mind.

Dragon Sect

Thinking about the dragonling, she couldn't deny there was something special about him. She had seen it when they had locked stares in the Hatching Warren. He was different from the others, but for some strange reason, that had only added to his allure. Unsure of how to act in a dragon's company, she had decided it best not to interact at all. Deep down, she knew that was wrong. Like it or not, the dragonling had awoken something inside her. Something she hadn't been aware she possessed. Something she was afraid to acknowledge.

Jyllana joined Kingstone on the far side of the promontory and whispered something Ouderling couldn't hear. If Kingstone responded, he did so without including her.

In the interval between heartbeats, Kingstone crouched and leapt off the edge of the promontory, catching his weight with long wingbeats. Rising into the air, he circled back to the steep mountainside above the ledge and made his way westward, scanning the clefts and ridges around Highcliff.

Ouderling patted the stone beside her. "Come! Sit! Kingstone will deal with whatever's out there."

Jyllana obliged but not until she had cased the perimeter of the promontory. Sliding her twin daggers into their sheaths, she adjusted her tight-fitting, leather breeks to allow her to sit comfortably.

"What did you say to him?"

Jyllana shrugged.

"Come on. It was about me, wasn't it?"

Jyllana shrugged again, not meeting her gaze.

"*Jyllana!*" Ouderling persisted.

Jyllana swallowed, her head bowed, looking at Ouderling from beneath downcast brows. "Don't be mad."

"Mad? How can I be mad if I don't know what you said?"

"I, um, told Kingstone that I was worried about you."

"Worried about me? Why?"

"You don't seem yourself."

Ouderling blinked several times in rapid succession, running fingers through her hair—absently noting how much it had grown since she had cut it. "What do you mean, I'm not myself? Who do you think I am?"

A nervous laugh escaped Jyllana. "I didn't mean it that way. I just mean…you've been distracted lately."

Ouderling made to interrupt but Jyllana looked up and said forcefully, "More so than usual. Ever since Kingstone's son proclaimed you as his rider."

"How would you expect me to behave?" Ouderling asked, anger seeping into her voice. "I never asked for it."

Jyllana stared hard. "It's a privilege to be selected by a dragon."

"For a commoner, perhaps," Ouderling said, ignoring the incredulous look Jyllana gave her. "I'm a princess, Jyl. I'll never really be a Guardian. I'm being groomed to rule South March."

"So?"

"So?" Ouderling shouted. "I haven't got time to throw my lot in with a dragon. Especially one with an attitude like that one possesses. No thank you."

Jyllana looked away. When she spoke again, there was a sadness in her voice. "What will you tell Kingstone and Hyperion. I doubt they'll take the news lightly. It'll be a slight to them, that's for sure."

Ouderling wanted to scream, *'It's not my fault!'* She hadn't come to Highcliff to become a dragon rider—not that the thought wasn't a pleasant one if she allowed herself to consider her true feelings.

She shuddered, recalling the relationship she had shared with Buddy. She couldn't imagine how deep a relationship she might forge with a dragon after centuries of being together. There was no way she wished to experience the crushing loss of breaking such a bond when the time came for her to ascend the Willow Throne.

She shrugged. "That's their problem, not mine. I didn't ask for this, Jyl. Don't lay the guilt on me."

An uncomfortable silence settled over the promontory.

Far over Crystal Lake, moonlight glinted off something flying along the distant shoreline. It was hard to see Kingstone for more than short glimpses, but every now and then, the bronze lining of his scales reflected the moonlight, allowing her to track his progress eastward.

Jyllana sighed. "Who said a princess, *or* a queen, can't have a dragon?"

Ouderling opened her mouth to respond but stopped as the truth of that simple statement sank in. It was as if the weight of the mountain behind them had been lifted from her shoulders, leaving her so relieved that she thought she might collapse.

Grabbing Jyllana by the face, Ouderling kissed her forehead. "You're right! What would I ever do without you?"

Jyllana's beautiful smile melted Ouderling's heart. She pulled her stunned protector into a tight embrace, not wanting to let her go.

Moonlight glinted off Kingstone's scales far over the lake as he flew beyond the last of the lava flows and turned north toward Highcliff.

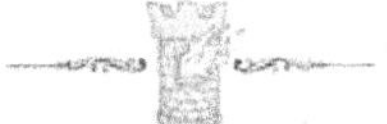

"Well, have you decided, or do I have to inform Hyper that her son will remain nameless for yet another day?"

Ouderling stared up at the green dragon without an inkling of fear for what the colossal beast was capable of doing to her should he ever wish her harm. "I don't get why I should be the one to name him. He's your son."

"Grimclaw's Law."

Ouderling rolled her eyes. "That makes no sense. Grimclaw doesn't even live around here anymore. Is he even alive?"

"Of a certainty. I would know if he had died. Like your mother, I sense these things," Kingstone said matter-of-factly.

"Right. You and the queen's affinity to nature's essence."

"You have it too."

"Ya, ya. So you and Aelfy keep telling me."

"Aelfy?"

Ouderling swallowed, realizing her slip up. She had repeated Pecklyn and Balewynd's nickname for High Wizard Aelfwynne when they weren't in the goblin's company. Though she thought it cute, it probably wasn't the best way to refer to the highest arcane power in the land. "Sorry. I mean, Master Aelfwynne."

Kingstone tilted his head, as if critically assessing her. *"You're an odd one, princess. For someone who's supposed to be capable of doing great things, I sense something unusual in you."*

"Ha! You're just figuring that out now?"

Kingstone frowned and pulled his head back. *"I'm beginning to understand Master Aelfwynne's initial reservation about you, if that's what you mean. As someone destined to become the future leader of the greatest realm this side of the Niad Ocean, you have a peculiar way about you. A presence that doesn't suit itself to becoming a sovereign."*

"Maybe its because I don't want the crown. If it were up to me, I'd remain here for the rest of my life and throw myself into being the best Guardian I could be. Perhaps then I could become a great dragon rider."

Kingstone's golden gaze flicked to Jyllana who merely shrugged and said, "I told you."

His troubled gaze returned to Ouderling; a hint of sadness reflected there. *"Would you prefer not to be my son's rider?"*

Ouderling heaved a great sigh. The dragons had accepted her from the first day she had escaped the Passage of Dolor. Never once had they questioned their loyalty to her as the heir to the Willow Throne. They had taken her for who she was, despite her own misgivings.

Looking into Kingstone's caring gaze, she couldn't bear to hurt his feelings. "Of course I want to be his rider," she lied. "I'd be honoured."

A great grin exposed the biggest teeth Ouderling had ever seen. Longer than her arm, Kingstone's white, meat-rending fangs filled his gaping mouth, encompassing a purple tongue big enough for her to sleep on. *"Then you have a name for our son?"*

Panic seized her. She had no idea what to name a dragon.

"Um, yes…" She stalled. Kingstone had become such a close friend over the last few months that it pained her to imagine disappointing him. His infectious manner had grown on her. His constant companionship, especially during the long days she had mentally hurt and doubted herself had been a godsend. In her mind, Kingstone was more than just a dragon. He was family. The blessing of his familial bond so special that she would gladly die to protect it.

A slow smile crept across her face. She dropped to a knee and bowed her head. "In honour of your friendship, Kingstone, a bond that has made you an important part of my extend-a-family here in Highcliff, your son will, from this moment forward, be known as Keaf. Short for, Kingstone's extend-a-family."

"Your Majesty, I am deeply honoured. Hyperion will be overjoyed to hear such a name. But you must never bend your knee to anyone." Kingstone looked around as if worried someone might see them. *"You're the princess. With the exception of Queen Khae, you suffer no superior. Please rise. I beg you."*

"I'm the princess of South March. I can bow to whoever I choose." She lifted her head to smile up at him. "Though I doubt it'll ever happen again toward another living creature, you, my good sir, are worthy of my obedience. When the time comes, may the exploits of Keaf and Ouderling honour your memory with the respect it is due."

Dragon Sect

The Throne is Already Lost

It had been a few days since Ouderling had named the dragonling, Keaf. Days that left her fretting whether to visit the private warren relegated to Hyperion and Keaf to protect the other dragonlings, and indeed, the caretakers who looked after their needs, or leave them be. Thankfully, the incessant demands of Balewynd, Pecklyn, and Aelfwynne had kept her too busy for anything but training and sleep.

One of these days, she vowed to get the better of Balewynd. Either by beating her in an endurance challenge or miraculously subduing her during one of their sparring contests. She smiled at that last thought. She had no misconceptions about matching the fierce Guardian's melee prowess. That day would never happen.

Of the three trainers, she enjoyed working with Pecklyn the most. The easy-going Guardian patiently walked her through saber training, never once looking down his nose at her shortcomings like the others were prone to do. Her worries were always a distant afterthought in his company. And the dragon training! She smiled. Who could resist falling in love with flying the skies on the back of the wondrous beasts? Thousands of feet above the ground, hanging onto a scaly back with nothing more than her hands and gentle thigh pressure, Ouderling had never felt safer—at least once she had acclimatized herself to the nuances involved in keeping one's balance.

"I'm not interrupting anything important, am I?"

Aelfwynne's raspy voice snapped her out of her musing, returning her attention to the yellow-paged tome open before her on a low, stone table that had been carved out of the floor.

"Um no. Sorry. Did I do it again?"

The goblin's stern glare was all the answer she needed.

"You were saying?"

Aelfwynne chewed on his lower lip, looking none too pleased. "If this is beneath Your Majesty, just say so and we can stop wasting my time."

"Oh, no. It's not. It's just that…" She struggled to finish the thought. Truth be told, she'd rather be doing pretty well anything else other than sitting cooped up in the drafty aerie of the high wizard's conjuring chamber set high in the rock face above Highcliff.

Aelfwynne raised hairless eyebrows in anticipation of the rest of her answer.

She sighed, her face regressing into a pout. "I'm sorry, Master. It's not your training, it's me."

"Obviously."

"I don't think I'm ready for this. I just turned eighteen a few weeks ago. Maybe I'm not old enough."

Aelfwynne's eyes narrowed. "Not mature enough, more like."

That rankled her. She had fought hard to shrug off her elfling persona since arriving at Highcliff—something she had cared little about back home. It proved difficult to keep the petulance from her voice. "How old was my mother when she began training her mind? Surely older than me."

"Suckling Nyxa's teat." Aelfwynne harrumphed and crossed his arms, daring her to refute his answer.

Not knowing what to say, she spat out the first thing that came to mind. "Things were different back then."

The look of contempt she received told her the high wizard didn't agree.

"My mother didn't have to run around the mountainside and fight hand-to-hand, day in and day out without fail."

Aelfwynne's unmoved demeanour spoke otherwise.

Her jaw dropped. "Well, she didn't have to learn to fly dragons."

"No," Aelfwynne agreed. "That she did not. But," he nodded as he spoke, "she could read and write what lies before you with great proficiency before her seventh birthday."

"What? Runes? I highly doubt that."

"Runes. Common. Man. Doubt all you want, Khae was fluent in all three before she was ten."

Flustered, she couldn't hold his penetrating gaze any longer. Resigning herself to the knowledge that whatever she said to the wizened wizard, he would always have a response to make her feel foolish, she refocused on the glyphs printed on the pages of an open tome. Three months ago, the runic text staring back at her would have been nothing but gibberish, but she found that with more than a little effort, she could read enough to make sense of it for the most part.

If she chose to believe the dour goblin, the ancient book sitting between them had been scribed by the hand of Gullveig—an account of his early life in what now comprised northern South March. He had grown up in the stretch of mountains known today as the Wizard's Sleeve.

Dragon Sect

The ancient text proved monotonously boring—pages upon pages of chores and menial tasks he had performed in the employment of an old magic-user, preparing potions and procuring ingredients from the land or in the marketplaces of the ancient city of Eldoon—known today as Urdanya.

The text blurred on the pages as she did her best to piece sentences together. It wasn't long before her mind wandered again.

"He'll be casting spells before you know it, my sweet," Xantha whispered into Aelfwynne's ear. In the darkness of their shared bedchamber, she lay with her arms wrapped around him, his back to her.

"Mmm." He nuzzled his head into her shoulders, feeling the press of her body against his. Her proclamation did little to ease his anxiety. In all of his eight centuries, he had never been responsible for a child. He had no idea how to be a father.

He smiled at that. It couldn't be much different than dealing with the princess. Probably easier. Dithreab didn't have the weight of the throne behind him.

"Whatcha thinking?"

Xantha's purring voice had always been exotic, especially when sharing a pallet together—something they had done less of recently due to the pressures of overseeing the upkeep and protection of the Crystal Cavern and nursing a baby. He shrugged in her grasp. "Nothing."

"Come on." She squeezed him. "There's never a time that the great wizard Aelfwynne's mind finds itself at rest."

He chuckled and held her wrinkled hands against his chest. She knew him too well. There was no point trying to put her off. Not if he wished to get any sleep. "Just the princess."

"Oh," Xantha said playfully.

Dragon Sect

A cold swept through him. He rolled over to face her in the darkness, his goblin's night vision allowing him to see the mischief on her handsome face. "That's just rude, my pet. She's eight centuries younger than me. Why she…she'd…" Flustered, he couldn't come up with the words he wanted.

"Kill you?"

"That's it," he snorted.

Xantha stroked his rough cheek, her pale, purple eyes staring into his. Her night vision had always been superior. "What troubles you, my sweet?"

"It's hard to explain. You wouldn't understand."

"Oh?" She raised her eyebrows. "Try me."

He held her loving gaze until he could organize his thoughts sufficiently to speak them. "I see a lot of her uncle in her."

Xantha frowned. "Orlythe?"

"Aye."

"That's not good."

"I'll say."

"What makes you think that?"

Aelfwynne sighed. Though he felt justified in his assessment, perhaps he was guilty of being overly pessimistic. "I'm finding it impossible to train her. She doesn't listen. Her head is full of so many fanciful ideas about what she's going to do when she becomes queen that she won't concentrate on what she must learn to become a successful ruler. I don't know how to get her to put aside her fanciful notions and accept the reality of what the Willow Throne represents."

"*Your* idea of a successful ruler," Xantha said, but offered him a sympathetic smile. "Don't you think she's capable of doing the things she speaks of?"

"Seriously? Centuries upon centuries of the same old problems assail the throne. Nothing ever changes but the name of the one sitting on it."

"I don't see the harm in trying. It's a noble sentiment, is it not? Even if it is, as you say, nothing but a fanciful notion."

"Bah! Waste of time. She needs to get her head out of the clouds and focus on the real issues facing South March."

"She's just an elfling, my sweet."

Aelfwynne's mood darkened. "And there lies the biggest dilemma of all. I hope I'm wrong in my thinking, but I'm pretty sure that I'm not."

"About what?"

"We haven't heard the last of the Dragon Witch Wraith."

Xantha's eyes widened as she took a sudden intake of breath.

"Aye." Aelfwynne nodded on his pillow. "If what I fear comes to pass, Ouderling will find herself ascending the throne sooner than the rest of us would like—especially Khae."

Xantha noticeably swallowed. "What should we do? Have Khae and Hammas come to live here as well?"

Aelfwynne had given that very thought much consideration as of late. "No. That would leave the realm vulnerable. If not the wraith, then surely the Grim Duke will take the opportunity to seize the throne. Besides, I know Khae. She would never abandon Borreraig Palace. She'll be safe enough there as long as she doesn't wander."

Xantha raised skeptical eyebrows. "So Odyne thought, as well."

Aelfwynne conceded the point.

"But there's more. I can see it in your beady, little eyes. Out with it."

Dragon Sect

A faint smile lifted his sadness as he gazed into her purple eyes, reminiscent of that night long ago when they had sheltered in a rundown tent while on a secret scouting mission for Nyxa Wys. A torrential downpour had soaked them to the skin for the better part of the day, forcing them to huddle miserably in the cold to await the morn. At some point during the long night, something magical had happened between them.

He blinked a couple of times, appreciative of the captivating hold his life mate held over him. "You're not going to like it."

Xantha made no attempt to keep her sarcasm at bay. "There's a surprise."

"If I'm to have any chance of defending either one of them, I must reclaim the Staff of Reckoning." Unable to think of a softer way to tell her the rest, he blurted, "I'm sending Ouderling to Castle Grim to retrieve it."

The shock on Xantha's face was expected.

"You're not serious?"

"She needs to be tested."

"But…But…You're talking about sending her into the clutches of the one who conspired to kill her last year. What good can possibly come of that? It's too dangerous."

He couldn't help but smile at the irony. "Strange hearing that come from the mighty Xantha."

"That's different, and you know it. I was never the heir to the Willow Throne. What if she gets hurt? Worse! What if she…" Xantha didn't finish the thought.

Aelfwynne's voice dropped to a whisper. "Then the throne is already lost."

Dragon Sect

Reluctant Warlock

Urdanya Castle had never felt so lonely. Walls of thick stone carved from the very mountain occupying the northern shoreline at the mouth of the Ors Spill made the formidable fortress almost impenetrable. As solid as the edifice was, it did little to reassure Braen Wys as to his safety. The Grim Duke had been spotted marching a considerable host of black leathered troops north of Alywind. By now they had likely entered Urdanya's sprawling city limits south of the river and would be making their way through the seedier part of the city.

Staring out of his bay window at the Niad Ocean's white-capped surf north of the castle, his only consolation was that it would take his uncle the better part of the day to reach the river crossing. With any luck, he wouldn't have to face the duke until the morrow. He grinned as he clung to the hope that Orlythe might suffer an unfortunate mishap before then. With any luck, the bridge spanning the river would give way beneath the crush of his troops and spirit them out to sea.

Off to the right, the Sea Witch Sceptre demanded his attention. Brooding and defiant across the arched causeway connecting it to the castle, the stone spire mocked his cowardice. Not once since his mother's demise had he garnered the nerve to revisit the ghastly edifice. The Witch Watch had patrolled the causeway day and night from that day forward, forbidding anyone from entering the mystic tower.

He sighed. Just as he had feared, his mother had dabbled in things she had no business toying with, and it had cost Odyne her life. As selfish as it felt, he couldn't deny her demise had cost him his life as well. Though no longer saddled by her overprotective watch, her death had burdened him with the responsibility he had never wanted.

Nobody's fool, Braen wasn't cut out to rule Urdanya. He could barely find it in himself to ask his servants to tend the morning fire or fetch his meals. The thought of others waiting on him hand and foot bothered him more than he cared to admit. He rued the reality of being princess Odyne's only child. Had his mother put more stock into creating a sibling for him, preferably female, he might have escaped the noose of the Sea Throne. As it was, he only dared occupy the uncomfortable symbol of power to entertain the monotonous duty of adjudicating the weekly petitions.

The irony of his situation wasn't lost on him. The security offered by the hewn rock of Urdanya Castle was tempered by the prison those walls represented. The highest-ranking citizen in Urdanya, and indeed the whole west coast of South March, enjoyed the least freedom.

"What a glorious day to be cooped up inside this drafty, old castle."

Braen stiffened at the voice he knew too well. He cringed and closed the cover of the tome in his lap. Setting the book aside, he jumped to his feet, casting a withering look at the helpless faces of the two Witch Watch standing behind his uncle.

"Oh, don't blame your lackeys. I ordered them not to announce me," Duke Orlythe strode past Braen's chair and spun to face him, his gaze taking in the book.

Braen shook his head at the Witch Watch, shooing them from the room. He held out a hand to greet his uncle, but it wasn't accepted. It was going to be one of those meetings.

Orlythe nodded at the tome. "Sir Stanley White, Zephyr Knight. Interesting. Never heard tell of it."

A jolt of fear tingled Braen's senses, not surprised that his uncouth uncle hadn't heard of the bard. He doubted the duke bothered to read at all.

"Zephyr knight, hmm? That means he's from…"

"The north," Braen finished for him.

"Should you be reading that?"

Braen shrugged. Not wishing to speak further on the subject he couldn't help from growling, "Why not? That book goes a long way to prove that man, no matter how barbaric we've been led to believe them to be, is capable of the most sublime civility."

"Indeed." Orlythe stepped closer and fingered the tooled, leather cover, taking the time to open it to a random page and read what was written there. He let the cover fall back into place and stepped to the bay window, his sweeping gaze settling on the Sea Witch Sceptre.

"She died up there, did she?"

Braen didn't trust himself to speak but a simple nod wouldn't suffice with the duke not looking his way. "Yes."

"And you witnessed this…this wraith with her?"

"Yes."

Orlythe nodded and turned to face him. "And you did nothing to stop it?"

Braen hung his head. "No, m'lord."

A boisterous laugh met Braen's response.

"Why not? Did you not care for your mother?" A cynical sneer lifted the side of Orlythe's face.

"Yes, m'lord. Of course, I did."

"Strange way to show it. I would have died to save mine..." He chuckled. "Well, once upon a time, perhaps."

"Of course, m'lord." Braen looked up. "I know what I should've done, but everything happened so fast."

Orlythe's shrewd gaze bored into Braen. "It makes no matter now. Your weakness cannot be undone."

The harsh words infuriated Braen. His uncle hadn't been there when the wraith had attacked. Biting back an angry retort, he said, "No, m'lord. I'm ashamed I couldn't help her."

"I guess that makes you the reluctant warlock."

Braen frowned. "I'm sorry?"

"It's no secret Odyne dabbled in the dark arts. So much so that the commoners referred to her as a witch. You being her son would make you a warlock."

The assertion was so bizarre, Braen didn't know what to say.

"A pity I wasn't allowed to attend her funeral."

"Yes, m'lord."

"Was it well-attended?"

"No, m'lord. The queen insisted it be a private affair. She and the king and a few others from the palace were there, as well as the old Guardian, Xantha, and a mysterious elf she travelled with."

"That would be the high wizard."

Braen's frown deepened. "No, m'lord. High Wizard Aelfwynne wasn't in attendance."

"Of course he was, you dolt. He was in disguise. If your mother had allowed you to attend Borreraig Palace for more than weddings and funerals, you would know that. The elf with Xantha was Aelfwynne."

"If you say so, m'lord." The connection made sense, but for the life of him, Braen would never have associated the handsome young elf with his memory of the old goblin.

"Another deception perpetrated by those who rule the land," Orlythe growled.

"Yes, m'lord." Braen sighed, wanting to change the subject. "What brings *you* to Urdanya?"

"You."

"*Me?*"

"As the current occupier of the Sea Throne, you carry great weight in the realm."

The term, 'current,' wasn't lost on Braen. "A weight I could gladly do without."

Orlythe nodded, his black eyes looking to the vaulted ceiling in thought. "You're unhappy in your present role."

The duke's words were a statement, not a question.

"Yes, m'lord. I don't covet the seat of Urdanya."

"Interesting," Orlythe observed, his gaze flicking to the old tome. "And just what *do you* covet?"

Braen didn't know how to answer that. He dared not reveal his innermost desires to the queen's brother.

"Perhaps you yearn for adventure, hmm?"

Braen's eyes widened. It was like his uncle read his mind. Though he doubted that was actually the case, one could never be too careful around magic-users, and the Duke of Grim reportedly possessed a high aptitude for the arcane.

"What would you say if I offered to watch over the Sea Throne while you do just that?"

Confusion narrowed Braen's eyes. "Do what, m'lord?"

Dragon Sect

"Go on a grand adventure. See the world. Enjoy the freedom you never had during your mother's tight reign. Does that appeal to you?"

Braen searched his soul, not believing what was being proposed. He would enjoy nothing more, but he wasn't senseless. He had heard the tales that had arisen after the Battle at the Gate—of the sudden dragon war that had nearly led to the capture of the Crystal Cavern by his uncle's wizard. If he chose to believe the rumours, Afara Maral had acted on the duke's behalf, and not unilaterally as Orlythe had presented it to the public.

Nor was he unaware that his relatives weren't on the best of terms. It was no secret Orlythe despised the queen. As far as his mother had been concerned, both Khae and Orlythe were welcome to their quibbling over the Willow Throne. He had long suspected that the only reason his mother had endured the yoke of leadership thrust upon her was due to the close proximity of the Sea Witch Sceptre. The mystic tower provided her the forum to entertain her true love in life—experimenting with dark forces she knew little about. He took comfort in the fact that she had never aspired to do anything untoward with her ability—at least not to his knowledge. Being hailed as the Sea Witch had been the only accolade she had ever desired.

Orlythe lifted the tome from the table with two hands and opened the cover, pretending to read as he flipped through the crackling pages. He nodded and looked at Braen from beneath lowered brows. "How about a journey into the savage lands? You may even find the author of this book, or another like him, if such a creature exists. Would that appeal to you?"

Braen stared at the enigma that was his uncle. The duke's physical prowess was enough to make most people wary of him, but it was the tales of the large elf's past that made Braen leery. To openly admit to the Grim Duke that he would like nothing more than visit the realm of man was a most dangerous proposition.

And yet, he couldn't negate the importance of what Orlythe advocated. Braen had dreamed of travelling north of the border since he was little more than an elfling. Well into his young adult years at sixty-six, he had never ventured farther than Borreraig Palace.

The prospect of his uncle's offer seemed too good to be true. "What about the Sea Throne? I cannot, in good conscience, leave it unattended. I have no heirs."

"You have family, Braen. Do you not think your uncle competent enough to watch over Urdanya in your absence?"

"Yes, of course, but—"

"Then it is settled. You desire to explore the world before you are straddled with the responsibility your mother has dumped in your lap at such a young age."

"Whoa. Wait a moment. It wasn't her fault. She was murdered."

"I'll admit she never asked to be murdered, but," the duke raised an eyebrow, "she should've known better than to entertain dealings in the dark arts. Only a fool would think nothing bad would come of it. It was inevitable that it caught up to her."

Braen was incredulous. "You think she brought the wraith upon herself?"

Orlythe shrugged. "Considering the forces she drew upon, there can be no other explanation."

Not happy about it, Braen had to concede the point. He could think of no further justification for the dire events of that fateful night. He shook his head.

Dragon Sect

Orlythe placed a large hand on his shoulder and squeezed. "Fear not, my nephew. The Sea Throne will be in good hands while you're gone. Uncle Orlythe will see to it that Urdanya and all of the elves that depend on the Sea Throne for guidance will be dealt with."

Dragon Sect

All is Lost

"**High** Wizard Aelfwynne commands an audience," Ashe, the elf with the peculiar grey hair, announced as he poked his head into Ouderling's bedchamber.

Ouderling tried to see beyond him into the hallway but couldn't. "Who's with you?"

Ashe looked over his shoulder briefly. "No one. Why do you ask?"

Ouderling considered the Guardian. Other than the day she had commandeered Zorain to fly her to Wyvern Beach, she couldn't recall the last time she had roamed the passageways of Highcliff without Jyllana, Pecklyn, or Balewynd in tow. Perhaps, if she was quick about it, she might be able to wander on her own for a change.

"Okay. Give me a moment."

Ashe said nothing. He just stood and stared.

"Close the door and wait for me in the hall."

He didn't appear like he was going to comply.

"I have to change."

"Oh."

The door closed with considerable force.

Dragon Sect

Ouderling stripped to her undergarments and sifted through a pile of previously worn clothing lying in a heap beside the wondrous armour she had been gifted last year, looking for something befitting Aelfwynne's summons. It was too late in the day for him to be wanting to train her, so whatever the reason for his summons, she imagined it must be important. The goblin never did anything for pleasure.

Grabbing her least filthy tunic, she pulled it on, quickly ran her bone-toothed comb through the worst of her tangles, and slipped into the passageway—allowing Ashe to lead her to the main tunnel and Aelfwynne.

"Sit and pour yourself some wizard's tea." Aelfwynne directed from across the small firepit where he sat on a low bench. Small flames licked at the air between the benches though no fuel was present at their base. Glowing crystals embedded into the dome of rock comprising the walls and ceiling of the cramped chamber cast everything in a dull, orange glow.

The high wizard waited until she had settled onto the opposite bench and poured herself a healthy goblet of the dark-hued liquid before he exposed a mouthful of pointed teeth. "Your lesson with Balewynd went well today?"

"Pecklyn, actually."

"Right. Right. How come I can't keep the days straight?"

Ouderling wanted to joke that he was getting old, but knew better. The goblin wasn't big on humour, so she spoke into her goblet as she smiled and sipped. "You keep a busy schedule."

"Aye. There's that."

She had no sooner ingested a mouthful of wizard's tea than a soothing calm released the tenseness inherent whenever she spoke privately with the high wizard. Though she had grown used to his mannerisms, and knew that he only had the best intentions with regard to the care of the Crystal Cavern and South March as a whole, she found she couldn't bring herself to relish a one-on-one meeting with the grumpy goblin.

An uncomfortable silence settled over the chamber—a foreboding of what was yet to come. Ouderling breathed deeply, staring into the mystical fire, afraid to break the silence. She swallowed and looked up as Aelfwynne set his goblet on the ground.

"You have been at Highcliff for over half a year now."

The high wizard's rasping voice gave her the shivers. She forced a wide grin and nodded.

"What have you learned?"

She blinked a couple of times, taken aback by the odd question. "I, uh…I've learned a lot, actually. I can run the mountain paths for long periods of time without having to rest. I can use a rapier to defend myself…well, to some extent."

Aelfwynne's beady stare held her gaze. "Go on."

She shrugged. "I can fly a dragon on my own. I, um, know a lot about the care of the Crystal Cavern."

"Is that it?"

"No!" She blurted more emphatically than she meant to. She wished he would stop glaring at her in that wizard-like way of his. "Oh, and because of you, I've learned to tap into my gift and perform small tricks."

Aelfwynne's eyes narrowed. "Is that what they are to you? Tricks?"

"Well, n-no…," she stammered. "I didn't mean it the way it sounded. I meant that compared to you or Scale, my magic is insignificant."

"Because you refuse to accept who you are."

She sighed, knowing where the conversation was going.

"Like it or not, you *are* your mother's prodigy. I sense in you the future of South March. The way you're going, it'll be a dire one at best."

She sputtered, about to protest, but stopped as his features hardened.

"Your refusal to accept your gift for what it is, won't end well. With the return of the Dragon Witch Wraith, the kingdom is in peril. Should anything happen to the queen, the Willow Throne will be lost."

"The wraith is gone." As soon as the words left her mouth, she knew she had erred.

"This is why I shunned you when you first came here."

She frowned.

"You don't act on knowledge. You assume. You're not mentally strong enough to take your mother's place." He nodded. "Aye. Things are unfolding exactly the way you and I talked about when you first arrived at Highcliff. The Duke of Grim forges a path to the Willow Throne. Even as we speak, he's set his eyes on Urdanya." He nodded at the shock on her face. "Odyne's seat sits vacant. If we don't act quickly, Khae's will soon follow."

"What?" Ouderling leaned dangerously close to the flames licking at the air between them. "My mother? What do you know?"

"Only this. If steps aren't taken to rein in your uncle, South March will lose its only practitioner of nature's essence. If that day comes to pass, our loose association with the Fae will be severed. When that happens, our ability to withstand the malignance of the soulless creature will be compromised. Should we lose touch with who we are as a people, an army of dragons at our back won't be enough to thwart the Dragon Witch Wraith."

Ouderling's jaw hung open. Gathering a semblance of her voice, she whispered, "What can I do?"

An evil grin transformed Aelfwynne's face. "Travel to Castle Grim. Once there, you must use your gift to retrieve the Staff of Reckoning before all is lost."

Dragon Sect

Sagora's Warning

Travelling the Wizard's Sleeve during the middle of the spring was both beautiful and hazardous. New growth clung to stunted trees and scrub brush vying for life amongst the rugged crags of a steep mountain pass. But the miracle accompanying the spring thaw also left the ground underfoot treacherous to anyone traversing the steep path known as the Wizard's Walk.

Two horses had already gone down hard, injuring their riders, and spilling their wares. One of the mounts had to be put down—never a good omen for a travelling host.

"How fare the wounded?" Queen Khae asked a large, middle-aged captain of the Home Guard dutifully riding along beside her—the vigilant elf ready to respond at a moment's notice should her white mare, Faelnyr, slip in the muck.

Captain Kall's angular features forever turned one way and then another, scanning the terrain in search of dangers only a highly trained Home Guard would be aware of. Serious to a fault, he regarded her without expression. "They'll live.

The scout's condition is serious, but it'll serve as a lesson to take better care of his horse."

Khae nodded, doing her best to keep the astonishment from her voice at how coldly he spoke of the scout's plight. "See to it they get the best care in Orphic Den."

"Yes, Your Highness."

Khae turned away to take in the rock wall rising up from the edge of the roadway on her right. The trail had narrowed to the point that only two horses could walk abreast in the heavy shadows of the ravine. She knew full well why Captain Kall was on alert. The constriction presented the perfect place to ambush their small brigade.

King Hammas had insisted she travel with a full host of Borreraig's elite Home Guard, but after a heated discussion, she had convinced him that until the Dragon Witch Wraith was accounted for, the palace was not to be left vulnerable. She hoped the last image of her husband wasn't going to be the unhappy one she had kissed good-bye to five and a half days ago.

"Does the king know we head to the wizard's lair?" Kall asked casually in his deep voice.

The captain surprised her. She wasn't used to being questioned by anyone other than Hammas. She stared hard at the expressionless elf but the way he returned her gaze eased her brooding discontent. He was doing his job. Loyal to a fault, Kall wasn't afraid to bear her wrath if it meant keeping her safe.

She forced a smile. "I believe by asking you already know the answer."

He nodded. "Yes, Your Highness."

"Then you also know that to have informed the king of our little side trip would have caused him undo stress. In my absence, the poor elf will have enough to worry about."

Dragon Sect

Kall dipped his head as if her explanation were enough.

The constant slosh of hooves sucked at the mud as their contingent of fifty Home Guard trod eastward into the Wizard's Sleeve. A least another league ahead, the hamlet housing the wizards' guild of Orphic Den waited unseen at the head of the pass.

"Do you think it unwise to venture thus?" Khae commanded Kall's attention.

"It's not my place to say, Your Highness."

"Perhaps not, but I'm curious of your view."

Kall seemed unsure how to proceed.

"I value your opinion above most others. You may speak freely."

"Very well, Your Highness. With all due respect, I don't trust this place." He searched the walls on either side of the trail. "Nor do I trust the elves of Orphic Den."

"You fear magic?"

"Not so much fear, Your Highness. I respect the harm magic can inflict. I've seen numerous strange things during my service to your parents. Enough to keep me wary whenever an adept is close at hand."

Khae nodded. She could only imagine the horrors the captain had witnessed during her mother's reign. Driving the human rabble back to the northlands shortly after battling the forces of the sorceress Urdanya and the Dragon Witch Wraith, it was a wonder Kall wasn't quaking in his boots as they neared the arcana stronghold.

"I can only imagine what you survived as a young elf during mother's rise to power, but that's not what I'm asking. What is it about this particular trip that bothers you?"

If he was on edge, he hid it well. "I didn't appreciate how you were treated by Headmaster Sagora and his house servants the last couple of times through here."

She could tell there was more. "*And…?*"

When he didn't respond, she raised her eyebrows. "I'm first and foremost, a practitioner of nature's essence. Like it or not, I know things most do not. There is a foreboding in you."

He swallowed. "Yes, Your Highness. You're correct. There's something about Headmaster Sagora I can't put a name to. Something shifty."

"Shifty?" Khae chuckled at the term, though she agreed with his assessment of the Master Wizard. "How so?"

"It's not in what he says, exactly, though he'd be well-advised to mind his tongue while in your presence."

"Indeed, he'd better," Khae averred. She valued Kall's faithfulness and appreciated the counsel of someone who had lived through what he had, but she knew she couldn't allow her personal feelings toward the headmaster cloud her judgement while dealing with him. "Leave him to me. It wouldn't do if one of my troops skewered the headmaster of the wizards' guild."

"Yes, Your Highness."

"That being said," she winked as she spoke, "I'd privately be the first to commend you for putting an end to one of my many miseries."

If Kall found her comment humorous, he didn't let on.

"What else bothers you about this side trip? I suspect it has something to do with Orphic Den itself."

"It is unnatural, Your Highness. Everything about the village and the keep it's named after. There's something sinister in the air. I taste it every time I set foot in the forsaken place."

She couldn't agree with him more. The angular, derelict-looking buildings hobbled together at the base of the brooding keep seemed to have a life of their own—the entire area perpetually enshrouded by a mist, that in all appearances, hid phantoms and ghouls within its swirling veil.

"I speak for no one but myself, Your Highness, but believe me when I say, I was close to wetting myself the last time we were through here after the Battle at the Gate."

Khae couldn't help but laugh. "If it helps, I may have soiled my underclothes a wee bit myself."

Her mirth dwindled as a wave of apprehension washed over her. "I can't stand the place either. I promise we'll be in and out as quickly as possible."

"I'll be by your side every step of the way, Your Highness."

She turned her attention forward and urged her horse to keep up with the ranks in front of her as she spoke to the daunting walls penning them in. "I'm counting on it."

"Your weapons remain here," a withered elf chamberlain snarled as he gave Captain Kall a once over. He stood with slumped shoulders in an open doorway that led from a small antechamber into Orphic Den proper.

The half dozen Home Guard stuffed into the waiting room stiffened but before anyone acted upon the gruff elf's command, Captain Kall grabbed the crotchety servant and yanked him into the room to stand before Khae, forcing him to his knees. "Kneel in the presence of your queen!"

The chamberlain's knees hit the ground hard.

Kall wrapped his fingers in the elf's wiry, grey hair and forced him to look at the ground.

Not a fan of forcefully making her subjects show her the respect her station was due, she struggled to keep a grin of satisfaction from her face, having dealt with this chamberlain before. The ease of how easily her strong Home

Guard had tossed the stricken chamberlain around filled her with an enormous sense of pride. Confident her safety was in good hands, she nodded for Kall to let him up.

Kall pulled the chamberlain to his feet by the hair and thrust him toward the open doorway. "Lead on."

The chamberlain appeared on the verge of retaliating as he glared at the captain. Despite his rough handling, he remained adamant. "Your weapons remain here."

Khae raised her eyebrows and glanced at Kall, her look giving him permission to deal with the situation as he saw fit.

Kall stepped up to the chamberlain. "The only way my weapons go anywhere other than with me by the queen's side will be in your dying body as I drag you kicking and screaming up yonder stairwell to drop your corpse at your master's feet."

Khae had to give the obnoxious servant credit for having the audacity to stand up to Kall for a few tense moments before he acceded to the captain's refusal.

Casting a baleful glare her way, the chamberlain stormed through the doorway and mounted a steep flight of flagstone steps beyond, not bothering to look back.

"Begone, you insolent oaf," a portly, grey-bearded elf in white robes ordered after a brief discussion with the old chamberlain. He looked at Queen Khae, an obnoxious smile on his pudgy face. "I apologize, Your Majesty. I don't know what goes on between his pointed ears some days."

Khae exchanged a knowing glance with Captain Kall, neither of them fooled by the headmaster's conciliatory tone. She put on her own mock face of pleasantness. "No apologies necessary. I have come to expect nothing less from the highest seat in the wizards' guild."

Dragon Sect

Before Sagora could take issue with her statement, she held up a stalling finger and added, "Second highest seat, actually. High Wizard Aelfwynne's voice still holds sway in South March."

Sagora sputtered, his face reddening, "Of course, Your Majesty. As you so adamantly pointed out the last time you graced our humble village with your presence after the most unfortunate of misunderstandings at the Battle of the Gate."

"Unfortunate misunderstanding?" Khae raised skeptical eyebrows.

"Yes, Your Majesty." Sagora bowed his head as if he were a humble servant. "If not for the betrayal of the treacherous human wizard, Afara Maral, I'm sure your brother would not have acted so."

"Indeed," Khae agreed with the statement for the sake of civility but wondered how deeply involved the wizards' guild had been in the whole affair.

"Has His Majesty travelled with you as well?"

Khae surmised Sagora already knew the answer to that question, but she humoured him. "He keeps watch at the palace. As you know, we're in the midst of troubling times. It wouldn't do to leave the royal seat unattended."

"Of course, Your Majesty. Prudence is always the best course of action."

Khae dipped her head in acknowledgement and followed the headmaster's direction to take a seat on the same couch she and Hammas had shared the last time they had come seeking the aid of Orphic Den. The day Headmaster Sagora had blatantly denied the wizard guild's assistance to her face.

Captain Kall took up a position directly behind the amply cushioned couch that sat beneath an overhang on the open-aired, eastern facing balcony several stories off the ground.

Judging by the pale sky visible beyond a thin veil of mist, the sun was setting in the west.

The six Home Guard accompanying them took up strategic positions around the large balcony, their attention on the doorway and the thick marble balustrade lining the exterior perimeter.

The headmaster clapped his hands and a diminutive servant materialized from the shadows beside a marble table set close to the doorway.

"Pour the queen and myself a healthy libation."

The female elf merely nodded and set about to do just that.

After receiving their silver goblets, Sagora held his goblet up from where he sat on the opposite side of a low table. "To Khae, the Queen of the Elves. May your reign be long and without incident."

Khae held up her goblet, nodding her thanks.

Not wasting time, Sagora took a long swig, wiped his thick lips on the back of his hand and cleared his throat. "So, what can the guild do for you?" He raised his eyebrows. "I'm correct in assuming you're here to ask a boon of Orphic Den?"

Khae struggled to keep her feelings from her face.

"Which, of course, is your right according to the changes that were unilaterally made to the long-standing accord between the guild and Nyxa Wys."

How the pompous dictator maintained a neutral demeanor when speaking the way he did to her face, she had no idea. Even without her gift, she would have seen through his façade.

She took her time indulging in her heady wine before answering. "A treaty made necessary due to the flagrant abuse of the intent of the original agreement."

"Of course, Your Majesty. Of course. An unpleasant oversight on behalf of the guild."

Khae inwardly shook her head. The arrogant elf would never allow the blame to fall directly on himself. She held his intimidating stare. "I hate to disappoint the *guild*, but the assistance of Orphic Den is not required. At least not in a physical sense."

Sagora finished his wine and brought the goblet down onto the tabletop harder than need be.

At once, the meek servant sprung into action, filling his goblet, and turning to Khae—bowing and extending the decanter between them. Khae shook her head and the servant faded into the shadows.

"I've come to inquire about the wraith we spoke of after the Battle at the Gate."

A furtive look passed across the headmaster's face for the briefest of moments—gone so fast, Khae questioned whether she had imagined it.

"What of the ghoul? Have you heard tell of it since its unfortunate interaction with your sister?"

Again, he used the word, 'unfortunate.' She couldn't help but wonder who the term was meant for. Storing the information to ponder later, she said, "That's why I've come to Orphic Den. I haven't heard anything of its movement since, and that worries me. It's been over half a year. Surely it didn't just decide to leave us alone."

Sagora sipped his wine with a little more decorum as he offered, "Perhaps it slipped back across the great ocean from whence it came."

"I've considered that. Hoped for it, actually, but I can't bring myself to believe it. That would be too convenient in my estimation. If I'm to trust my brother, which I don't by the way, the wraith was the one who conspired to kill

Ouderling in the Passage of Dolor, not him or his human wizard."

"To what end?"

"That's what puzzles me. Aelfwynne claims the wraith is the same one my mother fought against."

Sagora nodded. "The Dragon Witch Wraith."

"Yes. From what I've been able to glean from texts and stories handed down by the elders and chroniclers, the Dragon Witch Wraith never coveted the throne. Had no use for it, from what I'm led to understand. It was always after the Crystal Cavern. Something it couldn't attain on its own due to the repulsive power of the crystals whenever it gets near."

"Makes perfect sense."

"Then why kill my sister? What did it hope to achieve by murdering her? By Odyne's own admission, she wasn't a player when it came to the succession. Sure, she wanted the throne when we were young, but I firmly believe she cared little about becoming queen in her later years. Unfortunately, I had no choice."

"There is always a choice."

She hoped that her look was as scathing as she intended it to be. "I'm the only one capable of communing with the Fae. Not to mention, I'm the first born."

"First born female," Sagora stated and buried his face in his goblet as if afraid to meet her quizzical look.

"Have you spoken with my brother?"

Sagora paused a moment longer than Khae thought prudent.

"No, Your Majesty. At least, not since the last official function held at the palace. Near the end of last summer, I believe."

Khae nodded, caring less when that had been. There was something the headmaster was withholding, but she couldn't figure out what.

"Is there something you wish to tell me, Headmaster Sagora? Something that perhaps causes you angst? You may speak without judgement."

"No, Your Majesty."

Khae sighed, nodding to herself. He had blurted his answer much too forcefully. She held his gaze, daring him to break the stare first.

He spoke into his goblet, "There may be one thing you're not aware of."

The headmaster's delay in finishing his thought as he drained his goblet tested Khae's patience.

"Your brother is in Urdanya."

Khae was thankful she was sitting down. She blinked vacantly a couple of times, unable to respond.

"According to my sources, he arrived the other day."

"And he's still there?"

"Far as I know."

On the surface, for a duke of the realm to visit Urdanya, or any place in South March, wasn't out of the ordinary, but she knew Orlythe. He wasn't big on pomp and circumstance, and he certainly hadn't been an ardent supporter of their sister before her death. They had been inseparable while growing up, but after the fall-out between them prior to the onset of the Dragon Witch War, Khae had never known Orlythe to show an interest in his sister's affairs. Now that Odyne was dead...

"He travels with a formidable host."

Sagora's ominous words slapped Khae's sensibilities hard. "Why would he travel with an army?"

Sagora shrugged. "I'm not one to bother with the affairs of state, Your Majesty, but if I were you, I'd be wondering if Urdanya is but a stopover."

Khae gaped. Sagora's satisfied smirk irked her, but his next words left her cold.

"You were right not to leave the Willow Throne unattended."

Dragon Sect

Storm the Castle

"You sure you've got everything you need?" Pecklyn asked as he stood on the edge of the platform overlooking the black waters of Crystal Lake, its unusual glassy surface reflecting the myriad of stars overhead. "We won't get a second chance to storm the castle."

Ouderling straightened from where she bent over a small, leather rucksack at her feet and observed the assembled dragons and their riders as they prepared to escort her to Castle Grim. Her dark vision enabled her to see the intense faces of the brothers Ashe and Cynder waiting patiently upon the shoulders of their red dragons, Athgaan and Dagomar respectively.

The whistle of large wings cutting the air overhead drew her gaze to Kingstone and his rider patrolling the sky over Crystal Lake—Draakyr's black hair barely visible in the moonlight.

It had been well over half a year since the Battle at the Gate—a time that had required a heightened vigilance from everyone living at Highcliff. Without the aid of Aelfwynne's staff, the high wizard had feared things would not go well should the Dragon Witch Wraith discover a way to overcome the bane the earth blood presented.

Ouderling slipped the rucksack over her shoulders, one of the straps rubbing against her cheek and smearing the camouflage dye blacking out her face. She nodded. "Good to go."

Pecklyn used his thumb to repair the smudge as best he could. "You be careful when we get there. If you suspect something is remotely wrong, tell me or Balewynd and we'll abort the mission."

"Master Aelfwynne said we weren't to return without the staff," Ouderling whispered, wondering where the goblin had wandered off to. He had just been speaking with Balewynd and Jyllana sitting atop the blue dragon, Mirage.

Pecklyn scowled, an unfamiliar look on the ever-optimistic elf. "I don't care what he says. It's not worth your life. I'll deal with him if things go wrong."

"Not a good omen," a raspy voice directly behind them sent a cold jolt up Ouderling's spine.

Nonplussed, Pecklyn spun around and followed Aelfwynne's gaze over the lake. "For those who believe in superstitions, maybe."

"Don't get too cocky, young Ors. Sayings aren't fabricated from thin air. A mist-free night upon Crystal Lake is the harbinger that something foul is afoot." Aelfwynne lowered his voice. "Guard her with your life."

"If she doesn't make it back," Pecklyn's harsh whisper matched the high wizard's, "you can rest assured I won't either. I imagine the same goes for everyone on this quest."

"That's good." Aelfwynne glared at Pecklyn. "Your lives won't be worth living if you do."

Dragon Sect

With the threat hanging between them, the high wizard approached Ouderling who had heard every word. "You certain you can attune yourself to what needs to be done?"

She wanted to say yes, but stopped herself. She wasn't sure of anything. "I'll do my best, Master Aelfwynne."

"That may not be enough. Push yourself. Without the staff in my possession, the fate of the throne will be fraught with misery and loss."

Ouderling swallowed. "You're sure my uncle isn't there?"

"As sure as I can be. The Watchmen's last report has him at Urdanya Castle."

Ouderling nodded, not wishing to contemplate why her uncle had suddenly expressed an interest in her deceased aunt's castle. She felt sorry for her cousin.

Aelfwynne muttered as he hobbled past her and made his way into a small egress in the cliff face that had been fashioned for someone his size, "The future of the kingdom may well be decided tonight."

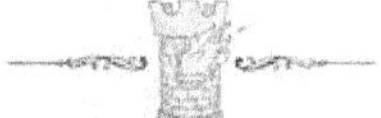

Seated behind Pecklyn, both of them clad in black leather, proved an uncomfortable flight for Ouderling atop Dawnbreaker's wide shoulders. She was glad her sword rested secure in its baldric—the ruby gemstone Eolande had infused in the tip of its pommel glinted above her shoulder in the light of the full moon. Far below, the glassy surface of Lake Grim mirrored the starry sky.

Ouderling hugged Pecklyn, pressing her lips against his ear to be heard over the rushing wind of dragonflight. "Do they know we're coming?"

"Unless they're sleeping, there's no way they can miss five dragons flying across the moon," Pecklyn laughed, leaning his head into her chest to look at her—his long hair whipping around her neck to mingle with hers.

Dragon Sect

"Won't they shoot us out of the sky?"

"We're about to find out." He smiled at the shock his words elicited. "With your uncle away, I doubt anyone will be brazen enough to give that order."

"What about his wizard?"

"Ryedyn?" Pecklyn shrugged. "It's unclear whether he travels with the duke. I guess we'll find out soon enough."

The hard lessons Aelfwynne had drilled into her over the last several months made Pecklyn's response irritating. "It's a good thing Aelfy didn't hear you say that."

Pecklyn released his hold on Dawnbreaker's neck and leaned into Ouderling's embrace, laughing. "I see he's rubbing off on you, too."

Ouderling rolled her eyes, desperately hanging onto the carefree elf lest he slip from Dawnbreaker's back. She pushed him forward. "Pay attention to what you're doing."

He regripped a scale on either side of Dawnbreaker's neck. "She wouldn't let me fall. She loves me."

"You two had best get ready. Kingstone's gone ahead to see if he'll draw fire." Pecklyn's purple-tinged dragon warned.

Instantly alert, all sense of merriment left Pecklyn's face.

Moonlight glinted off Kingstone's bronze-tipped scales, making it easy to follow his dive toward the black bulk blotting the north shore—Castle Grim's brooding keep aglow with flickering, candlelit windows, and wall-mounted torches along the top of the battlements.

Distant cries disturbed the night—the tell-tale sound of alarmed Grim Guard taking notice of the dragon formation descending on their position.

Kingstone levelled his flight at rampart height and glided gracefully across the entire sweep of the sprawling castle from west to east. Reaching the end of the outer wall, he spun a lazy circle, riding an updraft, and soared from east to west.

"All's good, so far," Dawnbreaker reported. *"Hang on."*

Ouderling didn't have to be told twice. She wrapped her fingers around Pecklyn's sword belt and leaned into him, trying to hide her body as best she could to adhere to their plan.

Led by Mirage, with Athgaan and Dagomar right behind the blue dragon, Dawnbreaker followed in their wake. Abandoning their side-by-side formation, the dragons dropped into single file.

Kingstone's timing coincided with Mirage's arrival—he had spun around at the eastern corner tower and led the group past the hulking keep. Tilting his wings, he crossed over the southern ramparts and continued past the towering spires of the great cathedral to fly out over the flatlands fronting Castle Grim's landlocked walls.

Mirage pulled up above the great courtyard separating the keep from the cathedral and hovered while the red dragons, Athgaan and Dagomar landed momentarily in the inner bailey along with Dawnbreaker.

Kingstone reappeared overhead and dropped quickly to the ground to allow Draakyr a chance to leap from his back, then rose into the sky to keep watch as Mirage touched down.

Steel boots clanged along the battlements, announcing the arrival of the castle's watch, a mixture of curious and alarmed eyes peering into the dark shadow cast by the cathedral.

At a nod from Ashe who had run across the open space toward the main gates where stairwells emptied from the top of the walls, Pecklyn, Ouderling, and Cynder jumped free of their dragons moments before they rose into the air, emitting a cacophony of ear-piercing screeches to draw the attention of the Grim Guard.

"Go," Pecklyn ordered with a harsh whisper.

Ouderling scrambled after the blacked-out faces of Balewynd and Cynder, their silent footfalls mounting the cathedral steps and carrying them through the doors at the top.

She paused on the threshold long enough to witness Pecklyn, Draakyr, and Jyllana join Ashe near the base of the wall. Hands in the air, they confronted an endless stream of Grim Guard that had spilled into the courtyard with weapons drawn.

Dragon Sect

The Path to Evermore

Khae stewed as Faelnyr picked her way along the sloppy terrain leading out of Orphic Den. Though Headmaster Sagora had offered to put her up for the night in the wizard's keep, she had refused his feigned hospitality. Even had she not despised the boor so, she owed her troops the courtesy to put as much distance between them and the eerie atmosphere of the wizards' guild as possible. They didn't deserve to spend one moment longer than required in the mystic village. She had enough to worry about.

Their spread-out procession rounded a long bend and entered one of the few level clearings along the Wizard's Walk. Captain Kall's voice in the darkness drew her from her gloomy thoughts. "We should camp here tonight, Your Highness. We're safely away from the Den and a long narrows lies ahead. I'd be amiss not to express my discomfort at marching through the cramped defile in the dead of the night. Especially with the news the headmaster imparted."

"By all means, captain. Give the order," Khae said, relief in her voice. Even with the stopover at Orphic Den, it had been a long day in the saddle. It would feel good to stretch her weary body and lie down for the night.

Captain Kall nodded and spoke to the Home Guard around him. The call to halt passed up and down the procession.

It wasn't long before Khae's pavilion was erected on the driest ground available. She smiled for the benefit of the beleaguered sentries posted outside her tent as she pushed through the flaps and was met by a blast of welcome heat that radiated from an iron brazier in the centre of the open space—its smoke wafting through a hole in the conical ceiling.

Standing on the far side of the makeshift hearth was the elf captain, Kall, warming his hands. "I trust this is adequate, Your Highness?"

Khae surveyed the spacious interior—large enough to house twenty Home Guard. A fur covered pallet had been assembled just beyond the captain, with a table erected on either side of the brazier—the smaller one contained food and drink while the larger table held an unrolled map of the region.

"Give my thanks to the troops, captain. As always is the case, they've done well considering the situation. Cold and weary, and no doubt preoccupied with whatever ghastly apparitions they endured back at the Den."

"No doubt, Your Highness." Kall dipped his chin in acknowledgement. "I shall pass on your kind words, though I would expect nothing less of them."

"Nevertheless, I don't want it said that their queen is an ungrateful ruler." She ignored the food table and strode to inspect the map. "Do you know where we are?"

"Here, Your Highness." Kall indicated with a finger. "It'll take the better part of tomorrow to reach Gullveig."

She sighed. "Very well. I suspected as much. I just wish I knew what he was up to."

Kall nodded, his manner suggesting he knew exactly who she was talking about.

She shook her head. "What does he hope to gain?"

"If banners are called, the Sea Throne will command a fair-sized army, Your Highness."

"An army that is accountable to the Willow Throne!"

Kall nodded, conceding the point, though he didn't appear convinced.

"You think the coastal towns will side with Orlythe?"

"I'm not privy to what goes on in someone else's mind, Your Highness, but stranger things have happened."

"Please. You may dispense with my title while we're alone." Khae's tone softened. "As a commander in the South March army, what does your gut tell you?"

Kall mulled the question over. He repositioned several hand-sized statues of rearing horses on the map, their surfaces glinting in the light of many candles. Satisfied with their placement, he looked directly into her eyes. "Given the proper leverage, I believe any local lord can be convinced to support a cause that is not to their liking. Should the Duke of Grim garner the support of Urdanya's troops, his forces will outnumber South March's standing army."

Khae gaped. It was a fact she knew well, but to hear it spoken so casually by one whose opinion she trusted implicitly shocked her.

"Aye." Kall pointed to the horse markers on two of the larger, southern settlements. "It's safe to assume that Alywind and Nayda will follow suit. With their close proximity to Grim Town, it would be in their best interest."

"Best interest?" Khae was incredulous. "To rise against their queen?"

Kall raised thick eyebrows. "Their geographical position leaves them little choice. Should they oppose such a move on the duke's behalf, Orlythe's forces would crush them outright."

"That's treasonous."

"Of a certainty, Your Highness. But it's also a matter of survival. Sure, the royal troops stationed in and around the southern towns may choose to stand against the duke, but the common folk will inevitably push to do what's best for their families. What choice do they have?"

"To rebel against the throne will cost them their lives! What could possibly possess them?"

"Again, I don't profess to speak for the masses, Your Highness, but if I were in their boots, I can see how they'd rather face a potential reckoning later at the benevolent hands of Borreraig Palace than be brutally slaughtered by the duke's forces."

Khae wanted to yell at the captain. To vehemently refute his reasoning, but as she poised herself to do just that, she found she couldn't find fault in his hypothesis. Chewing her lower lip, she fought to control her sudden, erratic breathing.

"Dammit, Kall. You've done nothing but upset me further."

Kall dipped his chin. "My apologies, Your Highness. I wish it were otherwise."

She sighed and patted his beefy forearm. "You need not be sorry for having the courage to tell me the truth."

He nodded.

"Come, sup with me." Khae crossed to the food table. "I'm honoured to have you by my side as we travel this uncertain path to evermore."

Dragon Sect

Her Mother's Essence

Cynder hugged the wall with his back and leaned forward to peer into the brightly lit corridor beyond. Deep in the heart of Grim Keep, Ouderling and Cynder had followed Balewynd through an underground warren that had originated from an access point in the floor of the cathedral—Balewynd's uncanny knowledge of the castle's hidden byways helping them avoid any real contact with elves of consequence. Twice they had come upon a servant going about their duties. Twice, they had incapacitated the servant, gagged and tied them, and placed them inside a room, hopefully not to be found until long after they had retrieved the Staff of Reckoning and returned to Highcliff.

"Clear," Cynder whispered, his long black hair tied in a ponytail; his face blackened by dye.

Balewynd clung to the wall behind him, her face as black as his. She nodded at Ouderling against the wall behind her, and together they slunk across the wide passageway and started toward a short flight of broad steps at its far end.

Balewynd had done well to get them this far. She claimed there was no way to access the castle wing she believed they needed to get to without proceeding down this stretch of corridor.

They reached the bottom step and froze. Muted voices came from somewhere close by. Ducking against the wall did little to hide their blacked-out appearance at the base of the beige marble stairs.

Balewynd pulled her curved, black-bladed dagger free of its sheath and held up her free hand for Ouderling and Cynder to stop. She mouthed, *'Stay here,'* and padded up the flight of steps without a sound. Keeping her body lower than the top step, she lifted her head enough to glimpse a corridor that ran off on either side of a small landing.

The voices came from the left. She rolled her eyes. *Of course they did.* Fortunately, the voices didn't sound like they were getting any closer. She waggled her fingers for Ouderling and Cynder to come forward.

"There's two, at least," Balewynd whispered. "They'll be guarding the duke's private chambers at the far end of the hallway."

Cynder nodded, but Ouderling frowned and asked, "I thought we're looking for your father's chambers?"

Balewynd took a deep breath. They didn't have time for explanations. She glared at Ouderling, not fazed by the red eyes staring back at her. She had witnessed the unusual trait in the princess many times over the past several months during their training sessions. Had been the reason for their hue on many occasions. Red eyes meant hatred or pent-up excitement that bordered on anxiety in the princess. She imagined both of those scenarios weren't far from the truth deep in her uncle's castle.

"Have you never been up here before?" Balewynd asked with forced patience.

Ouderling shook her head.

"Father was Orlythe's head chamberlain. Their quarters are next to each other."

Ouderling nodded.

"What's down the other way?" Cynder whispered.

It was all Balewynd could do not to yell at the two of them to keep quiet. Hoping to discourage further questions, she growled, "The hallway wanders around to the west side of the keep to where the rest of the higher-ranking staff members are lodged."

Cynder nodded and fingered the wisp of his mustache in thought.

"Now..." Balewynd held a finger to her lips. When Ouderling and Cynder nodded, she leaned forward to glance around the corner. Not bothering to look back, she held up four, black-gloved fingers.

Movement from behind startled Balewynd. She pulled back in time to watch Cynder mount the last couple of steps. She reached out to grab him but he was too quick.

The black-haired Guardian strolled casually down the right corridor, not bothering to look at the Grim Guard.

"Hey you! Stop!"

Cynder jumped into a run and disappeared from sight.

Ouderling made to go after him, but Balewynd grabbed her by the elbow and pulled her back, holding her against the wall at the base of the steps.

Heavy footsteps resounded down the upper corridor from the direction of Duke Orlythe's chambers. Three Grim Guard charged up the hallway, but as they approached the open space at the head of the steps, Cynder's voice kept their attention directed his way.

"You want to fight? You'll have to catch me first."

Dragon Sect

The sound of the Grim Guards' pursuit echoed down the western corridor, diminishing quickly, and soon died away altogether.

Ouderling glared at Balewynd and yanked her arm free.

Balewynd raised her brow. "Now there's only one."

Ouderling nodded and smiled. She held up a finger as she stepped past Balewynd, and stood on the landing, staring down the hallway at the last guard. "Excuse me. Do you know where I can find the duke? Oh, never mind." With that said, she rejoined Balewynd.

Not happy about the princess exposing herself, Balewynd gave her an appreciative nod, nonetheless.

"Hey! Miss! Get back here!"

Inhaling deeply, Balewynd calmed her mind, slipping into her fighting persona—prepared to react to whatever presented itself with a clear mind. This is what she enjoyed most about being a Guardian. She took pride in the fact she was good at it. Better than anyone else if she allowed herself the satisfaction of the truth.

Quick footfalls made her job easy. The lone Grim Guard had barely rounded the corner when a startled gasp escaped him.

Balewynd twisted her curved dagger as it slid beneath the guard's leather chest protector and angled up, under his ribs.

The guard appeared to weigh twice her weight but she eased his dying body against the corner of the wall and helped him slide to the ground, all the while staring into his stricken eyes.

Before the guard slumped to the ground, she was confident he wouldn't be bothering them any longer. She pulled her blade free and wiped it on his black leather breeks.

Not sparing him another glance, she scanned the corridor in both directions. "Come on. The way's clear."

Ouderling gave the dying guard a wide berth and followed in her wake. "Did you have to kill him?"

Balewynd didn't look back as she responded, "We don't have time to be merciful. He chose to come after you."

She knew that if she looked back to see Ouderling's reaction, a pervading guilt would consume her, and that, she couldn't allow. Weakness now would end up getting them all killed.

Stopping near the end of the corridor, an intense sadness washed over her as she stood before the plain, wooden door that marked her father's old quarters. The one she had shared with him as an elfling. She grabbed hold of the worn handle and paused long enough to take a deep breath, not knowing what she might find inside.

The door opened on a dark room without a window. From her time at Castle Grim, she knew the duke's quarters surrounded her father's on all sides but the corridor.

Ouderling followed her in. She didn't need to ask if the princess required light to see by. It had become apparent to Balewynd over the last year that along with the peculiarity of Ouderling's colour changing eyes came her exceptional dark vision.

She closed the door behind Ouderling and squinted to make out the furniture in the chamber. Everything appeared as she remembered, less her father's few possessions. Whoever the duke had elevated to the position of head chamberlain, they either didn't care to keep personal items out in the open, or they inhabited a different room.

Ouderling turned a slow circle, scanning the walls and the simple furnishings.

Difficult to tell in the absence of light, Balewynd thought Ouderling's eyes had changed from red to green.

Being in the room she had shared with her father was disconcerting—especially aware of how he had died. Thankful for the darkness to mask her sadness, she appreciated Ouderling's company more now than ever.

The princess had come a long way since her first days at Highcliff. Balewynd's first impression of the spoiled brat elfling that had ended up on their doorstep was one of a scared, naïve, impulsive teenager. She had agreed with Master Aelfwynne's initial assessment of the heir to the Willow Throne. Ouderling didn't belong at Highcliff.

Watching the confident elf now, slowly scanning the room with purpose, she had to admit how wrong they had been. Ouderling still had a long way to go to become someone to be reckoned with, but she was young. There was ample time to groom the princess for the future provided they found what they had come for and were able to escape the castle with their lives.

The pain evident in Balewynd's expression tugged at Ouderling's heart as she examined their surroundings. Her newly found friend—for that's what Balewynd had surely become over the past months of dogged training and mentorship—had not returned to Castle Grim since the Battle at the Gate. She couldn't imagine how traumatic it had been for Balewynd to witness her father's grizzly death. Revisiting his old quarters had to weigh heavily on the Guardian no matter how brave she tried to appear on the outside.

Blinking to refocus her thoughts, Ouderling concentrated on why they had come to the castle. The long hours of monotonous training by High Wizard Aelfwynne was about to be put to the test. As much as his instruction had been geared toward preparing her to handle a moment like this, nothing they had practised remotely equated to the pressure she faced now.

Her heart hammered in her chest. So many people depended on her.

Now that Cynder had alerted the Grim Guard to his presence deep within the stronghold, it was imperative she find the Staff of Reckoning as fast as possible.

There was also Jyllana, Pecklyn, and Ashe to think about. Facing down a horde of Grim Guard on the castle grounds, only the spirits knew how they fared. Had they been able to stall the hard-nosed brutes, or were they already in fetters? Or worse, were they…?

She swallowed her fear. According to Master Aelfwynne, speculating on things she had no control over was self-defeating. He had monotonously driven home the point that the only thing of importance during a crucial moment such as this was to clear one's mind and do what needed to be done. The others were responsible for their own part in the raid. For the moment, they weren't her concern.

Two, deep, cleansing breaths, followed by a third, just as Aelfwynne had taught her, centered her attention on what she was about to do. What her mother had always done. Communicate with the otherworldly realm of the Fae.

Not directly. That required more magic than she had at her disposal. Even the great Queen Khae relied on the ethereal presence of Grim Watch—the mysterious warlock tower located on Grim Ward Island in the northern reaches of the Ors Sea.

Employing what Aelfwynne had taught her, she eased her mind into a state of semi-consciousness, Fear and apprehension drifted into the background of her mind. All sound fell away—replaced by a profound level of self-awareness.

Dragon Sect

At first, she sensed nothing. A blank void confronted her where she knew she should feel the essence of her innate magic—a unique ability to cast her flitting thoughts to a mystical realm beyond her physical reality. It was time to become one with her gift. It was time to embrace the magic her mother had passed down.

A sudden spasm of dread threatened to extract her from the trance-like state she fought to maintain. On the cusp of losing focus altogether, she sought the lessons painstakingly imparted by the highest wizard in the land. Grasping desperately at the reassurances those teachings provided, her emotions settled sufficiently to allow her to assert the magic that was part of who she was. The magic that made her different from every other elf in all the realm. Every elf but her mother, and by extension, her deceased grandmother, the great warrior Nyxa.

Nyxa had been the first. The one who had found a way to harness their unique ability and transcend the mortal world to speak with the Fae.

A runnel of warmth trickled along her arms and up the back of her neck. She had finally found a semblance of peace with her grandmother's legacy. One she had vehemently denied while growing up in Orlythia.

Though not spoken, it was as if the thoughts of other beings had joined them in the chamber—directing her attention to the back wall.

"Pull the pallet away from the wall," she heard herself tell Balewynd.

Balewynd cast her a worried stare. Nodding slowly, she did what Ouderling asked.

The exposed black marble wall appeared no different from that comprising the rest of the room, but instinctively, Ouderling knew that wasn't the case. Near the bottom right corner of the chamber, her magic exposed a hollow section of wall behind the stone façade—the vision in her mind so clear that she couldn't understand how Balewynd couldn't see it as well. A section large enough to hold the Staff of Reckoning made itself apparent to her probing gift.

Balewynd watched on, her expression imploring Ouderling to direct her further.

Ouderling ignored her. Focusing on the wall, she mouthed the strange runic text magically etching itself across the thin section of marble in question, *'Only those who can summon the breath of the wind may pass beyond this wall.'*

If Balewynd saw the runes, the Guardian never let on. She frowned, seeking direction.

Only those who can summon the breath of the wind may pass beyond this wall. Ouderling couldn't fathom the meaning of the ancient script. *Summon the breath of the wind. The breath of the wind.*

Doubt crept along the fringes of her mind. In her heart, she believed she had located the staff's hiding place, but for the life of her, she couldn't figure out how to solve the riddle. Without knowing how she knew, it was obvious to her that they wouldn't be able to retrieve the priceless talisman without deciphering the meaning of the odd phrase. Short of using a heavy warhammer, she could see no way to discover the truth behind what her nature's essence told her to be true. Closer inspection of the smooth wall left no doubt that a trip lever wasn't to be found.

Her intense green eyes faded through a pallet of colours until they shone orange. A phenomenon that troubled her. The realization that she was losing her grip on her magic only accelerated its demise.

Dragon Sect

Her hands shook uncontrollably. A scream of frustration ripped free of her throat, obliterating the fragile link she had established with the Fae.

The floor rushed up to meet her.

Dragon Sect

Breath of the Wind

Balewynd jumped across the intervening space between them, catching the princess before she hit the ground. One moment Ouderling had been in a trancelike state, and in the next she had cried out as her legs buckled beneath her.

Arms dangling limp, Ouderling blinked up at her. "Wh-what happened? Why is it so dark?"

Balewynd eased her to the marble floor, helping her to sit in the middle of her father's old quarters. "You fainted."

"What?" Ouderling took in their surroundings. Her body tensed. "Oh my. We're in Grim Keep."

Balewynd offered her a hand up. "Yes. Searching for Master Aelfwynne's staff."

Ouderling nodded. "I remember." Her head snapped to the side to stare at the blank wall Balewynd had exposed. "Did you see them?"

Balewynd's head snapped to face the only door in the chamber, expecting the worst. "Who?"

"Not who? The words etched into the wall," Ouderling said as if to herself. She approached the back wall and bent down, running a hand along a section of marble. "I saw runes somewhere around here."

Balewynd squatted to get a better look, her attention distracted by who she feared they would soon see at the doorway. It wouldn't be long before the dead guard was found. When that happened, the entire floor would be crawling with Grim Guard. "I never saw anything. Your dark vision is better than most. What did they say?"

"It made no sense. It said, only those who can summon the breath of the wind may pass beyond this wall."

The princess couldn't have shocked her more if she had punched her in the face. She gripped Ouderling's forearm and squeezed. "Are you sure?"

"Yes, why?" Ouderling pulled her arm free.

Balewynd swallowed and stood, running a hand through her dishevelled hair. Of course. It made sense. Her father had stolen the Staff of Reckoning and hid it in the wall separating the duke's chamber from his own. A sad smile crossed her face. Leave it to him to hide the most important talisman in South March feet away from where Duke Orlythe rested his head every night.

The riddle Ouderling claimed to have seen was Balewynd's father's favourite. He had taunted her with it for years as a young elfling, daring her to solve it in order to earn a reward he claimed would allow her to soar on the wings of a dragon. The riddle had gotten so old between them that she had simply ignored him whenever he had mentioned it over the ensuing years.

It hadn't been until just before he had convinced the duke to allow her to train with the Highcliff Guardians that it dawned on her what it meant. That had been the first time she had spoken with a dragon.

Dragon Sect

Having snuck up to a tiny balcony surrounding the peak of the highest spire adorning Grim Keep, she had taken a moment to enjoy the breathtaking view of Grim Lake and the distant, volcanic mountains. Pleased with herself, she had successfully bypassed the human wizard's wards to get there. Nor had it been easy to slip past the Grim Guard patrolling the corridors at the base of the spire. Afara Maral had forbidden anyone access to his wizard's aerie years before. To Balewynd, the edict had been seen as a test. Through her dogged determination to rise to the challenge, she had finally realized her goal.

Mesmerized by the view, and more than a little anxious about what would happen were she to be found out, she had almost jumped to her death when a dragon had appeared out of nowhere and brushed past the low-walled walkway encircling the tower's pinnacle.

More alarming had been the strange voice that had entered her head as the blue dragon banked over the lake and hovered long enough to lock eyes with her. *"I knew I'd find you one day. If you ever have need of me, summon the breath of the wind and I will pass beyond these walls."*

Those words were the only ones spoken by the young Mirage, but they had instilled in her a longing desire to one day fly the skies on the back of a dragon. Something her father had miraculously arranged the following spring.

She tried to moisten her dry throat as she looked wide-eyed at Ouderling. "Show me exactly where you saw the runes."

Ouderling bent low and touched the black marble near the ground. "Here, I think. I don't see them anymore."

Balewynd crouched beside her, running her hand along the cold stone. It didn't feel any different than the area around it. Swallowing her doubts, she spoke to the wall as if she were saying hi to a friend. "Mirage."

Ouderling cast her a quizzical look.

An almost inaudible snick disturbed the silence, followed by a soft rumble.

Before their eyes, a thin, rectangular seam appeared on the wall, interrupting the surface's smooth sheen. Barely visible in the darkness, the section of stone fell into the room.

Balewynd's dragonlike reflexes caught it before it hit the ground. Easing it to the floor, absently surprised by the weight of the thick slab, her attention was drawn by Ouderling's gasp as the princess pulled a two-foot stick from the recess and placed it across her bent knees.

Though hard to see in the darkness, several of the grotesquely screaming faces carved along its length stared blankly back at her.

She stared in awe at Ouderling. "You did it. You found the Staff of Reckoning."

Ouderling nodded, a great smile on her wondrous expression.

As amazing as it was to have recovered the revered Staff of Reckoning, just the sight of it filled Balewynd with dread. Evil creatures sought Aelfwynne's cane. Beings who would not hesitate to deliver onto them an excruciating death in order to possess the talisman themselves.

She swallowed. Grabbing Ouderling's forearm to steady herself, she pulled the princess to her feet and dragged her toward the door. "We need to be gone from here!"

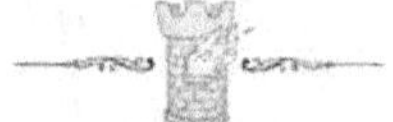

"What about Cynder?" Ouderling asked as they stepped past the guard Balewynd had killed and started down the steps leading away from the duke's chambers.

"He's on his own. He knew the risk of his actions." Balewynd took the steps three at a time, stopping momentarily at the bottom to ensure Ouderling made it safely.

Ouderling paused, but Balewynd shoved her forward.

"Go! His sacrifice will be for nothing if we're caught with the staff." Balewynd tore the talisman from Ouderling's hands and pushed her between the shoulder blades. "Move!"

Stumbling down the corridor, Ouderling couldn't help looking back. Not for fear of the Grim Guard, but in hopes of seeing Cynder appear from a side passage to join their frenzied flight through the levels of the Grim Keep maze. The servant's door closing behind them sounded like a death knell. They had left Cynder behind.

The hidden byways passed Ouderling in a daze. Heart hammering and breaking at the same time, her shoulders bounced off the narrow walls. If not for Balewynd's steadying hands, she would have fallen to the floor on several occasions.

Unsure of how long they had run, the narrow flight of steps that shot up at the end of the dimly lit tunnel they ran along, startled Ouderling. They had reached the cathedral.

Balewynd threw her shoulder into the marble, trap door, its weight evident on her face as the dim light of the building above illuminated her features. She held the hatch open long enough for Ouderling to clamber out of the ground before letting it slam back into place, unconcerned about the reverberations echoing off the vaulted ceiling.

The Guardian paused at the great double doors exiting the cathedral. "Let's hope Pecklyn and the others were able to keep the Grim Guard at bay."

The open space between the cathedral and Grim Keep was filled by elves in studded, black leather.

"There!" Balewynd pointed to the base of the castle's exterior wall. Their companions sat with their backs against the rampart, watched by at least a dozen attentive Grim Guard.

"Let me talk to them," Ouderling started down the wide steps fronting the cathedral. "They'll listen to me."

Balewynd grabbed her elbow and yanked her back. Giving her a once over, her gaze lingered on Ouderling's face. She touched Ouderling's cheek, black camouflage dye creating a dark smear on her finger. "How will you explain this?"

Finger and thumb between her lips, Balewynd emitted a shrill whistle, the moon reflecting in her blue eyes as she searched the sky above the parapets.

At the sound of her whistle, everyone in the bailey turned to stare at the cathedral steps.

So intent were the looks they received, Ouderling wanted to melt into the marble steps, but Balewynd surprised her.

"Take the staff. Whatever you do, don't let go." Relieved of the Staff of Reckoning, Balewynd's jagged dagger appeared in her hand. "Stay here and watch the skies. Be ready."

Ouderling nodded as Balewynd descended the steps. Slowly. Deliberately.

The nearest group of Grim Guard started toward them but stopped at the sight of her weapon and how she approached.

"Get her!" A large, female guard stepped ahead of the others. "There's only two of them."

"That's Balewynd Tayn," one of the guard's cohorts pointed out.

"I don't care if she's the queen. Don't let her escape."

Ouderling trembled at the top of the steps, not sure what to do. She couldn't let Balewynd face them on her own, but neither did she wish to disobey her. Balewynd had been emphatic that she was to stay put.

Dragon Sect

The Grim Guard pulled their weapons free and spread out around the fluted steps. Balewynd was trapped.

"Bale!" Pecklyn shouted from where he now stood with Ashe and Jyllana—the three of them daring the guards to come closer. "Don't engage! Just hold them."

Balewynd didn't respond. Facing the Grim Guard closing in around her, she feigned to lash out at them—the threat providing her a brief respite.

A large guard rushed her with a mace in hand, missed his swing, and cried out in pain. Dodging his attack, the keen edge of Balewynd's dagger sliced the leather covering his forearm.

The vocal female emitted a frenzied cry and lunged with her rapier, stabbing at Balewynd's exposed side—its point diving into her abdomen.

Balewynd grimaced, but spun away from the assault, her dagger slashing her attacker's cheek.

Hands grabbed Balewynd from behind and a press of bodies took her to the ground.

Ouderling pulled her sword in preparation to fend off two Grim Guard that had stepped beyond the writhing pile restraining Balewynd.

"Halt!" Ouderling shouted. "How dare you threaten the heir to the Willow Throne? Unhand my companion."

The two Grim Guard stopped halfway up the steps, their puzzled gazes trying to verify Ouderling's identity.

Face blacked out, and hair cut short, they would have a hard time identifying her in the moonlight.

The female Grim Guard with the slashed face started up the steps. "Get her, you fools."

"She claims to be the princess," the bigger of the two male Grim Guard protested.

"The princess is dead!" The female spat blood on the steps at Ouderling's feet, her rapier poised to strike.

A blood-curdling scream erupted from behind Ouderling. She turned in time to see Cynder burst through the cathedral doors and launch himself through the air at the female Grim Guard.

Whether the female acted on instinct or the jab had been a lucky coincidence, Cynder fell on the surprised guard—her rapier taking him in the stomach and exiting his lower back, burying itself to the hilt. Though she had defended Cynder's charge, the guard couldn't prevent being crushed beneath the momentum of his leap. Together, they tumbled down the steps, rolling into the Grim Guard struggling to restrain Balewynd.

Before Cynder and the one who had surely ended his life came to a stop, ear-piercing shrieks sent chills up Ouderling's back.

"Dragons!" Several Grim Guard pointed over the bulk of the cathedral, their eyes reflecting the fear the fanged and fire-breathing beasts instilled in someone who was about to be eaten.

Kingstone hit the ground hard near the base of the cathedral steps, his wings spread wide, separating the Grim Guard battling Balewynd from their peers. His great head scanned the bailey, briefly resting on the spot where Pecklyn and the others were being held. Without warning, he let forth a wide swath of dragon fire, incinerating anyone and anything in its path.

Pecklyn and Ashe whistled in time to divert the plummeting fall of Dawnbreaker, Athgaan and Dagomar as they dropped onto the castle grounds near Pecklyn's group, crushing several Grim Guard beneath them. Snapping viciously, the dragons scared off anyone foolish enough to remain behind.

"Where's Balewynd?" Mirage's voice sounded in Ouderling's mind.

"There!" Ouderling pointed with the tip of her sword. "Hurry!"

Two large Grim Guard had risen to their feet with a bloodied Balewynd in their grasp, her head hanging to one side. Pain-laced eyes watched as a third guard hefted a large warhammer over his shoulders and swung at her head.

The warhammer swept through the air but at the last moment its course was altered by a blur of black leather— the heavy weapon impacting one of the guards holding Balewynd with a sickening crack.

Jyllana drove through the hammer-wielding guard and tumbled to the ground.

Before the shocked Grim Guard could react, a blue missile of death dropped beside the one still clinging to Balewynd, and let out a terrific roar.

The remaining Grim Guard around the steps stumbled and fell over themselves as they scrambled away from the cathedral, their earlier bravado forgotten in the presence of the enraged dragon.

Ouderling sheathed her sword and rushed to help Jyllana lower Balewynd to her knees—throwing them to the ground as an arrow thudded into the dirt beside them. Two more arrows ricocheted off Mirage's scales in quick succession.

A distant cry rang out from somewhere above, "Arm the ballistae."

Mirage shrieked and flapped his wings twice, rising off the ground to blast the ramparts with a deadly swath of fire. Archers ducked, but not before two bodies toppled from the wall engulfed in flames.

Balewynd groaned beside Ouderling, and tried to rise, her bloody hands grabbing Ouderling by the tunic as she attempted to lift the princess to her feet, but fell back to her knees. "We have to get you out of here."

Ouderling nodded. "Grab the staff."

Balewynd did, allowing herself to be pulled to her feet. She wavered uncertainly and stumbled toward Mirage who had dropped back to the bailey.

Random arrowshot thudded against scales and impacted the ground around them.

Ouderling put her shoulder in Balewynd's armpit. With the aid of the staff, she hobbled the Guardian to Mirage's side and helped her climb onto his shoulders. Clambering in behind, she slapped Mirage's neck. "Go!"

Mirage sprung into the air and rose above Castle Grim, but not before the sickening sound of an arrow slammed into Balewynd's torso and dropped her limp across Mirage's neck.

It was all Ouderling could do to prevent the Guardian from slipping from the dragon's neck, desperately clinging to her trainer and the Staff of Reckoning at the same time.

"Faster, Mirage. She's hurt bad!"

A profound sadness infused Ouderling. Though the big, blue dragon never spoke a word on their hurried flight back to Highcliff, she sensed his terror for not acting faster to save his rider.

Tears streamed across Ouderling's cheeks as the cold, night wind buffeted the hair around her face. Unable to speak, she listened to the rest of their raiding party talking solemnly amongst themselves.

The lump in Ouderling's throat grew, threatening to choke her. Six Guardians had stormed the castle and six Guardians were returning to Highcliff, but not all of them flew a dragon.

Dragon Sect

Forming a makeshift guard of honour around Kingstone, five dragons winged across the expanse of Grim Lake, rising high to crest the distant volcanic mountains.

Dangling beneath the bronze-tinged leader, clutched within his claws, the breath of the wind blew Cynder's long, black hair behind his lifeless body.

Dragon Sect

To Catch the Fly

Compared to the manicured hedgerows and bountiful gardens synonymous with Orlythia and Borreraig Palace, the outlying hovels lining the roadway east of Urdanya always filled Queen Khae with a sense of failure. Astride her beautiful mount and surrounded by Home Guard, she couldn't help but feel like a spoiled child as she walked Faelnyr through the outlying tenements—the squalor and despair on the dirty faces of the elflings broke her heart. Doing her best to keep a warm smile on her face, what always struck her harder than anything else were the vacant stares of mothers who appeared powerless to alter their little ones' fates.

She spoke to Captain Kall, but her gaze remained on those they passed, "Did you arrange for the gifts?"

"Of course, Your Highness. The rear wagons are dispensing them as we pass."

She nodded. Though the provisions she had ordered brought with them to give to the impoverished elves would be welcome, the token gesture was little more than a handout. A pittance to appease her troubled conscience with the hopes of keeping from openly crying. No matter how hard she tried to do right by her citizens, there were always those who inevitably fell through the cracks. Judging by the number of shanties they had already passed, those numbers had grown since the last time she had come this way.

Sprawled outside the imposing walls of the edifice that was Urdanya Castle, she would have thought the unfortunate elves would be the benefactors of charity from the Sea Throne. Judging by what she witnessed, the system had failed them—right beneath her deceased sister's nose.

The sun fell in the afternoon sky, bathing the roadway in the lofty shadow of the mountainous keep, its parapets and spires resplendent in a golden hue.

Khae's gaze was compelled to the ominous tower that stood to the right of Urdanya Castle. The Sea Witch Sceptre stood stark above the surrounding coastline; its summit bereft of the mystical cloud cover rumoured to be attracted to the ethereal chamber in the sky. Discomforted by the dread the spire suddenly instilled in her, she swallowed. Odyne had been murdered up there.

The closer the brooding mass of the fortress became, the more Khae's prickling anxiety rose. She was thankful she had decided to make the journey west when she had. If the headmaster of the wizards' guild had the right of it, her brother had to be stopped before he dug himself in too deep.

A commotion up ahead brought the procession to a stop. Angered voices reached Khae where she sat her horse beside Captain Kall; the commander's angular features hardening as bits of information drifted down the line.

A lone rider galloped toward them from the front of the royal entourage, his headlong charge barely missing curious onlookers. He pulled up beside Captain Kall and leaned in to speak privately.

"Get back to the front and tell them not to engage under any circumstance unless they're attacked first," Captain Kall instructed.

"Understood." The elf scout turned his horse around and charged back the way he had come.

Khae held her breath as the captain's grim gaze met hers.

"It appears the duke's troops have barred our passage to the castle."

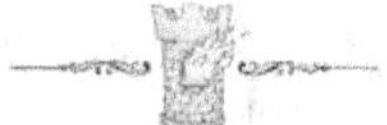

Duke Orlythe followed Ryedyn's gaze to the scene unfolding far below. Standing behind a floor-to-ceiling pane of thick glass at the pinnacle of the Sea Witch Sceptre, he took great pleasure in what he had orchestrated. Clad in royal green, over two score of the queen's mounted troops had come to a standstill along the northern roadway approaching the castle gates. A satisfied smirk lifted his pepper-grey mustache.

"Oh, to be a midge on the rump of her highness' horse."

Ryedyn chuckled, "More like you're the midge on her royal arse, m'lord."

Orlythe smiled at that. Something he seldom did.

His grin faded as a scout raced along the edge of the small contingent and stopped beside a high-ranking elf sitting his horse beside the queen—the scout likely informing them of the reason for the hold-up. He could just imagine his sister's indignant face as she learned that she was unwelcome in South March's largest city.

He thought of the raven he had received yesterday afternoon. The headmaster of the wizards' guild would have to be compensated for his timely information.

Oh, there would be a comeuppance for the situation unfolding far below, of that there could be no doubt. But it wouldn't happen today. By the time Borreraig Palace

Dragon Sect

became aware of the slight, it would be another week before a forced march brought about a serious response from the king. If things went according to plan, the bumbling fool would arrive too late to save his queen.

As such, there wasn't any question in Orlythe's mind that Hammas would lead the charge. That suited him just fine. With the crown's attention directed on the west coast, the vacant Willow Throne would be begging to be captured. Once the palace fell under his control, all he would have left to do would be to catch the fly that had escaped his web of intrigue last year.

He glanced sideways at the one who had promised to make it all happen. Coaxing his niece away from the safety of Highcliff would be his ultimate coup. While Khae and her pompous husband responded to the treasonous acts perpetrated by the Urdanyan Witch Watch, their little darling would be vulnerable. In the ensuing upheaval, the conniving queen would fall. Those who had chosen to remain loyal to his sister would either bow their head or lose it.

He nodded at Ryedyn. The magic-user was too young in his estimation to claim to be as powerful as he asserted, but he had to give the wizard his due. The stick-like elf had delivered what he had intimated back at Castle Grim. Spurred by events that would leave the queen and High Wizard Aelfwynne reeling, neither knowing what had happened until it was too late, the hierarchy of the kingdom was about to experience a monumental shift in its allegiances.

"You've done well, wizard. It's high time the Willow Throne entertained a magic-user to watch over it."

Ryedyn's broad smile beamed beneath a set of closely spaced, diabolic, blue eyes. "It has only just begun, m'lord."

Dragon Sect

Orlythe returned his grin, but something in Ryedyn's appearance unsettled him more than it ought to have. He took a deep breath and looked away, locating Queen Khae amongst the milling horses of the Home Guard. "What I wouldn't give to loose an arrow and be done with her."

"All in good time, m'lord. All in good time."

Orlythe growled and stepped away from the window to stare at the ancient tomes and tattered scrolls scattered about the octagonal chamber atop the Sea Witch Sceptre, absently wondering if it was always this cold up here.

Ryedyn was right, of course. If something were to happen to the queen before Ouderling could be drawn away from Highcliff, the Dragon Mage would never allow the princess to leave. Khae's death would have to wait a little longer.

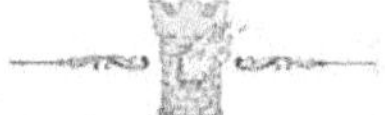

The duke's heavy footfalls echoed in the tight confines of the narrow stairwell carved through the core of the Sea Witch Sceptre.

Ryedyn waited until the duke's flowing black surcoat whisked across the arched causeway connecting the witch's spire to Urdanya Castle before turning to speak to the far side of the room. "You can come out now."

A pervading cold preceded the wraith as it detached itself from the shadows between two of the chamber's eight windows. "You've done well, wizard."

Ryedyn faced the tattered rags of the form that appeared to glide across the chamber. It stopped by the eastern facing window to regard him—pinpricks of fiery orbs the only thing visible within its dark cowl.

"Thanks to your instruction, all of the players are moving into position," Ryedyn spoke calmly, though he was certain his knees were close to knocking.

"Does the duke suspect anything?"

Dragon Sect

"Not that I can tell. He believes this is his plan."

"Very good, Ryedyn Danya. You have done your ancestors proud," the wraith's grating voice intoned. "I trust you learned more than what your heritage has given you during the time you spent with Afara Maral. That combination has allowed you to outlive his usefulness. Human magic is stronger than the elves give it credit. In conjunction with your elven magic, you possess the potential to rival the power your great-aunt commanded. Soon, you and I will come to realize the power of the Crystal Cavern. When that time is upon us, Urdanya's dream will be realized and South March will be yours to deal with as you see fit."

"And the duke?"

"He's but a means to an end," the wraith growled as it observed the bottlenecked, Home Guard contingent. "He's likely to become a casualty of the civil war that is about to ensue. You needn't worry about him."

"And should he survive?" Fearful of what the wraith ultimately had in store for South March and its inhabitants, including himself, Ryedyn wasn't afraid to speak his mind. Something he had always been known to do.

The wraith slowly turned, its fiery orbs growing in intensity. "When all is settled, and you sit upon the Willow Throne, you'll be in need of a court jester."

Dragon Sect

Clip-Clop

How it had come about so fast made Braen's head spin. One moment his intimidating uncle was confronting him— something the duke had done all of Braen's life—and in the next, he found himself on horseback trotting along a lonely road north of the town of Aelfwynne toward the barbaric lands above South March. Toward the land of man.

Armed with a hunting bow, a rapier, and his addled wits, Braen was thankful his roan, Seafoam, did all the walking, but if his conveyance was left to its own devices, Seafoam would likely have walked off the edge of the high escarpment that fell away on their left and plummeted them to the jagged coastline far below.

A brine-laden wind assailed their course, chilling him to the bone despite the fur-lined, leather cloak flapping around his slender form. Seafoam didn't appear bothered by the weather, but he suspected by how its ears pricked that it wasn't keen on the route they travelled. It was like Seafoam sensed they were leaving the false safety of the elven kingdom to venture into the wild lands lurking beyond the horizon—moving toward a realm fraught with uninviting adventures that would, in all likelihood, chill an elf's soul. Had he not feared what disappointing his uncle might mean, he would never have made it this far.

So much had happened in the last year. Before his mother's untimely death, life had been simple. Boring, if he cared to think on it. Since then, however, his life had been anything but. Presiding over the populace of Urdanya and surrounding countryside had proven more difficult than it had seemed when he had accompanied Odyne at court. The way his mother had adjudicated petitions had carried an air of excitement, but for some inexplicable reason, dealing with the commoners' discontent on his own had proven a thankless task. One that inflicted him with a massive headache before each day was out.

At first, he had put it down to the fact that he was new to the position. He quickly learned that was not the case. Dealing with the varied walks of life proved a delicate matter to say the least. Nor did he command the respect his mother had established with the masses. Be it because he was male, or something that ran deeper, he couldn't put a name to it.

Whatever the case, there were many times over the ensuing months after his mother's death that he had honestly believed his life was in danger. If not for the intervention of the Witch Watch, there was the very real possibility that he wouldn't be alive today.

Perhaps the most disturbing aspect of his journey toward the realm of man was the troubling rumour overheard during his stay in Erline, and then spoken in hushed whispers while he had passed through Aelfwynne. If he cared to consider the rabble in the streets as a reliable source for information, his aunt Khae had arrived in Urdanya shortly after his departure only to be denied entry by his uncle's forces.

Dragon Sect

As unelfly as it made him feel, he couldn't deny that he was glad to be rid of the Sea Throne and whatever storm was brewing between his relatives—the two most powerful leaders in all the land.

He sighed. His mother had ranked right alongside the queen. If not for his cousin Ouderling, Odyne would have been the second highest authority in all the land.

He took solace in the fact that his mother was better off where she had gone. She would have hated being caught in the middle of a power struggle. Like himself, she had cared little for the day-to-day posturing of the powerful houses of lords. He smiled ruefully. Perhaps she had foreseen this day and had made a conscious decision to facilitate her early exit.

A painful grimace twisted his clean-shaven face. There was no way his mother would have purposely orchestrated such a ghastly demise as the one she had fallen victim to. Perhaps her actions had brought about her death like his uncle insinuated, but the more he thought on it, the less convinced he had become.

There was no denying Odyne dabbled with forces she had no right to disturb, but never in all of his sixty-six years had Braen known her to summon something as maleficent as what he witnessed that gloomy night atop the Sea Witch Sceptre. Not many nights had passed since then that he hadn't woken in a cold sweat.

Nature in its uncanny way must have sensed his forlorn ruminations and bathed him and Seafoam with a blast of cold air. He shivered so hard he didn't think he could hang onto the reins; his numb fingers unable to feel the leather strap held within his shaking grip.

Cresting a high rise, he gazed across the iron-grey waves surging against the rugged shoreline—ship-wrecking reefs that sent great geysers of seawater into the air. Far to the north, the coastline veered westward to the horizon. He had never travelled this road, but being as well read as he was, he knew intrinsically that the dark blot of land jutting into the sea foretold of the beginnings of the kingdoms of man.

Whether it was that sobering thought, or feelings brought on by his commiseration of how ineffective he had proven himself to be as a high-ranking official of the elven realm, he couldn't help but despair. His muscles ached with the fatigue of shivering incessantly, much of that due to something deeper than the pervasive cold.

Perhaps the adventure his uncle had sent him on would be just the tonic he needed to overcome his futility. There was also the possibility that it might bring about the end of his meaningless life—an all too fitting demise for someone who had no right to claim an association with the Wys family lineage. Not that he wanted to die, but in hindsight, it might be the answer he was searching for.

Fighting back tears not borne on the wind, he heeled Seafoam in the flanks and said through chattering teeth, "Come on. The faster we get there, the sooner we'll be rid of this place."

Seafoam responded by tossing his head and breaking into an easy trot—the clip-clop of his shod hooves providing Braen with the only comfort he had known in many long days.

Dragon Sect

Wizard's Destiny

Aelfwynne glared up at him as only the high wizard could, his beady eyes full of contempt.

"What?" Scale asked from the back of the wyvern, Miragan, as he studied the solitary stalactite. "I did it exactly the way you told me to."

The grumpy goblin strutted around the perimeter of the glowing earth blood pool dominating the middle of the Crystal Cavern to get a different view of the Focal Stone. He pointed. "I can still see the crack, you bumbling fool. It looks bigger!"

Scale scratched at his head, careful not to conk himself with the iron mallet he held—his free hand steadying him on Miragan's shoulders. He saw it too. "I don't know what happened. That spell should have sealed it."

"If it breaks off, you'll be wishing you were still grovelling in Castle Grim's dungeons."

Scale rolled his eyes. It was unbelievable how the wise old goblin insisted on getting the events of last year wrong. He had never grovelled in the dungeons. Sure, he had been punished by the captain of the Home Guard for allowing

Dragon Sect

Princess Ouderling to leave the castle unguarded, but if it wasn't for his subsequent rescue of the ungrateful wizard, they wouldn't be having this conversation.

"Get down here before you bring the entire ceiling down, ya big galoop!"

"He's in rare form today," Miragan spoke inside Scale's head.

"Tell me about it. Just when you think he can't get any grumpier."

"I heard that, ya blasted imbecile!" Aelfwynne ranted, his clawed hands on his hips.

"Better take us down, Mir," Scale whispered and thought, *if he calls me a witless northerner, I'm out of here.*

Miragan landed on the far side of the earth blood pool and lowered her chest to the ground for Scale to dismount.

He patted her on the neck and jumped free. "Best you get away from here. I'll call you if we're to go back up again."

Miragan gave him a sympathetic look, leaped into the air, and flew to another part of the cavern.

"What happened up there?" Aelfwynne rounded the pool. "It shouldn't be that hard to mend a cracked stone."

Scale shrugged for he had no answer. The Focal Stone was no ordinary piece of rock.

"Think, you witless northerner! Does nothing I tell you sink through that thick skull of yours?"

Scale fought the urge to storm out of the cavern. This wasn't his fault. He firmed up his resolve and met the goblin's glare. "It's like I said. Something is preventing my magic from doing its work. Whatever is affecting the Focal Stone, it's like it's rebelling against the intrusion. I intoned the restorative spell exactly the way you taught me."

Aelfwynne held his stare, running his tongue between his bottom teeth and fleshless lip. After a time, he nodded. "It certainly sounded like you did."

Scale's tension eased somewhat. The wizard knew he hadn't made the mistake that had resulted in extra damage to the most important crystal in the cave. The loadstone crystal served to focus the collective power of the rest of the cavern, attuning it with the potent magic of the earth blood pool that bubbled away beside them. The crack that had formed around the spot where it dropped away from the cavern's ceiling was disturbing to say the least.

Aelfwynne lowered his gaze and studied the earth blood. "I don't understand what's happening to it. Why has it suddenly split?"

"I don't know, Master. It looks worse up close."

The high wizard's attention snapped back to Scale. "You think it'll fall?"

Scale shrugged, not wanting to admit it, but silence wouldn't sit well with Aelfwynne. He sighed. "I'm surprised it hasn't already."

The goblin's beady eyes were off-putting anytime Scale looked upon them, but the concern reflected on Aelfwynne's rough-skinned features alarmed him.

"That's not good," Aelfwynne mumbled, more to himself than for Scale's benefit. "Not good at all. If the Focal Stone falls, only the gods know what it'll mean to the future of Highcliff. If I'm not mistaken, and I rarely am, the Dragon Witch Wraith, the grotdraak, and all the unspeakable horrors that lurk within the bowels of the earth will be free to access the Crystal Cavern. When that happens, the kingdom will surely fall."

Dragon Sect

Scale swallowed, unsure how prophetic the wizard's words actually were, but he had learned the hard way to never doubt the almighty Aelfwynne.

He shivered—his wild imagination conjuring all sorts of chaotic scenarios that might befall South March. His mind inevitably returned to the scene deep beneath Grim Keep in which the wraith had handed Afara Maral someone's freshly claimed heart. A second shudder passed through him, stronger than the first. Should the Focal Stone fall, the future would be bleak indeed.

"Back to the lair," Aelfwynne muttered and wandered away.

Scale looked around. He imagined he was supposed to follow. Taking a last glance at the solitary stalactite, he issued a silent prayer for it to remain where it was until they could figure out a way to bypass whatever it employed to thwart their magical intervention.

He caught up to the slow-moving goblin before he had exited the Crystal Cavern. The steady beat of wyvern wings overhead informed him that although their future was tenuous, life invariably went on.

"Do you have any idea what's preventing our spells from taking hold in there?" Scale asked as they started up the main tunnel toward the front of the Highcliff complex.

"If I did, do you think I'd be walking away." Aelfwynne shook his head. "Seriously, Scale. Tell me what I see in you."

Scale fought an urge to snap at him, refusing to be goaded into a heated reply. He was beginning to think the surly goblin spoke the way he did to provoke him. Instead, he searched his memory. "Have you ever known magic to be used on it before?"

Aelfwynne's disgruntled face twisted in thought. He stopped to stare up at Scale, wonder softening his hard lines. "That's a good point. You may be onto something."

With that said, Aelfwynne nodded and started away, walking faster than his little legs usually carried him. "Yes. Yes! Soulbiter."

Scale scrambled to catch up to the high wizard, not caring for the sound of the goblin's last word.

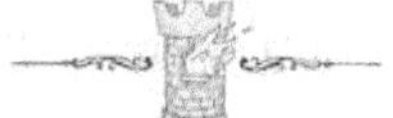

"Here. Hold this." Aelfwynne extended a plain sheath toward Scale, ivory hilt first. The high wizard had confiscated it from Ouderling's sleeping quarters on their way up to the high wizard's drafty conjuring chamber set above the promontory.

Aelfwynne had been so preoccupied since the mention of Soulbiter, muttering and talking nonsense to himself, that Scale had been loath to interrupt, but as he accepted the dagger, he asked, "How did you know she hadn't taken it with her?"

The high wizard ignored the question, his attention on a large tome he had retrieved from a sagging side shelf. He raised to his toes, sweeping several scrolls and a couple of spent candle stubs to the ground with an elbow before plunking the book down and blowing a heavy layer of dust from its surface.

Caught in the debris cloud, Scale turned away in disgust— covering his face with the crook of his elbow and coughing.

Aelfwynne continued to mumble as he searched the contents of the many pages. Part way through the book, he stabbed a finger at a certain passage. "Aha! I knew it."

Scale moved in behind to look over the wizard's hunched shoulder, but the text was difficult to decipher. Though Aelfwynne had spent many hours tutoring him and

Ouderling on runic verse, the princess had proven more adept at learning the difficult language.

"Pull the dagger free," Aelfwynne ordered without looking up.

Scale backed up and did as he was told. The gleaming blade, inlaid with intricate threads of gold and inset with tiny gems, had no sooner cleared the sheath than a stabbing pain shot up his arm, causing him to drop it to the floor.

Aelfwynne shook his head and sniggered but continued reading.

"You knew that was going to do that, didn't you?" Scale asked incredulously.

"Bah! You're not dead, are you? Pick it up."

Scale frowned, glaring at the back of the high wizard's head. If Aelfwynne thought he was touching the dagger again, he was sorely mistaken.

"Pick it up, I said. And be quick about it."

"But it…it bit me."

"If it wanted to harm you, you'd be on the ground gasping for breath."

"And you expect me to touch it again?"

"Don't be a big baby. You passed its test. You can wield it now."

"Passed its test?" Scale asked as he looked around the chamber. Retrieving a dirty rag, he bent down and carefully wrapped the hilt. "And what if I had failed." He straightened and held the dagger, blade first to Aelfwynne.

Aelfwynne took great care to relieve Scale of the blade by the handle. Discarding the rag to the floor, he looked Scale in the eye. "Then I'd be in need of a new apprentice."

Scale held Aelfwynne's gaze, biting back an angry retort.

"Now," Aelfwynne laid Soulbiter on the open tome and resumed reading, "if I understand this passage correctly, only magic from another world may be used on the Focal Stone."

"Another world?" Scale's voice cracked. "That's absurd."

"What do you consider the Fae? Your neighbour?""

"Of course not, but they aren't easily found. If the princess and the queen can speak to them, they must surely be part of this world."

Aelfwynne released a heavy sigh and looked up from the tome. "Does nothing register between those pointy ears?"

Before Scale could respond, Aelfwynne continued, "Where do you think the Dragon Witch came from? And the one named, Nayda. You remember me teaching you about Nayda, don't you?"

Scale nodded, feeling sheepish under the high wizard's scrutiny. "She was the Dragon Witch's companion. The one who tamed Grimclaw."

"Ah, you do listen. There may be hope for you after all." Aelfwynne nodded, returning his attention to the tome. "According to this, the Focal Stone's composition was originally altered by the confluence of earth blood, elven magic, and that of dragonkind."

Scale wondered at the relevance of Aelfwynne's musings.

"That, in and of itself, should be easy enough to deal with. Any Guardian with the assistance of a wyvern is capable of employing all three magics." Aelfwynne straightened up to hold a claw-tipped finger in front of Scale's face. "But, if I'm not mistaken, the introduction of Soulbiter changed all that. The otherworldly blade altered the Focal Stone's properties further. So much so, that unless I miss my guess..." His face darkened. "Don't say it...Unless I'm wrong, the stone now possesses a fourth magical presence. One foreign to our realm."

Dragon Sect

Scale frowned. He had no idea what Aelfwynne alluded to. Not that that was anything new when it came to dealing with the eccentric creature.

Aelfwynne reached back and plucked Soulbiter from the yellowed pages and brandished it between them. "This is not of our world. It was fashioned by man."

Scale's face twisted in bewilderment. "I thought you said it came from another world?"

"I did. The original Dragon Witch and her companion Nayda came from a world that is only infected by the race of man. No elves. No goblins. No dwarfs or giants. Just man."

Scale swallowed. "That's absurd. How can you know that?"

"It's a wizard's destiny to know things most others do not. That's where our mystique comes from." A ghastly smile split Aelfwynne's smug expression. "We learn things that are strange to the common population. When we divulge such knowledge, it tends to make people leery of us. They wonder how we can know things that lie beyond the scope of reasonable possibility."

Scale attempted to change the subject, hoping to avoid another one of the high wizard's drawn-out lectures that never made any sense. Aelfwynne was famous for rambling on about seemingly unimportant matters, leaving Scale wondering what he was supposed to retain and what to ignore. "So, what you're saying is that we need to get our hands on someone who not only possesses dragon and elf magic, but also man magic?"

"Exactly!" Aelfwynne jabbed Soulbiter at the air between them. "There may be hope for you yet."

"And just how're we going to find someone like that?"

"We don't have to. We have one in our midst." Aelfwynne raised his hairless brows twice in quick succession. "Well, at least he lives in South March."

Scale jumped back to avoid being jabbed by the vicious blade, unable to think of anyone other than Afara Maral who might fit that description. Elves weren't keen on man. Other than the duke's wizard, Scale had never seen one before. He couldn't help but ask, "Who?"

"Who, indeed." Aelfwynne walked to the thick glass window that fronted his lair and looked toward the distant mountains on the far side of Crystal Lake. After a while, he turned to face Scale. "You know, it's almost fitting that the one we seek ascended the Sea Throne last year."

It took a moment for Scale to grasp who he meant. "Braen Wys? Odyne's son? He's an elf."

"So sure, are you?"

"Princess Odyne was the queen's sister."

"Aye. But who was Braen's father, hmm?"

Scale frowned, searching his memory. "I don't think I've ever heard who his father is."

"Was."

"Whatever. Are you saying Braen's father was a…?" Scale wasn't sure what he was implying. "He wasn't a man, was he?"

Aelfwynne nodded. "But no one outside of this room knows that."

Scale absently searched the room. Only he and the high wizard were there. If he were to believe the goblin, then not even Braen or Khae Wys knew the true identity of Braen's father. "How is it that you're the only one in all the realm to know this?"

"Ah, you see. I'm right when I say that you don't listen."

Scale's frown deepened.

"It's a wizard's destiny."

A loud rap at the door made them both jump.

"Come!" Aelfwynne commanded.

The door flew open and in strutted the black-haired, mustachioed leader of the Watchmen.

"Draakyr!" Aelfwynne sounded alarmed. "What brings you up here?"

Draakyr bowed his head in reverence. "Zorain has returned with ill tidings, Master Aelfwynne. The Grim Duke has taken Urdanya and is denying Queen Khae access to Urdanya Castle."

Dragon Sect

The End of All Things is at Hand

Several days had passed since the arguably successful raid on Castle Grim to retrieve the Staff of Reckoning. The high wizard had been ecstatic to have his priceless talisman back in his possession. He uncharacteristically praised all involved, including the brave dragons, but Ouderling struggled with his concept of success. Cynder had lost his life. If not for Jyllana's heroic effort, Balewynd would also be dead.

Cynder's life companion, Dagomar, agreed with her sentiment. The crusty, red dragon had been inconsolable ever since.

Exiting Balewynd's chambers, Ouderling forced a smile for Jyllana's benefit as the Home Guard held the door open.

"She's looking better," Jyllana said, keeping pace as they made their way up a narrow tunnel toward the main corridor.

"She's lucky to be alive," Ouderling muttered, her eyes a pale red.

"That's twice now in less than a year. She's got to be the toughest elf ever."

Dragon Sect

"Or the unluckiest," Ouderling grunted as they hit the main tunnel. She glanced to the left toward the distant exit but decided to turn right and seek out the one Guardian whose company always provided her with a sense of calm whenever she felt like her world was spinning out of control.

After several months in exile, life as a Highcliff Guardian wasn't as glamourous as she had first believed it would be, notwithstanding the wondrous opportunity to fly the skies on the back of a dragon. It had been difficult keeping up with the intense daily trials and lessons delivered by three polar opposite personalities, but her recent pairing with a dragon who was to be known from this point forward as *her* life companion had overwhelmed her sensibilities. Keaf wasn't a normal, easygoing dragon. The little, green monster had been separated from the rest of the dragonlings because his disposition strikingly contrasted with the others.

Her mind drifted to the conversation she had been part of in the mess hall over breakfast. Aelfwynne had informed everyone present about the troubling events taking place in Urdanya; claiming it wouldn't be long now before King Hammas rounded the Wizard's Sleeve. A large force was reportedly set to sail the length of the Ors Sea to bolster his strength—gathering the troops that were amassing near the port city of Rhysa.

It was disconcerting to wrap her head around the idea of a civil war erupting in the west, but nor was she naïve when it came to her uncle. The Duke of Grim had made no bones about his dissatisfaction with regard to the current regime. If Aelfwynne was correct in his reasoning, Orlythe stood a good chance of coming out on top should such a conflict ensue. As much as she had despised her parents for banishing her from the palace, she hadn't slept much lately—worried about their welfare.

The glow of the Crystal Cavern pushed aside the dreary light of the main tunnel—a flickering, bluish-white haze pulsed from within. Crossing the cave's threshold, she searched the heights, locating three wyverns and their goblin caretakers flitting about the large crystal formations. Of Miragan and Eolande there was no sign.

Rounding the last bend before the earth blood pool, Jyllana pointed to the back of the cavern. "There they are."

The Home Guard had no sooner spoken than Miragan and her rider, Eolande, turned their heads in unison. A few wingbeats later, Miragan landed beside the gurgling pool, smiling at Ouderling and Jyllana.

"Ah, my dear friends." Eolande slid carefully from Miragan, his declining physical condition evident in the way he stretched his back and neck. He had never been quite right since their confrontation with Afara Maral.

"A little stiff, are we?" Jyllana chuckled.

Eolande's wide smile was actually pleasant considering it came from a goblin. Ouderling grimaced. It was a shame she felt that way. There wasn't a goblin caretaker in all of Highcliff that she didn't like. Perhaps her first encounter with Aelfwynne had tainted her perception of the humble, quiet folk. She smiled inwardly, thinking of Aelfwynne. *Well, most of them are humble and quiet,*

Vowing to move beyond her unfounded, preconceived prejudices, she realized that even knowing her perception was wrong, change would take time.

She sighed and offered her friend a genuine smile. A friend almost as dear to her as Jyllana.

Eolande nodded, "Let's see how stiff you become when you reach my age, hmm?"

"Only a mountain or lake has the ability to see as many years as you have, Eol." Jyllana's broad smile was infectious.

Eolande's chuckle was cut short as Ouderling bent low and wrapped him in a firm hug. "I wish I could squeeze the stiffness away."

The look on the goblin's face when she released him was worth any embarrassment the unusual act instilled in her. If her unsolicited affection wasn't enough to startle the head caretaker, Jyllana proceeded to hug him as well, leaving him gaping and sputtering—looking around as if he expected something profound was about to happen.

He staggered backward a couple of steps. "Wh-what was that for?"

"For being you," Ouderling said matter-of-factly. "Because we love you."

Eolande swallowed, more moisture in his beady black eyes than normal, and almost fell over sideways in fright as Miragan's large head nuzzled his shoulder.

"We all do."

"You tell him, Mir." Ouderling patted Miragan between the eyes, rubbing a knuckle on the bony ridge, marvelling how much the wyvern had grown since the day she had met Miragan in Perch's company.

Her smile fell away. The cavern wasn't the same without the old wyvern.

"Ah, good," a rasping voice from behind made everyone jump. "Just the two I want to talk to."

Ouderling and Jyllana spun as Aelfwynne hobbled around the bend in the pathway and confronted them, the Staff of Reckoning supporting him, though they all knew he didn't need it.

"I'll leave you, then." Eolande bowed his head. "Master Aelfwynne."

"Nonsense." Aelfwynne held up a claw-tipped hand. "I value your input. Yours *and* Miragan's."

"Very well, Master."

Miragan dipped her chin in reverence. *"Master."*

"Follow me," was all Aelfwynne said as he ambled past the group and started down the curving path deeper into the cavern.

Ouderling allowed Eolande and Jyllana to precede her; Miragan took to the air and disappeared over a hump of crystals.

"I've never been this far into the cavern before," Jyllana commented, one hand resting amicably on Eolande's shoulder as they walked.

"Not many pass beyond the earth blood. There's not much to see other than more crystals," Eolande said casually.

Jyllana's head swivelled one way and then another. "Pretty crystals."

If Ouderling didn't know better she would have thought Jyllana had never been in the Crystal Cavern before, such was the wonder on her face.

As big as the cavern appeared, Ouderling was surprised by how long it took to reach the end of the pathway. Rounding a sharp bend, the jagged back wall loomed before them on the edge of a great open space large enough to accommodate all of the wyverns if she had the right of it.

Miragan waited for them beside an older wyvern in the middle of the courtyard-like setting, surrounded by a circle of low benches.

Had the female goblin, Lylande, not suddenly appeared between two juts of crystal at the base of the wall, Ouderling would never have noticed a series of small egresses. "So, this is where you live."

"Of course. Where did you think the caretakers were housed?" Eolande said.

Ouderling shrugged. "I never thought about it before."

Lylande seemed surprised to see them. She smiled shyly, bowing her head to Master Aelfwynne. "Good day, Guardians. May I help you?"

Aelfwynne dipped his chin. "Good day to you, fair Lylande. We're looking for a place to talk. Please, go about your business."

"Of course, Master Aelfwynne." Lylande paused long enough to smile at everyone before approaching the small wyvern that spoke with Miragan. She patted Miragan on the shoulder, mounted the older wyvern, and was away.

Aelfwynne assumed a seat on a bench near Miragan and waited for the others to join him. "After discussing the disturbing events unfolding in Urdanya, Xantha and I have deliberated long and hard about Highcliff's response."

The high wizard's gaze settled on Ouderling. "Though it is yet to be seen what'll happen when the king's forces join Queen Khae on the city's outskirts, it's fair to assume Duke Orlythe will not be dissuaded from the path he's chosen."

"How *is* Xantha and little Aelfwight?" Ouderling asked. "We haven't seen much of them lately."

The question and nickname for Dithreab threw Aelfwynne. He cast her a dark glare, obviously not appreciating the change in subject. "They're fine. Dith's having a terrible time teething, but that's not important at the moment."

Seeing the dozens of pointed teeth bristling in Aelfwynne's mouth as he spoke, it was no wonder the little goblin elf was hurting.

Dragon Sect

"I have sought you and Jyllana out because there's something I need you two to do for me."

"Our pointed ears are listening," Ouderling's attempt at lightening the mood earned her a dour look.

"Yes. Right," Aelfwynne grumbled. He cleared his throat and sat up straighter, both hands resting on the top of his staff. "I want it known that if not for Xantha's strong recommendation, and Jyllana's performance at Castle Grim, I would not have entertained this request. Unfortunately, the rest of the Guardians are required to remain at Highcliff in case the queen has need of our assistance."

The gravity of Aelfwynne's words erased Ouderling's smile. Things were worse than she had thought, but his implication irritated her. "So, what you're saying is our services are useless?" She nodded to include Jyllana.

Aelfwynne's glare intensified. Ignoring her remark, he said, "I need you to find Grimclaw."

A surreal silence settled over the group. The hammering of iron mallets and the wing flaps of rider and wyvern working around the cavern were but a distant backdrop. Ouderling blinked rapidly, not sure she had heard him correctly.

Aelfwynne rose to his feet. "Trust me, it took much convincing on Xantha's part for me to see the merit in selecting you two for this important quest."

"I'm sorry," Ouderling sputtered, barely able to speak with her jaw hanging as it did. "You want us to do what?"

Aelfwynne nodded. "That was exactly my sentiment when Xantha broached the subject, but she's right, as usual. If the Grim Duke follows through with his perceived threat, your parents will be in grave danger."

"But why search out Grimclaw? We have dragons. Surely they can turn the tide should my uncle's forces come to blows with my mother…" Ouderling trailed off at the sight of Aelfwynne shaking his head.

"Demonic took more than half the dragon population with him. Others have left since then, not wishing to have anything more to do with our affairs. That leaves us with two Watchmen, eleven Highcliff dragons, and four dragonlings."

"And five wyverns," Eolande ventured.

Aelfwynne bowed his head toward Miragan. "True. And valuable allies they are, but they're needed to protect the crystals." His concerned gaze looked toward a solitary stalactite in the centre of the ceiling. "If the Focal Stone falls, we'll have bigger problems to worry about than a rogue duke."

The high wizard stopped pacing and turned to face his audience. "When Ouderling and Jyllana depart, our dragon numbers will be further depleted."

"But my parents." Ouderling threw her hands in the air. "You can't just abandon them."

"Rest assured, princess, should the time come that a dragon intervention is required to preserve the crown, Highcliff *will* respond. But know this. If that happens, it'll surely mean the end of all things is at hand. Highcliff will be vulnerable. Afara Maral proved last year that as valiant as our wyvern population and their faithful riders are, they are no match for a powerful wizard. I'm of the belief that if it comes to the point that we must save the queen, Highcliff will face something more sinister than a human wizard."

Ouderling's eyes reddened as they grew wide with realization. "The Dragon Witch Wraith."

"Aye, but his presence isn't the only one staining South March." Aelfwynne let that ominous statement hang in the air as he turned to Miragan. "This is where you come in, granddaughter of Perch."

Miragan bowed her head. *"Whatever is your wish, Master, you can count on me."*

"I know. That's why I'm asking you to fly the future of South March upon your shoulders."

Miragan bowed her head, her eyes closing momentarily in solemn acknowledgement.

"You're to fly the princess north of our border into the wild kingdoms of man on a quest to not only save the elves, but the future of dragonkind as well."

Dragon Sect

Arrowshot

Built on the north shore of the source of the Ors Spill where the Ors Sea drained westward across the land, the small port city of Rhysa had been much quieter since a small contingent of the royal armada had come and gone. King Hammas had arrived with heavily armed troops and horses, stopping long enough to conscript able-bodied adults between the ages of twenty and four hundred.

Why the king hadn't continued downriver by ship, Harek had no idea, but he had gleaned from the troops during their brief stopover that a dark storm was brewing in the great city of Urdanya. One that might spill over to other cities in the realm.

Harek spat off the top of the wooden parapet he patrolled. There was nothing 'great' about Urdanya other than its size. Even so, he had to admit that during his younger years he had enjoyed visiting the seedy city and partaking in the boisterous and carnal nightlife Urdanya offered. Growing older, he wanted less and less to do with the somewhat illegal, if not immoral, behaviour. If he never set foot in Urdanya again it would be too soon.

Dragon Sect

He squinted in the late afternoon sun, the glare on the slow-moving waterway painful to the eyes. Looking to the east, the Ors Sea crashed against a jut of lower crags that served to take the best part of the sea's fury from the surf.

Behind him, plumes of late day meal fires strung the city to a cluster of low-lying clouds perpetually clinging to the black peaks of the western spur of the Steel Mountains. There was good reason Rhysa received more rainfall than any other region in South March, even though the skies to the east and west were generally clear.

He wasn't bothered by the anomaly. During the oppressive heat of summer, the wispy cloud cover filtered the worst of the infernal sunshine, keeping the terraced fields between Rhysa and the mountain at her back sufficiently irrigated.

As if on cue, a raindrop splattered on his exposed forearm, followed by another, and then two more. He grunted and shook his head, looking once more to the west—into blinding sunlight. The weather along the south shore of the Ors Sea was unpredictable.

The rain increased in intensity, scattering the Rhysa Watch along the wall to where they cowered beneath wooden overhangs atop the watchtowers. Harek did likewise, bolting into the relative shelter of a narrow corner tower commanding a great view of the source of the Ors Spill and the Ors Sea's southwest shore. Comfortable with his own company, he was thankful no one else sought refuge in this particular tower.

Preceded by a wave of cold air, the rainfall increased to a torrential downpour. Wet and shivering, Harek couldn't wait until his shift was over. It wouldn't be long now. When the sun set, the night watch would replace the day crew. He would soon enjoy the welcome heat of his humble cabin's hearth, indulging in the thin ale his wife would have waiting for him.

Just the thought of the portly woman brought a smile to his weary face. No matter how bad things had gotten during their long life together, she had been his constant— grounding him whenever things seemed like they were spiralling out of control. Their many elflings grown and scattered around South March, he remembered those who had succumbed to disease or died accidentally. Hugging himself for warmth, a pervasive sadness gripped him. One that was never far from the surface of his thoughts. He doubted he would ever get beyond the loss of the three elflings that had gone on before him.

The rain lessened as fast as it had come. Before he knew it, it had stopped altogether. The sun's dying rays in the west heralded another beautiful sunset, glinting off the slow-flowing current on the city's western shore. A spectacular rainbow hovered over the Ors Spill; its ends lost in the woodlands on either side of the wide river.

Harek smiled at the wondrous sight, wishing he was an artist so that he might capture the moment and bring it home to his dear wife. With any luck, she had taken a brief respite from her chores to witness nature's glory.

The sun slipped behind the western treeline, easing its glare, but what it left behind staggered him. Unseen until now, a fleet of single-masted boats sailed toward Rhysa.

His breath caught. Boats on the Ors Spill were nothing out of the ordinary, but the sheer number reminded him of the king's fleet a few days past. And yet, he knew at once this was not the royal armada. They had returned to the sea to head back to Orlythia.

Dragon Sect

Nor did the flags flapping atop the masts belong to Queen Khae. They were black. The thin pennants of the Duchy of Grim.

It took a moment for Harek to appreciate the significance of what he observed. As the fast-moving boats sailed past his vantage point, black clad troops in studded leather and bristling with weapons lined the decks. Rhysa was under attack.

Swallowing the lump in his throat, his voice cracked in panic, "To arms! To arms! Look to the river! We're under attack!"

He turned to grab the rope dangling beneath a bell hanging from the roof for just this purpose, and pulled hard—the urgent peal quickly picked up around the city.

Harek checked to ensure his arming sword sat free in its sheath. Sweat soaked his uniform despite the cold. The thin suede would provide him little protection from the weapons he would soon be facing.

Releasing the bell pull, he stepped free of the tower overhang to join the other, elderly Rhysa Watch farther along the wall, but was brought up short. Pain erupted below his left shoulder, staggering him.

Eyes wide in terror, the fletches of a fatal arrow protruded from his chest, amidst a blossoming crimson stain.

He grasped the feathered shaft in both hands and dropped to his knees, the suns dying rays glinting in his eyes.

The angelic image of his beautiful wife flashed through his mind as he fell face first to the walkway, never to rise again.

Dragon Sect

Jyllana couldn't restrain her excitement. Nor could she forget the fear and grave responsibility that came with High Wizard Aelfwynne's request. She had never heard tell of another elf flying a dragon across the northern border into the kingdoms of man.

Aelfwynne's wizard's lair was littered with scrolls, tomes, and vials that were filled to varying degrees with only the goblin knew what—all illuminated by the dull grey sky visible through a floor to ceiling windowpane overlooking Crystal Lake.

Studying the charts spread out upon a stone slab in the centre of the cluttered space with Master Aelfwynne hadn't been much help to alleviate her nagging worry that she was about to get her and Ouderling hopelessly lost. Aside from two prominent mountain ranges on the largest map—one running the length of the western coast and another that originated out of a vast region of desert in the east to bisect the coastal range, there were only a handful of settlements indicated—most along the coast.

Dragon Sect

A second chart that depicted land north of the first one showed a couple more coastal settlements along the shores of what the map labelled as the Unknown Sea.

Jyllana pointed at the second chart. "Those are the only cities? That's a lot of land to cover."

"Huh?" Aelfwynne grunted, his usual snarl on his face. "You're to stay away from cities. You won't find Grimclaw in a house. He despises all races, with good reason."

"Are the maps to scale?"

"How should I know?" Aelfwynne shook his head and walked to a side shelf to pull out a scroll. "I didn't make them."

Blowing the dust off it, he returned to the central slab and carefully wriggled the aged, leather thong from around it. "Pay attention, for this might save you."

He unrolled the crackling parchment and placed pieces of volcanic rock on its corners to keep it from rolling back on itself.

Jyllana leaned over the opposite side of the table, following his claw-tipped finger to a long inlet. "What am I looking at?"

"As far as I know, this is one of the largest human settlements. Fly clear of it."

"Okay," Jyllana said hesitantly. "I'm assuming there's more to this chart than…," she squinted to read the faded inscription, "Madrigail Bay."

"Correct. Madrigail Bay is only a landmark to guide you, nothing more. Do I make myself clear?"

"Perfectly."

"Good, because it wouldn't do to underestimate the barbarians. They've proven in the past that they're capable of taking down a dragon."

"Speaking of which, are we both to fly Miragan?"

Dragon Sect

Aelfwynne rolled his eyes in disgust. "Of course not. She's just recently lived through her first dragon cycle. Were she a dragon, perhaps."

"She seems big enough."

"Aye, and strong too, but it's a long way to where you're going. If you encounter difficulty, I'd rather there be two dragons." He sighed and looked up from the map, his intense stare boring into hers. "Don't forget your role. If it comes to it, you must be prepared to sacrifice yourself and your dragon to save the princess. The future of South March depends on you doing your duty."

Jyllana's stare hardened. "Nothing will touch her as long as I draw breath."

Aelfwynne held her stare, as if ascertaining the conviction of her words. He nodded. "See to it that you don't stop breathing."

She swallowed, not sure if that was an attempt at a sense of humour. If it was, he had picked a fine time to show he had one.

Aelfwynne traced another long inlet north of Madrigail Bay. "North of Madrigail Bay, how far I have no idea, there's supposed to be a large valley dividing the mountain range along the coast. It's rumoured to extend many leagues inland. This may be it, but I have my suspicions that it's not as there's a settlement on either end of the gap."

Jyllana read the inscription of the settlement on the coast, whispering its name, "Thunderhead." She tried to read the name of the inland settlement but most of the text was faded beyond recognition, only the last three letters legible. "End."

"Huh?"

"Nothing. Just reading the names on the map." She forced a smile. "May I take this with me?"

"Are you daft? Do you know how old this scroll is?"

Dragon Sect

She shook her head.

"Me neither." He shuffled to a rickety cabinet that looked to have contained a glass front once upon a time. Reaching through the gap in one of its many empty framed doors, he retrieved a newer looking scroll, a stone inkwell, and a long feather—its metal tip stained black—and set them on the top of a smaller stone slab against the side wall. "Draw yourself a reference map."

Jyllana hesitated. "What about my dragon?"

"You don't have a dragon! You're too old to be selected."

"I'm twenty-six. Barely old enough to be considered an adult. Zorain chose Scale."

"That's different. Look, I don't make the rules when it comes to the scaly beasts. That's another one of Grimclaw's laws."

"Perhaps we need to change his laws. But whatever. Who am I flying?"

Aelfwynne tensed—her question seemingly making him uncomfortable. He grabbed his staff and considered its carved surface, as if beseeching the strange faces for an answer. Without looking up, he said, "Dagomar."

Of all the Highcliff dragons, other than the four dragonlings, Dagomar would have been her last guess. "Cynder's dragon? You can't be serious. From what I hear, Dagomar hasn't left his warren since we buried Cynder. He's not fit to fly."

"On the contrary. He's not fit to be considered amongst one of Highcliff's protectors."

"That's a cold thing to say." Jyllana struggled to control the disgust in her voice. "He just lost his life companion. How would you expect him to be?"

Dragon Sect

"I expect him to do his duty. The realm's on the brink of damnation. We haven't time to let our emotions control us. We must be strong."

Jyllana glared at the goblin, her chest heaving, but she held her tongue until she could speak without venom. "Has he been told?"

Aelfwynne sighed and looked away, his reply barely audible, "Not yet."

Dragon Sect

Dragon Sect

"**Thank you** for agreeing to see me, Master Aelfwynne."
Ouderling accepted a stone goblet of wizard's tea as she sat
on the low bench before the magical fire separating her and
the high wizard in the tight confines of his personal chamber.

"Of course, princess. All you need to do is ask."

Aelfwynne's change in attitude toward her was evident not
only in how he addressed her by title, but also in his reverent
tone. Something big must have happened to alter his usual,
crotchety demeanour.

She forced a smile. "I want to run something by you before
Jyllana and I take our leave."

Aelfwynne cocked a single eyebrow. "Oh?"

"Something I've been thinking about for some time now.
Because of your most excellent training, I've come to learn
that I need to embrace my birthright. Though nowhere near
as adept as mother, by tapping into it during the long hours
of the night while alone in my chamber, I believe I've
discovered how to achieve a higher level of consciousness."

Aelfwynne pursed fleshless lips and tilted his head, giving
her a knowing look. "That's good to hear. Very good, in fact.

And just what kind of inspiration have you derived from this, *higher consciousness*?"

"Well, um, it's hard to explain. I think it's enabled me to see into the future in an odd sort of way."

"Interesting." Aelfwynne nodded. "Makes sense. Nature often portends events we mortals can't foresee until it's too late. Do you think nature is speaking to you?"

Ouderling frowned. "I'm not sure. I'm at a loss to explain what I'm experiencing. It certainly leaves me breathless, I can tell you that. It's like I can communicate on a subconscious level with someone, or *something*, that I've never encountered before. The strangest part is that I sense this phenomenon is intimately familiar with me."

"Curious. And you do this without outside magical aid?"

The question surprised her. "Why, yes. It happens when I'm totally at ease."

"Interesting. Perhaps we don't require Rhysa's Diary after all." A wicked grin turned up one side of his face. "Please, do go on."

His scary countenance threw her. Nor had she ever heard of Rhysa's Diary. Taking a long sip of wizard's tea to calm her surging emotions, she took a deep breath and spurted, "With all due respect, Master, through this contact I've come to realize the shortcomings of our relationship concerning dragonkind."

Aelfwynne raised a curious eyebrow, but didn't interrupt.

"Don't ask me how I know this, but something deep inside me is urging us to expand on what we're doing at Highcliff. The way we employ the dragons must be honed to our mutual advantage."

"Fascinating. And has your communion shed light on how to go about this?"

Dragon Sect

She swallowed her unease, not sure how to explain what she had gleaned from her dreamlike rendezvous with…She sighed. She couldn't put a name to whoever or whatever it was that she communicated with. Speaking her deliberations out loud only served to fill her with a notion that perhaps it was nothing more than her wild imagination running amok.

Hoping her rapid pulse would slow, she answered, "I'm not sure what it means, to be honest. My gut tells me that in order to create a symbiosis…" She hesitated, wondering where that last word had come from. Shaking it off as something she had heard while communing with nature's essence, she swallowed her misgivings and continued, "In order to establish a mutually beneficial pact with dragonkind, especially outside of Highcliff, I feel we must create a secret group of dragon riders that can protect *all* of South March from enemies, both foreign and domestic."

Aelfwynne's brows came together. "Are you suggesting a clandestine society of dragons and elves that live apart from Highcliff?"

"You put that more eloquently than I ever could, but yes. A *dragon sect*, if you will." Hearing the words pass her lips, she feared the high wizard would view her suggestion as preposterous and give her that condescending look she knew all too well, but his thoughtful face gave her pause.

He blinked several times, mouth open, but said nothing as his beady eyes searched the walls and ceiling of his grotto in thought. Finally, he nodded. "I think I see where you're going with this. Leave it with me. Provided things don't fall apart while you're gone, it may be worth investigating deeper once the situation in Urdanya is resolved."

Speechless, Ouderling fought to restrain the triumphant smile threatening to cleave her face. She purposely drank the remainder of her wizard's tea slowly, her elation hidden behind the cover of the stone goblet.

"Whatever you do, don't mention a dragon sect to Grimclaw," Aelfwynne warned.

"Providing we find him, you mean."

"Oh, you'll find him, princess. After what you've just told me, I have complete confidence in your ability." Glancing sideways to where his staff lay beside him, his voice lowered to a whisper. "I must admit, I've been gravely mistaken about you. You *are* your mother's elfling in every way. Perhaps more so than Ordyl ever was. I only wish I'd recognized it sooner. We might have avoided all this…" He trailed off and gazed into the fire, his expression one of deep-rooted regret.

Ouderling knew it had nothing to do with her. "It's okay, Master Aelfwynne. You meant well. You had Ordyl's best interest at heart. I'm sure mother knows that."

Aelfwynne lowered his unfinished tea to the ground and said softly without meeting her gaze. "The only interest I had was my own."

Dragon Sect

May the Gods Help Us

"**Do** you remember me saying to you before all this started that I should just lay siege to his castle and be done with it?" Khae said to Hammas as they sat alone in their pavilion on the outskirts of Urdanya sipping wine.

"Yes. You got me all excited."

"I got myself excited." Khae smiled grimly. "Looking back, I realize now that that's exactly what we should've done."

Hammas remained quiet, but she knew him well. He refrained from saying what was on his mind to keep from upsetting her further.

"It's okay. Go ahead and say it," she urged.

Hammas took a deliberate sip of wine and lowered his goblet to the side table between them. "You did what you thought was right at the time. No one can fault you for that."

She raised her brows again. "Oh, I'm sure there are many who'll find fault with my inaction if Orlythe isn't brought to heel without bloodshed. Such is the burden of the crown, I suppose. No matter who I appease, I'm sure to offend someone else. I need to take a lesson from my mother and be more forceful. She would never have stood for his behaviour."

Hammas nodded. "No. Nyxa would have cut him down with her own hands long ago, despite the morality of such an action. She was a formidable ruler who didn't suffer anyone who didn't agree with her outlook on life."

·Khae held his gaze, choosing not to take offense to his last words. It wasn't in his nature to sling a sideways barb at her. Nevertheless, the inference was an apt one. "That's putting it nicely. Ruthless leader, more like."

"That's what was needed then. Times change. After South March became a unified realm, there were bruised egos that required massaging. The former chieftains dared not voice their displeasure while Nyxa still lived, but when you ascended the throne, they became more brazen with their demands. All the credit in the world to you for how you handled their grievances. You prevented an insurrection that we all knew lay beneath the tenuous veil of what the new regime stood for. You put an end to the bickering and South March has been better off as a result."

"Until now," Khae muttered.

Hammas said through a compassionate smile, "Until now."

He rose from his chair and knelt before her, grasping her hands. "We'll see this through. When the second fleet arrives with the bulk of our troops and blockades the river, your brother will have no choice but to submit."

She wanted to believe him, but knew Orlythe better than anyone. He was not to be underestimated. "And if he doesn't?"

Hammas' green eyes intensified. "Then, by everything we hold dear, we'll crush his rebellious resistance and put an end to this nonsense." He squeezed. "You'll see."

"I'm going to have to kill him."

Her simply spoken words startled the king. He shrugged. "That may be, but know this. He has brought it upon himself. He's fortunate you're the queen and not another. You've been more than fair. If he feels that strongly that he's willing to die for his misguided cause, that's on him, not you."

Khae sighed. She wanted to cry. If only Odyne had been born first. Taking a deep breath to steady her frazzled nerves, she returned Hammas' squeeze. "You're right, of course. You always know the proper thing to say to make me feel better. Thank you."

Hammas leaned in to kiss her long on the lips. Rising to his feet he pulled her out of the chair and hugged her tight, rubbing at the tension in her back.

She allowed a couple of tears to flow unseen, vowing not to shed a single one when she presided over her brother's lifeless body. Killed by her own hand.

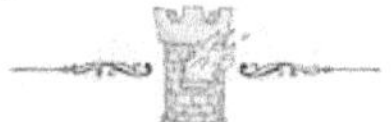

"The king's arrival is fortuitous indeed," Orlythe purred, from the embrace of the Sea Throne—a rather disgusting piece of furniture in his estimation. Constructed from crushed shells and skeletal segments of krakens, it proved more uncomfortable than the Lava Throne back at Castle Grim. "Are you certain our armada has engaged Rhysa?"

Ryedyn paced the empty receiving hall below the throne dais, his thin arms behind his back as he kept his gaze on the granite floor at his feet. He stopped, but didn't look up. "Indeed, m'lord."

"Very well. Send word to the Sceptre when we know if they were ultimately successful." Tired of the throne digging

Dragon Sect

into his nether regions, Orlythe stood and regarded the garish chair. He shook his head and growled, "Take this eyesore out of here and bring me a seat with a cushion."

Ryedyn looked up. "The Sea Throne has been the symbol of power in Urdanya for centuries, m'lord. It was built before the sorceress sacked the city once known as Eldoon."

"I care little of its history. Have it removed."

"The citizens might not take kindly to such an act."

"What the citizens think doesn't concern me. They don't have to sit in it!"

Ryedyn bowed his head. "Yes m'lord. What shall become of it?"

"Toss it off a bridge for all I care."

"Yes, m'lord."

Orlythe stormed past his wizard, not bothering to spare him a second glance. "I'll be up top if you need me."

"Yes m'lord."

The duke pulled his black surcoat around him as he stepped onto the arched causeway spanning the jagged defile between the castle and the base of the Sea Witch Sceptre.

Wind tussled his hair and flapped the hems of his clothing—the biting chill doing little to alleviate his conflicting emotions. As much as he despised his sister for allowing the kingdom their parents had left in their care to become one built on complacency—underachieving in his estimation—he couldn't escape the twinge of guilt that accompanied his plan to eliminate her. Seeing King Hammas dead would be a joyous event he hoped to witness firsthand, but Khae? They had been close once upon a time.

He threw open the tower door, thankful to escape the elements, and started the long climb to the octagonal chamber high overhead. Each plodding step drove home his determination. By the time he reached the top he was thoroughly livid at the unfairness of it all.

Far to the east, burnt-orange pennants fluttered around the massive camp of his sister's host. Unable to appreciate from such a distance, the simple image of the double-tailed dragon with its mouth wide open and its body surrounded in red flames struck him as a mockery of what the symbol represented as it fluttered over his sister's troops. It was the image of a war dragon. The name his mother's enemies had labelled Nyxa with.

He shook his head. How far the crown had fallen. The daughter of the War Dragon had allowed Nyxa's legacy to suffer a long, agonizing death.

A slow smile crept along his face, parting his unruly beard from his thick mustache as his gaze took in the Ors Spill meandering eastward toward the distant mountains. If his fleet of commandeered Urdanyan boats carried out their orders, it wouldn't be long before King Hammas' head adorned a pike that he planned to set in the ground before Urdanya Castle's main gate.

"A raven, my queen," the gaunt-faced falconer, Waryn, said as a husky Home Guard parted the tent flaps to let him through, accompanied by the day's first light, the tenth morning since King Hammas had arrived.

Queen Khae and King Hammas had been up well before the dawn, eating a scant meal while they studied the detailed charts of Urdanya and its outlying area, wondering where best to concentrate their push into the city when their reinforcements arrived. If their plans remained on schedule, the offensive would begin the following day.

She accepted the tiny scroll, eyeing Waryn's grave expression with suspicion. "Have you read it?"

Dragon Sect

"No, Your Highness."

Khae tilted her head. "But you know something, don't you? I see it in your face."

Waryn nodded grimly at the scroll in her hands. "Blood stains, Your Highness."

Khae frowned and regarded the little scroll. Turning its bound length in her fingers her eyes widened. There was indeed a stain that resembled dried blood on the yellowed parchment.

Wasting no more time, she stripped away the tiny loop of leather binding the scroll and broke its nondescript wax seal.

Hammas' attention flicked between Waryn and Khae, the missive too small for him to read while in Khae's possession.

Before Khae finished reading it, her hands began to tremble. The paper slipped from her fingers and fell to the ground at her feet.

"What is it?" Hammas asked with alarm, but didn't wait for an answer. He snatched up the parchment and fumbled at it until his thick fingers managed to unroll it again.

His face fell and his Adam's apple convulsed. Looking into Khae's stricken eyes he murmured, "May the gods help us."

Dragon Sect

Kingdom of Man

Crossing what he believed to be the imaginary border that separated South March from the kingdom of man, Braen chose to ride with his sword across his lap. Though he didn't know exactly when he had passed beyond the northern reaches of South March, he could tell by how the coastline veered sharply westward and continued on to the horizon that he was no longer on friendly soil.

He rolled his eyes. It wasn't like South March had been kind to him.

Not sure what to expect, he was surprised as the rest of the day and the day after that went by without incident. Thick forestland kept his course along the barely discernable path skirting the bluffs lining the Niad Ocean. Twice the trail dropped to a wide stretch of sandy beach before it rose back to the top of the high mesa, but it wasn't until sunset on the second day out of South March that he leapt from Seafoam and pulled the roan into the trees.

Almost imperceptible in the bright glare of the setting sun, he caught sight of several small vessels bobbing on the ocean. Lying on the edge of the drop-off so as not to be seen, he watched as they made their way toward shore, disappearing behind an embankment many leagues west of his position, into what appeared like the mouth of a large bay.

The sun had almost slipped beyond the distant waves before he crawled away from the brink and joined Seafoam amongst the trees. The sight of the boats had unnerved him more than he cared to admit. If not for his fear of disappointing his uncle, he would have climbed into the saddle and spurred Seafoam back home again.

Thinking of home, he considered the rumours of the queen being confronted by her brother. He nodded. It was better to keep moving north.

The sun hadn't quite achieved its zenith the following day when the trail Braen walked Seafoam along widened. Smaller paths appeared out of the woodland to join the ocean roadway as it veered north and afforded him his first real glimpse of civilization in many days. He swallowed his apprehension. That intimation depended on whether man could be considered civilized.

A wooden wall constructed out of tree trunks surrounded a large town on the far side of a large bay. Through his love of books, he knew the town to be Apexceal—the closest man settlement to South March.

He stopped Seafoam, absently fingering his pointed ears. It wouldn't do to bring unnecessary attention to himself. Not one to wear any sort of head covering, he feared his cowl might not be enough to hide his elven identity. He rummaged through the scant possessions in Seafoam's saddlebag and pulled out a spare black shift that was meant to go under his chainmail. Using his dagger, he severed a strip along its waistline and bound it around his head.

He could only assume how foolish he looked, but better to be laughed at for his headband than cut down because of his ears. Embarrassed, he donned his cowl.

Rounding the southern shore of the bay, the rest of the day went by without mishap. Wherever the small paths leading off the main trail went to, he never encountered a soul. Deciding it best not to arrive in a strange settlement after dark, he dismounted and walked Seafoam into the deeper wood to make camp for the night.

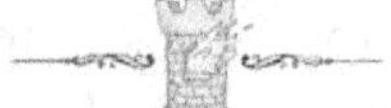

The sun barely cresting the distant mountains in the east, Braen plunged Seafoam into the shallow waters at the mouth of a wide river and slipped in amongst a procession of carts approaching the town's eastern gate laden with goods. Keeping close to a busy wagon train surrounded by men and women on foot and on horseback, he did his best to fit in—smiling warmly whenever one of them turned their attention his way.

Apart from seeming huskier than elves and possessing strange accents, the men and women didn't strike Braen as much different. Cruder, perhaps, with regard to their conversation, and of course, less the pointed ears, but all things considered, mankind could pass for elvenkind quite easily.

He walked Seafoam past the inattentive guards and through the wooden gatehouse without incident. Once free of the confined space, he dismounted and tied his roan to a hitching post alongside several other horses. Not sure what the practice was in Apexceal, he looked around, but nobody paid any attention to him.

Seafoam sniffed at his closed fist for only a moment before he opened his hand to expose a couple of pieces of withered carrot. "There you go. I'll be back soon with more."

Dragon Sect

It wasn't hard to discover the marketplace set one street back from the busy quayside. Carts entering the town creaked and groaned over uneven cobblestones that appeared to have weathered many centuries of traffic, on their way to the town bazaar.

Everything about the settlement of man was remarkably different than anything he knew. Simple things like rectangular doorways instead of the usual round tops of South March, and the lack of gargoyles depicting dragons along rooftops, set the architecture apart. Placards bearing script in bolder, more angular letters than that of common Elvish made them more difficult to read, but the words themselves were really no different, even if they weren't all spelled the same.

In order to perform the many rites in the Sea Witch Sceptre, his mother had made it a point of learning several languages and had insisted on teaching Braen as well. Dwarven, and Runic had proven a challenge at first—he wasn't sure which was tougher to learn—but with practice, he had mastered them enough to at least read their books. Luckily, the language of man differed little from elven, however, listening to the heavy accents in Apexceal, he feared he might make a spectacle of himself if called on to speak.

Entering the marketplace proper, the roadway widened to twice its width. Wooden stalls and faded tents lined the street, with many others set in between. Crammed with artisans, merchants, buyers, and the odd city watch, the pathways amongst the vendors meandered in every direction.

It wasn't until he found himself amongst the throng that he noticed the difference in his clothing. Though his travelling garb had seemed innocuous when he had set out, he felt out of place in what he estimated might be considered flamboyant attire compared to that of the people around him.

As different as the sights were to his senses, the delicious smells of the oddly shaped breads and selection of fruit displayed on an old table before him made his mouth water.

"You going to stare at my shingle all day, or are you going to buy something before it goes stale?" A gruff voice snapped him out of his reverie.

Braen's gaze fell on a rotund man wearing an apron, standing on the opposite side of the table; his dun-coloured clothing dusted with flour. He swallowed his fear of making a scene with his Elven accent and said slow and deliberate, "My apologies, good sir. No, I was just…" he struggled to find the right word, "…contemplating my choices."

The balding man squinted. Examining Braen's clothing, his inspection paused on the ratty cloth tied around Braen's forehead. "Judging by you're the way you're dressed," his gaze remained on the headband, "you must be down from the castle, I'm thinking."

"Um, yes. I-I mean no." Braen swallowed. He was butchering it already.

The baker tilted his head. "Well, what is it? You either are or you ain't."

"Both, actually," Braen said, attempting to sound convincing. He tried to recall from the books he had read where Nordicia Castle lay in relation to Apexceal. "I'm not from Nordicia. I was invited by the king to visit his castle." Panic set in. *What* was *the king's name?* "He, ah, suggested I make my way to your marketplace and indulge in the fine things it has to offer."

"Oh, he did, did he? Well bless his benevolent soul."

The sarcasm in the baker's tone wasn't lost on Braen. "Well, I may have asked him which town he would recommend to a wayward traveller looking for fine wares."

"Fine wares?" The baker scoffed, inspecting Braen's clothing again. "Where're you from? Ain't to be from south of the Wall, I'm guessing."

South of the wall? Braen grappled with the reference but luckily it came to him. "Yes. You're correct. I'm from north of the Undying Wall. From Madrigail Bay, actually." He hoped his geography was correct as he searched the crowd to where the harbour lay. "Actually, I'm looking for passage home."

"So, you're wasting my time then," the baker grunted and crossed forearms more muscled than Braen would have thought a baker might possess. "Be off with you."

Flustered, but not wishing to offend the man, or worse, draw attention to himself, Braen pointed to one of the breads he wasn't familiar with. "Not at all, good sir. In fact, how much is that one?"

"Same as the rest. A copper." The baker's pudgy face screwed up. "Can't you read my sign?"

Braen looked up and laughed nervously. The price was clearly written underneath the words, 'Baked Goods and Fruit.' Digging through a small leather purse on his belt, he pulled out a handful of gold and silver pieces. Pushing them around his wide palm with his finger, he uncovered a copper and handed it to the baker.

The baker eyed the money with obvious interest, but frowned as he examined the copper. "A wise guy, eh? Where'd you get this? I'm thinking I should be calling the Watch." He craned his thick neck, his gaze coming to rest on a man-at-arms three stalls deeper into the marketplace. He raised his hand, about to call out.

"No! Wait!"

The man left his arm in the air but indulged Braen.

"I was given that by a sailor." He looked at the elven coin in his palm, a flush of humility washing over him. How could he have been so foolish? He hoped his cheeks weren't as red as they felt. "Given all of this, in fact, as something to take back as a souvenir."

"That's quite a souvenir. There must be ten gold pieces."

Braen let all of the coins but one slide back into the pouch, and closed its flap. "Here. For your trouble. And I'll take an apple too."

The baker lowered his arm, his jaw dropping as Braen placed one of the silver pieces on the table between them and walked away.

Hoping he didn't look too suspicious, he slipped through the crowd with the loaf of bread, doing his best to keep it from getting squished.

Seafoam crunched the apple whole as he was untethered and led toward the wharves. Braen paused long enough in a tight alleyway to tear at the loaf with his teeth before walking alongside Seafoam and inspecting the quayside. It might not be a bad idea to distance himself from Apexceal just in case attention was brought to the coins he had used.

Up until his encounter with the baker, Braen hadn't really had a destination in mind, but now that he thought about it, Madrigail Bay sounded like a better place to start looking for individuals similar to Stanley White. The great port city was renowned for its shipbuilding and learned establishments, but from what he recalled of the kingdoms of man, it was a long way from Apexceal.

He surveyed the harbour as he picked at his bread. Sweeter than bread back home, he found the soft dough quite pleasant.

Dragon Sect

Masts of varying heights sprouted from a multitude of decks—adorned with yardarms and rigging, the amassed flotilla resembled a floating forest. Thick hawsers creaked with the strain of boats tugging at their moors on the gently rolling water.

Ignoring the smaller vessels, he approached a large jetty that housed two ocean-going ships preparing to cast off. Seafoam's hooves clopped loudly on the wooden dock slats.

"Excuse me," he said to a bare-chested sailor untying a hawser securing the nearest ship to the pier.

The sailor ignored Braen until he stepped in front of the man and raised his voice. "Excuse me."

"Ya talkin' t' me?" The sailor grunted, straightening up and rubbing a large hand over the top of his bald head.

Braen looked around. There was no one else close by. "Yes, sir. I seek passage up the coast. For me and my horse."

The man's stubble-faced scowl made Braen swallow.

"Look, laddie. Ya got the wrong ship. Now move on so as I can finish me business."

"Where are you headed?"

The sailor had bent over again but straightened to his full height—a head taller than Braen. Though his frame boasted a large stomach, his thick arms bespoke of formidable strength. "I thought I told ya to leave me alone? I ain't t' be tellin' again."

Braen dug into his pouch and held out three gold pieces. The look on the sailor's face made the gamble worthwhile. "I'm not from around these parts, but this should be fair recompense for passage."

The sailor looked around with a sly grin and held out his palm.

"Ah, ah. Not so quick." Braen pulled his hand back. "One up front and two when we get there safely."

The sailor snarled, not taking his eyes off Braen's hand. "Alright, but that's me price to get ya aboard. You'll be needing a couple silver fer me captain t' agree."

Braen almost balked. The man planned to keep the gold for himself. "You still haven't said where you're headed."

"We're t' be puttin' in t' several ports on our way t' Sea Hold."

"Is Madrigail Bay one of them?"

The sailor scrunched his face. "Aye. The first as a matter o' fact."

Braen's slow anger surfaced. "You're swindling me."

"I be doin' nothin' of the sort. Ya offered the coin an' I accepted." The sailor's eyes narrowed; one meaty hand fingering the pommel of a well-used dagger dangling from a loop on his belt.

Braen sighed. Wanting to be away from Apexceal, he nodded reluctantly and handed the sailor his gold piece, and two silver for the captain.

The sailor bit the gold coin, uncaring about its strange markings. "Best ya say nothin' about our little arrangement if ya know what's good fer ya, eh?"

The sailor's thick drawl was difficult to interpret, but his nonsensical tone drove the point home. Braen nodded. "Just see that I get there safely."

The sailor frowned and searched the people closest them. "It seems t' me yer tryin' to escape someone. Ya aren't in trouble, are ya?"

Not yet, Braen thought, as he followed the bandit down the pier.

"Excellent, Tyral. We can use another deck hand," a muscular man in a tight-fitting, high-collared tunic said to the sailor Braen had made arrangements with. He opened his palm to receive a single silver.

Braen gaped. *The swindler!*

Tyral shot him a warning smirk. Turning to the captain, he replied, "I'm always lookin' t' do what's best fer me mates."

"Yes, of course. Leave us now." The captain dismissed Tyral.

Tyral dipped his chin and walked away, but not before he raised his brow at Braen as if to say he was watching him.

The captain turned the coin over in his palm. "Where'd you come by this?"

Braen shrugged. "A sailor gave it to me."

"Interesting. What was the name of their ship?"

Braen's armpits dripped sweat. He hoped his discomfort wasn't evident on his face. "I can't recall, captain…?"

"Turse," the captain replied, his gaze flicking between Braen and the coin. "This is an elven coin."

"Really?" Braen looked as shocked as he could. "That explains why they were so eager to give it to me."

Captain Turse eyed him suspiciously, appearing on the verge of saying something more, but turned and walked toward the starboard steps leading up to the rear quarterdeck.

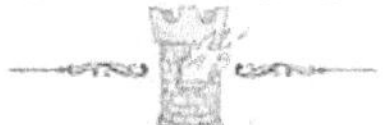

Had Braen known that he would be required to work as hard as he had since *Coastal Cutter* left its berth in Apexceal, he would have sought passage aboard a different ship. Several times over the next couple of days he had crossed paths with Tyral, but aside from a sneer that promised pain should Braen divulge their private accord, Tyral never bothered with him.

Despite what Tyral had said about Madrigail Bay being their first port of call, they made a stopover in the port of

Dragon Sect

Ember Breath later that same day to take on another passenger. One who wasn't expected to get his hands dirty.

Just before sunset, two days out of Ember Breath, that passenger joined Braen where he leaned on the midship port rail and nodded.

Braen nodded back, his gaze sweeping the deck. No one else was near. Though the crew hadn't been openly hostile toward him, he wasn't naïve. During the many hours of scrubbing the deck, he had overheard bits of conversation and accompanying laughter behind raised hands. He had done nothing to earn the unfair attention of the rough crew, but he knew better than to react. Their words couldn't hurt him unless he let them. Nevertheless, conscientious in the man's company, he slipped his cowl over his head.

The new passenger's golden locks blew around his face as *Coastal Cutter* sailed past a volcanic island farther out to sea, its heights shrouded in mist.

"Have you ever been to Ghost Island?" The newcomer asked, his gaze on the volcanic peak.

The man's amicable tone surprised Braen. He shook his head. "Never heard of it."

The angular-faced man locked eyes with him. "You're not from around here, are you?"

"Madrigail Bay. I'm on my way home."

The newcomer's brows raised skeptically but he said no more on the subject. Leaning both elbows on the rail, he said to the wind, "If one were looking for a place to lose themselves, Ghost Island would be a good choice."

Braen frowned at the odd statement. Had the man directed it at him?

"Unless, of course, someone was trying to avoid a dragon."

Braen fought hard not to react, but the sly smile of the other informed him that he had failed miserably.

"You should know there are members of the crew that mean you harm when we arrive at the Bay."

The information wasn't a great surprise, but to hear it confirmed was unsettling. "Who? Tyral?"

"Amongst others. They claim you carry wealth on your person."

"You could call it that."

"Valuable currency that isn't usually seen in Nordicia, *or* the realm of Madrigail, from what I hear."

Braen shrugged, trying to take the measure of the handsome man. "I'm Braen."

The man nodded. "Well met, Braen…?"

"That's it. Just Braen."

The man gave him a knowing smile. "Braen it is. They call me Alexis. I hail from the Kingdom of Carillon, east of Madrigail."

Braen had a working knowledge of where the kingdoms of man were situated. "Over by the swampland?"

"Aye. Our kingdom borders the Forbidden Swamp."

"Right.' Braen nodded. "That's what they call it."

Alexis gave him a curious look. "For good reason. We forbid our people from venturing there. Nothing good has ever been associated with that terrain. I would think someone from the Bay would know that."

"I forgot. My memory isn't the greatest at times." Braen settled back onto the railing, hoping to break the man's stare.

The bulk of Ghost Island lay to the stern. Before his eyes was nothing but the expansive ocean, its rolling seas set afire by the orangey sun sinking beyond the horizon.

The man settled in beside him. "If you ever find yourself in Carillon, be sure to ask for me."

Taken aback by the offer, Braen stuttered, "Uh-uh, sure. I will."

Dragon Sect

An odd silence settled between them. With the loss of the direct sunlight, a pervasive chill carried on the wind. The smell of the late day meal caused Braen's stomach to growl, but he knew there was no rush. He wouldn't be fed until the rest of the ship had eaten their fill.

Alexis pushed away from the rail. "I best be heading to the galley before the food's all gone." He placed a strong hand on Braen's shoulder, his gaze lingering on Braen's cowl. "Ware yourself well. It's plain to see there's more to you than you let on. Others have noticed it too. Watch your back if you wish to survive landfall."

Coastal Cutter's hold stank of animal excrement and wood rot, two days after Braen's conversation with the newcomer—neither aroma appealing to Braen's weak constitution. The ship had entered a long inlet, north of a smoking volcano. He found Seafoam penned in a mucky stall that hadn't been cleaned in many days.

Careful not to soil his soft suede boots too badly in the thick layer of dung and things he cared not envision, he removed his cowl and extended the carrot he had saved from his lackluster meal yesterday.

Seafoam nuzzled his hand and accepted the morsel.

Deck boards creaked overhead. The faint glow afforded by the day's dying light darkened. Someone hovered above the open hatch.

Braen ducked beside the stall.

A black boot found purchase on the ladder's top rung. "I knows yer down here."

The familiar voice of Tyral sent cold shivers up Braen's back. He straightened and watched the bald sailor and two of his mates jump from the ladder to confront him.

Dragon Sect

Braen stood, his right hand resting on his sword hilt. *Fat lot of good my blade's going to do*, he thought. He had never bothered much with weapon training; preferring the knowledge found in the books of his mother's plentiful library. "Shouldn't you be supping with the others."

"Supping?" Tyral laughed, looking to his companions who joined in his merriment. "Strange words from a strange *man*."

Braen didn't miss Tyral's gaze on his coin pouch.

"I'm thinking me an' me boys are t' be breakin' somethin' fast, eh lads?"

"What about our agreement? I paid you well to keep me safe." Braen pulled his sword free and held it clumsily before him. "Come no closer or I'll scream."

"Ha!" Tyral scoffed. If he was wary of the blade pointed his way, he showed no concern. "Scream like a maiden all ya like, pretty boy. Ain't no one gonna hear ya. Anyone who's anyone is forward, enjoying their evening meal. It's just ye an' us, an' ye have somethin' we'd be likin' t' relieve ya of." Again, his gaze fell on Braen's purse.

"But our agreement!"

"Let that be a lesson t' ya. It doesn't pay t' be trustin' someone ya just met."

Braen swallowed, resisting the urge of his latent magic to surface. Aside from the fact that he had no idea how to use it, he refused to become like his mother. "I'm not afraid of you." He tried to sound menacing but his attempt to inflict fear in his attackers was lost on them. His years of acquiring knowledge proved of little use to him now, other than providing him with the wisdom to realize he was about to die.

Dragon Sect

All Four

Dagomar appeared as unimpressed about the quest Aelfwynne had requested he go on as a disgruntled dragon could look.

Jyllana stood beside Ouderling who was searching through her small rucksack in the scant light afforded by the cloud covered moon; the princess trying to ensure she had packed everything Pecklyn had suggested. Water for the long stretches of dragonflight, and the crude charts Jyllana had drawn for each of them were lain on top of a slim ration of salted meat and root vegetables. Pecklyn had assured them that once they were out in the land, Dagomar and Miragan would provide them with all the food they required.

Aelfwynne waddled out of the Highcliff complex via the side tunnel connecting his chambers to the rock shelf through a maze of smaller tunnels. He stopped to speak with Dagomar, patting the despondent dragon's front paw and whispering words no one else could hear.

Jyllana watched the high wizard and the dragon they had selected for her to ride as she leaned close to Pecklyn. "You sure Miragan can't fly both of us?"

Pecklyn, smiley as ever, shook his head. He rubbed the base of Miragan's temple horn. "Mir is untested, and you have a long way to go. I'm sure she would try her best." He looked at the wyvern. "Wouldn't you Mir?" and then turned back to Jyllana. "It wouldn't be fair to her."

"We may need Dagomar's strength in battle where we're going." Miragan said and leaned into Pecklyn's knuckles, a contented grin on her scaly, black face. Unlike most wyverns, Miragan was more black than brown.

Ouderling slung her pack over her right shoulder, careful not to damage the fletches of the arrows protruding from her quiver. Clad in training armour, she nodded toward Dagomar and whispered, "Here comes Aelfy."

"Are you ready?" Aelfwynne's question incorporated all three of the quest participants.

"Yes, Master Aelfwynne," Ouderling said at once.

"Yes Master," Miragan said as well.

Everyone looked to Jyllana.

She lifted her chin, her green eyes intense as she stared at Dagomar. "I'm ready, Master, as long as he is."

Aelfwynne followed her gaze. "You have nothing to fear. He knows his duty."

The high wizard's words did little to ease her apprehension.

Aelfwynne turned to Ouderling. "You're in good hands, princess. Ordalf has proven capable of doing what needs to be done should things go awry. I need not reiterate Dagomar's role."

The high wizard nodded to Miragan. "If Miragan is a shade of her grandfather, I would venture to say that only Kingstone himself might provide you with better protection. Unfortunately, I can't spare him."

Jyllana bit back what jumped into her mind. Ouderling's safety should be paramount above all others, but she knew Aelfwynne was of the belief that if the Crystal Cavern fell, neither the queen nor her daughter would be left with a kingdom to rule.

"Go now. Make all possible haste. South March's survival may very well pivot on you completing your mission. Find Grimclaw. Convince him our need is dire."

"We'll do our best, Master Aelfwynne," Ouderling assured him as she clambered aboard Miragan's shoulders and adjusted her armour.

"Let's hope your best is enough," Aelfwynne muttered, motioning for Jyllana to go to her dragon.

Jyllana sighed. Hefting a small sack over her shoulder, she plucked a long-handled scythe from where it leaned against the wall outside the main entrance and approached the pale red dragon.

"Dagomar." She nodded and smiled for his benefit though her insides churned more than they had done in a long time.

"Jyllana."

Dagomar's gruff voice grated inside her skull.

"Do you know where you're going?" Jyllana asked, unsure whether she should just climb onto Dagomar's back or wait for some kind of signal from the dragon.

"North," was all he said.

Exasperated by the turn of events, she looked back to where Aelfwynne and Pecklyn watched her.

The goblin looked impatient for her to get on with it, which didn't help matters, but catching a glint of moonlight in Pecklyn's friendly, amber eyes did wonders to settle her nerves. The smiling Guardian dipped his chin as if telling her everything would be alright.

Dragon Sect

Inhaling deeply and letting it out again, she turned and mounted Dagomar. As she settled into place, she thought it wouldn't have hurt the dragon to kneel lower to make her task easier.

Without warning, Dagomar crouched and leapt into the air, his spring so fast that Jyllana nearly fell from her perch. Holding on tight to the sides of his neck, she hazarded a look back. Highcliff was already disappearing in the darkness. If not for the light reflecting off Ouderling's fancy armour she wouldn't have known that Miragan trailed not too far behind.

Dagomar flew eastward across Crystal Lake, rising high enough to pass between two mountain peaks before skimming the slopes deeper into the fathomless tract of the Dark Mountains.

They had left in the dead of night with the hopes of not attracting the attention of Grim Keep to what they were about. Though Jyllana didn't know of anyone living amongst the inhospitable crags bordering the entirety of South March's eastern frontier, Aelfwynne was adamant they take no chances.

As the cold night air left gooseflesh on Jyllana's skin, she couldn't help reflecting on Aelfwynne's decision to send the princess into a hostile land with only herself, a young wyvern, and a grieving dragon for protection. If she didn't know better, it was as if the high wizard deemed all four of them expendable.

She shook off the thought. That kind of thinking never ended well. Instead, she focused on the quest to find the infamous Grimclaw—hoping that Aelfwynne's plan to enlist the legendary behemoth's aid wouldn't lead to the death of them all.

Dragon Sect

Cursed

Scale looked up at Aelfwynne's untimely entrance into the high wizard's lair. Before him on the central pedestal sat a bronze bowl three-quarters full of a viscous liquid he wasn't used to employing. Sweat beaded on his forehead due to the extreme concentration required to perform the spell he was about to attempt—his anxiety heightened by the goblin's presence.

Aelfwynne hobbled in with the assistance of his cane, but he leaned it against a cluttered table along the back wall and shuffled over to inspect Scale's progress. Red eyes narrowed as Aelfwynne rose to the curved claw tips of his bare feet and peered into the bowl, his ever-present scowl in fine form.

The spell words Scale had rehearsed over and over again until he could recite them in his sleep suddenly left him. He frowned, trying to recall the next phrase.

Aelfwynne's large head swivelled on his tiny neck to stare at him. Looking back to the rippling liquid, he growled, "You're losing it."

The opaque substance began to agitate and then bubble, emitting wisps of thick steam.

Dragon Sect

"Easy now. Don't let it get the better of you." Aelfwynne stepped back. "Concentrate!"

Scale wanted to scream at the high wizard to shut up, but any lapse now might prove catastrophic. Aelfwynne had expressed faith in him earlier in the day that he was up to the task. Scrying great distances was a tricky matter. He knew only too well that should he let his hold on the high-level spell slip without properly backing out of it, there would be serious repercussions.

He sensed rather than saw the high wizard grab his staff and start toward the exit, skirting the edge of the lair.

"Scale! You're losing it!"

Scale's white knuckles trembled as they grasped opposite sides of the bowl's rim. He desperately tried to regain control of the power he had unleashed, but even as he spoke the words that were second nature to him, he knew he was lost.

An unusual glow took form around the scrying bowl.

"Scale!" Aelfwynne shouted, his raspy voice sounding far away.

Scale relinquished his hold on the bowl and ducked beside the solid stone slab, covering his head.

A thunderous detonation rocked the lair. Tomes and scrolls blew off various tables and slammed against the walls amidst shattering vials and splintering wooden tables. A loud clang resounded off the front wall as the floor to ceiling window fronting the lair exploded outward. The subsequent vacuum created by the opening sucked at unrolled scrolls and tore pages from scattered tomes—the priceless debris fluttering in the wind over the Highcliff promontory below.

It happened so fast, Scale had no idea how long he cowered against the slab, ears ringing and limbs trembling. He thought for sure he was about to die.

His eyes widened. Aelfwynne!

Dragon Sect

Staring in disbelief at the wreckage of the high wizard's lair, he wasn't sure that he was relieved to see the goblin rise from under pieces of broken table, shattered candles, and errant parchment, or not.

"You imbecilic, bumbling fool of a witless northerner, big galoop! Look what you've done! You've destroyed centuries of lore!" Aelfwynne admonished, his face agog.

Scale swallowed hard. Aelfwynne had never used all four of his favourite insults in one sentence before. He had half a mind to jump through the gaping hole where the great window had recently stood.

He staggered to the edge of the lair and peered out, observing the damage. Countless sheafs of paper fluttered down the mountainside—some resting momentarily on the promontory, amidst the shocked faces of Guardians looking up at him, before the wind whisked the priceless documents off the ledge to swirl to the lake far below.

Aelfwynne stepped up beside him, the goblin's jaw hanging in disbelief. He turned an incredulous stare toward Scale for a moment but was thankfully speechless.

Together they watched the fluttering paper and debris blowing in the wind. Elves and goblins wandered into the open, surveying the damage. Some stopped to gaze up at them while others ran around frantically attempting to salvage whatever they could.

Recovering his senses, Scale scrambled around the blasted lair, collecting scraps of loose parchment that were threatening to blow away—securing the piles with pieces of stone from shattered candleholders, and larger bits of table debris. Daring to look at Aelfwynne as he did so, the high wizard glared at him. Had Scale not known what was in Aelfwynne's hands, he would never have guessed the mangled object had recently been the scrying bowl.

Dragon Sect

Aelfwynne ambled over to the central slab with slumped shoulders and set the remains of the ancient talisman down with a clang.

"There has to be a better way," Scale mumbled, not knowing what else to say. Apologizing for destroying the high wizard's sanctum seemed a hollow thing to do. How could he ever atone for his mistake?

"That's the trouble with you," Aelfwynne muttered, not bothering to look him in the eye. "Always looking for a shortcut. Never content to accept that the old ways are the best ways."

Scale knew better than to argue. The old wizard was set in his ways. Nothing Scale said would change that…unless!

"Why not forge a magical vessel? Something possessing its own magic that can assist us in focusing our own inherent magic into something stronger. Much like the Focal Stone does with earth blood." As soon as he mentioned the unique crystal shard, he regretted it. Repairing the all-important stone had been another one of his recent failures.

Aelfwynne's angry eyes flicked up to meet his, the goblin's chest heaving.

Scale figured it was only a matter of moments before the high wizard smote him on the spot. He broke eye contact and stared morosely at his folded hands at his waist. Useless hands that were good for nothing but bringing trouble. He whispered, "Or like the Staff of Reckoning. Something that will allow the diviner an opportunity to view something without the constant threat of disaster."

Aelfwynne's eyes narrowed, his gaze going from Scale to his staff to the crumpled piece of bronze and back again. They opened wider in contemplation. Finally, he nodded. "You might be onto something, my boy. You might indeed."

Dragon Sect

It had been days since Ouderling and Jyllana had left Highcliff, and the surly high wizard was growing impatient to know how they faired. Losing the use of the scrying bowl couldn't have come at a worse time.

He paced around his wizard's lair, oblivious to all of the hard work his apprentice had put in cleaning the chamber and restoring as much of the damaged treasures as he could. It was disheartening to think about the ancient lore that had been lost when Scale's attempt to harness the scrying spell had gone awry. He wasn't sure he had forgiven him quite yet, but he couldn't fault Scale for his effort since.

News out of Urdanya had done little to alleviate the angst and stress caused by the unsettling events happening on the far side of the land. Seemingly out of nowhere, the kingdom faced the unpleasant prospect of civil war. Every city below the Ors Spill had thrown in their lot with the Duke of Grim. Whether out of loyalty to Orlythe or driven by the real fear of what refusal would mean to their communities made no difference to the outnumbered royal army. Any stakeholder south of Urdanya would be ground to dust under the sweeping surge of the duke's forces if they didn't capitulate.

Scale looked up from where he and Eolande were putting the finishing touches on a new sheet of glass they had fitted to the opening overlooking Crystal Lake. He cleared his throat to get Eolande's attention and the two of them faced Aelfwynne with a satisfied grin.

"Looks good but needs cleaning." Aelfwynne waddled over to inspect the pane. He touched it with a claw, drawing it across the surface with a frown. "What's wrong with it? Is the dirt on the outside?"

Scale lifted his eyebrows, but it was Eolande who spoke.

"Your *apprentice* and I took the liberty to add something special to its composition."

Dragon Sect

Aelfwynne wasn't fond of surprises. "You mean it'll always look this cloudy?"

Eolande shrugged. "More or less. We're not sure why that happened but I think you'll be okay with it when we show you why. Scale and I hope you can avoid what happened to Princess Odyne in her wizard's lair atop the Sea Witch Sceptre. Place your palms flat against the window and attune yourself to what your magic senses."

Aelfwynne frowned but did as he was told. Had it been anyone but Eolande, he would have balked, wondering if there was something sinister involved. Especially after mentioning the demise of the queen's sister. He was sure Braen's description of her attacker pointed to none other than the Dragon Witch Wraith.

The glass felt cool, its thickness firm beneath his touch. He didn't notice anything out of the ordinary but as he concentrated, an almost indiscernible hum made itself heard. At first, he put it down to the incessant wind on the outside of the window, but his aptitude in the arcane arts informed him there was more to it than that. Something had been enchanted into the glass.

A familiar essence called out to him, attempting to draw him in closer. The sensation melded into his palms, causing him to jump back with a start.

"What have you done?" Aelfwynne looked from Scale to Eolande.

"It was his idea," Eolande nodded at Scale.

Aelfwynne turned a dark glare on his apprentice.

Scale grinned. "We cursed your window."

Before Aelfwynne had a chance to ask, Eolande explained, "We imbued the glass with a protective ward."

Aelfwynne didn't know whether to be angry or thankful. Before he replied, a knock on the door elicited a response from Eolande.

"Come in."

Pecklyn stepped into the wizard's lair and greeted everyone, his gaze falling on Eolande. "You called for me?"

"No, I—" Aelfwynne started to say but Eolande stepped forward, interrupting him.

"Yes. Please, do come in."

Pecklyn strolled to the window and looked out. "I don't recall it being that misty today. Must be a volcano spewing somewhere nearby. I better go check."

Aelfwynne rolled his eyes. "Don't bother. It seems my apprentice and someone who should be attending to more pressing matters in the Crystal Cavern deemed it necessary to fog my window."

Pecklyn touched the glass. "Oh, that's a relief. Might help keep direct sunlight out."

"Ya. Like we get much of that around here," Aelfwynne grunted.

Eolande approached the large stone slab rising from the centre of the floor—its surface unusually bare. "If you'll all join me at the table, Scale and I will demonstrate the warding mechanism. With Pecklyn's help, of course."

As everyone gathered around the pedestal, Eolande asked Pecklyn, "You're pretty fast, aren't you?"

Pecklyn's smile twisted in thought. "I guess so. Why?"

"Would you say you're the most agile Guardian we have?"

"Mm? Pretty much. Balewynd might disagree, but yes."

"Good. Good. Scale and I need your help demonstrating our new invention."

Pecklyn shrugged, looking questioningly at Aelfwynne. "Sure. What do you need me to do?"

Dragon Sect

"Attack Master Aelfwynne."

Aelfwynne and Pecklyn stared at the Crystal Cavern caretaker like he had gone mad.

Eolande held his clawed hands up. "Not hurt him. Just take your sword out and feign like you're going to strike him. Make it appear real but be sure to miss him of course."

Pecklyn frowned.

"Trust me," Eolande said. "But, when you do pretend to strike him, you must immediately jump clear of the spot you're standing on. Make sense?"

Pecklyn laughed. "No, but whatever. You want me to swing at Aelfwynne but not actually hit him and then retreat."

"Yes. Retreat fast."

"Okay. I can do that." Pecklyn drew his sword and stepped clear of Eolande to confront Aelfwynne who stood with his back against the slab. He looked to Eolande who had stepped far back. Scale had done likewise. "Now?"

Eolande nodded. "Yes. But remember, you must vacate the spot you're standing on at once."

"Fair enough." Pecklyn brandished his saber and raised his eyebrows. "You ready Master?"

Aelfwynne rolled his eyes. "Sure. Let's get this over with so I can get back to work."

Pecklyn's saber sliced the air, barely missing Aelfwynne's shoulder and slammed the top of the pedestal sideways with a resounding clang. Faster than a dragon snapping at a troll, Pecklyn dove sideways, rolling onto his shoulder and springing back to his feet.

Aelfwynne stepped back, alarmed at how close Pecklyn's blade had come to hitting him, his perturbed gaze landing on Eolande and Scale. "Well? That was magnanimously disappointing."

"I don't know what went wrong." Eolande stepped over to the window to inspect its surface. He looked at Scale. "What a cursed project this has turned out to be."

Scale shrugged. "Maybe he has to actually hit him."

Eolande's face lit up. "Hmm? You may be right."

"Whoa. Wait a minute," Aelfwynne said. "That's not happening."

"Oh, but Master, it must. We need to know our wards are working. It might save you one day." Scale turned to Pecklyn. "Can you hit him in the shoulder with the flat of your blade?"

"Gladly." Pecklyn's eager smile fell seeing Aelfwynne's unappreciative reaction to his enthusiasm. He lowered his gaze. "I mean, sure, if I must."

"Okay. Go back to the pedestal. Both of you," Eolande said as he joined Scale on the far side of the chamber.

Getting into position, Pecklyn readied his saber, his grin broader than Aelfwynne thought it should be.

"Remember. Make it convincing, and then move fast," Eolande said from behind a smaller stone pedestal where he and Scale crouched.

"Are you ready Master?" Pecklyn waggled his saber, gripping it with two hands.

Aelfwynne raised his hairless brow. "Remember who's the high wizard. If that cuts me, you'll be wishing the window hadn't been replaced because that'd be the only way you'd be able to escape my wrath."

Pecklyn's smile grew wider. "Oh, I've been waiting for this day, Master Aelfwynne. I wish Bale was here to witness it."

Aelfwynne's dark look made Pecklyn laugh.

Holding his blade out wide, Pecklyn leaned away from Aelfwynne momentarily before his saber cut through the air.

The flat of the blade thwapped the goblin's exposed shoulder with such force that Aelfwynne yelped and staggered sideways.

The chamber flickered and a momentary hum preceded the crackling energy that formed along the edges of the windowpane. It coalesced to a focal point in the centre of the glass and discharged a lethal blast to the spot Pecklyn had just vacated. The jagged arc blasted a small chunk out of the floor, showering a very surprised high wizard.

"Yes!" Scale and Eolande shouted.

Aelfwynne stared at the scorched ground, then at the window, and finally at the two responsible for the defensive mechanism. Holding his pained shoulder with his opposite hand and brushing bits of rock dust from his person, he growled, "And what if Pecklyn had been an assassin and snuck up behind me to slit my throat?"

Eolande and Scale looked at each other, their triumphant faces falling.

Eolande conceded the point. "Then you'd probably be dead before the ward discharged. Hmm, I guess we've more work to do."

"Look on the bright side," Scale said with a hopeful smile. "At least the assassin would be dead too."

Aelfwynne shook his head and headed toward the exit, muttering, "Cursed apprentice."

Dragon Sect

Dragon Friend

Tyral came at Braen seemingly without a care, not bothering to brandish the cutlass hanging from a thong on his hip. "Careful ya don't stick yerself wit' that thing."

The brawny sailor feigned to rush him but stepped back as Braen's poorly-aimed sword cut the air between them. Faster than Braen knew what was happening, Tyral stepped in and grabbed his wrist. Pulling Braen toward him with ease, he smashed his forehead against Braen's face.

A sickening crack signalled the awful pain that ensued. Braen's sword clattered to the offal. Staggering backward into an empty stall, he sensed his building magic slip away as he fell addled to his backside.

Tyral stepped after him but stopped—his eyes widening. "You *are* one of them!"

Braen held his hands to his broken nose. By the way Tyral stared, he knew his bandana had slipped. With bloody hands he repositioned the headband, but the damage was done.

"Look here, lads. We got ourselves one of them pointy-eared devils in our midst."

Dragon Sect

The sailors appeared over Tyral's shoulders, their faces twisting into sneers.

One of them hocked and spat, a gob of spittle smacking Braen's forehead. He snarled, "I say we lop off his ears and present them to the captain."

Tyral nodded, an evil grin on his unshaven face. He pulled a filleting knife from a thin sheath and held the curved blade toward Braen. "I'm gonna gut 'im like the serpent his kind are and toss his entrails t' the krakens."

Braen scuttled backward in the filth of the stall, trying not to retch at the stench of the hold and textures squishing between his fingers. Blood streaming from his nose, he inadvertently pushed his sword through the slop with him.

Tyral grabbed his ankle and bent forward to strike, but a gasp of astonishment held his hand.

"Hey!" One of his companions shouted, dividing Tyral's attention between the dying sailor beside him and a well-dressed man with long, golden locks.

Before the second sailor could react, Alexis shivved him beneath the ribcage, driving his blade into the man with such force that the sailor briefly lifted off the ground.

"What the…?" Tyral released Braen's ankle and spun to face the newcomer. "Yer gonna die fer that."

His dagger lodged in the dying man's abdomen, the sailor's dead weight forced Alexis to his knees. He could only watch as Tyral brought his cutlass to bear.

Tyral lunged forward but jerked upright. Howling in pain, he dropped to the ground beside Alexis—Braen's sword stuck in the back of his knee.

Braen's sword pulled free of his clammy grasp. Breathless, he couldn't believe he had actually stabbed someone. Horrified, he curled into a ball, hugged his knees to his chest, and looked away.

Alexis jumped to his feet and located the first dead sailor's cutlass. Pulling it free of the man's waist, he held its tip against Tyral's throat. Sparing a glance for Braen, he said, "Get up."

Braen didn't have the strength—his hands and knees trembled in shock.

"Get up!" Alexis shouted.

Afraid of his savior, it still took everything Braen had to comply with Alexis' command. With the help of the back wall of the stall, he rose unsteadily to his feet, unable to control his shaking limbs.

Alexis stared at Braen, taking in his ears. "I suspected as much. What business do you have in Madrigail Bay?"

Braen swallowed, at a loss for something to say. He didn't know how to explain why he was travelling the realms of man. His gaze fell on his sword lying beside Tyral's damaged leg.

"Pick it up," Alexis said. "He won't bother you again."

Before Braen garnered the nerve to move, Alexis drove the cutlass he was holding into Tyral's neck.

The sailor convulsed once and fell limp at Alexis' feet.

Braen gaped.

Alexis dropped the cutlass with a disgusted look. "It had to be done. He knew who you are. At least, what you are."

Braen swallowed, nodding ever so slightly.

"Here." Alexis grabbed Braen's sword, wiped it on Tyral's shoulder, and handed it to him. "Now get yourself together. We'll be in port soon. It won't do for you to be onboard when we tie off."

"Wh-who are you?"

"That's not your concern right now. When the crew find their mates, they'll come for you."

Braen looked at Seafoam. "What about my horse?"

Alexis followed his gaze. "The roan?"

Braen nodded.

"I'll bring him to you in the bay. Wait for me by the stone arch at the river mouth."

Braen digested Alexis' words, knowing how spooked he must appear to the man who had saved his life. "But why?"

"Why did I help you?"

Braen nodded.

"That's a story best left for another day. Suffice it to say, I'm a dragon friend."

Braen frowned.

"My family was spared by your former queen."

"Nyxa?"

"Aye. I'm told she was a ruthless leader during the time of man's ill-fated incursion into your lands, but she wasn't heartless. Of that, there can never be any doubt. She spared my ancestors when most others in her position would not."

Braen had no idea what Alexis was talking about. His grandmother had mercilessly slaughtered the invading armies of man. Drove them from South March running and screaming for their lives. At least that's what his mother had told him.

"Now come. Follow me." Alexis looked at the darkened hatchway. "The sun's down. It's time to sneak you off the ship."

Holding his bleeding nose, Braen had little choice but to obey.

Dragon Sect

Look to the Dragon Fang

Miragan's exceptionally smooth flight surprised Ouderling. Though she had previously flown the wyvern, Perch, it had only been inside the Crystal Cavern. The only great distances she had ever flown had been on Dawnbreaker—the purple dragon's ragged wing flaps and scaly shoulders had always left her backside sore.

It hadn't dawned on her how big the realm of South March really was until she witnessed it unfold from Miragan's back. League after endless league of the Steel Mountains passed them by as they flew lower than the loftier peaks to escape the worst of the cold. Clad in her training armour, not nearly as fancy as the suit gifted to her by Xantha, she was thankful Pecklyn had convinced her and Jyllana to bring along fur-lined, leather surcoats for the trip up the mountains.

Aelfwynne had ordered them not to fly over the interior of South March for fear of them being spotted by Orlythe's troops. He had been of the belief that should the Grim Duke discover they had left Highcliff, they would be in grave danger. Ouderling had inwardly rolled her eyes. The high

206

wizard was sending them on a quest into the kingdoms of man!

After that first night out of Highcliff, they had resorted to flying during the day—the interminable mountain range safer to navigate in the light. Afara's deception and Demonic's subsequent abandonment had taken with it any kind of dragon assistance the duke had formerly enjoyed.

Midway through the third day, Dagomar spotted a high ledge with a thin waterfall cascading into its midst before spilling thousands of feet into a deep ravine separating two peaks. Their course had paralleled the western edge of the Steel Mountains, allowing them to witness the great expanse of the Ors Sea. They set down for a quick rest and a bite to eat.

Jyllana spread out a scroll on a sun-bathed rock and pointed to a spot on the makeshift map she had drawn, looking northwest as she spoke. "Those twin peaks in the distance are the Fangs of the Dragon."

Ouderling glanced up from the map in awe. She was right! "We're close to Orlythia."

Jyllana nodded. "Once we fly beyond the palace, Pecklyn said we're to start making our way to the coast and follow the shoreline…"

Her personal protector kept blathering on, but her words were lost on Ouderling. Guilt-ridden, since arriving at Highcliff, she hadn't spared much thought for the elf she had not too long ago imagined she would spend the rest of her life with. Though they had parted on less than amicable terms, time had allowed her to reconsider her last days with Marris with a clearer mind. The fault behind their discontent lay solely at her feet. The beautiful elf had not deserved how she had treated him.

Dragon Sect

At the time, she had selfishly convinced herself that Marris had betrayed her, and for reasons she couldn't comprehend at the time, her parents had unfairly exiled her to a remote dragon colony. Looking back to the time that seemed so long ago now, she had come to accept that everyone had acted in her best interest.

She sighed, fearing it was too late to make amends. Half of her wanted to fly straight to the palace and hug the horse groom, while her other half dreaded that by doing so she would discover Marris had moved on.

Dagomar and Miragan had flown off to search for food, leaving her alone with Jyllana on the windswept ledge. It became apparent that Jyllana had stopped talking. Snapping out of her reverie, Ouderling blinked several times.

Jyllana stared. "Are you okay? You look like you've seen a phantasm."

Ouderling gaped at the choice of words.

"Sorry." Jyllana looked to the ground. "Not sure what made me think of that."

"It's okay," Ouderling said. Being this close to the place where both of their lives had drastically changed because of such a creature, she couldn't blame her friend.

She smiled at the notion of 'her friend.' Though the redhead's primary role was to act as her personal protector, Ouderling didn't view Jyllana in that light anymore. She hoped Jyllana shared her sense of friendship. "I'm fine. Just thinking of…" She trailed off, mad at herself for allowing her eyes to mist up.

Jyllana's knowing smile told her that her friend knew her well.

"Do you think Marris misses me?"

"Of course." Jyllana allowed the scroll to roll back on itself and held it in a fist as she embraced Ouderling. "How could he not?"

"I treated him unfairly." Ouderling tried to refrain from crying. For months she had bottled up her feelings, afraid to allow herself to think about how much she missed him. Thankful for Jyllana's embrace, she held on until she was sure she could face her again without tears, and stepped back. "He deserves better."

"Don't be silly. I doubt a day's gone by that he hasn't thought about you."

Ouderling cringed. If only she could say the same. She nodded, not daring to speak lest her voice crack.

After a lean meal of fruit and nuts, they watched Miragan and Dagomar fly back to the ledge. If they had found something to eat, they had already devoured it.

Jyllana tied up her rucksack and got up from the same rock she had unrolled the map on earlier. "You ready?"

Sitting on the ground, Ouderling nodded and rose to her feet. Her gaze lingered on the Fangs of the Dragon for a moment. Even though she knew the answer, she asked anyway, "Do you think it would hurt if we visited the palace? Neither of my parents are home."

"You know we can't do that. If word gets back to Aelfy, we'd be in a heap of trouble."

"Aelfy?" Dagomar's voice sounded in Ouderling's mind, surprising her. Not because of its suddenness, but because he had bothered to speak at all.

Jyllana started to walk toward him but stopped and stared. "A nickname we call Master Aelfwynne. One he wouldn't appreciate, if you know what I mean."

Dagomar stared at Jyllana but said no more.

Jyllana's face lit up as she spun to look back at Ouderling. "You know what we could do, though?"

Ouderling was almost afraid to ask. The mischief on Jyllana's face promised nothing good would come of it.

"No. What?"

"Follow me." Jyllana skipped to Dagomar, bounded onto his shoulder like it was something she did everyday, and prepared herself for dragonflight.

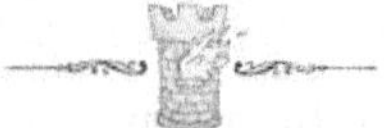

"I don't think Master Aelfwynne would approve, Your Highness," Miragan said as they followed Dagomar and Jyllana between the western summit of the Fangs of the Dragon and the eight-sided stone chamber built atop Grim Watch Tower. *"I sense a strong magical presence on the island."*

"That would be the essence of Grimlock. The warlock responsible for building the tower," Ouderling said, a fact she had been taught but had never thought about until this moment.

"There's more to that building than a warlock's presence."

"Does it frighten you?"

"Concerns me, would be more accurate," Miragan answered as the tower and the western fang receded behind them.

Ouderling looked over her shoulder, mesmerized by the daunting monolith. She had never visited it before. Judging by the creepy feeling it instilled in her, she doubted she ever would.

The last few leagues of the Ors Sea passed beneath them as they approached Orlythia and the impressive edifice fronting the north shore. Borreraig Palace rose out of the sea like a multi-spired leviathan sprawling along the length of the large city abutting its northern ramparts.

"Best we not fly too close!" Jyllana called back to them as Dagomar winged higher.

Miragan followed suit, gaining altitude with every wingbeat. The palace dropped away until it was no bigger in than an elfling's doll house.

Ouderling searched the eastern wing of the grand fortress, spotting the green pastureland surrounding the stable yard. She struggled to keep her eyes from misting up. Marris would be down there somewhere. She wondered if he was watching their passage. Two dragons would be hard to miss.

The more she thought on what they had just done, the more disturbed she became that they had risked needless exposure. She absently mused that even a few months ago she would have been the one encouraging such behavior, but as Borreraig Palace shrank to an indiscernible speck on the north shore, she appreciated the recklessness of their action. The king and queen were facing down her uncle at Urdanya, and here she was joy riding a dragon to satisfy her selfish desires.

If Marris was smart, he would have forgotten about her and her unpredictable temper long ago. Gritting her teeth against the pain of that thought, she steeled herself to the task at hand. Highcliff counted on them locating the infamous Grimclaw and somehow convincing him to assist her parents in a battle that was not his fight.

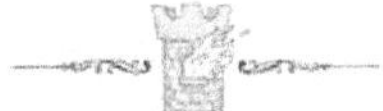

An indeterminable number of leagues of forestland stretched westward to the waters of the Niad Ocean. The only way Jyllana knew they had left South March was by listening to Miragan tell Ouderling that the large bay they flew over was a ship building port on the south coast of the kingdom of Nordicia.

She gripped the long-handled scythe she had learned to use under Pecklyn's tutelage. The unwieldy weapon was a useless implement while on the ground, but on dragonback, it was useful for both attacking troops on the ground as her dragon mount swooped low, or battling another dragon rider in midair. With Demonic's departure, she didn't believe there was much of a need to defend against another rider, but given the recent events, one could never be too sure.

The coastline continued west for the rest of the day, slowly turning from long stretches of sandy beach to hills and cliffs that grew into snow-capped peaks of a mountain range Miragan referred to as the Spine.

They settled on a remote beachhead for the night and were on their way again at first light. As the dying rays of the day blended into the waves, a loftier stretch of mountains bisected the Spine from the east and sank into the Niad Ocean, extending a few leagues into the surf along a rugged archipelago toward a large island far out to sea.

Two more days of incessant flight brought them to a large inlet.

"Didn't High Wizard Aelfwynne say Grimclaw would be found in a large canyon valley?" Ouderling called across the gap separating her and Miragan from Jyllana and Dagomar.

Jyllana recalled her conversation with the goblin wizard. "Master Aelfwynne said we'd come to a long inlet with a large city at the end of it. That would be Madrigail Bay."

"Should we fly to it?" Miragan asked.

Jyllana wasn't sure what to do. The coastline had been rife with inlets of varying sizes during their trip north, but none of them compared to the one they hovered over now.

"I say we fly down the inlet. If we see a settlement, we can always turn back!" Ouderling shouted to be heard above the wind.

"Okay, but if we see a city, we're to avoid it."

The inlet was much longer than any of them would have imagined, but sure enough, as they rounded a final bend to the right, a great port city sat nestled between two mountains rising up on either side of a mighty river mouth.

"That must be Madrigail Bay!" Jyllana pointed to where everyone was already looking. She lowered her voice, "Dagomar. Take us away from here."

The pale red dragon altered his flight and rose out of the confines of the inlet hemmed in by mountains on either side. Miragan followed close behind.

The following day, they came upon another wide inlet, this one more of a fjord—towering cliffs bisecting the land as far as the eye could see. A port city smaller than Madrigail Bay was built into the hillside that comprised the northern shore of the fjord's outlet. Tall masts bobbed at anchor inside the safety of the fjord's mouth, tied to numerous jetties jutting into the calmer water.

"Should we try this one?" Ouderling called out.

Jyllana remembered Aelfwynne mentioning a long inlet north of Madrigail Bay, explaining where he thought Grimclaw could be found.

'North of Madrigail Bay, how far, I have no idea, there's supposed to be a large valley that divides the mountain range from the coast to many leagues inland.' Were his words to her as he pointed at an ancient map scroll in his lair. *'This may be it, but I have my suspicions that it isn't as there's a settlement on either end of the gap.'*

She considered the fjord. "Hard to say! Master Aelfwynne doesn't know where we'll find Grimclaw! He said this stretch of land might be it, but he wasn't sure!"

Miragan altered her flight and shot up the fjord. *We may as well check it out.*

Jyllana agreed and said to Dagomar, "And I thought South March was big. The kingdoms of man go on forever."

Their journey down the fjord proved Aelfwynne's suspicions correct. Another port city lay at its far end.

Banking north as the sun set in the west, they set down deeper into the mountains north of the waterway and rested for the night.

As cold as it was on the high slopes, warmth was never far away when one flew with dragons. Despite Dagomar's reluctance to join in their company, aside from flying Jyllana, he was good about collecting large pieces of wood and setting them ablaze.

It's a wonder the surly dragon doesn't set the mountainside on fire, Ouderling thought as she huddled close to the welcome flames. She glanced around, her dark vision not much use beyond the brightness of the roaring fire. Hemmed in on all sides by jagged tors, she wondered if they would ever find Grimclaw.

She smiled. That prospect was okay with her. She didn't relish having to talk to the infamous dragon.

Endless days of flying had taken their toll. Yawning, she stretched out her fur-lined surcoat and laid back—blue eyes reflecting the leaping flames as she lost herself in the depths of the fire and a soothing dreamlike state that accompanied it.

Her inherent magic floated to the surface of her consciousness, allowing nature's essence to flow through her. The sounds and smells of the campfire drifted away, replaced by a heady aroma of damp loam, deep green pines, and something she couldn't quite place at first.

Musky, with the hint of leather and brimstone, a vision materialized out of the haze. An enormous beast bristling with sharp-edged, blue scales, talon-like spikes, and curved claws that appeared capable of rending stone, formed in her mind. Grimclaw!

As sure as she knew it was the dragon they sought, she was at a loss as to how to explain his presence infiltrating her idle thoughts. And yet, she knew without a doubt, that Grimclaw watched her. Waiting.

Her body convulsed in terror, expecting to fall victim to the ancient dragon's wrath.

Someone shouted at her from a long way off. She wanted to run, but something held her firmly in place, even though in her mind's eye she soared across endless treetops—the top boughs thrashing her face. She turned her head sideways to avoid the worst of the battering as a strange voice called to her.

"Look to the fang!" was all it said.

Opening her eyes, her breath caught. Everything disappeared and she fell into a yawning abyss.

Dragon Sect

The Crushing Tide of Rebellion

Hammas' incredulous face stared at the tent flaps of the royal pavilion. A scout who had infiltrated Urdanya had just left them after imparting unsettling news. Relating what he had found out, he had slipped back outside to find a way into Urdanya Castle and learn more about Duke Orlythe's intentions.

Forever grateful for the competent Home Guard surrounding her, Khae marvelled at how stressful it must be for her loyal scouts to do what they did every day. One slip up would surely mean their death. She bit her lips and sighed. Stepping in behind her husband, she wrapped her arms around his waist and pressed her cheek between his rigid shoulder blades.

They remained that way for a while, the brazier providing her little warmth. Hammas patted her hands and spun free of her embrace—the hollow shadows on his face, ghoulish. It had been a long stretch of days facing down her brother's troops. News out of Nayda had confirmed the destruction of their fleet and the repercussions had rung out like a death knell throughout her army.

Dragon Sect

If there had been any question about Orlythe's intent before, that brutal act of war had removed all doubt. She and Hammas were embroiled in a fight to the death with the one elf in all of South March who stood a chance to gain with their demise.

She swallowed the ever-present lump in her throat and put on a brave face. "It's only a matter of time until the rebellious towns south of the Spill pen us in from the east."

Hammas stared at her with tired eyes and nodded.

"I hate to say it, but unless we retreat, we're done for," Khae said—a grim fact that they both appreciated.

"And just where do you suggest we go? We can't cross the river. We can't return to Orlythia via the sea. If Orlythe has gained control of Erline, Aelfwynne, and Brysis, our land route north is cut off. That leaves the unpleasant prospect of scattering into the Wizard's Sleeve."

Khae's eyes opened wider. "That's it. We need to beat him to Gullveig."

Hammas frowned. "We won't find fighters there. They're merchants who're all about supplying the wizards' guild."

"Exactly. Orlythe may have numbers on his side, but we have an untapped community of magic-users."

Hammas' face had started to lighten, but fell with the mention of the guild. "Sagora is no friend of the crown."

"Friend or not, he's sworn to protect it."

Hammas' skeptical look sapped the life from the one hope she dared to cling to. That somewhere in South March, there existed a place, or group of elves, that could turn the fortunes of war in her favour.

She tried to take solace in the fact that there was always Highcliff. Surely High Wizard Aelfwynne was aware of the events happening in Urdanya.

She sighed. Highcliff's priorities weren't centred on the crown. Afara Maral's failed attempt to seize the Crystal Cavern had been the catalyst to deplete the dragon population loyal to South March—the rogue dragons following Demonic to only the Fae knew where. As such, Aelfwynne wouldn't dare risk leaving Highcliff unprotected again.

"We have no choice," Khae said, her voice on the verge of breaking. "If I must, I'll force the blasted headmaster to heed our call."

Hammas raised his eyebrows. "That won't go well."

Khae's shoulders slumped. "What else would you have me do? I refuse to send our troops into a bloodbath they cannot hope to win. No matter how well trained they are, Orlythe's numbers will crush us where we stand."

"I can't believe the entire kingdom has risen against us." Hammas shook his head. "You've done nothing to upset the masses. Everything you've done has been for the betterment of the realm. If anything, you've been *too* benevolent."

"And there lies the root of the problem. Many of the older generation believe Orlythe's vision of South March is the proper one. Their belief is likely spurred on by the memory of my mother's military prowess."

"Come on Khae, you know better than that. Nyxa never once desired to expand our borders. She fought to retain what we had, not conquer new lands."

"Of course I know, but the elders who fought with her think otherwise. Had she driven her army into the north, I haven't the slightest doubt South March would be a vaster realm today." Khae spun to glare at the flames leaping through the grillwork of the iron brazier, its thin mesh glowing orange. "If only I'd inherited her battle sense. She wouldn't have stood for Orlythe's insolence. She would've rolled over his traitorous army and squeezed the life out of the bastard with her own hands."

Hammas stepped in beside her and turned her into his embrace, holding her tight. "And that's what makes you special. You're not Nyxa. You're Khae. You have your own strengths. We'll find a way, you'll see. Even if you have to strangle Sagora with *your* own hands."

A tear slipped down Khae's cheek. The only one she was prepared to allow fall. There wasn't time for self-pity. She nodded into Hammas' shoulder. The crushing tide of rebellion facing South March was on the verge of overwhelming her troops. She had little choice but to enlist the aid of the wizards' guild. All she had to do was to convince the autonomous group that their best interests lay in her hands, not the Grim Duke's.

Taking a deep breath, she broke the embrace and lifted her chin high, her voice a feral growl. "Until the Grim Duke wrests the crown from my dying fingers, the wizard must heed my call."

Dragon Sect

Alliance with the Enemy

Coastal *Cutter* slipped into the wide cove dominating the centre of the great port city known as Madrigail Bay, under the cover of a starless night.

"You ready?" Alexis whispered from the shadows of the midmast, his head swivelling from bow to stern and back again.

Braen nodded, though he wasn't looking forward to what lay ahead as he clutched his boots in his hands.

Shouts from fore and aft preceded a cacophony of metal clinking and timbers creaking as the crew dropped anchor on either end of the large ship.

Rattled by the events below deck, Braen's nerves were on end.

Alexis stepped out of the shadows and strolled to the starboard rail, casually scanning the deck around him. Without a sound he gave a slight twitch of his head.

Braen drew a deep breath and did as he had been instructed, walking across the deck barefoot to stand between Alexis and the rail.

"Quickly now. Don't make a noise."

Dragon Sect

Braen didn't hesitate. Mounting the rail, he lowered himself to dangle over the hull. With Alexis hanging onto him, he grabbed hold of a railing post, and dropped his body along the curved hull of the ship. He couldn't fathom how he was going to fall into the water without making a noise. *Coastal Cutter* had anchored in the middle of the harbour for a reason. It was too big to berth.

"Hurry!" Alexis growled under his breath.

Braen inhaled deeply, wincing at the pain his nose was causing him. He closed his eyes for a moment to garner a bit of courage, and let go of the post. His body scudded along the rough hull of the ship and became airborne; the dark water rushing up to meet him. Arms flailing, he hit the water hard, creating a great splash.

The bay was colder than he had feared it would be. The sudden shock sucked the breath from his lungs as he surfaced and struggled to keep his head above water without making more noise.

"What was that?" A deep voice boomed from somewhere along the deck.

"Over there," Alexis answered, his hand the only visible part of him from where Braen treaded water. Alexis pointed to a spot far aft of his position. "It might have been a kraken!"

Though Alexis said that to divert the sailors' attention from where he floundered, just the thought of a kraken made Braen gasp. Searching the water around him, he half-expected to witness a leviathan rise out of the depths to swallow him whole.

A few tense moments later, Alexis' hushed voice asked, "You okay down there?"

"Yes," Braen croaked, struggling to hang onto his boots as he fought to keep his head above water without disturbing the surface overly much.

"Get yourself to shore. I'll try to keep their attention to port."

Braen had no idea if Alexis had left the rail. Eyeing the shoreline, it appeared farther away than it had while he was on deck. He swam across the open water, not daring to look back for fear of seeing the crew watching him, or something worse.

Halfway to shore, doubt seeped into him as the cold water sapped his strength, but one slow stroke after another brought him to an algae covered stanchion of a tall pier—the deck well out of reach. Resting at each subsequent stanchion, his feet finally touched the gravelly shore rising sharply to a rocky beachhead. Littered with overturned skiffs and larger boats on their sides, many with gaping holes torn out of their hulls, the solid ground beneath his wobbly legs was a welcome relief.

As cold as the water had been, spasms of intense shivering brought on by the night air wracked his body. He forced himself to stagger toward the shadows of a low building to wait out the night.

Huddled against the wooden slats of a ramshackle warehouse, his teeth chattered so hard he was afraid he might chip them. With nothing else to do, he reflected on why he had come to Madrigail Bay in the first place. For the life of him, he really didn't have an answer.

Not for the first time, he questioned why he had agreed to his uncle's plan to send him away. It hadn't made much sense then, but it made even less now. Sure, he had fantasized about finding likeminded individuals to the bard,

Sir Stanley White, but truth be told, he had never actually planned to do so.

Nor could he believe he had put his trust in the blonde-haired, highbrow passenger, for surely that was who Alexis was. The crew had avoided the man for the most part, but whenever they had any dealings with him, they had spoken with a reverence not afforded to the captain.

Duped into playing the game of those seeking power, for it started to dawn on him that that was surely his uncle's ulterior motive, he feared he had fallen into another web of intrigue that surrounded Alexis—a man no less!

He hugged his body in a futile effort to staunch his incessant shakes. What a fool he had become.

Clothing still damp, his skin white and clammy and riddled with gooseflesh, Braen approached the arched stone causeway spanning the mouth of a wide river that split the port city in half—the narrow roadbed barely wide enough to accommodate the rickety carts laden with goods trundling across its expanse in the early twilight.

Checking to ensure his poor excuse for a headband covered most of his ears, he pulled on his cowl, and tried to avoid eye contact with the citizens of the city. He imagined his face looked a mess. Thankfully, the people trudging alongside their carts with hunched backs and tired expressions weren't in the mood for small talk.

Coastal Cutter's mastheads caught the first rays of sunshine, the great ship's dark bulk floating close to another galleon on its port side. Braen had no idea if the other ship had been there when *Coastal Cutter* had dropped anchor, but as the morning light spread across the bay, he could make out the forms of people bustling about the decks of both ocean-going vessels—preparing to unload their cargo onto large, flat skiffs that were being paddled away from a couple of lower piers on the southern shore of the bay.

He walked to the far end of the causeway and left the rutted roadway, slinking down an embankment to sit against the stone wall of the bridgework. The fetid stench of dead fish and brackish seawater turned up his nose, but he didn't care. Watching the port city come to life, his eyes grew heavy. He hadn't slept in a long time.

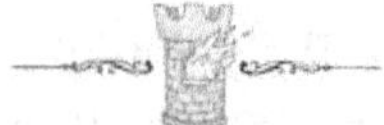

Head lolled to one side, a large smile on his face, Braen was startled awake by the toe of a boot jabbing him in the ribs.

"Hey. Get up," Alexis ordered. "And fix your headband."

Braen blinked rapidly, his foggy brain struggling to recall where he was or who was speaking to him. Fortunately, his eyes hadn't swollen shut like he had originally feared they might. As the reality hit home, he jerked upright and jumped to his feet, his hands going to the thin strip of black cloth around his head.

A whinny from the top of the embankment drew his attention beyond Alexis. Seafoam and a shiny, black warhorse stood tethered to the rocks lining the top of the bridge wall.

"Come on. We best be leaving," Alexis said, his concerned gaze resting on the *Coastal Cutter*. "When they discover their mates in the hold, they'll come for me as well."

Braen gaped. "You mean they don't know yet?"

"Doesn't appear so, but it won't be long now," Alexis muttered and started up the embankment, stopping long enough to toss him an empty waterskin that he pulled from inside his tunic. "We'd best be far removed when that happens."

Dragon Sect

"Where're we going?" Confused, Braen caught the leather bladder and followed in Alexis' wake, but the man never answered.

Untethering Seafoam, Alexis handed Braen the reins and untied the second horse.

Braen considered his unsaddled horse. It wasn't easy mounting Seafoam bareback, but he managed without help. Taking a last look at the *Coastal Cutter* in the middle of the bay, he directed Seafoam to follow Alexis up a dirt roadway rising eastward into the mountains, paralleling the river on their left.

Easing in behind his new acquaintance, he asked, "What about my saddle and bag?"

A dark look from Alexis chilled him more than his damp clothing had.

"You want to go back for them, have at it," was all the man said as he trotted away.

A shout of alarm echoed across the bay, taken up by several others.

Braen heeled Seafoam into a trot.

Once the sun had breached the mountain peaks, Braen's clothing dried enough to rid the cold from his bones. He removed his headband, feeling odd in the company of the man, but he needn't have. Apart from noting that he had done so, Alexis didn't so much as comment on his exposed ears.

They rode their horses at an easy gait, prepared to gallop away at the first sign of pursuit. The path lifted into the heights, circumventing unpassable, frothy chasms.

As they rode along a high ridge with the late afternoon sun on their backs, Alexis stopped his horse atop a high rise. The path they followed fell away into a green valley, the vista opening up before them and stretching wide to the horizon—a distant hint of another mountain range far to the east.

"You have just come through the one easy pass in all of the Spine," Alexis said looking back the way they had come. "There are only three navigable passes in the four southern kingdoms that reach the west coast. The other two lie far north of here."

Braen uncorked his waterskin and drank deeply. It had been no problem keeping them replenished along the narrow trail as many waterfalls had crossed their path, disgorging snowmelt from the towering peaks. He squinted. "Looks like a town down there."

"Aye. The Forke. A mining town built along the confluence of the Madrigail River," he nodded at the mighty river they had followed out of Madrigail Bay, "and the Frothe, a fast-moving river tumbling out of the mountains to the north. Supposedly gold to be had in the Frothe's riverbed if you're into fine minerals."

"And your home lies beyond that?"

"Oh, much farther to the northeast. Carillon City is about as far from civilization as one can get before entering the boundless swamplands beyond. But you can see the western edge of the kingdom of Carillon from here. Everything north of the Madrigail River and east of the Frothe is part of my realm."

"Your realm?" Braen asked, half joking.

"My father's, actually. I'll inherit it when he dies."

Braen choked on his water, his eyes widening at the revelation. He suddenly had a bad feeling about accompanying the man. "You're a prince?"

Alexis shrugged. "It's not as big a deal as people make it out to be. I'm the lord of a bunch of farmers."

"But your father's a king."

"Aye," Alexis laughed. "King of the wheat fields."

Braen nodded. Everything about how Alexis had been treated aboard the *Coastal Cutter* began to make sense. The wonder on his face dropped into a frown. "If the sailors know who you are, they'll know where to find you."

"Ha! Once we pass The Forke, we'll be safe enough. They wouldn't dare come after me in Carillon. My father's troops would see them dead before they set foot on the plains."

Braen had no idea what that meant, but it didn't matter. What concerned him most was that he travelled with a prince of the five kingdoms. One of the realms that had done battle with his grandmother. He doubted an elf would be welcome at Alexis' father's court.

The cork squeaked into place as Braen stowed the waterskin in his jerkin and thought of a polite way to break free of the man's company. "Um, perhaps it's time we parted ways."

Alexis appeared to stiffen. He turned a critical eye Braen's way.

"I appreciate everything you've done for me, really. I'd love to repay you somehow, but I lack the means." He tried not to look at the little money pouch hanging on his belt. "That being said, I'd hate to be a bother when we reach your home. I'm sure your people won't take kindly to someone like me."

"So sure of what you think, are you?"

Braen blinked at the man, not knowing how to answer that.

"Do you remember when I told you back on the ship that the Queen of the Elves spared my family?"

Braen nodded. "You said you were a dragon friend."

"That's right. Do you know what that means?"

Braen looked to the sky in thought but couldn't imagine what it meant. He shook his head.

"Let's just say that I believe fate has crossed our paths. I told you I believe there's more to you than your ears. Tell me I'm right about that, or should I have left you to be gutted in the hold?"

Braen swallowed, not sure he wished to divulge his true identity, but as he held Alexis' gaze, he couldn't detect any malice in the man's green eyes—more like a deep curiosity.

Inhaling deeply, Braen puffed out his chest, the false sense of bravado giving him the nerve to ask, "And what makes you think I should trust you?"

"Apart from me saving your life when I had no reason to care?" Alexis shrugged. "Let's just say, I felt at the time it was my way of honouring what your queen did for my family. Was I wrong in making an alliance with the enemy?"

Braen held his stare but didn't bother to answer.

Without another word, Alexis urged Char into a canter, riding down the steep trail toward a sea of golden grasses.

Braen sighed, debating whether to turn Seafoam around and be rid of the man who claimed to be a prince. Without a familiar face to be had for hundreds of leagues, and daring to consider the handsome prince a friend, he urged Seafoam after the receding man draped in vermilion, grimacing at the ever-present ache in his backside from travelling across the mountains without a saddle.

Dragon Sect

Hammer and Anvil

Ryedyn's days in Urdanya were numbered. Once the northern cities were brought to heel, the royal army would be swept beneath the rising tide of rebellion. The fact that it was being forced by the duke's hand made little difference. Nor did Ryedyn's mentor care how the populace viewed Orlythe's tactics once the queen was taken out of the equation. Provided the duke's campaign coaxed the high wizard from the Crystal Cavern, the Dragon Witch Wraith cared little what happened to the Wys family. With the power of the earth blood and dragon crystals at their command, no one short of a god would be able to stop Ryedyn or the wraith from achieving their ultimate goal.

Ryedyn's brow furrowed. What *was* the wraith's endgame? To subjugate the Crystal Cavern for sure, but to what end? It dawned on him that the soulless creature had never elaborated on his motive. It didn't appear to covet the throne.

Chin in hand, the duke's wizard blinked several times in consternation as he leaned against the southeast facing window in the chamber atop the Sea Witch Sceptre. A fleeting thought festered in the back of his mind. Once the magic source was in their possession, the wraith might not have further use for him. He swallowed—the implication was troubling.

Perhaps he had been wrong to conspire against the Grim Duke. The more he thought on it, the more unsettled the notion made him. He had assisted the wraith in duping the queen's brother to embroil South March in a war that would ravage it from border to border.

Should the queen somehow manage to find a way out of the conundrum her army faced, it stood to reason the kingdom would spiral into a prolonged battle. A war that had the potential to leave few troops standing before the dust settled. Confused by reeling emotions, Ryedyn wondered what the point was of usurping an empty throne?

His breathing grew heavier the more he contemplated the wraith's agenda. He had no idea where the creature had gone. After initiating the stand-off between the queen and her brother, and imparting a string of strange commands for him to follow, it had simply disappeared. Perhaps the most disconcerting part of it all was that he couldn't be sure if the wraith had actually left. It might be watching him now.

He shivered, turning slowly to examine the shadows in the octagonal chamber, a sheen of sweat dampening his forehead.

The sound of a Grim Guard clearing his throat caused him to jump. The elf's presence almost forgotten, Ryedyn blinked at the scraggly-haired elf. "Right. You were saying you just returned from Castle Grim."

"The Passage of Dolor, actually."

"Right…Right. Well, what of it? Has it fallen?" Ryedyn hadn't thought to ever hear from the group of elves he had sent to explore the passage under the Dark Mountains. It had been more of a knee-jerk reaction to see if the rumours were true.

"Fallen?"

Ryedyn shook his head. He didn't have time for this. "Is it still passable?"

"Depends on what m'lord considers *passable*." The Grim Guard wasn't daunted by the fact that Ryedyn was a wizard.

Ryedyn held his stare, his anger mounting at the elf's insolence, but he had to admit, he was surprised to be talking to someone from that expedition. Taking a deep breath, he said as calmly as possible, "Were you able to achieve your objective?"

"Oh, aye, m'lord."

Ryedyn's jaw dropped.

"We weren't able to get much, as the cavern is constantly tended, but we managed to grab this." The Grim Guard reached into his tunic and produced a forearm's length of crystal.

Ryedyn accepted the shard, its weight surprisingly light. "That's it?"

The Grim Guard's face darkened. "With all due respect, m'lord. Twelve of us went in. Only five made it out. Something big roams the Passage of Dolor. We came across a cavern littered with the charred bodies of elves and trolls."

Ryedyn barely heard the elf, his mind full of possibilities concerning the artifact in his possession. Nodding to himself, he mused, "So, Afara really did summon it."

"M'lord?"

"Nothing." He placed the shard on a side table and waved a dismissive hand. "Leave me."

The Grim Guard's face screwed up on the verge of saying something more, but his words were cut off as another elf entered the chamber.

"Ah, there you are."

A jolt of dread caused Ryedyn to jerk and spin to face the black clad duke. So immersed in his contemplation of the crystal shard, the duke's sudden appearance at the top of the stairwell had caught him off guard.

The Grim Guard bowed his head as the duke passed where he stood. Not waiting to be dismissed, he slipped from the room and descended the stairwell.

Duke Orlythe frowned at the departing elf, turning a quizzical eye on Ryedyn.

Ryedyn held his stare. "He came to report on the queen's movements."

"What's the matter, wizard? You look like you've been inhabited by a ghost." The duke joined him by the window and looked east.

Ryedyn did his best not to look at where the shard rested. If the duke discovered he was hiding something from him, there would be trouble. "I never heard you coming."

"Obviously." Orlythe purred, tapping the glass with his fingernails in thought. "If I didn't know better, I'd say you were up to something."

"Just trying to figure out the best way to deal with the queen."

Orlythe nodded, though he appeared unconvinced. "You sent the ravens?"

"Yes, m'lord."

The slightest of grins parted Orlythe's unruly beard. "It's only a matter of time now."

"Yes, m'lord."

Orlythe held his gaze a few moments longer. Looking out the window, he said, "I'm surprised she's still here. As much as I despise her, she's not stupid. She must appreciate her tenuous situation. The mobilization of the troops in the north can't be unknown to her."

The royal army's green surcoats stood out amongst the dun-coloured hovels lining the northeast approach to Urdanya. Even with the royal fleet sunk near the shores of Nayda, the royal host was sizable indeed.

"The queen's pulling up stakes!" Captain Drake announced from the top of the steps, his huge frame filling the doorway.

Ryedyn jumped again, his unease not missed by Orlythe. How the infernal duke and his lackey were able to sneak up on him like that was disturbing.

Orlythe's suspicious gaze lingered on Ryedyn a moment longer before he acknowledged the head of the Grim Guard. "Ah. Just what we were discussing. Excellent news, captain. Ensure your troops harry their retreat. I'm counting on you to force them into the Wizard's Sleeve. Don't disappoint me."

"No, m'lord. The queen will be coerced into the pass," Captain Drake answered and turned to go.

Ryedyn took advantage of the duke's distraction to put himself between Orlythe and the side table, inconspicuously covering the bulk of the shard with the edge of an open scroll.

"And captain," Orlythe called after him.

"M'lord?" The captain's lead boot hung over the first step.

"Until they've left, I expect you to put a high-level security protocol in place. Stricter than the norm. The queen's spies could be anywhere."

Drake nodded. His boots rang off the stone steps, the diminishing noise absorbed by the thick walls encompassing the stairwell.

Orlythe studied Ryedyn. "You do seem out of sorts. Is there something you're not telling me?"

Ryedyn forced himself not to look away, his voice as steady as could be under the scrutiny. "No, m'lord. I'm trying to take in as much information as I can from Odyne's scrolls and ancient books before we leave. I guess I should sleep at some point."

Orlythe's eyes narrowed. "Nothing's stopping you from taking them with you."

That took Ryedyn by surprise. He blinked dumbly, envisioning the monumental task required to transport all of the tomes and pigeon-holed cabinets stuffed with scrolls. There had to be five times the amount of lore in this chamber alone than the entire wizard archives at Castle Grim. Chests and deep shelves were crammed full of parchment from the ages, along with a separate storage closet at the top of the stairwell packed with vials of unguents and powders of who knew what.

"I'll have a detail sent to pack it. It'll make a great addition to Borreraig Palace, don't you think?" the duke said, looking around the chamber. His gaze lingered on the table where the shard was hidden beneath a haphazardly place document.

Ryedyn stepped between the duke and the table and forced a smile, imagining decades of solid reading in his future. It was almost incomprehensible to think of how powerful he might become if the duke allowed him to devote his time to learning everything contained within this chamber alone— not to mention whatever treasures were to be discovered at the palace.

Perhaps he had been hasty in throwing in his lot with the wraith. The duke seemed to genuinely appreciate his arcane talent. The more Ryedyn digested what was going on around him, the more he thought that ruling a kingdom wasn't something he desired. At least not yet. There was so much to learn from so many different places, he didn't have time to contemplate anything else.

The timing wasn't right. He saw that clearly now. Left to his own devices, he was confident the day would come when he *was* ready—provided he was afforded the leisure to pursue his indulgence in learning all of the arcane knowledge land had to offer. Equipped with elven magic *and* dragon magic, there would come a day that not even the wraith would dare stand in his way.

"Well?" the duke asked, eyeing him peculiarly again.

"Aye, m'lord, that would be appreciated," Ryedyn agreed, contemplating how else he might bolster his magical prowess. "If we can find a way to augment the present lore with that of Highcliff, the reign of Orlythe Wys the Invincible, will become one of great significance."

Orlythe's lips curved in a rare smile—a sincere look of pleasure that Ryedyn had never seen cross the duke's face before. The elf prince was quite pleasant to look upon when he allowed himself a moment of happiness—even if it did come at the expense of the rest of the royal family.

"Patience, wizard. All in due time. First, we employ the hammer and anvil. Once forged, South March's new reign will bring the kingdoms of man to their knees."

Dragon Sect

Valley of the Dragon

Visions of Keaf woke Ouderling with a start. The obnoxious dragon had pinned her into a corner and was threatening to attack. He had dropped into a crouch and sprung—rows of meat-rending teeth flashing before her eyes as he went for her throat.

Jyllana was on her feet so fast, she startled not only Ouderling, but Miragan as well who lay curled close to the princess for protection while they slept. Twin daggers in hand, Jyllana scanned the darkness. "What is it, Your Highness?"

An enraged shriek from the darkness beyond their camp sent chills up Ouderling's spine—Dagomar sounding exactly like Keaf had in her dreams. She swallowed, attempting to steady her breathing. "Just a bad dream."

Jyllana caught her embarrassed gaze, but walked around, inspecting the shadows. She stopped close to where Dagomar had slept apart from them. "You sense anything?"

Typical Dagomar remained quiet, but his great head swivelled back and forth, studying the terrain.

Dragon Sect

"Let us know if you do," Jyllana said and returned to the smoking firepit.

The mountains were dark but the eastern sky showed signs of lightening toward dawn. Though Ouderling hadn't slept in many mountain aeries, for some reason, the Spine felt more foreboding than the Steel Mountains back home. A cloudless sky eased her apprehension, promising a glorious day of flying ahead.

Jyllana knelt beside her. "You sure you're okay? You cried out shortly after you settled down last night. I wanted to wake you but Dagomar warned against it."

Ouderling yawned and stretched, her dark vision allowing her to see the pale red dragon ambling around the perimeter of the glade. "Interesting," she said quietly. "Perhaps he's coming around."

Jyllana's skeptical eyeroll informed Ouderling her friend wasn't convinced. She stood, stretching some more, and said, "He's been through a lot lately, Jyl. And not just losing Cynder. He was close to Demonic and Eldron before the Battle at the Gate tore everyone apart."

Jyllana leaned close and whispered, her eyes following Dagomar. "You think we can trust him?"

Ouderling shrugged. "Aelfy does."

"Dagomar's loyal to Xantha. He'd never do anything against Highcliff or go against the word of Master Aelfwynne," Miragan's voice informed them. *"We must be careful not to upset him further, but you're right, pretty lady. His friends' betrayal has upset him greatly."*

"I hope we can count on him when the time comes to do what's required," Jyllana muttered.

"Rest assured, according to Kingstone, if the need arises to defend either one of you, there isn't a dragon better suited for that role, with the exception of Dawnbreaker or

Kingstone himself," Miragan assured them. *"Master Aelfwynne chose Dagomar for a reason. His hope is that Dagomar's absence from Highcliff will help him come to terms with his loss, but know that Dagomar was sent primarily to protect you, princess. I pity even the great Grimclaw should he come against us."*

Hearing the name of the notorious dragon, Ouderling's séance with nature's essence the previous night slammed into her mind. "Speaking of the wayward dragon, I think I know how to find him."

The flight back to the coast and north along the rugged shoreline was uneventful. Avoiding the port city at the mouth of the fjord, they flew low over the waves, inspecting coves and small inlets as they went, but nothing stood out to Ouderling.

A hamlet tucked at the back of a small bay, its coastline protected from bigger waves by a series of jagged reefs, was the only sign of human occupation north of the fjord. A large promontory of black rock jutted out from a mountainside abutting the ocean less than a league north of the hamlet, its top surprisingly flat.

Temperature-wise, the first half of the day had been the most pleasant yet, but the monotony of examining endless tors and fissures in the vast reaching mountain range had everyone in the party desiring a midday rest.

"As soon as you see a suitable landing spot, take us down." Ouderling patted the base of Miragan's neck. "It's tiring enough for me and Jyllana, I can't imagine how exhausting all this flying is for you and Dagomar."

"I must admit, I think I'm reaching the end of my ability to carry you," Miragan said casually, as if she wasn't bothered at all.

Ouderling smiled. "Am I that heavy?"

"Oh no, pretty lady. It's just that other than warding the coast with the Watchmen, I've never flown this long before."

"But you've flown riders before, haven't you?"

A long pause confirmed Ouderling's suspicion.

"Seriously?"

"After Granddaddy died, Kingstone took me under his wing. I trained with Atsila. Although I recently flew Scale in the Crystal Cavern at Master Aelfwynne's insistence, Watchmen don't carry riders."

"Oh, I'm so sorry, Mir, I had no idea."

"It's okay. It's an honour to be a Watchman. Apparently, I'm the first wyvern accepted into their ranks." Miragan's voice dropped to a whisper, *"I'm sure Kingstone had a lot to do with that. He and Eolande are close."*

"No, I mean I'm sorry I didn't know you've never flown anyone before besides Scale. You must be exhausted."

"I would fly you until my wings gave out if you asked me to, pretty lady."

Deeply touched, Ouderling leaned in and hugged Miragan's neck, kissing a cold scale. "I know, and I appreciate it more than you realize, but I think that might turn out badly for both of us, don't you?"

It was the oddest thing to hear a wyvern laugh inside one's head. Ouderling patted Miragan's neck. "Come on, let's—" Her mouth dropped open. "Mir. To the right. It's the dragon fang!"

Miragan's long, temple horn scraped Ouderling's thigh as she craned her neck. *"That pillar of white rock?"*

"Yes. It's the same one I saw in a dream last night." Ouderling called across to Jyllana and Dagomar who had noticed the monolith as well, "That's it! The fang marks Grimclaw's territory!"

Dragon Sect

A small ledge rounded the towering rock formation. Miragan and Dagomar set their riders down and watched as Jyllana and Ouderling examined the odd-shaped formation.

"You saw this in your dream?" Jyllana asked, placing a hand against the side of her face as she stared skyward.

"Yes. It looks kind of plain up close, but from the sky, I'm sure it's the same one I sensed with my magic."

"You're nature's essence?"

Ouderling lowered her gaze to stare at Jyllana. "It must've been my nature's essence. I've never experienced it without having to concentrate on calling it up. It…it just happened."

"You better tell Aelfy when we return to Highcliff. I'm sure he'll want to know."

Ouderling listened but her mind drifted, considering what the revelation of her gift coming to her unprovoked actually meant. She wished she had paid better attention to her mother. She was fairly certain the queen had never done what she had last night.

A pang of homesickness gripped her. The first real sense of missing her parents since being exiled to Highcliff. She thought she had moved beyond the point of needing them, but a sudden longing to be held in her mother's arms or sit on her father's lap like she had as a wee elfling was too strong to ignore.

"Ouderling!"

A strong grip on her forearm snapped Ouderling out of her daze. She blinked.

"What's the matter?" Jyllana asked.

"Sorry. Nothing."

"Did you hear a word I said?"

"No. Not really?"

Dragon Sect

Jyllana rolled her eyes. "Dagomar claims a wide valley runs east through the mountains with no end in sight. It sounds like the valley Aelfwynne spoke of."

"We're close." Ouderling turned to Miragan, her mind reeling with the implications of her magic surfacing as she sensed something unusual stirring inside her. "Whenever you're ready, we should go."

"Eat first," Dagomar's voice jumped into the conversation. *"Neither of you will be of much use if you starve to death."*

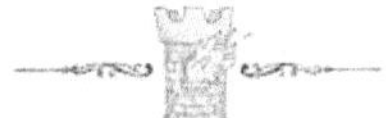

The excitement that had ensued the sighting of the rock formation subsided as the late afternoon sun settled beyond the peaks of the mountains in the west.

Sensitive to Miragan's needs, Ouderling could tell that the wyvern was flagging. As much as she hated to stop for the day, it was time to give their mounts a rest. Searching for a suitable place to make camp, a series of dark holes in the side

of a cliff face on the northern edge of the valley drew her attention.

"There!" She pointed at a sheer cliff face rising out of the forested valley floor—a wide river cutting a swath through the greenery. "That's Grimclaw's new dragon home!"

All eyes followed her outstretched arm. On closer inspection, dragon movement within the dark recesses drew their attention.

"You're right, princess," Dagomar's gruff voice filled Ouderling's head. *"I recognize several of the dragons down there. They're the ones who left Highcliff with him."*

"Do you think it's safe?" Miragan asked.

A long pause preceded Dagomar's answer. *"With Grimclaw, one can never be sure, but the princess' presence should temper the beast. He owes his life to her ancestors."*

A dark shadow enveloped Miragan and Ouderling, provoking an angered shriek from Dagomar.

"Look out!" Jyllana shouted, holding her scythe upright.

"Who dares enter the valley of the dragon without my permission?" a gravelly voice thundered in Ouderling's head, enticing her to cover her ears even though the sound resonated from within.

She looked up in time to see a leviathan plummet from the sky above.

Great, blue wings spread wide, the attacking dragon stretched murderous talons to take them in midflight.

Dragon Sect

Wand of Destiny

Scale noticed Aelfwynne's little body convulse. It happened so quickly that had he not have witnessed it before, he wouldn't have noticed. Examining the ancient wizard's beady eyes, he couldn't help worrying that something serious ailed the goblin. Something Aelfwynne refused to admit. The spasms were happening more frequently as of late. He decided he should take it up with Xantha when Master Aelfwynne wasn't around. She was the only one the high wizard would listen to.

"Are you paying attention, boy?" Aelfwynne snarled, not bothering to look at Scale when he berated him.

"Yes…What?"

Aelfwynne shook his head. "Grab that gemstone over there." He indicated a lone shelf between two high bureaus.

"This one?" Scale lifted the crimson gemstone they had confiscated from Afara Maral's body. The one that had hung around his neck that day in Crag's Forge when the human wizard had held the high wizard hostage.

"No, you bumbling fool. The invisible one next to it."

Scale frowned, searching the empty shelf.

"Of course, that one!" Aelfwynne shook his head again and returned his concentration to a small metal wand with a blackened tip that lay on the central slab in the wizard's lair.

Scale ignored Aelfwynne's rantings. He was used to the constant verbal abuse the goblin dished out. He had learned long ago that his only consolation for enduring the wizard's tirades was that Aelfwynne treated most everyone in the same manner.

He smiled to himself, taking pride in the fact that the high wizard had endeared him with four pet names. He doubted Aelfwynne had dubbed anyone else with that many.

Without looking up, Aelfwynne patted the slab beside the wand. "Put it here and fetch me the golden dragon scale dust."

Scale did as he was told and crossed the room to where the spell ingredients were kept under lock and key. He fumbled around the side of the cabinet until his fingers located the pressure point. Pushing on it, an audible 'snick' came from the unit's far side—a hidden drawer no bigger than his hand popped open, its red velvet interior bearing a large key with a winged dragon on one end. Inserting the other end into a slim hole hidden under the top lip of the cabinet, he turned it first one way, then the other, and back again. The cabinet's solid wood doors sprung open.

"I'm aging over here," Aelfwynne grumbled.

I doubt you can age much further, Scale thought, but was wise enough to hold his tongue. He opened a couple of small wooden boxes until he found what he was looking for and carried it to the central slab.

Aelfwynne looked up. "How many times must I tell a witless northerner not to leave that cabinet open?"

Unperturbed, Scale put the box down with a thump in front of Aelfwynne and returned to the cabinet to close it, thinking the magic they were about to enact was more like something a witch might perform. Wizards generally employed their latent magic through the use of words or mental thought—many times using artifacts to store their energy so as not to tire quickly should an arcane duel ensue.

"Get over here and pay attention to what I'm about to do with your wand. I don't want to explain this twice," Aelfwynne ordered as he lifted the finger-length, silver wand above the open box of powdered dragon scale. With his other hand he deposited Afara's gemstone—Scale had removed it from its necklace long ago—onto the golden grit and took a deep breath.

The litany of an ancient spell passed Aelfwynne's fleshless lips, the words vaguely familiar to Scale, but as the goblin intoned them, a white ball of light no bigger than a grain of sand lit up the blackened tip of the tiny wand—the light surprisingly bright considering it originated from such a small source.

He couldn't help but admire his mentor. He doubted there was a magic-user anywhere else in the world capable of wielding the many different types of magic the high wizard employed. He wouldn't be surprised if the crafty, old conjurer was capable of raising the dead under the right conditions. He shuddered at the thought, and silently hoped for a successful outcome to today's session. There was no telling what mood the high wizard would be in if the incantation failed.

He concentrated on the light, expecting to see it meld with the silver wand, but a flash of crimson from the jewel drew his attention. Not sure he had seen it at all, he held his breath. The ruby gemstone had begun to glow—softly at first, growing brighter with every spell word until Aelfwynne was awash in a reddish-purple hue.

Dragon Sect

Tendrils of auburn light emerged from the gemstone; curvy wisps that climbed to meet a singular white strand emanating from the wand's tip. As the magics merged, a loud snap of static energy made Scale jump back. Blinded by a radiant burst, he blinked rapidly, trying to see beyond the veins of light arcing across his field of vision.

His sight clearing, he was taken aback by the high wizard's evil grin.

Aelfwynne stared at the wand hovering in the air between them of its own volition—the goblin's hands resting on the slab. "Grab it, you imbecile, before it falls to the ground."

Scale extended a tentative hand and grasped the metal rod. He expected to be the victim of a magically induced pain when he touched the wand, but other than cold, smooth silver, he sensed nothing untoward in the talisman. Afraid to inquire if Aelfwynne's spell had worked, he held the wand close to his face and inspected it.

"Well? What do you think?" Aelfwynne rasped.

"I, uh…what did you do?"

"You can't sense it?"

Scale swallowed. "Sense what?"

"Give it here." Aelfwynne snatched the rod from his fingers. Pointing it at a thick candle stub melted to the surface of a wooden table across the chamber he said, "Celer-videtura."

The candle wick burst into flame.

Aelfwynne offered Scale a satisfied grin.

"Big deal. You can do that without a wand."

"Yes, but you could not." Aelfwynne raised his brow twice in quick succession. "Now you can."

Scale frowned, receiving the wand from the high wizard. "You mean it acts like a staff?"

Aelfwynne nodded. "Try it and see."

Dragon Sect

Scale examined the wand, a new level of respect for the inanimate object. He drew a deep breath and pointed the dark tip at the flickering candle. "Celer-evanescetti!"

The flame winked out, a black wisp of smoke wafting into the air above the wick.

"You can dispense with the 'celer' part of the command. I added it for effect," Aelfwynne said. "Nor do you need to point the wand at the object in question. Your brain knows where to direct the energy."

Scale digested his words. Not sure he believed them, he spoke the word, "Videtura."

The candle's flame leapt to life.

"Wow. That's amazing." Scale turned his back on the candle. "Evanescetti."

Unable to see any appreciable difference in the light in the chamber, he knew by Aelfwynne's smirk that the candle had gone out. He spun to confirm his suspicion, powerless to suppress his grin. "It worked."

"Of course, it worked, you buffoon. I transfigured the stolen magic stored in Arafa Maral's bauble into your wand."

Scale didn't care that his jaw hung. His gaze found Aelfwynne's Staff of Reckoning leaning close to the window. "You mean this wand is as powerful as your staff?"

Aelfwynne rolled his eyes. "Don't be a dolt. That'd require a much grander spell."

"But—"

"But nothing! What you hold in your hand is better known as a 'wand of destiny.' The first of many talismans you'll acquire on your journey to becoming a wizard."

The implication that he wasn't a wizard now didn't sit well with Scale. He could tell by the high wizard's softening features that Aelfwynne sensed his disappointment.

"You have much to learn before you can go forth in the world claiming you're an adept. If I were to send you to Orphic Den today, you'd discover you were nothing more than a first level acolyte. A bearer of bedpans if you will."

Scale's euphoria fell away. He had learned so much over the last year. To hear that his accomplishments were trivial was hard to digest.

Aelfwynne nodded. "Such is the life of a wannabe magic-user. It's not all glamour and praise like you were led to believe as an elfling. You have many, many years ahead of you—decades in fact, before you'll ever be considered competent enough to wear a wizard's robe. More likely, you'll be killed when an overextended spell backfires and reduces you to ash."

Scale gaped.

"Aye. The lifespan of most apprentices isn't a long one. Why do you think there aren't more elven wizards around?"

"What about Afara Maral's apprentice? He's not that old."

"Ryedyn? Pfft." Aelfwynne waved a hand in disgust. "He's a hack."

Scale sighed. Aelfwynne's explanation of a long journey ahead had sapped his excitement.

Aelfwynne held his troubled gaze. After an uncomfortable few moments, the high wizard grinned. "Fear not. You're in good hands. I wouldn't waste my time on you if I didn't believe you have what it takes." His smile faded. "There are days, however, that I wonder if my faith is misplaced."

Scale drew a deep breath. The goblin made it difficult to like him. His penchant for giving off-handed compliments followed immediately by a negative remark was not easy to deal with on a daily basis.

"Now that you've the propensity to perform more than just parlour tricks, I want you to lend your mind to something

Dragon Sect

I've been contemplating ever since we were assailed on the Path of the Errant Knight. You remember that day?"

"How could I forget? I thought we were dead."

"Aye. Unfortunate that would have been, hmm?"

Scale refused to answer. Had the goblin listened to his advice back then, they wouldn't have found themselves in the deadly predicament surrounded by a ravenous band of hideous creatures Aelfwynne had referred to as chazgul. Massive, humanoid beasts that crawled on all-fours—hairless, grey-skinned animals with grotesquely twisted faces. He had woken many nights since then, soaked in a cold sweat, dreaming about their brush with what would have proven a horrific death.

"I seek to emulate the magic of Dithreab's bauble."

Scale was dumbfounded. "You want to summon a dragon?"

"Not just *a* dragon, but any dragon." Aelfwynne nodded, deep in thought. "Nor do I want the magic to be a one-time event. If possible, I plan to discover a way of travelling great distances in a blink of time."

Scale frowned, unable to comprehend the possibility of making that happen.

"Oh, aye. You think me daft. I see it in your eyes. But, imagine for a moment, especially considering what Queen Khae is up against, the endless possibilities if Highcliff could dispatch a group of dragons and have them suddenly appear on the battlefield. I daresay the Grim Duke would require a clean pair of breeks."

"Along with their rider?"

Aelfwynne nodded enthusiastically. "Yes! You're right. I have to make allowances for an elf to be summoned as well."

"No, *you're* right. I think you're daft."

Instead of being angered by Scale's pessimism, Aelfwynne's evil grin expanded. "Now that I've bestowed your wand of destiny with an aptitude far above your casting level, you're going to help me achieve this dream."

Scale looked at the high wizard as if he'd lost his mind.

Aelfwynne's grin fell as quickly as it had formed, his voice dropping to a dangerous timbre. "We'd better get working. The queen's life may depend on it."

Dragon Sect

Fort Svelte

Alexis rode his black warhorse, Char, silently beside Seafoam; the roadway bisecting endless flatland of newly growing wheat and grasses, three days out of The Forke. Though the distance they had covered was far greater than traversing the Spine, the terrain afforded them easy travel.

They had crossed the Madrigail River in the mining town in the eastern foothills of the Spine and set out upon a well-trodden roadway northeast—taking them away from the course of the mighty river.

Braen observed the sea of gold and green, silently wondering how vast the kingdom of Carillon actually was. Nowhere in all of South March did his homeland posses such expansive fields. With the disease that had ravaged the elven crops last year, the winter months had been tough back home. If Queen Khae knew what a bountiful harvest was to be had in Carillon, she might yet be convinced of Duke Orlythe's vision for South March.

Unable to contain his wonder, Braen asked, "How many people live in Carillon?"

Alexis shrugged. "Not enough to consume half of what you've witnessed the last couple of days. Carillon's a peaceful nation. We prosper through trade. Wheat and horses are our mainstay, though other crops help keep our land prosperous."

"I see no sign of horses other than those pulling plows."

"They're raised south of here. Had we followed the Madrigail, we would've come to a town called Millsford. That's where you'll find the finest stock in the five kingdoms," Alexis said as their horses mounted a high ridge along the relatively flat terrain, affording them a spectacular view. He pointed southeast. "You can make out the distant range of the Muse. Millsford lies in its western shadow."

Braen nodded, struggling to appreciate the scope of the land.

"And, if you look this way." Alexis pointed northeast. "You can make out the wooden palisade of Fort Svelte and the surrounding city of Carillon proper."

Braen squinted. The vast stretch of farmland ended less than a league from where they had stopped, giving way to a what appeared as a great plain of short scrub grass and little else—the barren land running all the way to Carillon.

"Behold the Plains of Lugubrius," Alexis proclaimed, gently heeling Char into motion. "A stretch of useless land that has puzzled farmers for as long as time remembers."

Braen checked to ensure his head band was properly in place and followed the Prince of Carillon toward the plains.

The sun had set by the time Braen and Alexis crossed the Plains of Lugubrius—the flatlands wider than Braen imagined. Distances were deceiving when one could see clear to the horizon without interruption.

Dragon Sect

Approaching a set of tall, wooden gates comprised of full-length tree trunks with sharpened upper tips—Braen couldn't imagine how much work had gone into transporting them here—there hadn't been a real tree in sight since the day after they had left The Forke.

He marvelled at the size of the lake the city of Carillon was built against. It rivalled that of Lake Grim back home, but didn't appear to have any water source feeding it. No rivers or appreciable hills in sight, he surmised it must be spring fed, but its sheer size made that supposition incredible.

The guards manning the open gate recognized Prince Alexis. Bowing their heads, they greeted him warmly and let them pass.

Thatched-roofed, wooden buildings lined a maze of hard-packed dirt streets that meandered through the city beyond the walls; their odd routes allowing for multiple town-squares populated by vendor stalls and colourful tents. The marketplaces were mostly vacant as they passed through near the end of the day, but the prince made a point of stopping beside a rickety little table set beside a small firepit that was manned by a wrinkled hag with bulging eyes.

"My dearest lady, how fare you?" Alexis asked, nodding to her.

The hag scanned Braen with narrowed eyes and spat on the ground at Seafoam's feet. "You travel with a creature of darkness, Alexis of Carillon. Ware ye well, else the curse of Nyxa will find you."

Braen couldn't help but be taken aback by the crone's bold assertion.

She stared straight into Braen's wide eyes. "Aye, you know. The dark secret of your kind will be the death of all we hold dear." Turning her veined glare on Alexis, she added, "Heed me well, prince of the realm. You're inviting a beast to your table."

Alexis listened respectfully and bowed his head when the crone had finished. "I'll be sure to let my parents know of your concerns, m'lady. Good day to you."

The hag hocked and spat again, this time directing it at a copper urn between her feet, its filthy sides showing runnels of dried spittle. A soft 'ting' resonated as the yellowish wad impacted the inside of the rim and slithered into the body of the spittoon.

It took Braen a while to get over their encounter in the marketplace. The old hag's appearance had been unsettling, but it was her words that had made him more uncomfortable. He looked sidelong at Alexis, the prince smiling wide and greeting everyone they passed in the streets as if nothing had happened. The man seemed genuine enough, but Braen didn't know anything about him, other than he claimed to be a prince of men. A race notoriously despised by the elves. A race that had invaded South March not too long ago, killing thousands of elves in the process.

The cobblestone street they clopped along ended at a stone gatehouse, its low, twin towers flanked by a wooden palisade similar to that surrounding Carillon's outer district. Attentive guards with serious demeanours manned the gates.

Upon seeing who approached, one of the pikemen called up to someone atop the right tower.

Chains creaked and clanked, disturbing the tranquil twilight. Ironbound gates opened inward to allow Alexis and Braen access to a rushlight-lined garden pathway that led to a fair-sized, stone keep abutting the lake.

"Not much of a castle compared to where you come from, I'm sure," Alexis said. "But we've great plans for it someday."

Braen nodded. Alexis' statement was spot on. Raised in Urdanya Castle, not even the grandeur of Borreraig Palace came close to emulating the sheer size and engineering of his mother's castle. He frowned and shook his head—*his* castle.

"What is it?" Alexis asked.

The prince's question startled him. "Huh? Oh, nothing." He swallowed and forced a smile. "It has potential. These things take time."

"Ha! My great grandchildren shan't live to see its completion." The prince dismounted in a flurry of vermilion cloth, and golden hair.

At once, seemingly out of nowhere, two handlers appeared. The first bowed his head to the prince and accepted Char's reins while the second man waited patiently for Braen to dismount.

Braen looked around to see if anyone else was close by, adjusted his headband, and slid off Seafoam—his backside continuing to give him discomfort from riding bareback for the better part of a week. He rubbed at his aching posterior, slipped into his cowl to hide his identity even further, and followed Alexis.

Four guards manned the doubled doors atop a set of broad steps. Two moved to open the doors while the other two kept their eyes firmly on Braen—their no-nonsense demeanour and thick arms bespoke of fighters Braen had no wish of going up against. He almost laughed aloud at that random thought. He wouldn't wish to go against a lamb.

Inside the great entryway, a corridor ran along the inside of the keep walls, bisecting a wider one that led into the heart of the building. Alexis led him up the main passageway to the base of a short flight of steps topped by iron-strapped doors. Standing to the side of the open doorway, four of the meanest looking people he had ever laid eyes on, either elf or man, stood at attention with halberds in hand. Draped in vermilion surcoats similar to Alexis, sword and dagger pommels protruded from thick leather belts. He kept his eyes on the ground before him, afraid to meet their scrutiny.

Several steps into the great chamber beyond the threshold, Alexis stopped and nodded toward a podium built against the back wall of the poorly lit room.

Braen's elf vision allowed him to see a dark figure seated in a highbacked, wooden chair—the ornate furniture resembling a poor excuse for a throne.

The dark figure rose to his feet, his face hidden beneath a cowl. "Do come in, Braen Wys, son of Odyne. We've been expecting you."

Braen tried to back away, but Alexis gripped him by the elbow and forced him up the aisle.

The ironbound doors banged shut, closing off any chance of escape.

Dragon Sect

Zephyr Knight

The finality of the doors slamming closed behind Braen made him jump. A quick glance backward had him looking away again just as fast—the two, musclebound guardsmen blocking the exit didn't appear to be in a jovial mood.

Booming laughter raised the fine hairs on Braen's exposed skin. Striding boldly down the stone aisle, the dark figure who claimed to be expecting him threw back his cowl and shook out long, golden locks. He rose to accept Alexis' embrace, his palms thumping loudly in the relatively deserted chamber. "Well met, my son. I told your mother you were up to the task."

The man released Alexis and stood back to scrutinize Braen—his resemblance to Alexis leaving no doubt he was the king of Carillon. Not sure how to react in the foreign court, Braen dropped to a knee and bowed his head.

The king watched him for a few moments before he said, "Arise young Wys. I'll not have it said that a member of Nyxa the War Dragon's family was expected to take a knee in Carillon."

Braen hazarded a look up, expecting treachery, but Alexis' warm, green eyes set his mind at ease. At a nod from the prince, Braen gained his feet and accepted the meaty handshake of the king.

"Well met, Braen of Urdanya. You appear to have had some difficulty recently."

Braen noted how the king stared at his bruised face. "Thanks to your son, it wasn't worse."

The king nodded. "Indeed. How fares the lovely Odyne? Still dabbling with her magic books, I assume."

The king caught Alexis' head shake. "What?"

Braen extricated his crushed hand from the king's grip. "My mother was murdered last year."

The king gave Alexis a shocked look.

The prince nodded.

"I'm sorry to hear that. The queen must be devastated," the king said. "Come, you can tell me about it over some mead and a good meal, hmm?"

Without waiting for a reply, the king turned on his heels and strode deeper into the chamber.

Carillon Keep's feast hall was better lit than that of the drafty throne room—a warm ambience provided by two large hearth's crackling on either end of the great room.

Whatever dish had been set before him had satisfied the ravenous hunger Braen had acquired over the last few weeks. Chock full of the usual vegetables and some kind of poultry, the spices added had made for an interesting culinary experience. Having not eaten a decent meal since the day Orlythe Wys had darkened his threshold had gone a long way to help him appreciate the offering.

Aware of Braen's heritage without having been told, the king had invited him to remove his bandana, reiterating what

Dragon Sect

Alexis had told him in the hold of the *Coastal Cutter* and again on the road to Carillon—that he was in the company of dragon friends.

During the course of their meal, Alexis elaborated on the events that had brought him and Braen together and everything that had happened since. The king didn't say much, but nodded often.

Wiping his mouth on a cloth set on the table beside him, the king snapped his fingers and the dinnerware was promptly ushered away by an attentive staff. He waited patiently for a priceless-looking decanter to be set on the table before him, along with three fresh goblets, and poured the mulled wine himself. Raising his goblet, he said, "May new alliances be forged on the bones of old allegiances."

Braen clanked his brass goblet with Alexis and the king, and took a tentative sip. Nodding his approval, he drank deeper.

"Good, no?" the king asked.

"Very much so, Your Highness," Braen answered in all honesty.

"Ah-ah. We're newly found friends at this table. You're a prince of your realm. You need not address me by title. Call me Graham."

"But you're a king."

"By virtue of your grandmother, if that's what elves call their mother's mother."

Braen nodded.

"None of that matters now. What intrigues me is why the grandson of Nyxa Wys has come to the kingdoms of man. Surely not on a political venture for Queen Khae."

Still wondering how the king had known he was coming, Braen struggled to answer what should have been a simple question. Not sure what he should divulge—he doubted anything but a long explanation would account for his uncle's involvement in his decision to leave South March. Recalling his uncle's visit, a fleeting thought came to mind. "Actually, I'm searching for someone known as Sir Stanley White."

The king frowned. Looking to Alexis, the prince shrugged. Graham shook his head. "Never heard of him. Should I have?"

Nervous that he had made a big mistake in allowing himself to be brought to the castle of a man king, Braen added, "He's a Zephyr knight, if that means anything?"

The king exchanged a surprised glance with Alexis. More serious than before, Graham stared him in the eye. "A Zephyr knight? How have you come to know that term?"

Sweat formed on Braen's brow. He had unwittingly broached a touchy subject. "I read it in a book of the same name. One written by the knight's hand."

The king held his stare, an uncomfortable air hanging over the relatively empty feast hall. Stroking at his well-kempt, blonde goatee, Graham never blinked. "A book?"

"Um, yes. I found it in my mother's personal library. It looks quite old, actually. Perhaps the one I seek is no longer alive."

Graham nodded. "That would make sense. This person you speak of is not one of the present Zephyr knights."

A tingle of excitement crawled along Braen's skin. Perhaps his misgivings were misplaced. King Graham might be able to shed light on where Braen could find like-minded individuals such as Sir Stanley White. Unable to mask his enthusiasm, he blurted, "Can you tell me how to find them? It would mean a great deal if I could speak to one of them about the book."

Dragon Sect

King Graham sat back and folded his arms across his chest, but his stare never wavered.

Although Alexis fidgeted in his chair beside his father, Braen found he couldn't break the king's intense look.

Graham's demeanour never wavered. Taking a long pull of his mulled wine, he carefully placed the goblet on the table between them and said softly, "There are only two Zephyr knights remaining to the world." Exhaling a heavy sigh, he nodded at Alexis. "And you're in the company of both of them."

Dragon Sect

The Mighty Grimclaw

Grimclaw dropped from the sky—an avalanche of wings, horns, scales, and claws—for surely the blue-scaled beast had to be none other than the dragon they sought. Ouderling flinched in anticipation of the violent impact that was about to take her life.

Dagomar roared and Jyllana cried out, their voices lost in the rush of air marking Grimclaw's descent.

A stomach lurching drop in altitude and unexpected dip to the right had Ouderling clinging to Miragan's neck as the wyvern reacted to avoid the midair collision. Ouderling lost her grip, but the wyvern tilted left and flapped hard, deftly positioning her body to catch Ouderling's weight. The corrective action knocked the wind from Ouderling's lungs. Despite the pain, she managed to hang on.

Twice Dagomar's size, Grimclaw arrested his descent and banked tighter than Ouderling would have thought possible for such a huge beast—his great head craned in her direction.

"Who dares enter Dragonfang Pass?" A gravelly voice inquired.

Dragon Sect

"Grimclaw! Desist at once," Dagomar ordered, his voice redirecting Grimclaw's attention. *"You're in the presence of the granddaughter of Nyxa."*

"Dagomar?" Grimclaw winged behind Ouderling and Miragan, levelling off to match their altitude and speed. *"What possesses you to be in the company of one such as this?"*

"He means me," Miragan whispered inside Ouderling's head.

"Miragan is an emissary from Highcliff, entrusted with Princess Ouderling's care," Dagomar answered.

"They mustn't think too highly of their princess to send her on the back of a two-legged wyrm."

"Many things have changed since you left," Dagomar growled.

"Not for the better, I see. Princess or not, give me one good reason why I shouldn't tear her from the sky for riding such a lowly beast."

"Have you forgotten your vow to Nyxa?"

"I forget nothing!" Grimclaw's voice threatened imminent peril, black smoke puffing from his nostrils. *"Nyxa's dead. Her time has gone."*

"Nyxa sent her to us," Miragan interrupted.

Licks of flame escaped Grimclaw's nose slits. *"Silence, wyvern! You've no right to speak with real dragons."* He closed on Miragan's tail.

It was all Ouderling could do not to fall to her death as she twisted sideways watching the blue dragon bear down on them.

"Oh, but I do," Miragan answered.

Ouderling was impressed by Miragan's composure in the face of danger but given Grimclaw's attitude, she wondered if the timing wasn't poorly chosen.

"I've been entrusted with the future of South March by the High Wizard of the land," Miragan said before Grimclaw could say anything more.

"Who is this high wizard of the elves?" Grimclaw demanded.

"Aelfwynne, the Dragon Mage," Miragan pronounced with pride in her voice.

"The goblin still presides over South March? I can only imagine how well that's being received. A slight to elves and dragons alike."

"Unlike some," Dagomar interjected, *"Aelfwynne remains loyal to Nyxa's vision. Nor did he abandon us to deal with mankind's threat."*

Flames dripped from the corners of Grimclaw's mouth. *"You forget your place, Dagomar."*

"Oh, believe me, I know my place. It's you who has forgotten those who sacrificed their life for you. If not for Ouderling's ancestors, you'd never have been born, let alone survived to become the legendary figure spoken of in South March lore with a reverence you don't deserve. Hearing you now, I question whether your past deeds are greatly exaggerated."

Grimclaw's flight slowed, the great dragon falling behind. His massive head turned to stare at Dagomar as the cliffs passed by on their left—the dragon colony far behind.

A league of forestland and the winding river dominating the centre of the valley slipped beneath them before anyone spoke again.

"Follow me. I'll hear what you have to say." Grimclaw veered out over the valley and started back toward the dragon colony. *"Though I can't guarantee I won't eat your riders and the wyvern once you're done."*

Dragon Sect

Ouderling exchanged an alarmed glance with Jyllana across the gap separating their flight. Hunkering against Miragan's neck as the majestic creature followed in Grimclaw's wake, she wondered at the dissension apparent in Grimclaw view of wyverns. Miragan was physically different from Dagomar or Grimclaw, but that didn't detract from her beauty, both inside and out.

She struggled to understand how such disparity had come to divide the northern dragons from wyverns, but as they neared the colony, she recalled the kingdom they flew within, and the condescension began to make sense. Elves viewed man the same way Grimclaw's dragons considered wyverns. They didn't trust them because of their perceived differences. Because elves' pointed ears differed from man's round-topped ones.

She shook her head, unable to comprehend the senseless prejudices inherent in the world. A physical difference didn't make the person. It was what was in their heart and how they conducted themselves as an individual that was important.

Flying low over the treeline, Grimclaw flapped his enormous wings twice, lifting above the lip of the escarpment housing the dragon warrens, and landed gracefully in a small clearing on top of the cliff.

Dagomar craned his neck to regard Ouderling as if silently asking if this was something she still wished to entertain. She nodded and he rose in the air to settle down on the opposite side of the clearing from Grimclaw.

Cresting the brink on the back of a wyvern, Grimclaw's piercing, yellow eyes caught Ouderling's stare. She shuddered. It was as if the infamous dragon saw into her soul.

"You okay?" Miragan asked, her timing uncanny.

Ouderling considered the back of Miragan's head, wondering if dragonkind possessed the ability to perceive their rider's emotions. "I think so."

Miragan set Ouderling down beside Dagomar.

"Have dragon standards really lowered that much since my departure from Highcliff?" Grimclaw got right to it, his attention on Dagomar.

Dagomar's eyes narrowed to match Grimclaw's menacing stare. *"Only the brave and honourable remain."*

Ouderling gaped as the insult to Grimclaw hung in the air. As strong as Miragan claimed Dagomar was, she doubted he could threaten the gargantuan beast from Highcliff's past.

She tried to recall Grimclaw's age, wishing she had paid more attention to the Chronicler. The blue dragon had to be at least three centuries old. Perhaps four or five. His scales certainly didn't appear to be turning black as was the custom with aging male dragons.

Her grandmother had been quite young when Grimclaw was born, and Nyxa had died somewhere in her late three hundreds—middle-aged for an elf. Or was Grimclaw born before Nyxa? She shook her head, unable to recall. Regardless, she estimated him to be at least four centuries old—certainly not ancient by any means, but old enough to have learned how to defend himself. Given his size, she doubted there was a creature alive who could go up against him and survive.

The great dragon's gaze found hers again and held it, unblinking. He ignored the implication of Dagomar's words, but Ouderling was sure they had affected him.

Swallowing her fear of the creature, she said in a timid voice, "High Wizard Aelfwynne sent us to find you. The future of South March is in peril—"

Dragon Sect

Grimclaw boomed. *"Nyxa's barely cold in the ground and the kingdom falters already? Is the new queen that incompetent?"*

Ouderling fought to keep her tone civil. "Queen Khae has ruled for the better part of a century without trouble."

"What's a hundred years? If Khae's that anemic, then nothing I can do will save your kind. Perhaps the kingdoms of man were right in seeking the annihilation of the elves."

"Easy, pretty lady," Miragan whispered.

Taking a deep breath, Ouderling sensed her eyes turning red. "My mother ascended the Willow Throne at a young age. Considering her lack of experience at the time, she's done an admirable job ruling the kingdom."

"Apparently doing an admirable job isn't enough else the goblin wizard wouldn't have sent you to grovel at my feet." Grimclaw's eyes narrowed to slits, his voice a low rumble. *"How* did *you find my dragon home?"*

Chin held high, Ouderling said as pompously as she could, "I used my magic."

Grimclaw's eyes opened in mock incredulousness. *"Your magic? An elfling barely off her mother's teat claims to be powerful enough to locate my hidden colony? I find that hard to believe."*

Remembering how her mother and father handled themselves during the painfully long petition sessions at Borreraig Palace, Ouderling slid from Miragan's back and walked toward Grimclaw, pointing a finger at him. "It matters little what you believe. We're here on official business. Master Aelfwynne implores you and your dragons to make great haste and return to the kingdom of your roots. As is your duty."

Dragon Sect

It was like the clearing shook in the throes of a minor earthquake as Grimclaw laughed, his penetrating gaze never wavering from Ouderling.

Several dragons of different colours flew patrol overhead, aloof to the proceedings. They likely knew as well as Ouderling that the group confronting their leader posed no threat to the mighty Grimclaw.

"Duty?" Grimclaw growled. *"I have no obligation to South March. I did my so-called* duty *and what was I threatened with as a result?"*

He didn't wait for an answer. *"Let me tell you. I was faced with the ignoble honour of being subjugated by Nyxa's offspring. If I'd allowed Orlythe to have his way, dragonkind would've been reduced to nothing more than a pack of ravenous wolves, dying to further his ultimate plan."*

"That's exactly who we're fighting against! My uncle, Orlythe!" Ouderling stopped her advance halfway across the clearing, her courage draining with each step closer to the behemoth, but she kept her finger wagging between them. "My mother is facing the prospect of civil war to stop him."

"Your words reiterate my view of Khae's reign. No one competent enough to occupy the Willow Throne would have allowed affairs to degenerate to that point."

Ouderling reacted in the heat of the moment, pulling her sword free of its baldric and pointing it at Grimclaw. "You take that back."

The ground shook again as the great wyrm rose to his feet, smoke billowing from his nostrils and flames licking amongst his back teeth. He pulled his head back in the customary manoeuvre of a dragon preparing to spew fire.

Miragan leapt into the air to land between Ouderling and the enraged beast, smaller flames rippling along her jawline.

Dragon Sect

Grimclaw paused to sneer at the wyvern. *"I welcome the opportunity to kill a two-legged wyrm."* His head drew back farther, intense yellow eyes rivetted on Miragan.

Scythe in hand, Jyllana ran to stand between Miragan and Grimclaw. "Stop! This is insanity!"

Time stood still for everyone in the clearing as the red-haired elf placed her insignificant form between two ferocious, fire-breathing creatures many times her size.

"While we waste time primping our egos to determine who's tougher than the other, the fact that the Grim Duke's forces threaten the queen doesn't change."

Grimclaw paused his head in full recoil and glowered at Jyllana. Bouts of fire dripped from his hanging lower jaw. *"The infighting of royal houses does not concern me."*

Jyllana threw her scythe to the ground and crossed her arms. "If you're that ignorant to think that should Orlythe persevere that he won't subjugate the dragons loyal to Highcliff and come against the kingdoms of man then you're the one history will view as incompetent."

Grimclaw's ridged face twisted in consternation, his head tilting to one side.

"Yes. It's finally making sense, isn't it? Duke Orlythe won't be content to stop with the five kingdoms. He'll come for you and your dragons as well." Jyllana nodded, her voice exuding confidence. "How great will his army become with the mighty Grimclaw leading it?"

Grimclaw sneered, his huge head flashing forward to stop a whisper from Jyllana. *"You're a bold one, little elf, I'll give you that."*

The great dragon remained prone before Jyllana for many heartbeats. Finally, he dipped his chin ever so slightly and withdrew. *"You speak wisely, protector of Nyxa's prodigy. In appreciation of your wise counsel, I shall let you live."*

Dragon Sect

His gaze took in the others gathered in the clearing. *"You may leave with the knowledge that my dragon home won't fall to anyone—elf, man, or beast. We'll be ready when the vermin comes for us."*

Ouderling stepped beside Jyllana, placing a comforting hand on her protector's trembling shoulder. "You mean you won't help us?"

"I will not."

"The lives of those who gave you life are in serious danger. Doesn't that mean anything to you?"

"The ones who gave me life are dead. If Nyxa were still alive, I would lay my life down for her, but she's not. Don't speak to me of obligation, princess, lest I reconsider my decision to let you live."

"I guess the idea of a dragon sect is out of the question," Ouderling said without thinking, grasping for some way to change Grimclaw's mind.

Grimclaw frowned. *"What is this dragon sect you speak of?"*

An ember of hope sparked to life. Ignoring Aelfwynne's warning, she swallowed her reservations as Eolande's words came to mind. *'It's time to bestow your sword with a magic befitting a future queen. A queen who will walk the winds of fate on the back of dragonkind.'*

She nodded enthusiastically as the notion of a dragon sect clarified in her mind. "It's an idea of mine. One that would pair dragons with elves all across South March in a clandestine society of…wind walkers! Vigilantes if you will. Secret protectors of the realm."

"So you can subjugate us again?" Grimclaw's incredulous voice boomed. *"You're no better than your uncle!"*

Dragon Sect

The great dragon appeared on the verge of disgorging fire across the entire clearing, but he sprang into the air and flew northeast.

His trailing voice left no doubt as to what the visitors were to do. *"If you're still here when I return, South March will find itself less four souls."*

Dragon Sect

Haunted

Wizards!

Disgusted, Khae glared at the long pass leading into the Wizard's Sleeve with disdain. If the reports the scouts were bringing in were to be trusted, and there was no reason why they shouldn't be, the northern cities of South March had risen against her. Obviously because of Orlythe's heavy-handed manipulation, but that didn't change the fact that her grip on the Willow Throne was becoming more tenuous by the day. Not sure whether she wanted to cry or scream, for the life of her, she couldn't understand how the climate in South March had changed so drastically so fast.

Nor was marching the troops remaining loyal to her up the Wizard's Walk to enlist Sagora's aid sitting well with her. The headmaster of the wizards' guild had never made his feelings toward the crown a secret. Hoping for Orphic Den's support while the rest of the kingdom rebelled against her seemed like a fool's errand, but what choice did she have?

To make matters worse, Highcliff hadn't come to her aid either. Nor did she think it would. After the near fatal incident last year, she couldn't blame High Wizard

Aelfwynne for not wanting to leave the Crystal Cavern vulnerable again.

Shaking her head at the conundrum facing her, she pushed past the two hulking Home Guard who forever shadowed her, and entered the royal pavilion.

Hammas looked up from where he studied a large map spread across a table in the tent's centre, hunched beside the head of the royal army, Commander Keel. Joining her husband on the opposite side of the table was the elf responsible for her personal safety, Captain Kall, as well as Captain Hondrick, the elf in charge of the Queen's Shield.

Whenever away from Borreraig Palace, especially now that they were on campaign, ten of the Home Guard's most reputable fighters were assembled to form the Queen's Shield—their sole responsibility to ensure no one, not even the king, made it through without her personal approval.

A commotion arose outside the pavilion. It sounded like a scuffle had broken out. One that was quickly silenced.

"Who're you?" one of the Shield stationed outside, challenged.

"I bear tidings from Urdanya," the voice of the scout she had sent to find his way into her sister's castle answered.

"You're dressed like a traitor," another voice growled.

Everyone around the battle map stared at the entrance.

Captain Hondrick nodded to Khae and stepped past her, his face grim as he drew his sword and parted the tent flap.

Thrown on the ground, surrounded by several elves of the Queen's Shield, a battered elf in studded, black leather armour looked up.

Captain Hondrick studied the prostrate elf. Receiving a nod from Khae, he said, "He's one of ours. Let him through."

"Thank you, captain." The greasy haired scout got to his feet, dusted himself off with a sideways sneer for the elves who had assaulted him, entered the pavilion, and promptly dropped to a knee in front of Khae, eyes down.

"Rise and be at ease." Despite his ragged appearance, clad in the uniform of one of her brother's Grim Guard, Khae recognized him at once. She could tell by how he eyed the elf leaders and the king that he would never be comfortable in the presence of royalty.

The scout stood and folded his hands at his waist, not looking her in the eye.

She cupped his scruffy chin with delicate fingers, lifting his head to gaze into intelligent eyes. There was fear behind them, but she suspected that had nothing to do with his present location.

Through the grime on his face, she detected fresh bruising on his left temple. On closer inspection, crusted blood matted the hair above his ear. She couldn't imagine the dangers someone in his position endured on a daily basis, but it was his haunted look that spoke the loudest.

She forced a smile for his benefit. "It's okay. You're amongst friends."

The scout swallowed heavily, looking anywhere but at her.

She nodded to Captain Kall, indicating with her eyes the ewer set on a side table.

Captain Kall poured wine into a goblet and handed it to the scout.

"Drink," Khae stepped back to give the elf room.

The scout didn't appear like he was going to do as he was asked, his gaze following Hammas and Commander Keel who were rounding the table to confront him.

Khae held a hand up, her focus on the scout. "I insist."

Looking like he wanted to crawl under the table and disappear, the scout dipped his chin and took a tentative sip. "Thank you, Your Majesty."

Dragon Sect

Khae fought her impatience to learn what had happened. "It is we who should be grateful for your service. Do me a favour and drink up. By the looks of you, I'm sure you can use it."

The scout kept his gaze averted but wasted no time quaffing the contents of the sizable goblet. Wiping his mouth on a dirty cuff, he nodded his appreciation.

Khae caught the eyes of the four elf leaders, the concern in their gaze mirroring her own. "Now speak."

The scout bit his lower lip and took a deep breath. "I have failed you, Your Majesty."

"How so?" Khae asked.

"I was unable to reach the court of Duke Orlythe."

"That's understandable. I doubt anyone could've entered Urdanya Castle. Not with Orlythe's wizard present."

"Oh, I got in alright, Your Majesty. It was getting out that proved difficult."

Commander Keel stiffened. "Why would you want to come back out? You were tasked with infiltrating the castle. Are you saying you deserted your post?"

The scout took another deep breath. "It would seem so, my commander."

Keel's face turned livid. He opened his mouth to speak but Khae stayed him with a stern look. There was more to the scout's story. She could sense it. "You're hurt."

The scout didn't respond. His furtive gaze flicked to the commander and the king—shame evident in his bearing.

Khae caught her husband's attention and whispered, "Leave us."

Hammas nodded and returned to the table. "Keel. Kall. Hondrick. Show me again what we're up against."

Hondrick and Kall joined Hammas immediately, but it took an insistent glare from Khae to get Commander Keel to step away from one of his troops who had admittedly abandoned his post. His lingering stare promised he would deal with the scout in due course.

Khae grabbed the scout's filthy hand and led him to where two padded chairs sat before a second brazier in the pavilion—one upholstered in red velvet and the other in burnt orange. She indicated the burnt orange chair with her free hand.

The scout balked. "Oh, no, Your Majesty. I can't."

"I insist," Khae said sternly. "It's only a chair."

The scout swallowed again, something he seemed to do a lot in auspicious company. "Please. I'll stand."

"Look. I've had a long day. You're my guest. As such, I cannot sit until you have. So, unless you wish to see me fall to the dirt in exhaustion…"

Not meeting her gaze, the scout sat in the queen's chair—the horrified look on his face priceless.

She grabbed a small flagon from a side table and poured two goblets of wine. Handing one to the scout, she folded her robes beneath her and sat on the edge of Hammas' chair. "Tell me what happened."

"Yes, Your Majesty." His gaze flicked to the elves around the map table who were staring at him.

Khae rolled her eyes, her annoyance plainly obvious.

They looked away.

"Don't worry about them."

The scout stared at his wine. "When I left you outside of Urdanya, I went straight to the castle. I confiscated a Grim Guard uniform and made my way inside."

Khae raised her eyebrows, taking in the scout's torn and cut black leather armour. "Confiscated?"

The slightest of smirks passed his lips. "You don't want to know, Your Majesty."

She smiled. "Would it surprise you if I said I did?"

"No, Your Majesty. I-I mean…" His grimy cheeks reddened.

Khae chuckled for his benefit and patted his near hand. "It's okay. Carry on."

"Once inside, the Grim Guard patrolling the corridors were behaving differently than the troops in the streets."

"How so?"

The scout shrugged. "Hard to explain now that I'm not there. There's a heightened tension amongst the Grim Guard inside the castle."

"Makes sense given my army was camped on their doorstep."

The scout took a moment to indulge in his wine. "Yes, but it was more than that. They were questioning their own. It was only a matter of time before they figured out I wasn't one of them."

Khae nodded. "So, you left."

The scout looked up with wide eyes. "Oh no, Your Majesty. I would never do that."

"But you're here."

The scout looked away.

Khae patted his hand. "It's okay. I can't imagine what you deal with on a daily basis. Help me understand why you abandoned your post. Was your life in danger?"

"No, Your Majesty…Well yes, but that's not important."

"Then why did you leave?"

The scout looked her straight in the eye, his haunted look chilling her to the bone.

Jaw hanging open she urged him to elaborate.

"Because, Your Majesty, I know how the mean to kill you."

Dragon Sect

The Price of Magic

"**Am** I disturbing you?" Scale entered Xantha and Aelfwynne's chambers, quickly averting his gaze as he realized baby Dithreab was suckling—the elder Guardian seemingly unperturbed by his presence.

"Not at all, Scale." Xantha looked past Scale. "Though I must admit I'm surprised to see you without your sidekick."

Scale kept his gaze on a fur rug made from a large animal unfamiliar to him. He could only imagine it had been killed in the Mardeireach—likely along the Path of the Errant Knight. "Perhaps I should come back another time."

"Don't be silly. No worries at all." Xantha readjusted Dithreab and covered up, patting thin lips with a rag, and switching him to rest on her shoulder. Gently rubbing his back, her voice took on the oddest of timbres as she spoke to him. "You were just finishing up, weren't you my little Aelfwight."

Scale took a tentative glance at the legendary warrior. The sight of a tiny elf-goblin—for he had no better way to describe the child—held in Xantha's once powerful arms was odd to behold. Never one to be considered loving in her day, motherhood had certainly altered the way Xantha carried herself.

"What's bothering you?"

Scale swallowed. Was he that predictable? "Um, not me, exactly."

"Then who?"

"Master Aelfwynne."

"What's he done now?" Xantha frowned, readjusting Dithreab and eliciting a long burp from the darker-skinned baby. "If he told you he's done with you, not to worry. I'll talk sense into him."

Her words shocked him—it was as if Aelfwynne had brought up the subject of not training him any further to Xantha before. "Um, no actually…Is he thinking about getting rid of me?"

A rare smile softened Xantha's usual serious expression. "No! Not at all. Now, what's on your mind?"

The way she answered told Scale she was lying, but he let it slide—he wouldn't dream of questioning her. "I'm worried about Master Aelfwynne."

Xantha's smile fell. "Oh?"

"I've been noticing for quite a while now…Well, ever since he took me on as his apprentice actually, that something isn't quite right with him."

"You're just figuring that out now?" Her attempt at humour fell short. "Tell me what you mean."

Scale shrugged. "I don't know. I can't put my finger on it, but I'm worried he's getting sick."

Xantha's frown deepened. She stood and placed a drowsy Dithreab in a stone bassinet lined with plush blankets. Turning back to Scale, she nodded to a smaller chair beside her own. "Have a seat."

Dragon Sect

Scale crouched and carefully put his weight on the edge of what was obviously Aelfwynne's chair, afraid he might break it. When the chair held, he said, "Have you ever noticed that Master Aelfwynne suffers from spasms?"

A look of understanding crossed Xantha's purple eyes. She nodded. "You mean the magic sickness."

It was Scale's turn to frown. "I'm sorry?"

"The price of magic is a heavy burden. Have you never heard of the detriments of being a wizard?"

Scale shook his head.

"Interesting. I would think everyone pursuing arcana would be aware of the toll it takes on one's body."

"But…" Scale struggled to grasp the inference. "I thought magic-users lived longer than those who aren't gifted."

"Oh, yes. Some do for sure. Many in fact. But they also suffer greatly as a result. The agues, aches, and pains, and what you refer to as spasms, are part of a wizard's life. You cannot expect to shape nature and use it at will in whatever way you deem fit and not have an adverse reaction. The power employed must draw its energy from somewhere. It doesn't just happen. No one is simply…" Xantha shrugged, "lucky to be able to wield magic."

Scale didn't care that he gaped. Aelfwynne had never mentioned anything of the sort. Being the son of a military elf who had little use for Scale's dream of one day exploring his magical potential, he had never heard of what Xantha was telling him.

"That doesn't make sense. If the price of magic means the detriment to one's physical well-being—"

"And mental," Xantha added.

Scale's eyes grew wider. He nodded. "And mental. How can a wizard live so long?"

"Through the tools that they employ," Xantha said as if that answered everything.

His brows knitted together as he searched the rough stone ceiling of the cool chamber, trying to understand. Thinking on it, an incredulous look gripped him. He stared into Xantha's beautiful eyes. "The Staff of Reckoning."

Xantha nodded. "Exactly. Without its support, Aelfwynne would have died centuries ago. He draws strength from it. The lives that went into the making of that grotesquely carven talisman sustain him." She glanced at Dithreab cooing softly. "For that, I am eternally grateful."

Scale grappled with the revelation. He pulled his finger-length wand from the pouch at his waist and held it between them.

Xantha nodded knowingly. "Your Wand of Destiny. Aelfwynne said he crafted you one. Congratulations. Your first step to acquiring your wizard's staff."

Scale gulped.

"Oh, yes. Don't take his gesture lightly. Not many aspiring wizards live long enough to acquire their own staff of power. You have much to learn. May the Fae grant Aelfwynne the longevity to see you to the fruition of your journey."

"How long does it take? How will I know when I get there?"

"Oh, you'll know, trust me," Xantha's voice exuded confidence in the knowledge she imparted.

She stood and paced a couple of circuits of the room, tapping her chin in thought. She stopped on the far side near the exit door. "I'm no wizard, but I've been around them long enough to know this. There are certain events that happen in an apprentice's life that shape and define their future—events that are out of their control. Suffice it to say, they just happen."

She nodded and crossed to stand before him, holding out her hand to accept his staff to inspect it. "The first such event happened the day you risked your life to rescue him from Crag's Forge. That was your first major step in becoming a wizard." Her gaze took in the contents of the bassinet. "The second happened the day you returned to Dithreab's lair to inter my son's namesake."

Scale frowned. "I don't understand. I didn't do anything other than bury the wood sprite."

She handed him back his wand and surprised him by grasping his hand and kissing it. Straightening to her full, impressive height, she nodded at the wand. "Not everything is measured by how powerful you appear on the outside. The greater struggle is defining how powerful you are on the inside. By doing what you did for someone you didn't know, aside from your brief encounter, speaks to your character."

Abashed, Scale shrugged. "It was the decent thing to do. Dithreab gave his life so that we might live another day. It was the least I could do as a way to express my gratitude."

"You're right, of course, but that doesn't belittle your actions. Only one of true virtue may aspire to practice the dangerous arts that lie in your future and not be subverted by the power you will one day wield. Does that make sense?"

Scale turned his wand around in his fingers, staring at the thin silver stick, his mind elsewhere. Finally, he nodded and gazed into Xantha's compassionate eyes. "I guess."

She raised her brows at his choice of the word, 'guess.' "Good, because that's as best as I can explain it to you." She glanced at the doorway. "You best be gone from here before you-know-who comes back. If he discovers you've been questioning me about his health, I fear you may not live long enough to realize what future he has in store."

Dragon Sect

Rondou Wainwright

King Hammas dragged the scout from Khae's chair by the collar, his face a whisper away from the bruised and battered elf's. "What did you say?"

"Hammas!" Khae intervened, separating them, but Hammas' fists remained firmly locked in the elf's pilfered Grim Guard armour, his intense green eyes glaring death.

"What do you mean, you know how they're going to kill her?" Hammas shouted. When the scout didn't answer quick enough, Hammas lifted him to his toes. "Speak, dammit! What do you know?"

Khae forced herself between them, having to pry her husband's hands free. "By the Fae's gossamer wings, Hammas, give him a chance to respond. He's not the enemy."

Fists clenched, Hammas took a deep breath and stepped back, his stare never leaving the shaken scout.

Wild-eyed, the scout searched the faces crowding in around him. "Please, Your Highness," he spoke to Hammas, but couldn't break eye contact with Commander Keel. "I tried to reach you before you made it to Gullveig but your army moves fast."

Commander Keel growled, "What's so important about Gullveig?"

"Nothing, commander. The Wizard's Walk is the problem. Orlythe plans to trap the Royal Army where we stand."

"In order to trap us in the Wizard's Walk, the duke would have to control both Gullveig and…" Startled revelation washed over Keel's face. He exchanged glances with Hammas and Khae. "That means he already controls Orphic Den."

"Nonsense, commander," Khae spat, though even as she spoke, she realized she had no way of being certain about anything anymore. Up until a few weeks ago, she was the leader of South March—her biggest fear, other than the unknown whereabouts of the Dragon Witch Wraith, was the trouble with the crops.

Given everything that had happened last year, it wasn't a stretch to imagine Orlythe's troops marching in her army's wake and taking Gullveig by force once they had travelled through it on their way up the pass. If her brother had managed to force the hand of the wizards' guild, her tenure as Queen of the Elves would quickly come to an end.

Her dark glare forced the king and the army leaders to step away from the scout. Grasping the unnerved elf by the shoulders, she clung to the little patience she had left. "So, the Grim Duke plans on killing me in the pass?"

The scout swallowed. "Yes, Your Highness. But there's more."

Khae sighed, barely able to contain herself. "Go on."

"I'm not sure I understood what I heard."

Khae bit her lower lip, but raised her brow for him to keep talking.

Dragon Sect

"Apparently the duke's forces are to hold you in the pass until they can provoke the jewel free." He shrugged. "Those were the exact words. The Grim Guard I overheard as they were preparing to march never clarified what that meant."

Khae stared at the scout, going over his words again and again. Her eyes widened in comprehension. Turning to Hammas, his face mirrored her own. She searched the commanders' faces, seeking an answer to avert the impending horror the message implied. "We have to get word to Highcliff before it's too late."

"What have you learned, Your Highness?" Commander Keel asked.

"My brother is using us to coax Ouderling out of hiding. She's the jewel the guards speak of, I'm sure of it." She dropped his gaze to yell at the pavilion's entrance. "Guards!"

At once, the tent flaps parted. Several guards rushed in with weapons drawn.

"Bring the falconer at once!"

Relief evident on their faces, the vigilant members of the Queen's Shield slipped back into the night.

Not wasting any time, Khae addressed the scout, "I need you to do something for me."

"Anything, Your Highness."

"I'm running out of elves I can trust, but you've proven yourself worthy. I have no right to ask this of you after what you've endured, but I don't think I can assign this task to anyone else."

"I'd be honoured, Your Highness."

"Even at the cost of your life?"

"If that's what's asked of me, it will be done."

Her heart felt like it skipped a beat. Who was she to deserve such undying devotion? Steeling herself, she said, "I need you to go to Orphic Den ahead of us."

Dragon Sect

The scout managed to keep a straight face, but Khae didn't miss his Adam's apple convulsing.

"I must know the mood in Orphic Den before I subject my troops to what might be waiting for us. If it's indeed a trap we're walking into, we'll be hard put to survive the magic of the wizards' guild."

The scout swallowed again, but nodded, fierce determination in his eyes. "You can count on me, Your Highness."

"Thank you." Khae patted his shoulder, giving him a heartfelt smile. "You've faced so much danger in my service and I don't even know your name."

"Rondou, Your Highness. Rondou Wainwright."

"Rondou." Khae clasped his grimy, rough-skinned hands with clean, delicate fingers and raised them to her lips. "I thank you for your service. You and those like you are the reason South March is worth fighting for. The crown will be forever in your debt."

Clearly embarrassed, Rondou swallowed a third time, and dropped his gaze to the ground.

"I'll need you to leave before dawn's first light with a note I'm about to write, but not before you get a decent meal into you."

Without looking up, Rondou said, "That would be appreciated, Your Highness."

The sun sat high overhead, eliminating the usual shadows that had clung to the canyon walls for the better part of the day. It was colder higher up in the Wizard's Sleeve, but Commander Keel had insisted they move their camp to the widest part of the Wizard's Walk where his troops would be better equipped to defend the eastern and western approaches.

Dragon Sect

Khae reflected on the terse note she had sent with Rondou. Though she wasn't one to resort to threats, the position of Headmaster Sagora had left her with little choice. Perhaps referring to him as a self-serving weasel had been a bit harsh, but she hoped the derogatory term would let him know how dimly she viewed his treasonous response to the crown's time of need.

Khae stood outside her recently erected pavilion, staring up the canyon. "How long do you think it'll take Rondou to reach the Den?"

Commander Keel followed her gaze to the dark pass beyond the encampment. "I imagine he made it there before noon. Depending on what he finds out, we should hear from him by sunset."

Khae sighed. "I hope he was mistaken about what he overheard."

"Time will tell, Your Highness. Until then, we'll be ready for whatever comes our way. He was right about the duke's forces. Our latest reports say that thousands have gathered on the outskirts of Gullveig. Rest assured, our troops are prepared."

She placed a hand on his forearm and squeezed. "I know I'm in competent hands. Be sure to see to their needs while we wait." She nodded at a couple of the Queen's Shield standing at the ready close by. Without having to look, she knew there were others scattered around the bulk of the royal pavilion.

Commander Keel nodded and started away, pausing briefly to say something to one of the Shield before he left.

It took her a while to search out where Hammas had gotten to, but a knot of elves near the eastern approach caught her attention. Captain Kall's intimidating hulk stood out amongst the elite guard. He had accompanied Hammas who was personally speaking to as many of the troops as possible about the rumours filtering into camp regarding the rapidly deteriorating state of affairs in the kingdom. Hammas and Kall's simple gesture would go a long way to improving the troops' falling morale.

A chair was brought forward, allowing her to bask in the splendid sunshine and enjoy the warmth whenever the cold breeze sweeping up the pass abated. If only her troubles could be swept aside so easily.

On their trek up the pass earlier in the morning, she had given Waryn missives for his ravens to carry north and south. It was imperative she got word to the high wizard and warn him not to allow Ouderling to leave Highcliff under any circumstances. She also wanted to alert the guards left behind at Borreraig Palace to be prepared to defend the Willow Throne in her absence.

She may have misjudged Orlythe's ambition, but now that the wheels of his war machine were turning, she was confident he would set his sights on the throne regardless of the statutes of elven law. Past dealings and her intimate knowledge of her brother told her that he had no qualms about breaking the rules that governed the land. If only she had dealt with him last fall.

She shuddered. Should Orlythe achieve his goal, the dragon question would come to a head. Allowed to pursue his misconstrued ideals uncontested, Orlythe's next step would most likely be to assemble a dragon army and push into the kingdoms of man.

Khae didn't profess to know everything about their northern neighbours, but she knew enough to realize that a full-scale assault would lead to a wholesale massacre of elves and dragons alike. South March had barely survived the human invasion during her mother's reign.

Dragon Sect

As much as she prided herself in her rule, she wasn't naïve. She was not her mother. Add to that knowledge that only three of the kingdoms of man had participated in the war, taking the fight to the man kingdoms would not end well for the elves should all five unite.

The sun had begun to set in the west by the time Hammas slipped inside the loose ring of Queen's Shield and rejoined her. She accepted his brief kiss and smiled for his benefit. If they were still camped here tomorrow, she would take it upon herself to do exactly as he had done today. Show her loyal followers that she was not just their leader but was devoted to their welfare as well. Aside from her fancy tent—its size more to provide a base of operations than to offer the royal couple a luxurious place to lay their heads—she made sure she didn't indulge in anything finer than the lowest ranking troops were afforded.

A commotion from the eastern edge of the camp drew their attention. Khae stood and placed an arm around Hammas' back, following his gaze. "That's Rondou's horse, isn't it?"

Hammas didn't answer. Instead, he said to Captain Hondrick who was never far from Khae's presence, "Watch her."

Without explanation, the king joined Captain Kall who had materialized from around the back of the pavilion and went to meet Rondou's black charger.

"What do you think, Hondrick?" Khae asked.

"That's Rondou's horse alright, but there's no sign of the scout." A frown replaced his squint. "Looks like a large cage fastened to the side of the saddle."

Khae swallowed a deep sense of foreboding. "A cage?"

"That's what it looks like."

Not caring about the protocols put into place to keep her safe, Khae started toward the scout's horse.

Hammas and Kall stopped short of a group of elves gathered around the charger, shock twisting their faces.

"What is it?" Khae stepped beside Hammas—an exasperated Captain Hondrick running up behind her.

Hammas shot the captain a dark look, but spoke softly to Khae, "If I didn't know better, I'd say we're looking at the remains of Rondou Wainwright."

Dragon Sect

Never be Broken

Horror-stricken, the Queen of the Elves fought the urge to vomit. Protruding haphazardly from within a grisly mass of butchered meat, shreds of studded, black leather surrounded what appeared to be a disfigured, elven head. Hard to tell at first, she realized she was looking at the remains of the scout, Rondou—his face contorted and elongated to resemble a weasel's snout, complete with whiskers that appeared to twitch of their own accord.

Khae held her hands over her mouth and turned away, dry heaving. The headmaster of the wizards' guild had answered her plea for assistance with a poignant statement. There would be no aid from Orphic Den.

"Take that disgusting thing away and burn it," Hammas said with revulsion. He patted Khae on the back and helped her stagger back to the royal pavilion.

"Oh, Hammas. What have I done?"

"You've done nothing, my pet. Sagora's to blame for this. Him and the Grim Duke."

It wasn't lost on Khae that Hammas hadn't referred to Orlythe as her brother. Stepping into the warmth of her tent, she stepped free of Hammas' embrace and stared at the flames licking at the wood in the central brazier. He was right of course. Whatever Orlythe had become, he had long ceased being the elf she had considered family. It was time to treat him, *and* Sagora, as the enemy they were.

She turned a haunted look on Hammas. "What would my mother have done?"

Hammas' brow lifted, no inkling of the usual kindness in his eyes. "She would have razed Orphic Den to the ground and spat on the devastation she left behind."

Khae nodded, but his answer provided her little solace. Nor did it enlighten her on how to respond to the blatant insult delivered by the second highest ranking magic-user in the land. With the power of the wizards' guild at his disposal, Sagora was arguably the most powerful elf in all of South March. More powerful than the Queen of the Elves.

Even supported by her loving husband, and surrounded by capable commanders and elite fighters, she felt alone against the world. She was the ruler of the realm. Everyone looked to her for answers she didn't have.

The sound of the camp coming to life reached her as the tent flaps parted to admit Commander Keel, Captain Kall and Captain Hondrick. The military leaders surrounded the war table to study the map.

Hammas joined them and addressed Keel. "What're our options?"

Keel placed his purple-plumed helm on a side table and ran his fingers through damp hair. "I don't rightly know. The guild opposes us here," he jabbed a finger at Orphic Den on the map, "while Orlythe's troops hold this end of the pass. Short of a nasty climb through the wilds of the Wizard's Sleeve, one that will inevitably lead to its own kind of hardship and death, I recommend we fight our way through to Gullveig."

"If the reports are true, Orlythe's troops outnumber us five to one," Hammas said.

Keel nodded. "More or less."

"And you believe that's our best option?"

"Orphic Den hasn't mobilized yet," Keel paused and cast Khae a concerned look. "One can never be sure when it comes to their kind. For all we know, they're watching us as we speak."

Everyone in the pavilion looked around.

"Remaining where we are could prove a fatal mistake should the guild march on us when the duke's forces attack. If we move on Orlythe's position now, we'll only have to concern ourselves with our forward flank."

Hammas nodded grimly and joined Khae between the tent flaps and the table. "How do you think Highcliff will respond to your missive?"

If she were Aelfwynne, she knew what she would do, and it wouldn't be to leave the Crystal Cavern unprotected. Surely, he could spare a few dragons though. "I don't know. After last year's events, I'm inclined to think we're on our own." She sighed. "At least Ouderling is safe. As long as she remains at Highcliff, the duke cannot claim the crown."

Hammas raised skeptical eyebrows. "I wouldn't be too sure about that. If he has the backing of the rest of South March, there'll be no one left to gainsay his claim."

Khae's look darkened.

Hammas threw up his hands. "I'm just being realistic, Khae. Heir or not, if he seizes the Willow Throne, it'll take a miracle to take it back again." He glanced at the elves watching them from the war table. "If we can't find a way to win free of this mountain pass, the succession will become a moot point, whether Ouderling lives or not."

Khae cringed hearing one of her darkest fears confirmed. Hammas had an uncanny knack of cutting through conjecture and what ifs and honing in on what the real probability of the outcome of Orlythe's offensive would mean. Even if Aelfwynne responded with a full-scale dragon attack, however much the creature's numbers had been depleted, the resulting carnage would make the Willow Throne an empty seat without meaning. South March would, in all likelihood, revert back to the clans of old. To a time of unrest where elves fought amongst themselves. She snorted. Much like they were doing now.

The tent flaps parted to admit one of the Queen's Shield. The flaxen-haired elf dropped to a knee before the royal couple, bearing a bloodstained piece of paper in his hand. "Your Majesties. We found this stuck in the remains of the scout."

Khae exchanged glances with Hammas but it was Captain Hondrick who relieved the elf of his grisly burden. Squinting to make out what was written—the ink smeared and obliterated by blotches of dark crimson—he read the note aloud. "The wrongs committed by those entrusted to oversee South March shall be remedied with the new moon."

Khae frowned. "That's it?"

Hondrick examined both sides of the stained parchment. "Yes, Your Highness."

Khae inquired of Commander Keel, "How much time does that give us?"

"Until the new moon? Seven days, Your Highness."

Khae's widening eyes searched the king's. Swallowing her unease, she hardened her resolve. Taking in the concerned faces around her, she declared, "I must act quickly if I'm to sever the headmaster's head from his insolent carcass before the kingdom is lost."

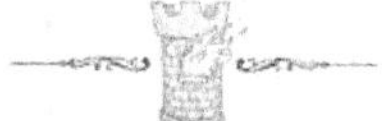

Sleep was not a luxury Khae could afford. She had paced the remainder of the day away inside her pavilion, speaking little, but her mother's mantra clawed its way up from the deepest recesses of her mind. *'Life's tendency is to bend you in its wind. Bend back. Never be broken, for only then can the darkness claim you.'*

'Never be broken...Never be broken...Never be broken,' over and over again as the formation of a desperate plan took shape. Her mother would have never shied away from a fight. By the Fae's gossamer wings, neither would she.

Hammas had watched her with concern throughout the day, likely fearing what she was about, but had gratefully restrained from bothering her. Her parents had been correct in sensing the dear elf's intellect from an early age. Hammas knew the right things to say at the right time, but he was also wise enough to know when to say nothing at all. Latching onto the semblance of an outlandish idea, she required peace and space to forge it into a workable plan.

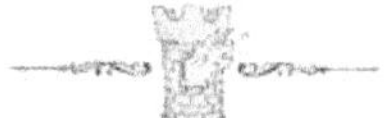

Lying in her cot well into the night, she opened her eyes briefly. Though hard to see in the poor light of the tent, sure enough, Hammas remained awake, speaking quietly with his three commanders on the far side of the pavilion, leaving her by herself to do what she felt must be done. He hadn't been happy when he discovered the nature of what she was about to attempt, but he respected her enough to support her decision. She smiled. Given what they were up against, what choice did they have?

Seldom did she ponder the actions she entertained, but never in her wildest dreams had she believed that one day she might pursue it. Though she had no way of appreciating the consequences of what she had in mind, she feared that by invoking the powerful magic, she ran the real risk of trapping her soul in the spirit world. Should that happen, she believed her corporeal body would simply cease to exist and everything her mother had fought so hard for would amount to nothing. That was something she refused to allow.

Taking a deep breath, she closed her eyes, concentrating on emptying her mind of the maelstrom of emotions and dark thoughts that threatened to break her. It took a while, but slowly her worries eased. The occasional clink of armour from the vigilant elves patrolling the camp receded into the background, along with the hushed voices of Hammas and the commanders.

The faint crackle and pop of the brazier soothed her, allowing her to drift into a state of semi-consciousness and open an inner channel to access nature's essence. As disorienting as it was to indulge in the strong magic, a profound awareness of the mystical Fae that were always present on the edge of reality grew until something otherworldly informed her she had bridged the gap and entered the faerie realm.

Vaguely aware of her physical body, it was as if she watched herself from afar. She rose from her cot and paced the perimeter of the pavilion, passing the warmth of the brazier. A wave of cold buffeted her. Uncaring of her surroundings, the tent slipped behind her—the night sky twinkling around a quarter moon.

Voices without meaning rose around her, but if they spoke to her directly, she paid them no mind—her attention on a tall structure appearing through a bank of mystical mist.

Dragon Sect

As impossible as her rational mind knew it was, the Fangs of the Dragon coalesced into a solid mass. Having flown on the back of a dragon with the legendary warrior Xantha, the sensation of dragonflight still flushed her with goosebumps. Adjoined to the western fang by a small bridge, Grim Watch Tower materialized before her eyes.

An abrupt change in angle left her dizzy—her viewpoint banking steeply upward. Without warning she was deposited within the same chamber high atop Grim Watch where her mother's shade had appeared alongside Rhiannon, the Queen of the Fae. It had been the White Witch's warning that had set last year's events into motion.

A pang of remorse gripped her, threatening to absolve the magical trance enthralling her surreal state of consciousness. What if Rhiannon had ulterior motives? Were the Fae conspiring to rid the mortal realm of the elves?

She swallowed, refusing to entertain such a possibility. If she were to have any chance of saving the kingdom, and by extension, Ouderling, she had to trust that her rapport with the nether realm had been one of mutual respect.

Somewhere in the back of her mind, she sensed a set of firm hands restraining her physical body, but through the ancient magic rooted in the soul of the living rock of Grim Watch Tower, she knew there was a deeper arcane force at play. The taint of the being responsible for the construction of the enchanted edifice brushed the fringes of her lifeforce—its unsettling presence extending through an otherworldly veil to bolster her command of the nature's essence at her command—helping her manipulate the forces rooted in the very fabric of the land.

A gust of wind teased her unkempt hair, lifting long tresses off her shoulders and buffeting them around her face. A drawn-out series of lightning flashed all around the eerie tower, but it was some time before thunder answered.

Difficult to see past the hair whipping around her face, she leaned into the face of the southwest window enclosure to counteract the fierce wind that threatened to lift her off the ground.

A jagged flash of light etched across the sky—visible from the southwest opening in the circular chamber—and slashed into a line of distant mountain peaks. As the surge of light disappeared far over the Ors Sea, the wind died. Reeling to regain her balance in its absence, she leaned out of the southwest break in the curving wall—her breath escaping in a frantic rush.

Rising above the peaks of the Wizard's Sleeve, a shimmering, expanding ring of vapourous light originated from what she perceived as a great confluence of discharged magic. The strange phenomenon spread across the night sky in every direction.

She ducked but needn't have bothered. The ring of power shot by high over the tower and out of sight to the northeast.

Staring into the ensuing darkness, she became aware of the shockwave moments before it struck. Her jaw dropped at the realization of what was about to happen.

One moment, she was staring into the night, and the next, her spiritual body was blasted from its feet, thrown toward the Fangs of the Dragon along with the crumbling circular chamber of Grim Watch Tower.

The rickety bridge spanning the desolate twin peaks exploded under the weight of flying chunks that had been blasted from the top of the ancient tower—splinters and frayed rope adding to the fury of the storm, littering debris upon the inaccessible slopes of Grim Ward Island.

Dragon Sect

Flight with Destiny

"**You** did what?"

For such a little goblin, Aelfwynne's penchant of instilling fear in everyone he met whenever they had the misfortune of raising his dander was a hidden talent. At least, Ouderling tried to assure herself, such was the case whenever she did something the high wizard didn't agree with. That seemed to happen more often than not lately.

She made a point of holding his menacing glare. "It kind of slipped."

"Kind of!" Aelfwynne threw his arms in the air and stomped around the wizard's lair, oblivious to the faces watching him. "No wonder the blasted varmint didn't want to help us."

Scale and Eolande stood hunched over a side table, working at repairing what looked like a piece of a stalactite from the Crystal Cavern. Ouderling absently wondered what good that was going to do since it no longer hung from the magical chamber's ceiling, but couldn't be bothered to inquire at the moment. She had known her conversation with Aelfwynne would likely go sideways.

Jyllana cleared her throat beside her and said, "It wasn't like Grimclaw was open to anything we might have suggested. He has to be the rudest creature I've ever dealt with."

Aelfwynne turned his dark look on Jyllana. "You speak to contentious creatures on a regular basis, do you?"

"No, but—"

"Grimclaw isn't an ordinary creature. He's legendary."

"With an attitude like his, I can see why people remember him," Ouderling mumbled.

Aelfwynne's gaze flicked back to her. "What would make you mention your idea in the first place. *Especially* after I forbade it."

Ouderling swallowed, but lifted her chin in defiance. "I said it in the spur of the moment. He was getting all righteous and aggressive. I thought he was going to kill us."

Aelfwynne gaped. "And you believed that bringing up your silly idea of a clandestine society of dragon riders to defend South March would appease the beast? Do you not hear anything I say?"

"Yes, but—"

"How can you? Grimclaw left Highcliff for that very reason. Tired of dragons being used by elves to fight our battles. What could possibly make you think that the mention of a dragon sect would persuade him to help your mother?"

Ouderling sighed and dropped her gaze to her hands folded in front of her. "I wasn't thinking straight, I guess."

Aelfwynne's beady, red eyes flared as her last word left her lips. "You're damn right you didn't *think*! Now I'm left with the unenviable decision on whether to allow the Queen of the Elves to fend for herself in a battle she cannot hope to win, or leave Highcliff vulnerable to an evil creature much worse than your short-sighted uncle."

Dragon Sect

"I'm sorry, Master Aelfwynne," Ouderling fought back an urge to cry—the sensation maddening her. She was only eighteen, but she had matured greatly over the last six months. She wasn't foolish enough to think she was anywhere near ready to assume the responsibility that would be thrust upon her if her mother was killed, but she hoped she was strong enough to find her way through the aftermath should that unfortunate scenario unfold in the not-too-distant future. If she listened to Aelfwynne's view on how volatile the situation had become regarding the crown, that day might arrive much sooner than she had thought.

"Go. Get cleaned up and rest," Aelfwynne dismissed her and Jyllana with an impatient flick of his hand. "You may be flying a dragon again sooner than you think."

Ouderling held his angry stare a few moments longer before looking away. Without a word, she led Jyllana from the wizard's lair.

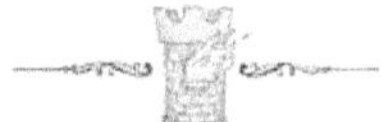

"Where're you going? Our rooms are this way." Jyllana stopped at the mouth of a side passageway leading off the main tunnel.

Ouderling took a couple more steps and stopped. Her shoulders stiffened, but she didn't turn around.

Jyllana stepped up to her. "What is it? Are you okay?"

Ouderling knew her eyes were red, and not just because she had been unable to keep her tears of frustration from spilling down her grimy cheeks. She bit at her lower lip, unsure if she had the nerve to go through with the crazy idea consuming her.

"Come on, Oud. He wasn't there. You acted the way you did because you were trying to salvage the situation." Jyllana smiled, the gesture obviously forced. "How were you to know what Grimclaw's reaction would be?"

Ouderling kept her eyes straight ahead, mulling over the preposterous notion forming in the back of her mind.

"Have you ever met Grimclaw before?" Jyllana asked, then answered for her, "No. Were you there when Grimclaw decided to abandon Highcliff and the elves? Of course you weren't. Perhaps old magic pants, who's older than dirt, knew what Grimclaw's response would be because he was there all those centuries ago. You weren't. You tried your best and you failed. You're only elven. You're not a seer."

Ouderling swallowed, slowly turning her attention on Jyllana. If her protector only knew how wrong she was about being her being a seer, but Jyllana's diatribe had given Ouderling an idea. "You're a genius."

Jyllana was hard put to keep up to Ouderling as the princess broke into a jog. "What is it? What did I say?"

Ouderling ignored Jyllana, her concentration on what she was contemplating. She had given up too easily. If she didn't act quickly, her parents would be left to bear the consequences of her failure.

The glow of the Crystal Cavern pulsed softly ahead. Entering the magical cavern, Ouderling called out, "Miragan! Are you here?"

The flight of several wyverns wavered momentarily as riders and beasts paused to see what the commotion was all about.

A smaller wyvern broke away from the ceiling and dropped to the path. Its rider offered them a warm smile. "Greetings, princess. Miragan's not here."

Ouderling recognized the old goblin as Lylande and nodded hello to the female caretaker. "Do you know where she is?"

Lylande shook her head. "We haven't seen Miragan since she left with you many days ago. How was your flight?"

So preoccupied, Ouderling didn't bother responding. She started back up the main corridor in a run. Jyllana's footsteps fell behind, but her protector caught up as she broke onto the promontory and slowed to study the deep shadows bathing the rock shelf—the moon hidden behind the perpetual cloud cover.

Kingstone and Dagomar sat quietly on the far end of the ledge—if they spoke to one another, their voices weren't being shared with Ouderling.

Walking to the edge of the promontory and searching the dark sky toward the orangey-reddish glow of the lava fields on the far side of Crystal Lake, Ouderling curbed her desire to cry out in dismay. The last thing she wanted was to attract Kingstone's attention, although she knew he was of her. The head dragon never missed a thing.

Jyllana stepped in beside her, pulling her tunic tight, and whispered, "Why are you looking for Miragan?"

Ouderling had half a mind not to tell her, but the more she thought on it, the more it made sense to include her. As much as she was dedicated to what she knew she had to do, it would be comforting if her one constant in life was beside her every step of the way. "I'm going—"

The ledge shook momentarily beneath their feet—the mighty Kingstone had taken flight, his large frame diminishing quickly in the darkness of the surrounding mountains—and then he was gone.

Ouderling swallowed, pausing a moment to allow time for her sudden apprehension to fade away. The departure of the head dragon eased her reluctance to voice what was on her mind. Taking a deep breath, she cast a wary glance at Dagomar who also appeared on the verge of flying off, and whispered so softly that Jyllana had to lean in, "I'm going back for Grimclaw."

The stunned look on Jyllana's face would have been comical had the situation not have been so dire.

Ouderling held a finger to her lips. "Aye. I know. Crazy huh?"

"Does Aelfwynne know about this?" Jyllana whispered harshly back.

Ouderling glanced at the tunnel entrance. "Of course not."

"Aren't you going to tell him? He deserves to know."

"Are you insane? If he gets wind of my plan, he'll forbid the dragons from coming anywhere near me. I need to find Miragan. She'll take me."

Jyllana frowned, her attention on Dagomar. "Then we're going too."

Ouderling followed her gaze. "Oh no. Don't say anything to him. He'll ruin everything."

"You don't know that."

Ouderling rolled her eyes. "Seriously? Aelfwynne trusts him almost as much as he does Kingstone."

"Okay, okay. But you can't go on your own."

"I'll have Miragan with me. I daresay she can handle herself, *and* she knows where we're going."

"You know what I mean. I'm not letting you go by yourself."

"I'm not. I want you to come with me."

"And how do you suppose that'll happen. I haven't learned how to fly yet. You have to let someone know what you're thinking of doing."

Ouderling sighed. "You're forgetting something here. I'm the princess. I can do what I want, when I want."

Jyllana shook her head. "No, it's you who is forgetting her station. At Highcliff, you're no more important than the next Guardian. Including me." Her voice rose louder than appropriate with Dagomar close by.

Dragon Sect

"Keep your voice down!" Ouderling admonished, her voice louder than Jyllana's had been.

"Is there trouble over there?"

"Oh great. Now you've done it." Ouderling glowered. Giving Dagomar a false smile, she said as innocently as she could, "No. Not really. We're just…having a disagreement."

Dagomar took a couple steps toward them but stopped, his crimson eyes watching Ouderling as if they possessed the ability to delve into her soul. The great dragon nodded his head a couple of times before springing into the air and winging away.

Ouderling watched until he was well over the middle of the lake. "That was close. If he were to find out and say something to Aelfy, I'd have to walk." She started toward the entrance to Highcliff, muttering, "It's a good thing he didn't. My parents don't have that much time."

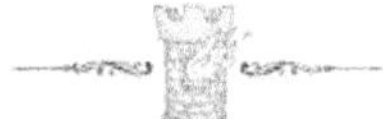

Jyllana sat on the edge of the promontory, her legs dangling over the dark waters of Crystal Lake barely visible through the mist. She had decided to remain behind after Ouderling went back into Highcliff in search of Miragan. If the princess found the wyvern, they would have to come back this way before taking off.

Life in the magical aerie high in the Dark Mountains had been quite an adventure over the last several months. Ouderling had matured a great deal since the day they had set out from Borreraig Palace on Queen Khae's order, but Jyllana wasn't fooled. The princess was still young and naïve to the ways of the greater world.

She scoffed at that. It wasn't like she was much older. Having to learn responsibility at an early age, Jyllana had matured faster than her peers—mostly due to her desire to one day join the Home Guard. A position she had obtained at an early age. Becoming one of the youngest elves to ever be accepted into the royal household, she had taken her duty more serious than most. As such, she had been rewarded for her efforts after Ouderling's previous personal protector had been let go.

The barely audible scrape of a soft-soled boot brought Jyllana to her feet.

"Ah, there you are," Ouderling said as she exited Highcliff. "Why are you still out here?"

Jyllana shrugged, absently marvelling at how long the princess' hair had grown. "Just wanted some air."

From the look on Ouderling's face, the princess didn't believe her.

"You mean a fortnight riding Dagomar wasn't enough?"

Jyllana shrugged again, her gaze on the cliff rising up from the back of the platform. "What can I say? I don't enjoy being cooped up in there."

Ouderling sat on the edge and swung her legs over the precipice—something the two of them enjoyed doing. "Don't let me stop you." She patted the stone beside her. "Come. Tell me what you've been thinking about."

Oh, you don't want to know, Jyllana thought as she eased herself down beside Ouderling. "Nothing much. Just reflecting on our recent quest."

"And?"

"Nothing special, really. I was just wondering if we could have handled it differently, but the more I think on it, the more I'm convinced we couldn't have. That obnoxious dragon didn't give us a chance."

Ouderling nodded. "And that's why we have to go back."

"We?"

"Of course. I'm not foolish enough to think I can shake my persistent tail."

Dragon Sect

The reference to how she used to keep tabs on the princess at the palace made her smile. What a chore that had been. When Ouderling wanted to elude her, the princess had found ways to do just that.

It had taken Jyllana quite a while to discover the private retreat Ouderling and the groom, Marris, liked to steal off to. A secluded little lake at the end of a narrow cleft. Only by the slimmest of timing on that first occasion had she found them—lucky to avoid witnessing the intimate bond they had shared.

As much as she wanted to believe that they hadn't realized she was close at hand, she had an inkling there was more to the horse groom than he had let on. Though he never spoke a word to her, Jyllana was sure by the way he looked at her that he was aware of her presence while he and Ouderling visited their mountain retreat.

Whether the princess knew or not, she had never brought up the subject lest bad feelings arose as a result. To remove the thought from her mind, she asked, "Were you able to find Mir?"

Ouderling shook her head. "No one knows where she went after dropping me off."

"Pecklyn might. He seems to know everything there is to know when it comes to dragons."

"I never saw him either. Nor Balewynd for that matter. Weird."

Jyllana mulled that over. It wasn't unusual for Balewynd and Pecklyn to disappear together. If she didn't know better, she might think the elite guardians were having an affair. She blinked at that and smiled. They would be good for each other. If opposites truly attracted, Balewynd's aloof, morose mannerisms were certainly on the far extreme from

Pecklyn's exuberant personality. The Fae only knew how much Balewynd needed someone like Pecklyn in her life.

"What're you thinking about?" Ouderling asked.

Jyllana blinked several times as she realized the princess was looking straight at her. Her smile faded. "Nothing, really."

Ouderling raised her eyebrows but didn't press the issue.

"So," Jyllana whispered, looking around before continuing, "Even if you do convince Mir to take you back, how am I going to go with you? She barely carried *you* there and back. There's no way she can carry both of us."

Ouderling chewed on her lower lip, her eyes widening, "What about Zorain? He'll do anything for me."

Jyllana gave her a condescending look. "No, anyone but him. It wouldn't be fair to get Zorain into anymore difficulty with Master Aelfwynne *or* Kingstone. Your excursion to Wyvern Beach landed him in enough trouble."

"Ya, I guess you're right. Hmm?" Ouderling chewed her lip some more and stared out over Crystal Lake. She looked back just as quickly. "We could ask Dagomar!"

Jyllana was glad she was sitting down. "Are you crazy? You just finished saying not to mention anything to him."

The frustration was plainly evident on Ouderling's face. "We have to do something. We can't just—" Her breath caught in her throat.

Dagomar landed on the platform directly behind them, shaking the ledge to the point that Jyllana feared the section they sat upon was about to break away from the cliff. Before she could scramble to her feet, Miragan touched down behind the red dragon—her landing more graceful.

"If you're serious about this," Dagomar's gruff voice sounded in her head, *"you'd better grab your gear before Kingstone returns."*

Dragon Sect

Jyllana shot Ouderling a puzzled look.

"I overheard everything."

Jyllana turned on Dagomar. "You were spying on us?"

"Not necessarily. Kingstone asked me to keep watch, so I landed on the ledge above Master Aelfwynne's lair and did just that."

"But how do you know what we're talking about if you aren't spying on us?"

"It's not my fault dragons have exceptional hearing."

"And where did Miragan come from? Does she know too?"

"She was up there with me. Been there ever since you two returned."

"Ever since grandfather died," Miragan whispered, *"I like to sit up there and watch the lake. It gives me peace."*

"So, you were spying!"

"Jyl. He's offering to help," Ouderling interrupted and walked up to Miragan. "And you too?"

"I would do anything for you, pretty lady," Miragan said solemnly.

"But what about Master Aelfwynne?" Ouderling asked.

"What Aelfy doesn't know can't hurt us," Dagomar said in his gruff tone. *"At least not until he catches us."*

Jyllana didn't care that her jaw dropped. Not only had the serious Dagomar referred to the High Wizard by the nickname nobody with any sense would say to his face, but what he suggested seemed preposterous coming from someone in his position. "I…I thought you answered to Aelfwynne."

"Please. I'm a dragon. I answer to no one."

Ouderling's grin threatened to cleave her face in two. She turned and held Jyllana by the shoulders, bouncing on the balls of her feet. "There's your answer!"

Dragon Sect

Grabbing Jyllana's wrist, she yanked so hard that Jyllana cried out, "Hey!"

"Come on!" Ouderling dragged her toward the tunnel entrance. "We don't want to miss our flight with destiny!"

The faint glow emitted by the moon dropping in the western sky did little to banish the lengthening shadows on the promontory of flat rock abutting the entrance to Highcliff.

Ouderling didn't mind—her dark vision good enough to see what she needed to as she secured her quiver and yew bow in the harness strapped across her back—its leather cinch buckled at the top of her stomach.

Clad in a low cut, green suede tunic and matching hip cape, she climbed aboard Miragan and adjusted her leather pants, ensuring the metal knee guards sat securely above knee-high boots that were protected by hammered brass shin guards. She pulled on a lined, leather surcoat to protect her from the pervasive cold synonymous with dragon flight. Of all the dragon riding attire she had acquired since arriving at Highcliff, aside from the heavy surcoat, she preferred the simplicity this outfit offered. If she needed to move quickly on foot when they arrived at their destination, she wouldn't be impeded by the heavier plate armour, and yet her lower extremities were shielded against arrowshot from the ground should a crisis occur while in flight. Given the state of the kingdom, and indeed the hostility of the region north of South March, she felt it a wise choice of apparel.

Jyllana waited nervously astride the base of Dagomar's neck, her watchful eyes darting from the skies to the complex entrance and back again. Should Kingstone return, or one of the resident Guardians decide to go for a late-night stroll, their secret quest would be a short one.

"Ready?" Ouderling asked, satisfied her gear sat properly.

Jyllana didn't have time to answer. Dagomar leapt into the sky and winged away to the east, following the route they had taken before.

"I'm ready, pretty lady. Hang on," Miragan said.

Dropping into a crouch, the wyvern sprung from the ledge, her wings quickly negating the resulting pull of gravity.

As Highcliff disappeared behind a bank of mist, Ouderling shuddered.

Miragan must have sensed it. *"Is everything okay?"*

Ouderling craned her neck, trying to see through the fog. Her nature's essence had taken hold of her conscious thought, informing her they were being watched.

She swallowed her apprehension. They were airborne now. Whoever, or whatever, it was, wouldn't be able to stop them now.

Forcing herself to look ahead, focusing on the barely visible form of Dagomar, she patted Miragan's neck. "Everything's fine, Mir. I'll be happier when we're far away from here."

As if her answer were an unspoken command, Miragan increased her speed, quickly closing on Jyllana and the rebellious red dragon.

Dragon Sect

To Ensnare a Witch

Urdanya Castle was much quieter since the bulk of Orlythe's troops had gone in pursuit of Queen Khae's army, but Ryedyn didn't fool himself. The temporary calm would not last. The sound of heavy footsteps tromping up the steps of the Sea Witch Sceptre confirmed his suspicion. With a knowing smirk, Ryedyn took a deep breath to compose himself. As confident in his ability as he was, it was never wise to antagonize the Duke of Grim. At least not yet.

He eyed the length of burlap stashed in the shadows at the back of the chamber, the length of crystal hidden underneath, and smiled. No matter the outcome between the duke's troops and the queen's army, he had in his possession a piece of the Crystal Cavern—an artifact that promised to place stronger magic in his hands. In time, he would become more powerful than Afara Maral ever was.

Bursting into the chamber, two Grim Guard took up positions on either side of the open door. Duke Orlythe strode between them and stopped in front of Ryedyn. "Who gave the order for the troops to hold at the bottom of the Wizard's Walk?"

Dragon Sect

Ryedyn held the duke's menacing stare, unable to keep from swallowing his discomfort. His confidence in dealing with Orlythe had been bolstered through private consultations with the Dragon Witch Wraith, but the creature was no longer in Urdanya. If the duke decided to have him killed, there wasn't much Ryedyn could do to prevent such a fate—other than doing his best to take Orlythe down with him in the process. He still had to bide his time.

Lifting his chin, he said, "I did, m'lord."

Orlythe's eyes narrowed, and his chest swelled. Leaning close enough that his scruffy beard itched Ryedyn's face, he bellowed, "You? How dare you command my army?"

Ryedyn struggled to keep the hint of fear from his voice. "It was done under advisement."

Confusion twisted Orlythe's purple face. "Under whose advisement?"

"The Soul."

Orlythe leaned back. "The wraith? How do you know this?"

Ryedyn feared this was where things might go sideways. "It told me itself."

Orlythe frowned. "It was here? In Urdanya?"

"In this very room, m'lord."

"Why wasn't I told?"

"There wasn't time. It remained long enough to leave instructions with me and left again."

"Where did it go?"

Ryedyn shrugged and said truthfully, "I know not, m'lord. Said it was off to contain a threat. That's all I know."

Orlythe stepped to the east-facing window—gazing toward the distant peaks of the Wizard's Sleeve and said under his breath, "What are you up to, wraith?"

Ryedyn stepped in beside him. "What's that, m'lord?"

"Nothing," Orlythe growled. "So, what now?"

Ryedyn shrugged. "We wait."

"For what?"

"According to the Soul, your men only need to prevent the queen from escaping. With the guild not answering her call, her troops will have no place to go."

"I don't like it. We have her cornered. We should strike while we have the chance. The mountains aren't entirely impassable. Should Highcliff intervene, we'll lose the advantage of our superiority."

"True, m'lord, but the wraith said it has something special in store for your sister. Something imminent that will change everything. It claims it won't be long before the queen seals her own fate, and thus that of the crown."

Orlythe turned a menacing glare on Ryedyn. "What's that supposed to mean?"

"I don't know, m'lord, but it assured me the queen will soon be dealt with. When that occurs, it said you can release your dogs—its words, not mine—and destroy the remainder of the Royal Army at your leisure, including the king."

Orlythe took a deep breath, obviously fighting the urge to break into a fit of rage. "What of Highcliff? If Aelfwynne responds, my troops will be helpless to defend themselves in the confines of the Wizard's Sleeve against a wing of dragons."

Ryedyn dipped his head in agreement with the duke's sentiments but kept his thoughts to himself.

"I need to equip them with dragon killers before it's too late," Orlythe muttered, appearing on the verge of one of his infamous tirades. Casting a last glare at the mountains in the east, he stormed from the chamber, his retainers following in his wake.

"Not much in this world scares me, Festyr, but I would be amiss to boast that the otherworldly lich doesn't instil in me a profound sense of revulsion."

The stoop-shouldered, old chamberlain sneered. "Aye. It reeks of an evil not of South March. I daresay it isn't elven."

Sagora's ample stomach jiggled with his amusement at that statement. He looked around, lowering his voice, "Indeed it is not. More of the man persuasion if you ask me. The sooner we're rid of it—"

The headmaster's words caught in his throat as a penetrating cold heralded the re-emergence of the Dragon Witch Wraith. Where it had gone since first announcing itself at Orphic Den was a mystery—one Sagora decided was better to be left alone.

"You were saying," the wraith's voice grated.

Smoother than he thought possible given the circumstances, Sagora replied, "We were just discussing what a pleasure it is to consider you one of our staunchest allies. The Queen of South March is a formidable foe, but not one that cannot be dealt with in an expeditious manner now that we enjoy the benefit of your aid."

"Be careful what you believe," the wraith growled. "The spawn of Nyxa is more formidable than you might think. If not for her penchant of not wishing to appear overbearing in her subjects' eyes, Khae Wys would be more remarkable than her mother. Trapped or not, she will not go down easy."

Sagora choked. "Please. The queen is nothing like Nyxa. She's nothing but—"

"Your death if you keep speaking of things you know nothing about!" The fiery glow of the wraith's eyes within its ratty cowl intensified. "Underestimate Nyxa's child at your peril. She might lack her mother's military prowess, but I assure you, the queen's mastery of the elusive magic that links our world to that of the Fae will bring about disaster for all of us if we allow her to follow its course."

Sagora capitulated, though he knew not why. His interactions with the sovereign of the elven nation had exposed her as someone unable to make the hard decisions her position demanded. Had he been in her place and faced with the insolence he had blatantly shown her on her last few visits to Orphic Den, he would have responded much harsher than she had. In fact, her head would have quickly found itself adorning the impressive, wrought-iron candelabra in the great hall of Orphic Den. Her inaction after being denied her request for aid, even after she had made it quite clear that his attitude would not be tolerated, spoke volumes to her conviction. In his estimation, she was not anything like her mother. Khae was weak. The current state of the kingdom proved that assertion.

Nevertheless, Sagora didn't relish debating the issue with the creature hovering before him. Even with all of the power contained in the trinkets adorning his fingers and hanging around his neck, he doubted he was a match for the Dragon Witch Wraith.

He bowed his head in deference. "Of course. I assume by your unexpected visit that you have remedied that situation."

"You're wiser than you appear, Headmaster."

Sagora fought his rising anger and dipped his chin so that he wouldn't have to look at the wraith head on. "What is it you require of the wizards' guild?"

"Of the guild…Nothing. It is you I require."

Sagora looked up, unable to keep the contempt from his glare.

"Only you are strong enough to do what must be done."

Sagora put aside his misgivings and puffed out his considerable chest. "And what is that?"

"The queen will come for you."

Sagora swallowed at the ominous proclamation. "She wouldn't dare."

"So sure, are you? Left with no other choice than to seek out those more powerful than us, I'm of the belief that Khae will enact a magic unheard of in our times."

Sagora frowned. "What's that supposed to mean? She's no wizard. What talisman does she wield?"

"The love for her daughter is all the power she will require to transcend the mortal veil separating our world from that of the White Witch."

"Rhiannon? Impossible!" Sagora sputtered, his bravado losing its enthusiasm as he met the wraith's resolute glare.

"I've come to learn the Fae consider Khae Wys as the crown jewel of our world. Someone they feel worthy of their intervention. Their aid last year in keeping the princess from harm until Khae could be convinced of the necessity to send Ouderling to the only place in all the realm where she would be safe from the likes of you and I is solid proof of what I speak. That alone speaks loudly to the value they place in Khae. Not even Nyxa enjoyed the loyalty of the Fae. If we're to survive the queen's wrath, we must defeat her on her turf."

That made no sense at all. So aghast, Sagora had trouble speaking loud enough to be heard. "And just where would that be?"

"In her mind, Headmaster. In her mind."

Sagora frowned deeper.

"If you wish to survive what's coming, you'd best be prepared to meet your death."

Dragon Sect

Raven's Death

Scale had no idea how he knew it was going to be a bad day but know he did. Rolling off his scratchy, straw pallet, he stepped on an errant boot and rolled his ankle. Bone impacting the stone floor, the resulting pain was so intense that he initially believed he had sprained the joint, but after a considerable litany of curse words, a few he made up on the spot, he found he was able to walk on the injured leg with little more difficulty than a slight limp.

Stumbling into the wizard's lair after the sun had crested the eastern mountains did little to alleviate his disposition. Aelfwynne's dark glare informed him the high wizard wasn't impressed by his tardiness.

"Thought you'd taken the day off," Aelfwynne grumbled and returned his attention to the crystal fragment on the central table.

Scale flashed him an unseen smile. What else could he do? Worried about his swollen ankle, he had sought out the healer, Lylande. By the time she had drawn herself away from whatever she and her wyvern had been working on in the back recesses of the Crystal Cavern, he had missed the serving of breakfast. But there was no sense sharing any of that with the high wizard. Aelfwynne wasn't one to offer sympathy.

"What do you make of this?" Aelfwynne straightened enough to expose the thicker end of the crystal where it had broken away from the cavern's ceiling—the third one in as many days.

Scale positioned himself around the opposite side of the table. "I'm not sure what I'm looking at."

"A shard, you buffoon."

Obviously, Scale thought, but kept that to himself. Aelfwynne was in a bad enough mood already.

"These marks." Aelfwynne ran a claw tip along several scores in the crystal's surface. "They're not natural."

"One of the caretakers, maybe?"

Aelfwynne shook his head, his dark glower unnerving. "They're not barbarians. Someone's been hacking at the stone."

Scale frowned. "If not the caretakers, then who?"

"If I knew that, do you think I'd be wasting my breath telling you?"

"It doesn't make sense. Only the Guardians have access to the crystals."

"Then we have a mole."

Scale frowned.

"A spy, you witless northerner."

Scale stepped back, stunned. He quickly went over every elf, goblin, dragon, and wyvern at Highcliff. There wasn't one in the bunch that roused even the faintest of suspicion. "Who?"

Aelfwynne gave him his famous, contemptuous glare. Shaking his head, the high wizard stomped over to the smoked-glass window and stared out.

Scale stepped in beside him. The sun was indeed high in the morning sky. He swallowed and tried to think of something to say to change the subject. "How's Eolande making out with the summoning spell?"

Aelfwynne didn't answer right away, but when he did, the worst of his angst had dissipated. "If you'd been paying more attention, you'd know that he's been able to move objects back and forth between caverns."

Scale blinked. "Impressive. That's good news, at least."

Aelfwynne directed Scale's attention to a side table close to the edge of the window.

Not sure what he was looking at, Scale observed an arch-shaped piece of stone.

"That used to be one of those," Aelfwynne grumbled, his gaze switching to a granite candleholder sitting on another table.

"Oh."

"It's not all bad. At least he's been able to summon them. He needs someone like you to help him take the next step."

Scale's eyes widened.

"Relax, ya big galoop. I don't mean by summoning *you*." Aelfwynne shuffled back to the crystal shard and stared. "Though, that's not a bad idea."

Scale swallowed, his gaze lingering on the melted stone candleholder.

"I want you to help Eolande in the Crystal Cavern. He claims he needs a human's touch, *but*, thanks to someone destroying our scrying bowl," Aelfwynne raised his brows, "we have no way of finding Braen. Rumour has it he's fled the kingdom."

That snapped Scale's attention away from the deformed experiment.

"Until we can locate another such individual with ties to man, we're not going to be able to do anything for the Focal Stone."

"Do you think it was tampered with by the same people who did this?" Scale pointed at the shard.

"No. I think the use of Soulbiter is to blame for the Focal Stone. The cursed dagger is tainted with dark magic. Using it to cut off the tip likely weakened its constitution. Eolande should never have allowed Ouderling to do what she did, but it's done now."

A commotion drew their attention to the chamber's exit. Pecklyn's feet slid on the smooth stone as he arrested his headlong dash into the wizard's lair, a lump of something black in his hands. "Master Aelfwynne! Tidings from the queen!"

A jolt of cold surged through Scale's body.

Pecklyn unloaded his burden on the stone table next to the shard.

A mottled raven fell to its side, its ribcage heaving erratically—the golden band around one of its ankles denoting it as one of the queen's personal carriers.

Aelfwynne looked with concern into Pecklyn's eyes. The raven had obviously been charmed by Khae's falconer to fly as fast as possible, nonstop to Highcliff. Judging by its condition, it was a wonder it had made it at all. Grasping the ailing bird, Aelfwynne undid the thong that secured a tiny missive to its leg.

Unrolling the parchment, the high wizard staggered as he read aloud, "Beset on all sides in the Wizard's Sleeve. If the duke commands the guild, we're finished. The throne mustn't fall into his hands. The heir's safety is paramount. Protect her at all costs. Khae."

Dragon Sect

The slip of paper fluttered to Aelfwynne's feet as he hung onto the side of the stone table. "It's worse than I thought." His haunted eyes searched Scale's and then Pecklyn's. "Thank the Fae, Ouderling made it back yesterday. Bring her to me at once."

"Yes, Master." Pecklyn bolted from the lair, using a hand to help swing him into the descending passageway beyond.

Scale didn't know what to say. He stroked the exhausted raven, trying to smooth its unkempt feathers and lost track of time watching Aelfwynne aimlessly pace the chamber; the high wizard stopping from time to time to stare forlornly out the window.

The sun had risen high over the lake when the sound of rapid footfalls approached the lair.

"Master Aelfwynne, come quick! Hyperion needs you!" Ashe cried out, bursting into the chamber.

The spasm that shook Aelfwynne who stood staring blankly at the broken crystal shard and the dying raven was clearly visible. Scale grabbed his upper arm to steady him.

Aelfwynne's large head wavered on his shoulders as he regarded the elf with peculiar hair. "What's happened?"

Ashe exchanged worried glances with Scale—the Guardian apparently noting the high wizard's frail appearance. "Her dragonling's gone."

Aelfwynne blinked dumbly. "Gone? What do mean, gone? He must be in the complex somewhere."

"Hyperion can't sense his presence."

Scale didn't know all there was to know about dragonkind, but he knew enough to appreciate that if Hyperion claimed she could no longer sense her dragonling, that either meant he had flown off or was dead.

The pressures of being the high wizard, especially with the significant happenings of the moment, had visibly affected

Aelfwynne. The goblin wavered in Scale's grasp, his wizard's sickness afflicting him—evident by sporadic bouts of trembling.

Taking charge, Scale ordered, "Check the tunnels and send someone to search the shoreline below the promontory."

Ashe nodded and bolted from the room.

Sweat soaked Scale's tunic. About to release his hold on the high wizard, he decided he'd better hang on a moment longer as Pecklyn stormed into the lair, his face paler than his hair.

"She's gone!" Pecklyn said, taking in the fact that Scale hung onto the goblin.

Aelfwynne's insignificant weight threatened to pull free of Scale's grasp as his body attempted to slump to the floor.

"Nor could I find Jyllana."

Scale gripped the side of the stone slab, not sure whether he would be able to support Aelfwynne much longer. Easing the high wizard into a sitting position—the goblin's back against the side of the table, Scale said, "Have you asked the dragons?"

Pecklyn visibly swallowed. "According to Kingstone, Dagomar and Miragan are missing as well."

Not knowing what to do, Scale searched the chamber as if the answer would magically present itself. His gaze settled on the raven. The bird lying motionless beside the broken crystal shard was too much to bear. As if the raven's death symbolized the dire events unfolding across the kingdom.

Sliding to his rump beside the high wizard, Scale stared blankly past Pecklyn to the chamber's exit wondering if the world had come to an inglorious end.

Dragon Sect

Eyes of a Watcher

How the dragons knew where to find the same place they had camped deep in the mountains of the kingdom of man the last time they had flown this way was a mystery to Jyllana. After starting a fire for her and Ouderling, Dagomar and Miragan had flown away to forage for themselves.

Ouderling finished her meagre meal of fruit and nuts, and washed it down with a long pull from her waterskin. Putting the leather vacuum on the large rock she shared with Jyllana, she smiled through a face-devouring yawn. "I can't believe how tiring it is to ride all day. I can't imagine how Miragan feels carrying my sorry carcass around for as long as she has."

Jyllana nearly choked on a mouthful of food. Ouderling was lucky to weigh half of what she did. Restraining her laughter, for some reason, she was reminded of a question she had wanted to ask the princess for a long time now. "So, what really happened to your previous protectors?"

Ouderling frowned in mid-stretch. "What would make you ask that?"

"Don't know. Just thought of it."

Ouderling let her arms drop to her side, regarding Jyllana in thought. "Different reasons, really. My protector while growing up was amazing. I loved her. She played with me and introduced me to my love of horses."

"You mean old lady Meeran?"

Ouderling smiled warmly. "Yes. That's her."

"She wasn't a Home Guard."

"No, I guess she wasn't. Didn't really need one when I was young. I answered to her without question."

"What happened to change that. She's still alive, isn't she?"

Ouderling's smile faded. "Yes, but she's not right in the head anymore. Babbles on about things that don't make sense. Poor thing. She was such a happy elf."

"That's a shame."

"Ya, but I'd be happy to reach seven hundred and be as spry as she was until recently."

"That's true. Not many of us will reach that age." Jyllana nodded appreciatively. "And that's when…," she frowned, "the one with long, blonde hair, much like your own, took over?"

Ouderling chuckled. "Ya. Good old, Hertrude. I liked her actually, but mother didn't. Apparently, Hertrude took advantage of her position."

"Really? How?"

"Funny you bring it up. I'd never given it much thought before. Now that I think on it, I see what mother was talking about. It didn't happen at once, mind you, but before long, Hertrude was receiving the same attention I got from the chamberlain staff." She nodded, eyes widening with the revelation. "More even. The staff ended up paying more attention to her than me." She shrugged. "Not that I cared.

She was more than welcome to it as far as I was concerned. Anyway, mother got wind of it…Through Ryona, I think."

"And that's when Braunhilde took over?"

Ouderling's eyes darkened, matching her tone. "That witch. Father said we should've beheaded her."

Jyllana gaped. She had heard rumours regarding the abuse the former Home Guard had inflicted on Ouderling—physically and mentally if she remembered correctly.

"Oh, don't worry." Ouderling rolled her eyes. "He would never do such a thing. Father's been known to say mean things in private, but he never actually follows through with them. He's too nice, though he sure can berate someone who's done him wrong."

Jyllana nodded. She wanted to ask about Braunhilde's transgressions, but it wasn't her place. The more she had gotten to know Ouderling, the more she considered the princess a friend rather than someone she was supposed to protect. Even so, she didn't think their relationship had grown intimate enough to broach a subject as delicate as that.

Ouderling's head snapped sideways, intense eyes searching the darkness beyond the campfire's glow.

"The dragons?" Jyllana asked, her daggers in hand before her feet hit the ground.

"Shh," Ouderling warned.

The light of the quarter moon did little to illuminate the crags towering around them. Dark shadows concealed ravines and crevices that stared back at them—the ledge they rested on dropped away sharply on three sides.

Ouderling pulled her dagger free—the wicked-looking blade's tiny gems and finely-wrought ribbons of gold gleaming in the fire's glow.

Jyllana swallowed despite herself. Eolande had spoken to her about the princess' dagger. Soulbiter was rumoured to have come from another world. She wasn't sure she believed that, but when asked, Ouderling had confirmed the reaction she had experienced when first touching the ivory-tusked handle. The blade had seemed alive. If Soulbiter's edge was sharp enough to sever stone, she hoped to never have to face its business end.

Stopping on the brink of the ledge, careful not to step on anything loose, Jyllana prepared to grab Ouderling should the need arise.

The princess stared at a spot high in the mountains, across a wide chasm separating them from the next peak.

Responsible for the princess' safety, it frustrated Jyllana to no end that Ouderling's dark vision surpassed her own. She whispered, "What do you see?"

Ouderling didn't respond at first, her narrow-eyed gaze intent on a certain spot. "Nothing, but I'm sure something's out there, watching us."

The tension eased from Jyllana's taut muscles. They were in the mountains. All kinds of animals lived on the heights. Many of them nocturnal. The campfire would stand out for leagues around, its unusual light surely enough to attract an animal's curiosity.

Not taking her eyes from the distant slopes, Ouderling asked, "Can't you sense it?"

Jyllana concentrated on their surroundings—listening intently to the incessant buzzing, croaking, and hooting of various creatures. If there was something, or *someone*, nefarious watching them, it wasn't making itself known to her, but she respected the princess' magic. She could only assume that Ouderling's nature's essence had detected the eyes of a watcher. They would be well advised to heed the forewarning. She squinted, but it was no use. "Not really. What do you think it is?"

"Hard to tell from here. Whoever it is, I'm getting the feeling I've met them before."

Jyllana frowned—the simple statement heightening her concern. If the watcher didn't mean the princess harm, there was no reason not to show its face. Searching the skies, she silently called for the dragons' return.

As if in answer to her unspoken plea, a screech disturbed the night—the hair-raising sound echoing eerily into the distance.

Jyllana's nerves jumped. "We should get away from the edge."

Thankfully, Ouderling didn't argue.

A higher-pitched shriek reverberated off the slopes.

"There!" Walking quickly in the direction of the campfire, Ouderling pointed back to where she had been looking.

It took Jyllana a few moments to detect the movement amongst the murky backdrop of the distant heights, but there was no doubt that a shadow had separated itself from the darkness and was winging its way toward them.

An ear-piercing shriek behind them shot a jolt of cold fear up Jyllana's spine—the blast of wind overhead causing her to duck. Miragan dropped out of the sky, landing between them and the brink—the wyvern's attention rivetted on the silhouette crossing the valley.

"Mir, what is it?" Ouderling asked.

Before Miragan answered, Dagomar appeared from below the ledge and hovered; flames dripping from his open maw. *"No need to be alarmed, pretty lady. It seems your dragon has followed us."*

"My dragon?" Ouderling turned a perplexed stare at Jyllana. As soon as the words left the princess' lips, her jaw dropped. "Keaf?"

Oh, great, that's all we need, Jyllana thought.

Dragon Sect

The original screech they had heard sounded again, closer, its high pitch making Jyllana's teeth ache.

The green dragonling that had terrorized the Highcliff Hatching Warren appeared from beyond Dagomar, flying around the red dragon and landing on top of the campfire. Ashes, flames, and dislodged logs scattered in all directions.

Standing amidst the obliterated campfire, Keaf flapped his wings, steadying his erratic landing. Appearing satisfied with himself, he folded his wings against his body and tilted his head; intense amber eyes staring at Ouderling.

The princess latched onto Jyllana's forearm for support, her knees threatening to buckle underneath her. "Keaf. What're you doing here?"

Keaf bowed his head. *"Your dragon companion has arrived."*

Dragon Sect

Life Debt

King Graham Alexander Svelte, as Braen had come to know the monarch of Carillon, steepled his fingers in front of his face to regard Braen across a small table separating them in the king's private chambers. The last few days spent in a castle of man had been interesting. Braen had ostensibly wanted to venture north in search of enlightenment—albeit, it had taken his uncle to force his hand. He had secretly desired to prove his theory that man, as a race, didn't epitomize the evil that his fellow elves had made their race out to be.

After a couple of whirlwind days in which Alexis had shown him around the keep of Fort Carillon and the surrounding city, introducing him to the locals that the prince claimed were in the king's trust, Braen was called to King Graham's private chambers, to ask him more about the conditions in South March—the ever-present king's guard asked to leave so that they might speak openly.

Braen considered the guard's dismissal unusual, but as their discussion evolved, he came to understand that the king's benevolent attitude toward the elves was one that would land him in trouble with his peers should word spread through the kingdom of Carillon and beyond that he sympathized with South March's plight.

"Before I say anything further," King Graham said through his hands. "What's so special about the book you mentioned the other day?"

Braen wasn't sure how to respond without sounding condescending. He remembered saying to Duke Orlythe when his uncle had asked him the same question, *'That book goes a long way to prove that man, no matter how barbaric we've been led to believe them to be, is capable of the most sublime civility.'* He didn't dare say that to the two men before him.

Clearing his throat in hopes of finding a delicate way to answer the question, he said, "There are those in South March who believe the kingdoms of man are…How can I say…?"

"Uncouth?" the king suggested with a raised eyebrow.

Braen swallowed, embarrassed.

The king smiled. "It's okay, son of Odyne. I'm of the view that this sentiment isn't far from the truth." Casting a glance at Alexis, he added, "Present company excepted, of course."

"If it makes you feel any better," Braen said, "not all elves think that way. Every race has its shortcomings."

"Especially those in Sarsen Rest."

Braen didn't know what to make of that, but when the king dropped his hands to reveal a slight smirk, he chuckled. "They'd be the first to laugh at that, I'm sure. But I defy you to find a harder working people."

Graham nodded. "Or meaner if crossed."

"I can just imagine."

Dragon Sect

Alexis sat up straighter. "From everything I've heard, Father, I think it's time we pay a visit to our friends south of Nordicia."

"I'm inclined to agree. However, if events in South March are as dire as our mutual friend makes it sound, I fear the resulting fallout will bring with it considerable ramifications to the kingdoms of man," Graham remarked, and turned his attention on Alexis. "That said, I'm loath to leave Carillon without a proper Zephyr Knight to ward her. You're to accompany Braen to South March on your own and determine the state of affairs firsthand. Travel the path of the dragon and let those who need to know that there may be need to enact the protocol. It's imperative the Knights of the Wind are prepared to march should banners be called."

Alexis dipped his chin.

Graham addressed Braen, "Should Carillon's assistance be required, seek out the Queen of the Elves. She'll know how to get word to me in an expeditious manner."

Braen struggled to keep his jaw from dropping.

The king picked up on it. "You're understandably naïve to the ways of the greater world, elven prince. Rest assured, the Zephyr Knights will answer the call should your aunt have need of our aid. Our name holds sway in many regions of the five kingdoms. The house of Svelte will honour our life debt to Nyxa the Fist."

"I…I don't know what to say," Braen whispered. "Without trying to sound ungrateful, I'm finding it difficult to fathom how fate brought Alexis and I together, and thus cannot help wondering if there is something else at play here."

Graham's tone was firm. "Not everything is as magical as the elves, I'm afraid."

Braen frowned.

Dragon Sect

"I've been keeping an eye on your kingdom for some time now. Ever since Princess Ouderling arrived at Highcliff."

Braen no longer cared that his chin dropped.

"From everything you've told us, it's starting to become clear why I haven't heard from my source for some time now."

"Your source?"

"My spy, if you will."

Braen's frown deepened.

"How do you think my son found you? I assure you it wasn't by chance. The five kingdoms cover a large area. Without the aid of the ancient warrior, there's no way we would've known about your travels north. Even with that information, it was fortunate Alexis was already in the south and spotted you haggling with a baker in Apexceal."

Braen cocked his head. "Ancient warrior?"

The king sat back, folding his arms below his broad chest. "As the son of Princess Odyne, you certainly must know of the infamous elf who terrorized the kingdoms of man and the lands of the elves alike during Nyxa's rise to power. According to legends handed down for generations here in Carillon, unless one had a wing of dragons at their back and a battalion of seasoned fighters at their side, they would've been foolish to engage Nyxa's Demon Rogue."

The name meant nothing to Braen. Being Odyne's son, he hadn't been as involved in court life as his cousins Ordyl or Ouderling. "I have no idea who you're talking about."

The king seemed surprised. "You must know the mighty Xantha. She's been feeding Carillon vital information regarding the movement of the elves since well before Nyxa's demise."

Flummoxed, Braen was glad for the support of the wooden chair beneath him, for surely he would have hit the ground.

Dragon Sect

Ouderling's Folly

"**Marris,**" Ouderling whispered longingly as the stable yards outside the eastern ramparts of Borreraig Palace slipped by far below. It was all she could do not to insist that Miragan take her down. It had taken almost three-quarters of a year to realize what a miserable wretch she had been toward the love of her life. The poor groom hadn't deserved to be treated the way she had dealt with him during those last days before her exile.

Obvious to her now, he had acted in her best interest. If he had done what she had suggested back then and just up and left Borreraig Palace with her, she would likely be dead. Her eyes misted over to the point she could barely see Dagomar and Jyllana flying off to the side. Marris would also be dead.

Thankful for the wind drying her cheeks, she pulled her attention away from the receding palace and looked forward. Jyllana had been correct this morning when she had mentioned that nothing good would come from flying over Orlythia, but being the stubborn elf she was, she had insisted.

She gritted her teeth. Never again. Marris was better off without her. Trying hard to accept the fact that she had ruined the best thing that had ever happened to her, she swallowed deeply and held her chin high. She didn't have time for trivial entertainment. She had the king of the dragons to tame.

Her breath caught in her chest. Convincing Grimclaw to come to the aid of her parents wasn't her only concern. Flapping far below, the irascible green dragon, Keaf, flew by himself, somehow keeping pace. She had believed, hoped in fact, that he would have fallen behind long ago and given up, but so far the independent cuss showed no sign of tiring.

Begrudging her rotten luck, she couldn't imagine spending the rest of her life dealing with the unruly beast. And yet, something deep inside her toyed with the thought of having her own dragon when she became queen. In light of her uncle's actions, it was becoming clearer every day that a queen who ruled with a dragon would be a more formidable sovereign to disobey.

She sighed. If only her dragon had been normal.

"Are you sure it was the princess?" Orlythe asked. Urdanya Castle was a lot quieter since Khae had withdrawn her forces into the Wizard's Sleeve.

"Yes, m'lord. Verified by three independent sources," Ryedyn answered from the far side of Braen's personal chambers where he had been going through the Prince of Urdanya's bookshelves before the duke had found him. He ruffled the pages of the thick book in his hand, intently looking at what was written on the pages. "Appears this isn't the first time she's been spotted flying north of the palace."

Orlythe had barely been able to contain his excitement at the news, but the added comment darkened his mood. "Why wasn't I informed of her previous flight?"

Dragon Sect

Ryedyn shrugged. "It's the first I've heard of it myself. It's rumoured she made a similar flight several days ago."

"Do they say where she went?"

"No, m'lord."

"I'll have to have a word with our Orlythian spies when I seize the throne. How current is their information?"

"The raven was sent yesterday."

"So, for all we know, she's returned to Highcliff."

Ryedyn replaced the book he had been looking at and ran his long pointer finger along the spines of the books next to it. "Hard to say. If our dragon allies hadn't abandoned us, we might know more."

The subliminal barb wasn't lost on Orlythe, but he let it pass. If he had paid more attention to Afara Maral's business, he might still have Demonic and those loyal to the rogue dragon at his command. Were that the case, it would have been a simple matter of dispatching the remaining royal contingent holed up in the Wizard's Walk while tracking down the wayward princess. When the business of usurping the Willow Throne was behind him, he fancied hiring a necromancer to bring his despicable human wizard back to life so he could kill him again with his own hands.

"I find it puzzling Aelfwynne has allowed Ouderling to roam the kingdom," Orlythe mused. "Regardless, we need a faster way of communicating her whereabouts. Surely that overstuffed magic-user at Orphic Den has a way to track her."

Ryedyn pulled another book free and blew the dust from its pages. "I imagine he has a scrying device."

"Can you not communicate with him quicker than raven flight?"

Ryedyn shrugged. "Yes, but I doubt Sagora would agree to it."

Dragon Sect

Orlythe's breathing came quicker. Jumping free of the comfortable embrace of Braen's chair, he stomped up to Ryedyn. It took all he had to keep from smacking the book from the wizard's hands. "I care less what the headmaster thinks. There's a reason the arrogant spellcaster was passed over for a goblin."

Ryedyn put the book back on the shelf and faced Orlythe.

"Go back to the Sea Witch Sceptre and make it known to Sagora that not only do I expect him to locate Ouderling, I implore he communicate at once whenever she leaves the safety of Highcliff.

"I'll broach the subject with Headmaster Sagora, though I doubt he'll be responsive to the order," Ryedyn said, holding Orlythe's stare for a moment before dropping his gaze and slipping from Braen's quarters.

Orlythe watched the exasperating wizard slink from the room, not bothering to close the door. Taking a deep breath to keep from screaming, he found himself commiserating with his sister. At least on one thing. From the outset of her reign, she had decided not to harbour a resident wizard at Borreraig Palace. Of the view that wizards had their role to play in South March, Khae had made it clear that they weren't to influence the political agendas of the duchies that comprised the realm. Thus, the wizards' guild had been given leave to house the land's most gifted personnel within a setting of like-minded individuals, with the goal of combining their knowledge to further the common good.

Orlythe snorted. He'd love to know how his headstrong sister felt about her decision now. Being faced with the prospect of an imminent battle against an entire community of wizards had likely not entered into her thinking way back then.

Dragon Sect

He located the book Ryedyn had expressed an interest in when he had first entered the room and pulled it from the shelf. *Chizel's Grimoire*. Leafing through the pages didn't do much to enlighten him as to the significance of the thick tome's contents. Ironically, Orlythe thought, he had been complicit in the death of the one member of the family who would have understood the magic book. Odyne had been the Wys' resident expert on all things arcane.

He sighed. It was times like these that he wished he had paid attention to the Chronicler and invested more time learning magical theory. His proficiency in simple elven spells had instilled in him an attitude of not needing to bother wasting his time with his nose in a book. He had been of the belief that he had known everything while growing up. Recent events, however, had prompted him to realize that perhaps his superior attitude had left him seriously lacking.

His parents had seen his potential. Had fostered it by bestowing in him responsibilities that were considered above one of his tender age while growing up. If only he had had the foresight to grasp that potential back then, he might not require the use of petulant wizards to perform the tasks that were proving beyond him.

Slamming the heavy book back into the shelf, he strode back to the bay window and stared up at the daunting chamber atop the Sea Witch Sceptre. The last place the Dragon Witch Wraith had revealed itself.

Just thinking about the creature made his skin crawl. With any luck, it had left South March in pursuit of other prey. The way things were working out with Khae's forces trapped within the Wizard's Walk boded well to further his plans. Once the Willow Throne accepted his bulk, the dragons of Highcliff would come under his control and the kingdoms of man would know a fear like they had never known before.

Dragon Sect

Everything revolved around Khae's demise, but that would have to wait until Ouderling was taken care of. A task that until this day had seemed insurmountable, but the reports of the princess leaving the sanctum of the high wizard had changed everything.

A ruthless smile crossed the Duke of Grim's face. Ouderling's folly would be the death of her mother.

Dragon Sect

Gritian Enclave

The natural dip in the terrain along the faint animal trail Alexis led them down didn't seem out of the ordinary to Braen. Earlier the previous day they had passed the southern reaches of a ring of mountains the man prince had referred to as the Muse. Other than the way the peaks sprung up from relatively flat ground, there didn't seem to be anything special about them, but Alexis had spoken of the small chain with reverence.

Cresting the northern lip of a wide, bowl-shaped basin, the animal track ahead descended into a narrow trench at the depression's bottom and continued toward the southern rise.

Curiously, Alexis halted their progress halfway down the slope and scanned their surroundings. Nothing but rugged hills rolling away on all sides of the grassy basin met their eyes—undulating hills covered in featureless scrub and pockmarked with exposed rock. The man prince dismounted and attached a lead to the front of his black warhorse's saddle. "We're being watched."

Braen swallowed deeply, but for the life of him he couldn't see where someone might be hiding. Casting a puzzled glance at his travelling companion, he thought it odd the man would dismount in the face of danger. There was no place for them to hide in the desolate landscape.

"Relax," Alexis chuckled. "As long as you're with me, you won't come to harm." Without another word, the Prince of Carillon walked his horse into the depression.

Not sure what to do, Braen slid from Seafoam's saddle—his backside appreciative of the saddle provided for him by the well-provisioned Svelte stables. Scanning the basin in all directions, expecting to see someone coming for them, he led Seafoam after his riding companion. Aside from the clip-clop of their horses' passage, the only sound that reached him was the carefree birdsong and an incessant buzz of insects.

The horses' hooves resounded within the confines of the stone trench proper but stopped as Alexis paused mid-trench to examine the western-facing wall—its lip several feet higher than his head.

Braen walked Seafoam alongside Char and examined the wall. "What're you looking for?"

"Not what. Whom."

Braen frowned, but before he could question the prince further, rock grated, rumbling the ground—the sensation lifting the fine hairs on his arms.

A slender section of the western trench recessed into the wall and slid sideways, revealing a large man with wild black hair and matching beard.

Braen's first thought was that his Uncle Orlythe stood before him. As silly as that notion seemed, it took him a terrifying moment to realize he was mistaken.

"Alexis Svelte!" the big man exclaimed as he wrapped the prince in a bone-crushing embrace, lifting his captive into the air. Looking over Alexis' shoulder, the man's shrewd, brown eyes narrowed to mere slits—focusing on Braen's exposed ears.

Braen's stomach fell at the realization of the oversight. Aside from the various animals they had encountered on their way south from Carillon, they hadn't crossed paths with another soul. He chastised himself for not donning his cowl when Alexis mentioned they were being watched.

The bear of a man lowered Alexis to the ground and stepped free of the tunnel. "And what do we have here?"

Alexis' gaze followed the newcomer's to Braen's ears. He smiled. "Viliyam, meet Prince Braen Wys, son of Odyne." He winced. "Son of the late Odyne."

Viliyam tilted his head, taking measure of Braen. "Scrawny things, these elves." He held out a hand to Braen. "Hard to believe what all the fuss was about during the Elven Wars."

"Indeed," Alexis agreed. "And yet, they sent man's sorry tail scrambling back to cower in their holes."

Viliyam turned a questioning look on the prince, but when he spoke it was to Braen. "I'm sorry to hear about your mother. A great loss to South March, I'm sure."

Braen nodded his thanks, extricating his hand from the man's painful grip.

"What brings the son of the late witch to the kingdoms of man? Surely you realize your very presence puts you in danger."

Cupping his smarting hand with his other one, Braen wasn't sure what to make of the term, 'witch,' but let it go, not wishing to cause trouble. At a loss at how to respond, thankfully Alexis answered for him.

The man prince's wary eyes scanned their surroundings. "Our elven friend comes bearing grim tidings." He tipped his head toward the gaping hole in the trench wall. "Perhaps we'd be best to discuss this inside."

Viliyam stared long and hard at Alexis before nodding his agreement. "Let me fetch someone to attend your horses."

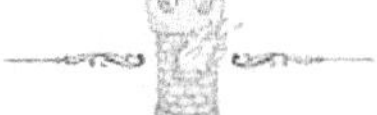

Braen wasn't sure what he thought he might see underneath the ground, but the tunnel Viliyam escorted them along was underwhelming to say the least. Viliyam led them deep into the underground complex, passing a smaller tunnel that took off to the right. "To the dungeon level and troop barracks," he said. At the next fork, the main passageway veered right in a long swooping arc that ended at the entrance to a great cavern.

"Someday this will become a most important audience hall if I have anything to say about it." Viliyam puffed out his chest. "Picture, if you will, a long aisle stretching straight down the middle of the chamber to the far end, flanked by row upon row of seating to accommodate the masses." He spread beefy arms wide. "The aisle will terminate below a grand stage lined with tiered seating for visiting nobility and their families to watch from. The greatest minds in the lands will come together in this very hall and put into motion ideas that will ultimately lead to the betterment of man…" he smiled at Braen and dipped his heavily bearded head, "and the other races too."

Viliyam had no sooner finished speaking when a sharp clang resounded from deep within the cavern, directing their collective gaze to the distant, rear corner. Noting the look of astonishment on Braen's face, he clapped a meaty hand on the elf's shoulder. "Sarsen Rest has been gracious enough to loan us the use of a team of stone masons."

"Dwarfs?" Braen asked in wonder.

A deep laugh escaped Viliyam. "They're surely not giants!"

Brae's cheeks reddened as he stared at the squat, bearded masons in leather caps swinging pickaxes and shoveling chunks of rock that appeared much too large for someone their size to move around as easily as they did.

Viliyam took note of Braen's surprise. "Have you never met a dwarf before?"

Braen shook his head.

"Oh, you're in for a real treat." A genuine smile lit up Viliyam's face. "Come, I'll introduce you," he said as he started along a meandering path around the bases of massive stalagmites rising to the lofty ceiling that was barely visible in deep shadows high overhead.

Left with little choice, Braen followed Viliyam into the subterranean chamber.

"Oi!" Viliyam bellowed to get the attention of three, dust-covered dwarfs breaking rock several feet off the cavern floor.

A red-bearded dwarf halted his pickaxe in mid-swing to look over his shoulder while his mates paused mid-shovel. Lowering his pickaxe to the ground and leaning on it, he wiped his sweaty forehead with the back of a filthy hand, smearing his face with grime. "Och, Vili. What in the god's name have you unearthed?" He squinted, examining Braen. Puzzled, his hard look returned to Viliyam. "Consortin' with pointy-ears now, are ya? That's not to go o'er well wit' yer neighbours."

"Ha! They tolerate Sarsen Rest's outcasts."

"Aye, but them's afeared o' me axe. Judging by 'is appearance, I'm doubtin' they'll be afeared o' the likes o' him. Ain't nuttin' t' the lad."

Dragon Sect

Viliyam reached up to accept the red-beard's hand and help him jump to the ground. "How quickly your folk forget the Elven Wars.

"Bah! Ain't t' be forgettin' nuttin'. Those were different times. The War Dragon was in charge back then. Ain't much to be afeared of now. Perhaps it's high time ya got yer act together and hit them agin. I daresay the elven leadership has fallen to a sorry lot."

Viliyam's grin grew.

The dwarf stared up at him, squinting one eye. "What ain't ya tellin' me, Vili?" His gaze went from Viliyam to Braen and back again.

"Unner Hill, son of O'er Hill, allow me to introduce to you, Braen Wys," Viliyam said and paused momentarily.

Braen's last name wasn't lost on Unner. The dwarf's eyes widened as Viliyam nodded.

"*Prince* Braen is the son of the late, Odyne Wys, who was of course, before her untimely death, second in line to the Willow Throne," Viliyam finished, smug satisfaction beaming from his face.

Unner looked dumbfounded. He swallowed and regarded Braen. Doffing his leather cap, be dropped to a knee and bowed low. "Me deepest apologies, me prince." He shot Viliyam a nasty sneer. "I meant ya no disrespect."

The whole scenario unfolded like an unwelcome dream. Never comfortable with his position in South March, Braen was at a loss as to how to respond to the stocky figure straight out of folklore kneeling before him.

"Oh, now you grovel." Viliyam laughed and winked for Braen's benefit. "Get up, Unner. Braen isn't one to be offended by someone as lowly as a dwarf, are you, elven prince?"

Braen swallowed his discomfort. "N-not at all. I mean, no offense taken, Mister Hill."

"Ha!" Viliyam belted out. "Mister! That's a rich one." Viliyam helped Unner to his feet.

Unner's mates scrambled down the rock face to stand on either side of him. Removing their debris-covered caps they bowed low.

"Allow me to introduce you to Unner's more civilized companions," Viliyam said and nodded to the black-bearded dwarf. "Chaynz Gor and," his gaze switched to the blonde-bearded dwarf on Unner's other side, "Smyte Garroch. master craftsdwarfs from Sarsen Rest. Their presence in the Gritian Enclave is due to this man's father." He indicated Alexis.

"It's an honour to meet you, Smyte, Chaynz, and of course, Unner," Braen acknowledged the dwarfs. "South March's history is rich with dwarven involvement. May it become so again in the years to come."

"My prince," the dwarfs said in unison.

Braen smiled and turned a slow circle, taking in the immense scope of the natural cavern. "From what Viliyam tells me, the construction of this audience chamber is quite an undertaking."

Unner squeezed his cap between grimy fists, barely meeting Braen's gaze. "Och, tis nothin', Your Majesty. Me an' me mates will 'ave 'er done in less than a turn."

Braen searched his memory. He had heard that phrase before. Likely from a book. At a loss, he asked, "What exactly is a turn?"

Unner looked up with a gap-toothed grin. "A century, Your Highness." He nodded and his companions did also.

"A century?" Braen gasped. "That's a long time."

"'Tis nothin' but a blink o' the eye when ya love what yer about. The score o' us'll have 'er done an' polished afore the stone changes hue."

Braen searched the cavern. "You mean there's more of you from Sarsen Rest?"

"Of a certainty, Your Highness. Fancy rock like what's required ain't t' be had in the Gritian Hills. Many are required t' harvest the lustrous rock we'll be needin' t' make the chamber befittin' a king. Why, there'll be two rows o' columns spanning a wide aisleway from the entrance clear t' the rear wall. Polished marble pillars will encase the rock drippin's from floor t' ceiling, givin' the hall an impressive feel, eh?"

Braen didn't know much about the geography of the region, but he figured the barren terrain he and Alexis had travelled wasn't conducive to mining finer stone. He recalled the mountains they had passed and was impressed. "You mean to tell me you're hauling stone all the way down from the Muse?"

"Och no, Your Majesty. If it were that easy. Hah! We found a stash of quality stone deep in the Undying Wall."

Braen's corresponding frown elicited a response from Alexis. "The Undying Wall is a formidable land break that separates the northern and southern kingdoms of man. Days south of here. We'll cross the divide once we've finished our business with Viliyam."

Braen raised his eyebrows and turned his attention back to Unner and his mates. "Sounds like you've got a lot of work ahead of you. I'm sure it'll be impressive. I'd love to see it when it's done."

"Och, you're a wee flatterer, Your Majesty. Perhaps we may be of service in the southlands in a turn."

Dragon Sect

Braen smiled. "I'm sure your expertise would do an elven court proud."

Seated beside Alexis and across from Viliyam in a small grotto deep within the Gritian Enclave, Braen placed his empty platter on a low table between them. Thankful for the hot meal, and the mind-numbing effects of the mulled wine, the past few weeks had taken their toll on him physically and mentally. The brief respite in Carillon had done little to ease the aches and pains of his long journey.

Still unsure what he searched for, being in the company of a man he'd recently met, but who on all outward appearances accepted him for who he was—specifically an elf—had done wonders for his spirit. Meeting the dwarven craftsmen had been one of the most unique experiences in his life. He had read so much about them, but to see one in person and confirm they weren't just folklore to be read about in old tomes left him giddy on the inside.

Viliyam dabbed at his mouth with a hand towel and placed it on top of his empty platter. During the course of the meal, Alexis had taken the opportunity to inform him about the situation unfolding in South March. Sitting back, Viliyam nodded at Braen. "I commend your bravery. Venturing this far into the kingdoms of man could not have been a decision you made lightly. I don't have to tell you the peril you've been in since leaving your realm. Will be in, in fact, until you return to South March."

If Viliyam knew my uncle, he might change his mind as to which kingdom might be safer, Braen thought. He flashed Alexis a look as he responded to Viliyam. "Don't be so quick with your praise. Truth be told, I hadn't come in search of aid. In a roundabout way, my intent was to flee the events unfolding in South March. Bravery's not something I'd attribute to my actions."

Viliyam considered him long and hard. Folding his arms across his girth, he nodded. "And yet, here you are."

"If not for Alexis' timely intervention, I'd be lying at the bottom of the ocean. He's the courageous one."

"That's true. The Prince of Carillon is a man to be taken seriously. That being said, if Alexis deems you worthy of saving, I'll not question his motives. King Graham obviously concurs, else we'd not be having this conversation." He turned his attention on Alexis. "Am I right in assuming this is more than a courtesy visit?"

"You are," Alexis confirmed.

Viliyam raised his eyebrows for Alexis to continue.

"Father wants me to rally the Knights of the Wind."

Viliyam nodded. "You're following the path of the dragon, I take it."

"For the most part. I decided in the name of expedience it would be best if Braen and I didn't take the time to visit the Birth, though they definitely should be roused."

"Leave that with me," Viliyam said. "Are we to mobilize?"

"Not yet. We'll send word through Queen Khae should the situation prove as dire as we suspect. Just be sure to have your people ready to march on a moment's notice."

"Will you bother with Nordicia?"

Alexis sighed. "I don't have much of a choice."

"They'll likely not take kindly to…" Viliyam nodded at Braen.

"Ya, that's what I'm thinking as well. I'll have him wait in the woods."

"Now that I think on it, I don't believe the King of Nordicia is a big fan of your father either. He'll suspect something's amiss if you suddenly show up on his doorstep."

"I know." Alexis sighed again. "But it must be done. I'm thinking we'll need every knight we can muster. Not only is the Nordician contingent substantial, but they control the only land access to South March west of the swamp. I don't envy sending the Knights of the Wind through the wastelands. It would take too long."

"Aye. Should they survive, you mean." Viliyam said matter-of-factly. "Better the enemy you know, I guess. I wish you luck. Rest assured, there'll be war amongst the kingdoms of man if you come to harm."

Dragon Sect

To the Queen

Pecklyn pulled on the cinch securing the flap on his leather rucksack for the umpteenth time as he awaited the arrival of Aelfwynne on the promontory fronting Highcliff. Ever conscious of the rigours of dragonflight, he hoped that one day his routine of securing his equipment over and over again might save his life. To his left, Dawnbreaker and Mirage squatted on the edge of the platform, keeping their own counsel.

Movement from the main entrance drew his attention. Balewynd appeared, followed closely by Xantha and Aelfwynne—the odd couple's difference in stature comical had the events that had prompted the upcoming mission not have been so dire.

Balewynd broke away from the high wizard and the elder Guardian, making her way to Mirage. In a movement so graceful and fast, it was hard to tell how she mounted her dragon's neck. Firmly astride the base of Mirage's neck, she leaned in to speak softly to her life companion.

There was no evidence in the high wizard's demeanour or the way he carried himself that he retained any lasting effects from the unusual breakdown he had suffered a couple of days before. Since then, he had held long talks with everyone living in Highcliff with regard to what their next move should be. An uncommon occurrence for the regular Highcliff Guardians as the goblin rarely consulted anyone before making a decision, except for perhaps his soulmate, Xantha.

"Master." Pecklyn dipped his head in respect.

Never one for small talk, the high wizard got to the point. "You're to fly straight to the Wizard's Walk and extricate the queen and king from harm's way. At no point are you to engage Orlythe's troops. Is that understood?"

"Yes, Master Aelfwynne."

"Do *not* deviate from the plan, even if the queen tells you otherwise. Once in the air, she'll have no choice but to accept it," Aelfwynne said, his tone brooking no argument.

Pecklyn couldn't imagine going against the queen's wishes should she demand to be flown elsewhere.

Aelfwynne must have picked up on his reservation. "If they give you a hard time about coming to Highcliff, I'll deal with them."

"Yes, Master." Pecklyn dipped his chin again, pulled on the cinch strap of his rucksack, and started across the platform, but Xantha's hand on his shoulder stopped him.

The elder Guardian nodded toward Balewynd who was scanning the misty skies over Crystal Lake. "Take care of that one."

"Of course," Pecklyn responded with a frown, the request seeming an odd one. Xantha knew them well enough to know that they always looked out for each other.

"I sense in her a recklessness," Xantha elaborated.

Pecklyn blinked at that. He had thought the same thing recently. His best friend hadn't been herself since the Battle at the Gate, but lately, she had taken her usual aloofness to a new level. He couldn't recall the last time he had seen her pretty smile.

He nodded and went to pull away but Xantha's grip was remarkably strong for someone her age.

"I fear she's becoming more like I was when I was her age," Xantha whispered.

Gooseflesh flushed Pecklyn's skin. Xantha was rumoured to have been the meanest fighter in Queen Nyxa's army. If anything, the elder's comparison was a great compliment to Balewynd.

"She teeters on the brink of a warrior's madness. There is bloodlust in her eyes. I can see it clearly as I was once stricken by it. In her is a greatness that hides behind a protective barrier, keeping the worries of the world at bay. Things are likely to go sideways when you arrive in the Wizard's Sleeve. Your dragons' presence will undoubtedly invoke a response from the wizards' guild. Should that happen," Xantha nodded again toward Balewynd who now sat impatiently staring at them, "I fear she'll try to take on the guild by herself."

Xantha released Pecklyn, her voice dropping to a whisper. "I know I would have."

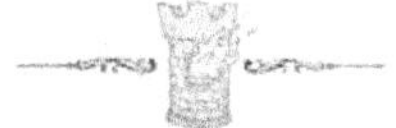

Taking a westerly berth around Castle Grim to avoid being seen, the flight north was uneventful. In tune with nature, Dawnbreaker and Mirage pointed out signs of mass troop movement above the Scale River along the main roadway toward Urdanya. They veered inland north of Alywind, winging northwestward across a seemingly endless tract of deep forest.

As the sun dropped over the distant ocean, the unmistakable stain of Urdanya marred the land. Even from the great distance separating them, Urdanya Castle stood stark against the skyline. Pecklyn had the urge to visit the coastal city and confront Duke Orlythe, but he was careful not to voice that to Balewynd. His brooding companion would likely take him up on the idea.

Leaning over Dawnbreaker's thick neck, he asked, "How're you making out? If you need to rest, let me know."

Two, long, graceful wingbeats later Dawnbreaker's gruff voice sounded in his head. *"I will fly until Queen Khae is safe."*

Pecklyn smiled and rubbed her rough skin beneath a large scale. "I know you will, m'lady, but we've a long way to go before we reach the queen."

"Master Aelfwynne said she was in danger. My duty is to protect her."

"You'll be no good to her if you fly yourself to death."

"Nor will I be if she dies before we reach her."

Pecklyn had to concede the point. As much as his thighs, hips, lower back, and shoulders were aching with the effort of clinging to Dawnbreaker, he would endure the pain until he fell from her shoulders if it meant the difference to the queen's life. "You know your limits. Just remember to keep up your strength. A short break to eat and drink will likely do us all the world of good."

In the lengthening rays of the dying day, Dawnbreaker and Mirage set their riders down in a small clearing in the centre of the midland forest and left them to forage for game.

Before the twilight faded into night, they were airborne again—the two dragons flying faster than Pecklyn deemed sustainable. Having flown across South March before, he knew that even at their increased pace, if they flew straight through the night, they would be lucky to reach the Wizard's

Dragon Sect

Sleeve before midday tomorrow. Once there, the Fae only knew where they might find the queen.

Silently urging Dawnbreaker to fly a little faster, he shrugged in a futile attempt to relieve his shoulders of the ever-pressing weight of his rucksack's straps. When Dawnbreaker said something, she always followed through.

It promised to be a long night.

Dragon Sect

Wayward Prince

Lylande landed her wyvern beside the Focal Stone to allow Scale and Aelfwynne to dismount.

Without a word of thanks, the high wizard stepped up to the earth blood pool and stared at a stalactite high overhead, scratching his head.

Embarrassed for his master's lack of manners, Scale dipped his head to Lylande and muttered, "Thank you."

"You're most welcome, young Scale," Lylande said in a meek voice. "If you have further need of our assistance, just think Sarafinious, and we will come."

"Sarafinious?" Scale asked.

"My wyvern, of course."

"Oh. Oh yes! Sorry, I'm still new here."

"No worries. I imagine an adept's mind has more important matters to dwell on than those of the caretakers."

"Adept! Pfft." Aelfwynne grumbled, not taking his attention from the cavern roof. "There ain't much going on in the big galoop's head."

Lylande, Sarafinious, and Scale stared at the goblin.

Dragon Sect

Scale rolled his eyes for Lylande's benefit. "Don't mind him."

"Master Aelfwynne bears the weight of the world. Someday, perhaps, you may rethink your decision to become the next high wizard."

Looking around, Scale realized the female voice in his head could only belong to the wondrous creature, Sarafinious. Her statement regarding his future shocked him. He had never once contemplated becoming the high wizard. In fact, he had never thought beyond his dream of being able to use his magic with a little more ease than he could at the moment. True, he had learned a lot under Aelfwynne's tutelage over the intervening months since rescuing the goblin from Crag's Forge, but he didn't fool himself. He had a *long* way to go.

All he could do was blink at the diminutive wyvern.

Sarafinious nodded her head. *"Master Aelfwynne wouldn't waste his time training a simple wizard. For him to put any effort into your development can only mean he deems your magical ability superior to most."*

Scale gaped, flashing a quick look at the high wizard, expecting a snarky response.

"Oh, don't worry about him. I know better than to speak thus in his presence. Only you can hear me." Sarafinious ruffled her wings and crouched, ready to spring into the air. *"Don't let his snarky disposition undermine your confidence. As much as he may snip at you, know this: he doesn't suffer fools. You're more powerful than he may lead you to think. Believe in yourself, and the world will follow."*

Before Scale could respond, Sarafinious leapt into the air, her rapid wingbeats ruffling his hair as she flew Lylande to a distant part of the cavern ceiling.

"It's getting worse."

Aelfwynne's sudden growl snapped Scale's attention from Sarafinious' receding form. "I'm sorry."

"Hmph. A truer statement has never been spoken."

Scale frowned.

"The Focal Stone, you witless northerner. The crack is expanding. It's weakened state is a presage of disaster."

Scale blinked in confusion at the goblin's words. "Presage of disaster?"

"An omen, you imbecile. A portent of things to come. I said before, had you cared to listen, if the Focal Stone should fall, Highcliff will as well."

"That's not good."

Aelfwynne's brow knit together, considering Scale with consternation. "Of course it's not good. It never ceases to amaze me the things that come out of your mouth."

Scale wondered why he bothered saying anything at all.

Chin in one hand, Aelfwynne stared at the earth blood, obviously contemplating something serious. His over-sized goblin head began to nod, imperceptibly at first but more vigourously as his beady eyes widened. "We're running out of time. I must find a wizard with a man's taint." His eyes flicked to Scale. "Call your dragon. I need you to locate Odyne's son and bring him to me."

Scale's jaw dropped. "You want me to find Braen?"

"Did Odyne have a son I don't know about?" Aelfwynne growled.

"No, but—"

"Of course, Braen, you bumbling fool. Who else would I be talking about?" Aelfwynne started along the path toward the exit, walking faster than usual.

"It's just that…" Scale trailed off, falling into step behind him. There was no use explaining himself when the high wizard was in one of his moods—which was always.

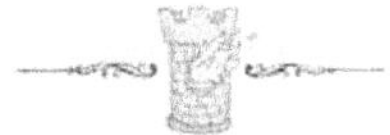 Dragon Sect

"You sure you have everything you'll need?" Xantha asked. In her arms, Little Dithreab reached out to touch Scale with small, claw-tipped fingers.

Not comfortable around babies, Scale stepped back, thinking that he'd never seen an uglier baby in his life. He smiled despite his revulsion—Aelfwynne's son was so hideous, he almost appeared cute. He shrugged, his fur-lined tunic of thick leather heavy, and patted the rucksack cradled in his arms. "Um, yes. At least, I hope so. I've never really flown anywhere before."

"I'm glad you're wearing your cold weather gear. The mountains in the north can be cold year-round."

"Bah. Do him good to learn the hard way," Aelfwynne grumbled. The goblin turned away from Zorain who waited for Scale in front of the stone benches that were carved into the base of the cliff, midway along the inside of the ledge.

Zorain and the high wizard had spoken at length, not bothering to include the others in their conversation. Scale made a point to ask his dragon about it once they were airborne.

"Well, boy. I don't have to tell you the world is depending on you not to mess this up. Remember everything I taught you. With any luck, you'll prove me wrong and actually succeed at something for a change."

"Aelfwynne!" Xantha admonished.

"Um, thanks, I think," Scale said, diverting his eyes so he didn't have to witness the scathing glare of his mentor. Although used to the high wizard's treatment, for some reason Aelfwynne's remarks cut him deeper than they normally would have. Taking a deep breath to keep from reacting to the abuse, he said, "I'll do my best."

"That's what I'm afraid of," Aelfwynne grumbled.

"Don't mind him," Xantha interrupted, forcing Dithreab into Aelfwynne's arms—the high wizard not appearing to appreciate the act.

She embraced Scale and whispered, "If cranky-puss thought anyone more capable of finding Braen, he would've sent them. Just make sure you come back safe."

Scale stepped back and nodded, his cheeks reddening—a warmth flushed his skin. The esteemed warrior of bygone days had echoed the sentiments of the beautiful wyvern, Sarafinious. "Thank you, Elder Xantha. I won't let you down."

"If you stand around any longer, we're going to all die of old age," Aelfwynne grumbled.

Scale swallowed. "Yes, Master."

He forced a smile for Xantha and left the bizarre couple. Clambering aboard Zorain, he patted the white dragon's neck. "Let's get out of here."

As the mountainside fell away, so did Scale's anxiety—regardless of the fact that he didn't have a clue where he was going or how he was going to locate the wayward prince.

Dragon Sect

In the Presence of Certain Death

"*Grimclaw's* not likely to be any more receptive to you when we confront him again, pretty lady. I fear for your safety."

"It'll be okay. You'll see." Ouderling patted Miragan's neck, unsure of who she was trying to convince, Miragan or herself. Though she had fallen asleep at some point last night, it didn't feel like she had gotten much rest. Coupled with the arrival of Keaf, her anxiety about their upcoming meeting with the king of the dragons wouldn't allow her to think of anything else.

In order to save her parents, she had to persuade the great blue dragon to put aside his resentment of how the elves of the past had manipulated the dragons to achieve their own goals. Certain elves, she corrected herself. Not everyone viewed the majestic creatures as a means to an end. Unfortunately, a certain high-ranking elf had been at the heart of the issue. She gritted her teeth. Her uncle's deeds had done a lot of damage to the realm of South March. It was hard to believe he was related to her mother.

Dragon Sect

A grim smile crossed her face. What Orlythe needed was for her grandmother to return from the dead and throw him over a knee and spank a lick of sense into him.

She sighed. It was too late for that. The irrevocable harm had already been done. There could be no redemption for her uncle. Somehow, out of the infinite goodness of her mother's heart, the queen had found a way to forgive him after the Battle at the Gate. Well, perhaps not forgive him for his complicity in the heinous events that had transpired, but to grant him a begrudging clemency at having being duped by his human wizard and the Dragon Witch Wraith. She doubted he would be afforded such leniency a second time should her parents survive.

As if sensing her fear of her parents' impending doom, Miragan increased her speed.

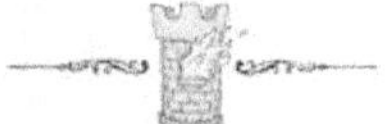

Rounding the white obelisk that marked the western end of the pass that housed Grimclaw's dragon colony, Ouderling was sure she was about to throw up.

On Dagomar's order, he and Jyllana assumed the lead.

Far below, skimming the course of a winding river bisecting the forested, valley floor, Keaf's erratic flight did little to ease her tension. As much as she hadn't asked for the dragonling's attention, she couldn't help but feel responsible for his safety. Their impending rendezvous with Grimclaw placed them all in peril.

Though profoundly beautiful, the wide valley of Dragonfang Pass was basically identical in appearance for as far as the eye could see. It hadn't been that long since they had flown this way, but Ouderling couldn't recall how far they had to fly to reach the cliffs where they had found Grimclaw.

"Dragons."

Dragon Sect

Dagomar's voice startled her. Looking forward, Ouderling spotted them. Two dragons drifted over the valley, seemingly flying to intercept them. As she watched, several more broke away from the cliffs on the northern edge of the pass—winging their way toward them. Hard to tell from such a distance, Ouderling was sure Grimclaw was absent from the greeting party.

The last words Grimclaw had spoken to them reverberated through Ouderling's mind as six dragons spread across the valley, *'If you're still here when I return, South March will find itself less four souls.'*

There had been no doubt in the tone of his voice that he wasn't afraid to back up his claim. If they were to survive their encounter with the infamous creature, she needed to say something so profound that it would quell the fire roiling in the back of his throat. She swallowed hard, wondering for the life of her what those words might be.

"You dare return with the two-legged wyrm?"

A voice thundered in her head, though she couldn't tell which dragon had spoken.

Dagomar slowed his flight to drop immediately in front of Miragan and Ouderling.

Jyllana hefted her scythe in one hand and shook it. "Come no closer or we'll drop you from the sky!"

Ouderling cringed, gaping at her protector's back. Had the elf lost her mind?

At once, the oncoming dragons surrounded them, fire dripping between spiked teeth and smoke billowing from their nostrils. Two reds, a yellow, an orange, a green, a purple, and a blue—all at least as big as Dagomar.

Cynical laughter filled her head. *"A Highcliff dragon and a wyvern? You don't stand a chance against us. Turn around or die."*

"You don't scare us, so you'll just have to face us." Jyllana proclaimed, brandishing her long polearm at each dragon in turn. "*Nobody* threatens the heir to the Willow Throne and gets away with it. Who wants to be first?"

If Dagomar resented Jyllana's bluster, he never let on—traces of flames escaped the corners of his mouth.

Miragan tensed. A wave of heat wafted back over Ouderling—the usual, gentle wyvern preparing to defend them. Miragan's fire at the ready, brimstone permeated Ouderling's nostrils. She didn't doubt for a moment that the larger dragons confronting them were in for the shock of their life if they underestimated the ferocity of her wyvern.

Hovering high over the valley floor, tense moments ensued. Just when Ouderling thought they were about to come to blows, the orange dragon winged away. *"We'll let Grimclaw decide your fate."* Diminishing laughter followed in his wake.

Two dragons split off to either side, and the blue dragon fell in behind as they made their way to where Grimclaw awaited them on the far side of the same ledge they had met days before. Of Keaf, there was no sign.

The orange dragon settled in beside Grimclaw, prepared to face Dagomar and Miragan who had landed in the centre of the clearing. The remaining dragon escort landed at various points around the clearing.

Grimclaw emitted an ominous growl. *"You're either braver than you look or dumber than your two-legged wyrm, daughter of Khae. I warned you what would happen should you return. There's no place for your kind here."*

Out of the corner of her eye, Ouderling noticed Jyllana dismount. To prevent her protector from making a fatal mistake, she leapt from Miragan's shoulders and stormed across the ledge ahead of Jyllana. If she had taken the time to consider what she was doing, she would have fallen to the ground in a quivering mess, but something deep inside urged her forward.

Stopping dangerously close to the behemoth, she pointed a thin finger at Grimclaw. "You ought to be ashamed of yourself!"

Grimclaw drew his head back in shock, his features darkening, but before he could respond, Ouderling continued, "Taking advantage of your size and numbers to threaten the prodigy of the queen who gave you life."

"Khae had nothing to do with my birth."

It was as if the very cliffside trembled when Grimclaw spoke. Hoping it wasn't obvious how badly her knees knocked together, Ouderling lifted her chin in haughty defiance. "I'm not talking about my mother. If you took the time to appreciate what's really important in life and stopped relying on your misguided perception of how things should be, you'd realize what a sorry excuse of a dragon you've become. Refusing to honour the memory of the elf queen who gave you life, you've set into motion the end of everything that is good in the world."

Grimclaw appeared to choke on an angry retort, but Ouderling didn't give him a chance to speak.

"Your loss will be welcomed by the decent creatures left behind in the wreckage that's about to befall *every* kingdom."

She wasn't sure what a dragon looked like when it gaped, but she surmised by Grimclaw's stunned expression that she had thrown him off balance. Fueled by pure adrenaline in the presence of certain death, she carried on, "As the heir to the Willow Throne, and an up-and-coming purveyor of nature's essence, your reluctance to assist in the war against the evil of the Dragon Witch Wraith will eradicate any good you might have previously done for our world. As Princess of South March, I hereby proclaim that your refusal to stand with Nyxa's prodigy is a grave insult to the War Dragon's legacy."

She nodded, cutting him off again. "That's right...I'm Nyxa's prodigy. The White Witch made herself known to my mother with the hope of saving me from the danger that has descended upon our world, and yet, you, an almighty *beast*, are blinded by your arrogance. Shame on you. On behalf of Queen Khae and in the spirit of Queen Nyxa's memory," she hocked and spat on the ground between them, "I say good riddance to Grimclaw and the sorry dragons who follow him, for everything the legendary creature of old stood for, the Grimclaw my grandmother admired is surely dead to the world."

A ghostly wind whistled across the ledge, ruffling wings and buffeting hair—the only sound disturbing the surreal silence in the wake of Ouderling's denunciation of the most feared dragon in all the lands. It was all she could do to keep from dropping to the ground—her hands visibly shaking at her sides.

In the presence of a creature so mighty that he could crush her without a second thought, she stared the old curmudgeon down. If the legendary dragon of elven lore deemed her cause unworthy, let him burn her on the spot. She couldn't imagine living if her parents were slaughtered as a result of her failure to enlist his aid.

Dragon Sect

Wizard's Spell

From high overhead, it wasn't hard to spot the queen once they had located the spires of Gullveig nestled at the foot of the Wizard's Walk. The black army of Duke Orlythe blocked the pass about a league east of the mountain-bound city, their mass a dark stain on the landscape. Though hard to estimate the size of the duke's forces, as soon as Pecklyn laid eyes on the royal contingent camped in a wider section of the pass farther east, he knew at once there was no way the queen could hope to win free without the aid of the wizards' guild. Unfortunately, there was no indication of Orphic Den's presence within the queen's ranks.

Whether out of an abundance of caution, or because the royal troops clad in green remembered the dragon assault at the Battle at the Gate, Pecklyn feared the archers watching their approach might launch an offensive against them before they had a chance to announce themselves. Luckily, Commander Keel stayed their hand. Forced to land on the opposite side of the small clearing from where the queen's pavilion was erected, they were surrounded by archers with bows at the ready and warriors with weapons drawn.

Dragon Sect

Pecklyn and Balewynd waited patiently on a tall elf who walked his horse free of those warily eyeing the dragons—the elf's shining armour and purple-plumed helm denoting him as the head of the South March army.

Commander Keel sat straight upon his armour-plated warhorse; the magnificent creature draped in a dark orange surcoat matching the queen's banner fluttering above a knot of elite elven guards. The powerfully built commander rode confidently up to Dawnbreaker and Mirage—his well-drilled horse comfortable in the company of dragons.

"Well met, Guardian Balewynd, Guardian Pecklyn. Highcliff dragons are a welcome sight. With them at the head of our army, we may yet win the day."

Balewynd nodded stoically at the commander. Pecklyn knew her keen eyes took in every aspect and nuance visible in the pass, including an intense inspection of the warriors watching them.

"Commander Keel." Pecklyn dipped his chin in acknowledgement. "It gladdens us to have found you, though our presence here is temporary."

Keel frowned at Pecklyn as the Guardian slid from Dawnbreaker's back.

"We're under strict orders from High Wizard Aelfwynne to extricate the queen and king and fly them to Highcliff."

Keel stared hard at Pecklyn. Though no emotion crossed his face, Pecklyn knew by the way the commander's stern gaze flicked between him and Balewynd, who had remained firmly astride Mirage, that the news shocked him.

A commotion rippled through the ranks from the direction of the pavilion as King Hammas followed the captain of the Queen's Shield through the crowd. Dark rings around his eyes, the king appeared haggard.

Dragon Sect

Pecklyn dropped to a knee and bowed low. "Your Highness."

Hammas nodded to Balewynd and the dragons, and surveyed the sky overhead. "Arise, Guardian Pecklyn."

Pecklyn did as he was bidden.

"Walk with me," Hammas indicated for Captain Hondrick to lead them across the camp. Lowering his voice, he said as they walked, "Your arrival during our time of need is certainly welcome, but it puzzles me. Has something happened at Highcliff to prompt Aelfwynne to deplete his protective circle of dragons?"

"Master Aelfwynne deemed it a necessary risk, Your Highness. Due to unforeseen circumstances, and to ensure the Willow Throne doesn't consider itself abandoned, he instructed us to extricate you and Her Majesty from harm's way."

Hammas put a hand in the middle of Pecklyn's chest and stopped him—his shrewd eyes causing Pecklyn discomfort. The king was as wise as the rumours proclaimed.

"What of Ouderling?"

Pecklyn swallowed, struggling to hold Hammas' gaze. He whispered, "She's gone missing."

"Gone missing?" Hammas bellowed. "What do you mean she's gone missing?"

Pecklyn searched the concerned faces around him but found no comfort there. Even though Ouderling's disappearance had nothing to do with him, Pecklyn felt guilty under the king's scrutiny. "We believe she and her protector left on dragonback. I was hoping she made her way to your position, but I see that's not the case."

"She was sent to Highcliff to be protected! Or has Highcliff forgotten the Dragon Witch Wraith has returned?" Hammas sounded upset enough to spit.

Dragon Sect

Nor could Pecklyn blame him. The Highcliff Guardians hadn't been as vigilant as they should have. On Ouderling's arrival last year, Aelfwynne had made it incumbent upon everyone that Ouderling was not to be left alone at any time unless she was within her sleeping chamber. Regarding the worried face of the king, he didn't know what to say.

Hammas shook his head. "Come with me."

It was all Pecklyn and Captain Hondrick could do to keep up with the king.

They passed beyond four attentive guards who began to challenge Pecklyn's approach but were warned off by the king's snarl, "He's with me."

Pushing through the tent flap, two of the biggest elves Pecklyn had ever seen watched him trail Hammas to a large war table in the centre of the tent.

The captain appointed to oversee the queen's personal safety watched from the far side of the table, his expression bleaker than that of the king.

It wasn't until Pecklyn stopped before the table, and was able to see what lay beyond, that he came to appreciate the gravity of the situation. Lying on her back with her hands folded across her stomach, Queen Khae stared vacantly at the tarpaulin roof.

Pecklyn struggled to find his voice. "Is she…?" he couldn't bring himself to say it.

The king knelt beside Khae's pallet—his voice enough to bring tears to Pecklyn's eyes. "She might as well be. Her spirit has flown."

Pecklyn blinked, unable to comprehend the king's meaning. "I-I don't understand, Your Highness."

Commander Keel's deep voice whispered, "We believe Her Majesty's spirit is trapped in the realm of the Fae."

Dragon Sect

The explanation did nothing to alleviate Pecklyn's confusion.

"In order to save us from certain doom, she stretched her considerable magic beyond its limits. As a result of her efforts, her spiritual essence has not returned."

"Th...that's awful. We need to get her to Master Aelfwynne."

"No!" Hammas said emphatically and stood to face them, his eyes red and glassy. "We dare not move her lest her soul not find it's way back from the wizard's spell that has ensnared it."

Pecklyn frowned, at a loss.

Commander Keel answered for the distraught king. "Judging by the lightning storm we witnessed over Orphic Den, we're of the belief that Her Majesty's essence is being prevented from returning to her body by Headmaster Sagora."

The queen's pavilion reeled around Pecklyn as he tried to make sense of what he was being told. Bewildered, the import of the king's words wasn't lost on him. If what the commander claimed was true, the future of South March was in worse shape than those at Highcliff had originally thought.

Recalling High Wizard Aelfwynne's recent breakdown, he couldn't imagine bringing the news back to him. The queen's plight would surely kill the goblin outright.

Hammas rose from Khae's side, and turned to face Pecklyn, despair on his gaunt face. "You have to help us get her back."

"Of course, Your Highness. I'll do whatever it takes."

Hammas nodded, unabashed by the tears streaking down his cheeks. "I need you and your dragons to break Headmaster Sagora's spell."

Pecklyn's eyes widened. He nodded because that was what the king would expect of him, but deep inside an unusual sense of terror gripped him. He said as calmly as possible, "It will be done, Your Highness."

Not afraid of much, Hammas' next words almost made Pecklyn's legs give out.

"Bring me the traitor's head so that we may charge against Duke Orlythe's troops with the grisly talisman perched on the end of a pike. It's time to show the rebellious elves what happens to those who rise against the rightful ruler of South March."

Dragon Sect

Faster than Dragonflight

Zorain's position as a Watchman in the Highcliff garrison had conditioned him to fly longer than was usual for most of dragonkind. If Scale wasn't mistaken, the pace of the white dragon was faster than normal as they flew north of the Steel Mountains above a terrain so vast, it was hard to tell how much ground they were covering.

The mountainous region had given way to a vast stretch of swampland. The Forbidden Swamp. A name he had read in one of the books in the Chronicler's library back at the palace.

If he remembered correctly, the Forbidden Swamp sprawled northward past three of the five kingdoms of man. Hoping to avoid detection by the barbaric race, he decided it best to keep out of sight until they reached the northern border of the kingdom of Carillon before venturing west to begin their search for the wayward prince. But as the day waned into twilight, other than a spell when they were forced to fly over an odd wall of mountains bisecting the land from east to west, the scenery never changed.

Dragon Sect

Aelfwynne's deteriorating physical and mental condition plagued Scale's thoughts. If something were to happen to the high wizard, especially considering the plight of the queen, South March would succumb to an evil fate. Should Aelfwynne die and leave South March without the only wizard who had the crown's interest at heart, the duty might fall to him. He almost fell from Zorain's neck just thinking about it.

What a disaster that would turn out to be if the crown was forced to rely of him for its salvation. In Aelfwynne's words, the realm would be at the mercy of a big galoop armed with little more than rudimentary magical skills and a finger-length metal talisman that Aelfwynne claimed was his 'wand of destiny.'

He scoffed at that. Some destiny. What could he do with the blackened wand? Open simple locks and light candles. Big deal. He laughed out loud as he recalled his first encounter with the goblin. He had come perilously close to killing the high wizard of South March.

"What's so funny?"

Scale laughed louder. "Me."

"Whatcha do this time?"

Scale stared at the back of Zorain's head. Even his dragon considered him a bumbling fool. "Nothing yet, and that's the problem. Master Aelfwynne thinks I'm something I'm not."

"And that is?"

"A wizard."

"I sense magic in you. More now than when we first met."

"You mean when you tried to fry me and Aelfwynne on the Path of the Errant Knight?"

Zorain's bulk trembled beneath Scale amidst a bout of dragon laughter.

"That wasn't my fault. Let's see how you feel if you and Eolande ever figure out how to summon something without destroying it."

"Exactly. If." Scale agreed. "Every time I set out to do something, I make a mess out of it."

He scanned the endless tract of marsh and sighed. "Apparently, Master Aelfwynne is grooming me to take over for him when he's gone. I can't even imagine that, can you?"

Zorain's silence thundered his answer.

"Ya. Me either. It's okay. After working with Master Aelfwynne, nothing offends me anymore."

A long silence ensued. Stretching northward, bog after swamp after marsh carried on to the distant horizon. Far to the west, the swampland gave way to barren landscape, while in the east, it appeared to abruptly terminate on the edge of a vast desert.

"Hey," Scale recalled Aelfwynne and Zorain's private conversation before they had left Highcliff, "what were you and Master Aelfwynne talking about on the promontory?"

Many wingbeats passed before Zorain said, *"Nothing."*

"You were talking about me, weren't you?"

"Perhaps."

"Well? What did he say?"

"That's between the high wizard and me."

"Come on. You can't hold out on me. We're bonded. We should never hold back from one another, or what's the point of being life companions?"

The endless terrain drifted by far below for a long while.

"Don't ever let him know I told you."

"Of course not."

Another spell passed before Zorain said softly, "He told me not to let you use your magic for anything other than the little you know."

Dragon Sect

Scale frowned at the back of Zorain's head.

The dragon shrugged in mid-wingbeat. *"That's what he said, more or less."*

"More or less?"

"You know how long-winded he gets. I think he's afraid to lose you."

"Lose me? To what?"

Again, the disconcerting shrug between Scale's straddling legs.

With sadness in his voice, Zorain elaborated, *"I don't think he expects to be around much longer. From the rumours I've heard amongst the dragon community, I believe he intends to recommend you as his successor to Queen Khae…If she survives, of course."*

Scale gaped. He'd heard the rumours before, even from Xantha, but for it to be common knowledge amongst the dragons went a long way to substantiating the rumour as fact. He swallowed his apprehension and let the matter go, afraid to consider the ramifications of Aelfwynne's untimely demise.

Left to his own thoughts, he pulled his little wand free of the pouch on his belt and considered its blackened tip. Sure, he had almost killed the high wizard in Crag's Forge, but his magic *had* proven strong enough to break a supposedly unbreakable lock. He was told that only a high-end magic-user would be able to do what he had done without much thought.

A touch of humility settled in as he recalled the ease at which the wood sprite, Dithreab, had disabled what remained of the restraints. He couldn't help wondering if the magic he had discharged in the forge had been housed in the wand all along and had nothing to do with him. Whatever the case, he needed to find the son of Odyne fast. Should the

Dragon Sect

Focal Stone fall, he doubted Aelfwynne would ever forgive him.

Waving the wand before him, pretending to cast a mock spell, the semblance of a wild idea came to him. Despite what Zorain had just imparted, he couldn't help thinking that he had to try it. Nodding to himself, he thought, *'why not.'* What could it hurt? It wasn't like he was going to locate Braen Wys any time soon. The endless land stretching clear to every horizon confirmed that the kingdoms of man comprised more area than that of South March.

Rubbing at the base of one of the blue, crystal-like horns on Zorain's neck, he asked, "What would you say if I told you I *might* be able to make you fly faster?"

"I can fly faster."

"No, I mean, really fast."

Zorain didn't answer but his flying slowed.

"It's really quite simple, now that I think on it."

"What are you up to Scale?"

"Nothing I haven't done with Eolande while trying to perfect Dithreab's summoning spell. It all boils down to acceleration. The faster an object moves, the more chance it has of jumping forward to a different place altogether."

"And you know this to be true?"

"Well, not exactly. But in theory, it should work."

"Should?"

"Well…We've never slowed the process down enough to prove it, but I'm pretty sure I can replicate it without it going sideways."

"Pretty sure, are you? That's not reassuring."

"More or less. I've done it with a candle."

"A candle?" There was no mistaking the incredulousness in Zorain's voice. *"I'm thinking this is what Master Aelfwynne warned me against letting you do."*

"Don't listen to him. Besides, I've worked on this with Eolande." Scale shrugged. "Granted, he doesn't think we're ready to try it on a living creature yet."

"Perhaps we should listen to the old goblin."

"Normally I would agree, but we're running out of time. I fear for Aelfwynne's health. I don't think he has much longer. Nor does the Focal Stone. Without either of them, we'll be in no position to assist Queen Khae against her brother. We may already be too late."

"And what would Eolande say if he knew what you're contemplating?"

Scale emitted a nervous laugh. "He'd likely punish me for even considering it."

"Then I believe you have your answer."

"Come on. When have you ever listened to authority?"

"I'm a Watchman. I'm duty bound to follow the rule of the High Wizard."

"Oh, like the time you flew Princess Ouderling to Wyvern Beach?"

"That was different. It was at the bequest of the princess."

Scale thought hard, He needed to find a way to convince Zorain that the kingdom's need superseded their responsibility to Highcliff. "The same princess whose parents are about to die unless something drastic is done?"

He felt the momentum of Zorain's flight skip ever so slightly.

"The same princess who's gone missing and could very well be in danger from those who sought to kill her last year? If the duke discovers she's left Highcliff, her life will be in jeopardy."

Several wingbeats later, Zorain said softly, *"Do it."*

Dragon Sect

Even with Zorain's permission, it took Scale a long while to fully appreciate what he was about to attempt. If his spell failed, he might kill Zorain—an unwelcome prospect for them both considering how high they flew above the world. Staring at the charred tip of his wand, he took a deep breath. They were Highcliff Guardians. Risking their life for the greater good was expected of them. And, according to Aelfwynne, Braen had to be found fast.

"Should I land?"

Scale blinked at the back of Zorain's head. "Um…no. I think it would be better done while in flight."

"I don't suspect the candles that you and Eolande experimented on were flying."

"No, they weren't. Perhaps that's where we fell short. I have a theory that the inertia involved in getting a stationary object moving presents a serious detriment to the effectiveness of the spell. I'm of the belief it requires more force to start an object travelling than to merely increase its speed while in flight."

Long moments of silence passed before Zorain asked, *"What does Eolande think about your* theory?"

"He doesn't. I just envisioned it now."

"Great."

The sarcasm in Zorain's voice wasn't unexpected. He was asking the dragon to place his life in an unproven wizard. The fact that Zorain trusted him at all was humbling. During their short time together, Scale had come to realize how special the bond was between a rider and a dragon. Something that had to be experienced to fully appreciate. He swallowed deeply. Playing with Zorain's life was the last thing he wanted to do, and yet, what choice did he have? If Braen wasn't found soon, everything Zorain stood for would be for naught.

As if Zorain sensed his apprehension, he said, *"If you believe you're capable of enacting this theory of yours, I want you to know that I trust you. Despite how Master Aelfwynne belittles your magic, no one else in the realm rescued him from certain death."*

"I nearly killed him when we first met."

"But you didn't. Nor did anyone else brave the Path of the Errant Knight to bring him safely back to Highcliff in time to rescue the princess."

Scale's cheeks reddened deeper than the effect the wind had on them. "I had nothing to do with what happened on the Path of the Errant Knight. Aelfwynne protected us until you arrived to send the chazgul scurrying away."

"Nevertheless, you were the one with the high wizard. No other," Zorain said with feeling. *"Nor can you refute the fact that it was* you *who slew Afara Maral. If not for your heroic actions, the Crystal Cavern would have fallen, and we wouldn't be having this conversation. Learn to believe in yourself as I do."*

Scale's vision blurred—his breathing constricted by the lump forming in his throat. Zorain's confidence in him made him feel even guiltier, knowing that what he proposed to do may very well lead to their deaths. If only the swampland would come to an end and save him the trouble of attempting the spell.

He sighed. Even if they reached the end of the marshland, they had so much ground to cover on their search back down the kingdoms of man. A search that would put them in harm's way for as long as they remained north of the South March border. He chastised himself for not searching from the bottom of the lands northward. If he took any consolation from what he was considering, it would be that should he be successful, he will have discovered a way to elude the men who would undoubtedly try to kill them.

He took a deep breath to steady his nerves and patted Zorain's neck. "Alright. I'm ready."

"Nice and slow. You've got this."

Clearing his mind, Scale concentrated on what he was about to enact. An acceleration of Zorain's flight to the point that, in theory, they should leap across a great distance. Not having a reference point to focus on as to where to aim their jump, he recalled what little he knew about the geography of the kingdom of Carillon—its northern border supposedly lined by snow-capped peaks and lofty crags similar to those of the Steel Mountains back home.

With little else to rely upon, he chanted the words he and Eolande had put together to augment the casting. The wand of destiny warmed in his fingers—a comforting testament that the spell was taking effect.

Almost indiscernible at first, Scale sensed a change in the air. The cold wind had turned bitter. Not daring to break his concentration, he channeled his inherent gift into the wand, willing it to enhance his magic, adding a stronger arcane presence to the enchantment.

Rain began to fall, lashing at his exposed skin, making it hard to keep his eyes open. Lightning flashed and thunder rumbled—the phenomenon troubling.

Attempting to ignore the lingering doubts that whispered to him along the periphery of his mind, it dawned on him that moving a creature the size of Zorain might require more magic than shifting a simple candle and its stone holder. A *lot* more.

He pushed aside the thought, enunciating the crucial part of the spell exactly as Eolande had taught him. Finishing with a flourish, he held his breath.

Dragon Sect

A piercing light shrouded the length of his wand, pulsing as if on the verge of discharging the pent-up power evoked, but aside from the bizarre storm that had formed out of a fairly clear sky, nothing else happened.

"Did it work?"

The land below was lost in the heavy downpour. "I'm not sure. I don't think so. Something's missing."

"Eolande?"

The absence of the goblin's magic affecting the outcome of the spell hadn't occurred to Scale. He assumed it just meant he had to augment Eolande's missing magic with his own. Something he hadn't believed would be a big deal as Eolande wasn't a strong magic-user to begin with.

The rain eased and the winds died down enough to allow him to see the ground again. Endless bogs and swamps enshrouded in mist, the terrain no different from what it had looked like before the spell. If anything, Scale worried that his invocation had slowed their progress to little more than a standstill.

"What if I add my magic to the fold?"

Scale did a double take. He had never thought of enlisting Zorain's aid. A profound elation flushed him. Dragon magic! That's what he and Eolande had been missing.

He tempered his enthusiasm. That's what he *believed* they were missing, but the more he thought about it, the more it made sense. Dragons flew. Candles did not. From what he knew of dragon magic, it wasn't far removed from that of the Fae.

His body trembled with excitement. Of course! Since he had never met anyone like Dithreab before, he was by no means an expert on wood sprites, but from what he had gleaned during their short time together, Dithreab's world was closer to that of the Fae than it was to mankind. If what he contemplated was true, Zorain's magic could very well be the missing ingredient in the Summoning Spell.

The pulsing radiance of his wand had faded to a dull ebb, but he hoped the power of the unused magic was still available to him. He didn't have the fortitude to conjure it again without a good night's sleep.

Afraid to lose what little of the spell that remained, he dared to ask, "Do you really think you can add your magic to mine?"

"Please. I'm a dragon."

Scale took a deep breath and refocused on his wand. Not sure if he needed to say the spell words again, he almost lost his hold on Zorain as a foreign presence infused life into the metal talisman.

The winds picked up and the rain intensified. Below them, the land was lost to sight. Lightning flashed several times in rapid succession without the usual, accompanying thunder.

Almost too hot to hang onto, the wand of destiny flared brighter than ever before.

Swallowing his fear of killing them both, Scale chanted the words to unleash the combined magic begging for release from his wand of destiny. Closing his eyes tightly, the strangest sensation gripped him, threatening to toss him to the wind.

Dragon Sect

Cassava

Nordicia Castle seemingly materialized out of the forest floor before Braen's eyes. One moment he and Alexis were trotting their mounts through heavy woodland, and the next, the tree line gave way to a wide clearing. In the centre of a grassy meadow, a stone-walled fortress shot up from the ground, dominating the open space. The only other buildings visible were small, pillared mausoleums scattered amongst leaning and toppled gravestones running alongside the castle's western rampart.

Alexis eyed Braen's bandana, causing the elven prince to pull his cowl over his head.

The Prince of Carillon said, "I'll go on my own from here. The road continues on the far side of the castle. Take Char and make your way through the woods. Wait for me there. If I don't make it out by sunset, something's happened. Should that happen, make sure you're well clear of here before morning."

Braen adjusted his poor excuse for an ear covering and nodded, unable to take his eyes from the ancient keep. Had Alexis not said he was going to the castle to meet the King of Nordicia, he would not have believed that anyone lived within the deteriorating rock walls.

Remaining on the edge of the forest long after the squealing, iron-latticed gate rose to accept the prince, Braen shivered. Something about the place didn't feel right.

The squeal of the rusted gate rising again got him moving when he realized the Prince of Carillon wasn't one of the rough-looking men-at-arms galloping toward him.

Urging Seafoam off the well-trodden roadway, they led Char into the undergrowth, pausing momentarily to watch the passage of the dark clad men. His heart skipped a beat. If not for their round-topped ears, he might have believed they were part of his uncle's Grim Guard.

Crouched behind a screen of fallen brush several paces off the roadway leading south out of Nordicia Castle, Braen removed his cowl and fretted about what exactly Alexis considered sunset. When the sun dropped below the western tree line? Or perhaps after the lengthening shadows had dissolved into the murky gloom of nightfall in the heart of the Nordic Woods. Whatever the case, he knew something must have gone wrong long before the moon appeared above the clearing to illuminate the walls of the crumbling keep.

Not wanting to leave the man who had rescued him from certain death in the hold of the *Coastal Cutter*, he fretted—at a loss as to what to do for Alexis. Walking up to the castle gate and demanding entrance didn't sound like the wisest plan, and yet, he couldn't just leave the man prince to his fate. Or could he?

He gritted his teeth in frustration, wishing not for the first time that he was as brave as he liked to pretend he was until an actual situation arose to prove him otherwise.

He looked toward the south roadway. Were he to walk away now, no one would be any the wiser. Surprised at himself for contemplating such an action, he didn't honestly believe his feet would carry him in the direction of Nordicia Castle, and thus the conundrum.

He wanted to scream at his cowardice but realized making unnecessary noise wouldn't end well for him either. Taking a deep breath, he shook his head, trying to ignore the panic gripping him. Hands trembling, he checked to make sure his rapier sat secure in its sheath and took a moment to string his hunting bow. He laughed quietly at the weapons—useless in his hands. Taking stock of the dozen finely fletched arrows that had never been loosed rattling about in the quiver, he paused to consider the madness of what he contemplated. As brave as he tried to convince himself he was, he knew without the slightest bit of doubt that should someone confront him, he would freeze on the spot and soil himself.

Patting Seafoam on the side of the neck he said, "This may be goodbye my friend. Thank you for getting me this far. I wish I could've been the warrior you deserve to carry into battle."

Swallowing hard, he stepped away from Seafoam on his way to the castle but cried out in alarm as a hard, pointed object pressed his high collar against the side of his neck.

"Don't breathe or I'll end you."

Braen wasn't sure what surprised him more. The dagger held against his throat, or the strange accent that belonged to a female.

"What're you doing here?" The exotic voice purred, a musky, cinnamon scent accompanying her presence. "You're far from home…elf."

Braen swallowed again, afraid to answer lest she slit his throat.

The blade's pressure increased. "Speak now or breathe no more."

"I-I'm Braen Wys. I-I don't really know what I'm doing here. Waiting on a friend."

The woman withdrew her blade and pulled him into the cover of the trees with such force that he stumbled and fell to his backside beside Seafoam. Rubbing at his neck, relieved to discover that he wasn't bleeding, he looked up to stare into the intense brown eyes of a dark-skinned female.

He absently noted her round-topped ears, but there was something in her bearing that screamed she didn't belong in the kingdoms of man either. "Who *are* you?"

"Your death, should I deem it."

Braen shook his head. "Oh no, m'lady. I won't harm you."

"Why are you skulking about the woods, spying on the castle?" Her keen eyes stared at his dislodged bandana. "An elven assassin, I'm thinking."

Braen almost choked on the audacity of her statement. She looked more like an assassin than he ever could. He let forth a nervous chuckle, unable to wrest his gaze from the long daggers the woman held in each hand—their guards bent upward to give the blades three stabbing points should the full length of the dagger be employed. "I assure you, I'm the farthest thing from an assassin."

Tightly braided, black hair tucked behind her ear, casually fell over her right shoulder across a gridwork of metal and leather armour and came to rest above her hip. Three spiked-leather straps wrapped around her right thigh overtop of snug-fitting, black leather breeks, while a half skirt draped her left hip. Whoever the woman was, her calm demeanour bespoke of someone Braen had no wish to offend.

"Please. If it's all the same to you, m'lady, I'll just untether Seafoam and be on my way. My business here is done."

Not a wrinkle on her high forehead, the woman pursed plush lips and shook her head. "Not until I'm sure of your motives."

"Motives?" Braen blurted. "My only aim is to live to see the morrow."

"Judging by the condition of your face, you have a strange way of going about it, Braen…*Wys*." She spoke his last name as if its significance registered in her mind. Her shrewd eyes narrowed.

He swallowed and nodded. "I'm a minor player in the house of South March. Inconsequential, if you will."

She studied him for a long moment. "You're the prince of Urdanya."

"I am."

The spinning of her daggers made Braen flinch and scooch backward, but he need not have feared. She expertly inserted them into thin scabbards set across the back of her shoulders and bent at the waist to hold out a hand to him.

At a loss for words, he accepted her help.

"Well met, son of Odyne. I'm Cassava, Queen of Aldebaran. I've come for King Drannor."

Braen gaped at the woman claiming to be a queen. He searched the underbrush, expecting to see an army of warriors hidden there.

Cassava followed his gaze; her hands moving so fast that Braen marvelled at how fast her daggers appeared, ready to strike.

He stepped back. "Easy, m'lady. I'm alone. I was looking for your retainers."

Cassava frowned, her gaze taking in both horses. "I have no need of…" she struggled with the word, "retainers."

Braen frowned. "You're here by yourself?"

"Why would I not be?"

"Because…" Braen considered the enigma standing before him, "You're a queen."

She tilted her head and pointed a dagger at him. "I'm queen because of my deeds, not by virtue of who I was born to."

Braen couldn't help but focus on the tip of the thin blade pointed his way. "Whoa. I'm not questioning you. If you have business with King Drannor," he indicated the shadowy walls of Nordicia Castle barely visible from where they stood, "then by all means, be my guest."

Cassava tilted her head to the other side, her tight braids dangling free. "You're a strange one for an elven prince."

"That would be an understatement, Your Highness."

Her eyes narrowed beneath a furrowed brow, the tip of a dagger zipping up to rest close to his face. "I am not *your* queen."

Braen stumbled backward and ducked low, his hands in the air. 'Whoa! Easy! There's no need for violence. At least not with me. Judging by your accent and clothing, I'd say you're not from the kingdoms of man at all, if I have the right of it."

She stared long and hard, as if deciding whether or not it would be better to kill him and be done with it. Finally, she lowered her blades, but didn't put them away. "From farther away than you, Braen of Urdanya."

Braen puzzled over that. "You're from south of the Dark Mountains?"

"I know not of what you speak. Aldebaran lies off the coast of southern Nordicia. Halfway to the mystic lands."

Braen nodded, recalling learning about the island nation somewhere—likely within the pages of a book. His mind drifted to Alexis, wondering what had befallen him. "Are you going to the castle now?"

"There's no better time than under the cover of darkness."

Braen laughed nervously. "Um…right. Would you mind doing me a favour when you're inside?"

Cassava tilted her head, waiting for him to continue.

"Can you inquire after Prince Alexis Svelte?"

"Is he Drannor's son?"

"Hardly. He's the Prince of Carillon."

Cassava nodded slowly, absorbing the information. "I'm going straight for the king."

"That's fine. When you talk to the king, I'd appreciate it if you could inquire about what has happened to Prince Alexis."

Cassava gave him an indignant look. "I'm not here to talk to the king. I'm here to kill him."

Dragon Sect

Pact with a Beast

Grimclaw's menacing stare promised a painful death for Ouderling Wys upon the bare rock clearing, high atop an escarpment bordering a wide valley within the northern Spine in the kingdom of Madrigail.

Jyllana stood frozen with fear for her charge—the princess' mid-back length, white hair blowing around Ouderling's head and shoulders. Eyes red as hot coals, Ouderling stood firm—her biting accusations enraging the only dragon Jyllana knew was larger than Kingstone. Looking at her pitiful daggers, Jyllana knew despair. She wondered if the scythe she left beside Dagomar would have served her better.

The mighty Grimclaw appeared on the verge of speaking but tilted his head this way and that in what Jyllana surmised as deep thought. Black puffs of smoke escaped his nostrils, but the flames dripping from the corners of his mouth had subsided. He dipped his chin several times, a jagged smile etching its way across his scaly jaw.

"You're bold for someone so tiny." He nodded deeper. *"I like that. But you're no Nyxa. Nor do I care what you think*

of my legacy. You're naïve to the greater world. Only if you grow to my age shall you earn the right to make such a claim. Like it or not, dragonkind doesn't answer to the other races—nor are we responsible for their shortcomings."

Ouderling made to interrupt, but it was Grimclaw's turn to cut *her* off.

"You're an enigma, Ouderling Wys. One that I can't wrap my mind around. You're young, headstrong, and petulant, but you're also braver than you have a right to be. Or more foolish. Not many amongst those gathered here would dare speak to me in such a manner. That speaks volumes about your courage. You and your companion are easily the weakest creatures present, but you act as if you are the fiercest." His attention shifted pointedly to Jyllana. *"That being said, just what exactly does your companion think she's going to do with her eating utensils? I get bigger shards of bone stuck between my teeth."*

Jyllana lowered her daggers. Looking around, aside from Dagomar and Miragan, who she didn't doubt would give a good account of themselves if matters deteriorated, there was no way she could save the princess should Grimclaw attack. She regripped her daggers with sweaty palms, prepared nevertheless to try—her spirit bolstered somewhat by the fact that they were still alive.

Ouderling turned sideways to look at her. "My protector is twice the warrior than you *or* your rabble. Regardless of what you think of her weapons. Unlike you, she's not afraid to use them to defend what she believes in. A pity you're not as brave as Jyllana Ordalf."

Jyllana tried hard not to gape. If Ouderling was attempting to rankle the agitated dragon further, she was doing a good job.

Dragon Sect

Renewed flames limned the back of Grimclaw's lips. His eyes narrowed and his head shot forward, stopping a breath away from Ouderling and Jyllana who were too stunned to move.

Breath smelling of brimstone was hot on Jyllana's face. Unable to see anything beyond the rough scales of Grimclaw's lower jaw and the bottoms of his fanged teeth, she resisted the urge to drive her daggers into his lip. This close to the gargantuan beast, his words rang true—her daggers would present nothing more than a nettle in the dragon's hide.

"Don't push your luck, princess. If not for the blood of Nyxa coursing through your veins you would already be just a rumble in my belly," Grimclaw thundered. He pulled his head back and rose to sit taller than some of the trees lining the clearing. *"If you're as brave as your attitude proclaims, I'm willing to offer you a proposition."*

Jyllana sensed it was all Ouderling could do to remain standing—the princess's skin as pale as she imagined her own must be. To Ouderling's credit, she lifted her chin in defiance.

"I didn't come to strike a bargain with you," Ouderling's voice was surprisingly strong. "I'm here on official business from Highcliff. A place you once swore allegiance to."

The clearing rumbled beneath their feet as Grimclaw let forth a hearty laugh. *"I have never sworn allegiance to anyone. Especially an elf! I chose to fight beside Nyxa out of the respect she had duly earned. I answer to no one."* His head closed half the distance separating them and snarled, *"Should you desire to leave here alive, I suggest you do what I'm about to ask."* His voice dropped to a dangerous growl. *"Do I make myself clear?"*

Dragon Sect

Ouderling appeared to struggle with an answer. In the end she merely returned his glare.

"Ironically, I find myself in need of your help. Well, in need of the help of someone as small as you. As I cannot suffer the company of man, two elves will have to do."

"Help *you*?" Ouderling spat incredulously. "After refusing to help my parents, you expect me to help you in return? You're crazier than I thought you were the first time we met."

Jyllana swallowed hard, her gaze darting around the clearing, looking for some way to extricate the princess from her mounting peril. Even with Dagomar and Miragan's help, she could see no way past the dragons watching them from the ground. She looked up. And the sky.

"Regardless of your petty criticism of my character, I'm prepared to ask this of you anyway. I recently commissioned a team of dwarfs from Sarsen Rest to build a dragon temple in honour of our presence in the land." He craned his neck to indicate a conical peak rising above the trees to the northwest. *"Alas, since the last time you came through here, the dwarfs have disturbed an ancient creature that lives in the depths of the volcano and find themselves trapped beneath the surface. I would be much obliged if you and Ms. Ordalf could rid us of this unforeseen hindrance."*

Ouderling frowned. "Why should I make a pact with a beast? If you're so mean and tough, why don't you rid the tunnels of the creature yourself?"

"Because the creature has trapped the stone masons within tunnels too small for us to enter."

Ouderling's frown deepened. "If the dwarfs can't defeat the creature, how do you expect Jyllana and I to?"

Dragon Sect

"With magic, Ouderling Wys. Prove you're the prodigy of Nyxa and perhaps I might change my mind about helping your parents."

"Perhaps?" Ouderling shouted.

It was as if the great dragon shrugged. *"Or perhaps I'll eat you."*

Dragon Sect

Den of Deceit

Orphic Den was just around the bend in the small animal trail—Pecklyn could sense it. He had travelled to the wizards' guild on several occasions in the past to deliver messages from Aelfwynne to the surly headmaster. It was no secret there was no love lost between the two prominent magic-users. Extending his magic divination, he satisfied himself that the land around them was free of trip wards. He subtly waved his hand in the air, making sure not to drop the thin coil of rope draped over his shoulder.

On cue, Balewynd scurried ahead, keeping low to the ground—her supple, black leather boots not making a sound. The faint path they followed descended to the base of the keep built on the eastern edge of Orphic Den. Hunkering behind a jag of rock, she peered into the tendrils of mist marking the boundaries of the mystical village. After a moment, she nodded for him to join her.

Staring ahead, Balewynd whispered, "Who's guarding Aelfy now that we're away? Xantha won't be much use with a babe stuck to her."

Dragon Sect

Pecklyn did a double take at the odd question, considering where they were and what they were about to do. He shrugged. "I imagine Scale will."

"Scale?" Balewynd scoffed. "He can barely put fire to a candle wick."

"He's come a long way since he joined us."

"Seems incompetent to me."

"He's just unsure of himself."

"That's a kind way to put it. Let's hope nothing bad happens to Highcliff until we return."

"Kingstone will handle it," Pecklyn said, more to mollify his own misgivings about being so far away from the high wizard during the dangerous times they were living in. Swallowing his discomfort, he followed Balewynd's stare.

Barely visible through a veil of swirling fog, the upper spires of the ominous keep pierced the mystic vapour. Already knowing what awaited him, he sent magical feelers into the mist and immediately recoiled at the vileness that infused him. Though not physically dangerous, the spectral fog contained a malevolence more prevalent than on previous occasions.

As if sensing his uneasiness, Dawnbreaker snorted, her bulk hidden on the slopes far behind them where she waited with Mirage. "Keep alert, m'lady. There's definitely a foulness in the air."

"Let Mirage and I burn the village to the ground," Dawnbreaker growled.

"Easy girl. There are powers here that none of us are equipped to handle. If the headmaster is responsible for the queen's malaise, he'll get what's coming to him."

Balewynd pulled her black-bladed dagger free, its curved, jagged edges promising an agonizing end to anyone who crossed her. "It's time to rid the den of deceit of the traitorous wizard."

Despite the revulsion the ethereal veil instilled in him, Pecklyn maintained his probing divination. There were likely dangerous wards and watching eyes hidden within the gloomy mist. If he missed one, their foray into Headmaster Sagora's bastion would not end well. He nodded for Balewynd to proceed.

Stealthier than an unspoken whisper, Balewynd eased into the village, one cautious footstep at a time—her intense eyes taking in things Pecklyn knew he would never see. Doing his best not to lick at the sickly sweetness of the mist on his lips, he trailed a step behind his companion—the two of them acting in practiced unison, their identical movements so precise it was as if they were one being.

Pecklyn purposely trod a little harder on his left foot. In response, Balewynd stepped left—the almost imperceptible sound her cue that he perceived danger to their right.

The path they had followed out of the mountains placed them near the northeastern spire of the keep. Her back to the rough, damp stone, Balewynd's constant scrutiny of their surroundings never wavered as she waited for him to join her.

Shoulder to shoulder, Pecklyn shrugged free of the rope and handed it to her.

The ability in which the lithe Guardian was able to scale a sheer wall always amazed Pecklyn. He had referred to her as a spider the first time he had witnessed her uncanny prowess, but watching her ascend the slick, ivy covered rampart was a sight to behold. Although he prided himself for his own climbing ability, he would never be able to ascend the keep's wall like Balewynd did.

Dragon Sect

In the time it took him to check that his saber sat secure in its scabbard, she had reached the underside of a small balcony, two stories off the ground. Undeterred by the impediment, she sprung from the wall like a squirrel hopping through tree branches and clutched the outer edge of the overhang.

Swinging her lower body beneath her, she thrust her legs forward and curled them over a low balustrade lining the balcony.

Pecklyn's breath caught, but he need not have worried. Balewynd's black clad body disappeared from view. Moments later, the rope dropped from the sky.

Magical tendrils searching their surroundings, Pecklyn made quick work of the rope and joined Balewynd outside of a solitary, wooden door. She indicated the door with her eyes and shook her head, her gaze lifting to another balcony farther up the side of the keep.

Ignoring the putrid essence prevalent in the mist, he probed the upper ledge. Sensing nothing untoward, he nodded.

Balewynd untied the rope, coiled it over her shoulder, and stepped onto the low, stone railing to begin her next climb.

The sound of muffled voices and the scrape of a boot sent a chill up Pecklyn's spine. He let out a sound imitating a bird's chirp and looked up. Hard to see from where he stood, Balewynd's stretched form had stopped moving.

Peering over the edge of the balcony toward the front tower of the keep, he extended his ability. If there was magic at play, it was overpowered by the pall of the mist, but something moved just out of sight.

Before he could probe deeper, two figures in flowing robes materialized, walking along the base of the keep, their hooded cowls directed at the ground before them as their male voices reached him.

"You see that lightning the other night?"

"How could I not? The storm came out of nowhere. Hit hard, and then it was gone."

"How about the bolt that hit the keep? I thought for sure it had blasted the roof off."

"You're not kidding. I've never seen anything like it. The lightning just kept coming. It was bizarre. I'm thinking it wasn't natural."

"Ya, bizarre is a good word to describe it."

"Talking about bizarre, do you think the high wizard will retaliate against the duke?"

"Don't see he has much choice. I'm surprised he hasn't already."

"Maybe he's in league with Saggy."

Pecklyn held his breath as they stopped just beyond the balcony, directly below Balewynd.

"Don't be daft. Saggy would like nothing better than to cook the goblin and feed him to the dragons."

"A shame the duke's dragons left him."

"Ya. This business with the queen would already be done."

"You think we'll be marching?"

"I doubt it. Not if Saggy has anything to say about it."

"What about that…that thing?"

Both figures looked around, as if searching for something.

"I shudder just thinking about it. Rumour says it's straight out of a nightmare from the time of Urdanya and the Dragon Witch."

"What's Saggy doing consorting with the likes of that?"

"Beats me," the elf lowered his voice. "I'm not sure about you, but I might have to rethink my position here. If the Soul *has* returned, I don't want anything to do with it."

They searched their surroundings again, their gazes seemingly coming to rest on Balewynd.

"Come on. Let's get back inside."

The other male grunted and together they shuffled into the mist.

It took Pecklyn a few moments to compose himself enough so that he could muster another bird chirp. He swallowed his reservations concerning what they were about to do. It didn't seem like the patrol had spotted Balewynd, but only time would tell.

Extending his ability toward the last place he had seen the two figures, he attempted to push aside the malevolent taint on the mist. A soft slap against the wall beside him and the brush of something against his shoulder almost made him cry out. Balewynd had thrown him the rope.

He shook his head and checked to ensure the rope was secure. With a last look into the mist roiling along the base of the keep, he took a deep breath and followed his companion up the wall.

Dragon Sect

Under the Graveyard

Cassava's presence did little to ease Braen's misgivings about being this close to a castle of a man king—especially after dark.

She searched the clearing for a long while before stepping free of the tree line with her daggers held casually at her hips. Looking over her shoulder, she asked, "Are you going to stand there and collect dew?"

He blinked dumbly at her. "I'm sorry?"

She rolled her eyes. "If you want to know what happened to the one you're looking for, you'll have to find out for yourself. I don't plan on being in the castle long enough to talk to anyone, but I can get you inside."

Braen swallowed. "Oh no. I couldn't do that. They'd kill me on sight."

Cassava shrugged indifference. "Suit yourself."

Watching the Queen of Aldebaran skulk across the clearing left him feeling more cowardly than usual. If the woman was serious, she must know of a way to get inside the castle walls without detection. Perhaps she was familiar with the night guard. Whatever the case, he may never get a better chance at finding out what had delayed Alexis. He owed the prince that much. All he had to do was convince himself that he was up to the task.

The sudden fear of being alone gripped him. The Queen of Aldebaran was nowhere to be seen. Stepping backward, he decided he'd be better off mounting Seafoam and putting as many leagues as he could between himself and Nordicia Castle before daybreak, especially if Cassava carried through with what she was about to do. Were the guard to find an elf lurking within the woods, they were sure to blame him for the king's death.

The faint moonlight glinted off a metal surface near the graveyard. Squinting, he caught sight of Cassava's silhouette passing alongside a small mausoleum on the edge of the graveyard.

Just the thought of following the mysterious woman set the fine hairs on the back of his neck on end. He pulled his cowl over his head to ward off the sudden chill her presence instilled in him.

Unable to believe what he was about to do, he patted Seafoam's neck. "Wait here and rest. I'm thinking we'll be needing to be gone from this place as fast as you can carry us when I return."

Seafoam nuzzled his hand and let forth a soft nicker.

"Shh!" Braen looked around in alarm, but no one was about.

It took him a moment to locate her again. Skulking around a raised mound, Cassava disappeared beyond its crest. He took a deep breath, checked behind him, and sprinted across the clearing.

Whether the open space between the forest and the castle was greater than he had first thought or he was in worse physical shape than he cared to admit, he wasn't sure—likely the latter he decided as he fought to catch his breath alongside the first mausoleum. He had to hang onto the edge of his cowl to keep it on his head.

Had he been able to breathe, he would have screamed outright when a dark figure appeared around the corner of the small building and threatened him with a triple pointed dagger.

Eyes wide, he fought to still his hammering heart. "For the love of the Fae…you scared…the life out of me."

Cassava glared at him, her facial expression none too happy. "Are you *trying* to get us killed?"

He gaped.

"You make more noise than a skinned troll. You'll have the castle guard on us."

Speechless, all he could do was look sheepishly back at her. He thought he was being stealthy.

"If you want to live, keep up."

He nodded and tried to swallow enough spit to utter more than a croak. "Where are we going?"

She gave him an exasperated look. Without answering his question, she left him at the mausoleum.

Unable to staunch the violent trembling of his limbs, it was all he could do not to bolt across the clearing, mount Seafoam, and gallop off. Taking a deep breath, he peered around a crumbling pillar that supported the stone eave above his head and searched for Cassava. A pang of fright gripped him. She'd only been out of his sight for a moment, but the woman had disappeared. Again.

"Psst!"

Barely visible in the yawning doorway of a larger mausoleum set beyond the central mound in the graveyard, Cassava waved a dagger at him.

He took a quick look around and made his way amongst the burial mounds, tripping several times on the uneven ground. Reaching Cassava, he was startled further when she slipped into the mausoleum's interior. "Where are you going?"

"Under the graveyard."

He blinked after her several times as his muddled brain tried to come to terms with her answer. Not relishing the fact that he now stood outside in the graveyard alone, he entered the dark building, the light so poor that his dark vision had difficulty identifying where the stone sarcophaguses were placed inside.

He was sure his heart had stopped when the sound of stone grating on stone rumbled through the interior—the floor vibrating beneath his feet. Where Cassava had found the torch she sparked to life was a mystery, but she watched him from the far side of an open sarcophagus with a satisfied grin. "After you."

Braen stopped and backed up a couple of steps. "Um, no."

"Suit yourself." Cassava hiked a leg up and straddled the thick stone side wall of the coffin. She paused. "Last chance. Once I'm inside, the lid will close, and you'll lose your chance to find out what happened to your friend. Unless," she winked and cast a gaze around the creepy interior, "you know which corpse to sweet talk."

It was as if the roof and walls pressed in from all sides, threatening to squeeze the life from him. His legs felt leaden, but he managed to drag himself to the coffin where Cassava waited impatiently—the look on her face telling him she enjoyed his discomfort far more than she ought to.

Peering over the lip of the coffin, he was relieved to find that there wasn't a body inside. Instead, a narrow stairwell dropped steeply into darkness—the weight of Cassava's foot seemingly forcing down the false bottom of the stone casket.

From where he stood, damp earthen walls draped in thick spiderwebs met his horrified gaze. He looked at her as if she were mad. "You expect me to go down there?"

She shrugged. "You can always knock at the front gate."

Taking a deep breath, more to keep from fainting than because of the queen's sarcastic remark, he swallowed and hoisted a leg over the side wall, his arms and legs shaking as if he were losing the strength in them. Try as he might, he couldn't coax his other leg over.

Cassava leaned in to purr in his ear, "Anytime now would be great."

His nerves jumped. He forced himself onto the top step but was afraid to continue into the ground.

Cassava lifted manicured eyebrows and smiled. "It'll be dawn before we know it."

He nodded and inhaled deeply, not believing what he was about to do. One tentative footstep followed by another, he descended into the earth, unsuccessfully avoiding contact with the myriad of silken traps. A warm presence in the cold dampness moved in behind him as the grating rumble of what could only be the lid of the sarcophagus closing overhead shook the ground.

"Are you waiting to be devoured by…?" Cassava indicated with the torch a fist-sized, bulbous spider sporting furry legs. It skittered away from the heat, disappearing beneath a rotting cross brace.

Most of the light from Cassava's torch was blocked by his body in the tight confines of the tunnel, but he was okay with that. The less he saw of his surroundings, the better. It was nearly impossible to avoid brushing against the imperfect walls or keep his head from disturbing the low ceiling. He was thankful for his cowl.

"If you go any slower, elf prince, we'll be joining those resting above our heads before we reach the castle," Cassava said as if she were having a casual conversation with a close friend.

He considered the ceiling with horror and started walking. The tunnel widened briefly, allowing the fearless woman to push by him to lead the way at a brisker pace.

Consumed by fear, he stumbled after her, flinching every time his shoulders careened against the walls, causing him to slap at his clothing to rid himself of imaginary spiders. The odd sensation he had experienced in the hold of the *Coastal Cutter* tingled inside him, but he feared its release more so than his discomfort of where the maniacal woman was leading him.

The tunnel wound around without apparent purpose. In no time at all he had lost all sense of direction. For all he knew, they were walking away from Nordicia Castle. Ducking below a section of roof littered with dangling roots, he shuddered at the thought of what else those roots passed through.

"Aren't you afraid of ghosts?" he asked in an effort to keep from screaming.

Cassava looked over her shoulder, raising a cocky eyebrow. "I'm responsible for putting many of them in the ground." She shrugged and nodded. "If they wish revenge, this *would be* the best place to have at it."

He thought about bolting the other way but was too afraid. The only thing he could think of that would be worse than following a maniacal assassin into a castle of man was the thought of finding himself trapped in a dark tunnel crawling with spiders beneath a graveyard should he not be able to open the lid of the sarcophagus they had entered through.

Realizing Cassava had started forward again, he gulped and followed the diminishing torchlight.

Up ahead, Cassava stopped at a sharp bend and directed the flames' light down a section of tunnel he couldn't see.

Her stance stiffened. Dropping the brand to the ground, she covered her head and cowered—a blood-curdling screech ripping free of her throat.

Dragon Sect

Castle in the Sky

"**Castle!**" Scale shouted above the deafening crack of thunder that sounded as if it had originated from their position in the sky. A pervasive cold that hadn't been present a moment before caused him to shiver uncontrollably. One moment he had been casting a spell, the power of the enchantment bolstered by Zorain's dragon magic, and before he could draw his next breath, his stomach had lurched into his throat, accompanied by a flash of white light. And then, without warning, the pristine walls of a large castle rose up before them.

Zorain dipped hard to the right, his flight barely missing a round corner tower.

Scale struggled to maintain his seat. If not for the cluster of blue crystal horns protruding from Zorain's shoulders, he would have fallen to his death. Righting himself, he focused on the top of the wide corner towers and the prominent gatehouse, relieved to see no sign of dragon killing ballistae.

His immediate fear for Zorain forgotten, he studied the imposing bastion. Surrounded by clouds, the base of the castle was built upon a solitary peak with a roadway carved into its side that fell away, out of sight.

He shook his head, attempting to rid the vertigo gripping him. His mind reeled with the ramifications of what his eyes were telling him. They no longer flew over the vast stretch of swampland east of the kingdoms of man.

His jaw dropped. Judging by the extreme cold making his breath visible, and the sting of the wind on his cheeks, his spell had worked. Almost afraid to speak what his senses told him was true, he gasped, "It worked."

"It would seem so," Zorain answered, gliding more than flapping as they circled the sky fort. *"Do you know where we are?"*

Scale chuckled nervously, "I know where we're not."

"And that is?"

He swallowed. "Highcliff."

"That's going to make it difficult to find our way back."

Zorain's comment lost on him, he remembered he had envisioned mountains similar to those back home while intoning the last words of the complicated spell. Other than having no knowledge of a fortress this large amongst the mountains of South March—for surely it wasn't Orphic Den—the extreme cold led him to believe they had leapt a great distance.

"Do you happen to know how big the kingdom of Carillon is?"

"I've never flown over any of the man kingdoms. The closest I ever get is flying off the shore of southern Nordicia."

Not knowing what to say to shed light on their present location, Scale said, "Drop through the clouds. It might help to see the land below."

Dragon Sect

Zorain altered the angle of his wings, dropping away from the castle into the cloud cover—a thick mist obscuring their vision.

A sudden shriek was the only warning Scale received. Blinded by clouds, he was thrown against Zorain's neck as their downward momentum abruptly ceased. A distinct crack of ice and a crashing wave of frigid water washed over them, taking his breath from his lungs.

Frantic wing flaps lifted them out of the water and back into the mist. Breaking through what they had perceived as cloud, they hovered close to the opposite end of the castle from the gatehouse. The back wall was dominated by an angular tower that breached the middle of the crenellated rampart—the structure constructed of stone different from the rest of the fortress.

Dripping water and shivering uncontrollably, Scale stared at the fortress. There was something odd about its appearance. He spoke through chattering teeth, "D-do you s-see anyone on the w-walls?"

Zorain veered alongside the castle, keeping out of arrowshot. *"I do not."*

"F-f-fly closer."

Zorain flapped several times, rising above the high tower set amongst the rear wall and swooped over the castle in a slow glide.

Thick walls and prominent corner towers adjoined by stone walkways surrounded a rectangular keep in the central courtyard, the castle appearing as an empty shell—the inner bailey built upon the bare rock of the hill it had been built upon.

"It looks deserted."

"Rightfully so. Who in their right mind would want to live here?"

Scale couldn't argue with that. "Take us in closer."

"Do you think that's wise?"

"There's only one way to find out."

"I see why Master Aelfwynne frets over you."

"I've been right so far, haven't I?"

"Lucky, more like," Zorain answered but did as Scale asked. Hovering above the out of place tower along the back wall, he added, *"I sense a strong, magical presence emanating below us."*

Scale felt it too. "A wizard?"

"Too strong for a wizard. It's not human." Zorain fought to maintain his position as a strong wind blew against their back. *"Nor elven."*

"Then what?"

"If I'm not mistaken, the castle itself is infused with…" he paused, his voice dropping to a whisper, *"earth blood."*

Scale swallowed, the relevance shaking him to the core. Aelfwynne had mentioned that there was another source of earth blood in the world. The high wizard hadn't known where exactly, but claimed it was hidden in the northern kingdoms of man.

The significance of Zorain's words were staggering. If man had learned to harness the power inherent in earth blood, South March's future was in greater jeopardy than the old goblin feared. Should the Dragon Witch Wraith discover this castle, it wouldn't need to bother with Highcliff. As much as that scenario would rid them of the incessant fear they presently lived under, it would exacerbate the dilemma the world faced.

"We need to go down there and investigate."

"An abandoned castle that looks as if it were just built, sitting in the middle of nowhere. I'm thinking there's more to it than we're seeing."

"I agree, but someone must live down there. Perhaps they're hiding. It's not every day a dragon comes calling."

"Or," Zorain said with an air of caution, *"they're not overly concerned about our presence."*

The simple comment made Scale sit up straighter. "Who in the world wouldn't be afraid of a dragon?"

Zorain shrugged between wingbeats. *"There are many creatures we've never encountered before. Magical beings like the Fae who aren't concerned about their inferior size."*

Scale caught himself nodding. The wood sprite Dithreab was one such creature. It would be presumptuous, and potentially fatal, for them to believe a fledgling wizard and a dragon were superior to everyone they encountered— especially in a strange land. A land that Scale was beginning to think was not part of the kingdoms of man.

Second guessing the desire to visit the castle, he recalled his brief time on the Path of the Errant Knight. If the grounds were infested with creatures like the chazgul, his foray to seek out the magic Zorain sensed might be the last thing he ever did. Nonetheless, he knew what Aelfwynne's reaction would be if they returned to Highcliff and told him they hadn't taken the time to verify their belief. Death might seem like a better alternative than listening to the crotchety goblin carry on.

"Take us down. Close to the odd tower."

Without a word, Zorain adjusted his flight. Winging a wide circle over the mist shrouded castle, he dropped into a graceful glide until they cleared a rear corner tower and reared up with a flurry of rapid back flaps before settling onto the bare rock lining the inner bailey.

Scale remained on Zorain's shoulders. "Do you sense anything?"

Dragon Sect

The white dragon's head moved from side-to-side. Bringing his attention back to a high-topped, double wooden door, his eyes narrowed. *"Whatever's emitting the magical taint, it's definitely coming from inside that tower. The rest of the castle appears to be nothing but cold stone."*

"But you can't tell what's responsible?"

Zorain sniffed at the air. *"No."*

Taking a deep breath, Scale resigned himself to the fact that he would have to enter the tower on his own. "Great. Keep an eye out for anything unusual. I won't be long." He swallowed and added to himself, *I hope.*

Pushing on the right side of the double doors, Scale was unpleasantly surprised when it squealed on its hinges to expose the gloomy interior of a grand foyer, its dust covered, flagstone floor cast with eerie shadows in the dim light of high window slits surrounding the round chamber beyond.

Unable to penetrate the murky shadows high overhead in the poor lighting of the eerie tower, it seemed to be hollow all the way to the top. Spinning a slow circle, he struggled to comprehend the reason for the tower. Aside from an odd window slit randomly inserted into the sloping walls, there was nothing remarkable about the empty interior. Just dust and bits of crumbled rock debris that appeared not to have been disturbed in centuries.

"What do you see?"

So engrossed in his observations, Zorain's deep voice made Scale's heart skip a beat. Catching his breath, he glared at the exit—the white dragon's orange eye dominating the space beyond the open door.

"Nothing. There's absolutely nothing in here. No furnishings, no rooms…Not even stairs. It's bizarre. It must be the stone itself that's exuding the magic."

Dragon Sect

"Of a certainty, the stone has been enchanted," Zorain agreed. His eye disappeared from view to be replaced by his probing snout—great nostrils contracting as he sniffed at the air inside the tower. *"Yes, the stone is infused with a magical essence. Almost guardian-like, if that makes sense?"*

Scale frowned. "You mean like the stone is alive?"

Zorain didn't answer right away, but as his snout disappeared from where it sniffed at the doorway, he said, *"As strange as that sounds, that would be a fairly accurate assessment."*

Scale swallowed and started to back out of the great chamber. "I have a bad feeling about this place."

"I agree. Something's not right."

Before Scale had a chance to take another step, Zorain's voice thundered in his head, *"Scale!"*

Spinning around in alarm, Scale jumped backward in fright.

The door squealed and slammed shut, locking him inside.

Dragon Sect

Confronting a Nightmare

"I don't like this," Miragan cautioned as she winged after Grimclaw and several other dragons.

Ouderling couldn't argue with her, but their flight was short-lived. They had barely risen above the tree line when they descended into a small clearing set between a newly constructed wall with an arched entryway and a gaping hole at the base of a cliff—the volcanic mountainside rising high overhead.

Dagomar dropped in beside Miragan, his crimson stare intent on Grimclaw sitting beside the tunnel opening.

Jyllana slipped from Dagomar's shoulder with her polearm and held out a hand to steady Ouderling as the princess dismounted.

"Ware yourself well, spawn of Nyxa. Where you're going, death awaits," Grimclaw growled. *"I'm almost of the mind to recant my demand."* A jagged grin formed along the blue dragon's great mouth revealing massive teeth. *"Almost."*

"You're insufferable," Ouderling gave him a disgusted look. "Rest assured, oh once noble dragon, should we die doing your bidding, so will any chance you might have had to save dragonkind." She offered him a smug smile of her own. "I've foreseen it."

Ignoring the surprised look from Grimclaw and his lackeys, Ouderling strung her bow, adjusted how the quiver sat on her back, and walked toward the tunnel entrance with Jyllana by her side.

"An arrow will not save you, silly elfling," Grimclaw growled. *"You must rely on your magic."*

Ouderling kept walking but stopped and turned on the tunnel's threshold and pointed a finger at Grimclaw's incredulous face. "It's you who must rely on my magic. I hope for your sake that it'll be enough, otherwise your demands will doom everything you hold dear."

Struggling to keep her limbs from trembling with the absolute fear gripping her, Ouderling forced herself to enter the mountainside—her bout of bravado had taken its toll on her nerves. She didn't think she had ever been more frightened in her life.

She took a deep breath. Walking into the dark passageway, she thought of another time when her fear had nearly incapacitated her. She would never forget almost wetting herself as she faced down Afara Maral. The knowledge that Scale and High Wizard Aelfwynne would not be coming to her aid this time only heightened her present terror.

The sound of the dragons and wind in the trees fell away as she travelled down a roughly hewn tunnel into the heart of the mountain. It wasn't long before she and Jyllana had to rely upon their dark vision to navigate the relatively straight passageway. Though it seemed like an interminably long time, it wasn't long before a reddish-orangey glow suffused the darkness ahead.

Dragon Sect

Jyllana placed a hand on Ouderling's forearm to stop her, the Home Guard's eyes wide with comprehension. "That's lava up ahead."

Ouderling nodded. They hadn't passed another tunnel since entering the volcano. She glanced absently at Jyllana's polearm, wondering how effective something that unwieldly would be inside the tunnels. Taking a deep breath, she broke free of Jyllana's restraint.

A welcome warmth bathed their exposed skin, the heat quickly rising as they approached the end of the tunnel.

Whether due to the tension of what they were about to face or the mounting temperature of the mountain's interior, Ouderling wasn't sure, but sweat beaded on her forehead as she stepped free of the entry tunnel. Gasping at the sight before her, she stopped on the brink of a large crater that dominated the inside of a gargantuan cone-shaped chamber—its open-air ceiling high overhead accessible by a long, impossible climb or dragonflight.

Two paces wide, a ledge curved away from where they stood, encircling the interior of the volcano they had entered. Careful to keep away from the brink, Ouderling resisted the urge to back into the entrance tunnel to escape the mesmerizing sight of a great lake of lava bubbling and churning in the depths of the crater. Great spouts of molten rock shot up from the lava's surface at random intervals, bursting in loud 'plops' and falling back into the ooze.

"I'd hate to fall down there," Jyllana said beside her, using her polearm as a walking stick in the spacious chamber.

Ouderling nodded. "I can't imagine why anyone would dream of building a temple inside an active volcano."

"Well, it *is* a dragon temple."

"I doubt dragons can withstand a volcanic eruption."

Jyllana shrugged and cast an inquisitive stare around the cavern's interior, her face dripping. She indicated dark shadows farther along the ledge they stood on. "Looks like more tunnels lead into the mountain."

Ouderling followed her gaze. "I wonder where they go?"

Jyllana shrugged again and opened her mouth to speak, but an angry roar reached them, its hair-raising tone muted in the volcanic chamber.

A heavy thud accompanied a slight tremor in the ground.

Ouderling stared at Jyllana in alarm. "What was that?"

Looking everywhere at once, she needn't have asked. She could tell by the look on her guardian's stricken face that Jyllana wondered the same thing. They were close to finding the creature Grimclaw had sent them after. Or more precisely, the ancient creature had found them.

Jyllana held her polearm horizontally in two hands and walked cautiously around the crater to the right. "This way, Your Highness."

Another thunderous growl reached them, quickly followed by two earth-shaking impacts.

Ouderling pulled an arrow from her quiver and knocked it, sheepishly recalling Grimclaw's warning, *'An arrow will not save you.'*

Whether that would prove true or not, she couldn't follow Jyllana unarmed.

'You must rely on your magic,' the second part of Grimclaw's warning echoed in her head so loudly that she wondered if the dragon had spoken the words again.

She rolled her eyes at the thought. A fat lot of good speaking with the Fae would do for her against a creature capable of holding a band of dwarfs at bay.

The ground shook again with such violence that Ouderling feared the ledge they trod might crumble away and cast them into the lava lake as they continued around the ledge toward more tunnel entrances farther along the interior of the crater.

"In here, Your Highness."

The Home Guard's natural predilection to refer to her by her royal honorific during a time of duress didn't faze her, but it seemed like such a trivial thing given the ordeal they were about to face. Looking over her shoulder to ensure they weren't being chased, she followed Jyllana onto a small landing at the head of a steep flight of steps carved into the bedrock.

As soon as they entered the side tunnel, Ouderling knew they were headed in the right direction—the distant sound of battle could be heard from deep with the bowels of the volcano.

Jyllana peered over her shoulder momentarily before starting down a steep stairwell—struggling to keep her polearm from getting caught up.

The darkness in the close confines of the precipitous descent was so absolute that Ouderling's exceptional dark vision struggled to reveal the roughhewn surfaces of the stairwell. Out of instinct, she ducked, fearing to bash her forehead off the ceiling—all the while intent upon the increasing furor unfolding somewhere below.

The sound of gruff, individual voices shouting hysterically separated themselves from the guttural roar they had been hearing. The roar of something Ouderling was sure she did not wish to confront. If her parents weren't facing such dire straits, she would have ran from the unfinished temple. Confronting a nightmare was not something she relished doing, for judging by the commotion below, it could be nothing less.

Dragon Sect

The faint glow of torchlight filtered into the bottom of the stairwell. Even without having seen it, she knew that whatever they had to face awaited them just beyond.

Jyllana stopped at the bottom of the steps and put a finger to her lips before leaning out of the stairwell to scout ahead. Eyes wide, she pulled back.

"What is it?"

Jyllana shook her head, her pale face whiter than normal.

"The creature?"

Jyllana nodded.

"Let me see," Ouderling whispered, struggling to manoeuvre her strung bow past Jyllana.

The light from many sconces was barely sufficient to illuminate a large, cylindrical chamber that appeared to have no bottom—its domed ceiling vaulting high overhead. Jyllana moved in beside her as she stepped onto a landing at the head of a rickety, wood and rope bridge that spanned a yawning abyss.

A quick glance told her they stood upon a flange of an immense sculpture carved into the side of a great shaft that dropped out of sight.

The platform below their feet was carved in the shape of a larger than life-sized book—held by the stone hand of a female caricature hewn out of the wall behind them. Draped in robes, the beautifully chiselled woman bore a staff in one hand and held aloft the book they stood upon with her other—her hair, high overhead, etched into veins of marble that shot through the dark granite walls.

Sculpted bodies of fallen men, women, and dragons lined the walls encircling the abyss, their anguished forms set amongst massive, stone tree trunks climbing high overhead. In the brief glimpse Ouderling could afford, tree limbs spread out to form the cavern's ceiling—a myriad of gemstones sparkling with a life of their own accord within the entangled branches like tiny faeries dancing around the petrified canopy—their wondrous light illuminating the chamber in an ethereal glow.

As spectacular as the chamber was, nothing could have prepared Ouderling for the beast that had stopped what it was doing and looked straight at them.

Rising from a platform on the far side of the chasm spanned by the rickety bridge, a stone creature stood beside the gaping mouth of a lava stone, dragon head. The bipedal creature stood almost as high as a large dragon.

The troll-like creature's raw eyes grew wide. A great bellow of rage escaped its throat, causing Ouderling and Jyllana to cower in fright.

The creature bent low, plucking a chunk of discarded lava stone bigger than Ouderling's torso from beside the larger-than-life sculpture—the dragon head's enormous mouth parted to reveal a small cavern of its own within the fang-infested maw.

Enrapt in the spell the vision of the dragon's head instilled in her, Ouderling yelped when Jyllana latched onto her upper arm and manhandled her back into the stairwell moments before the wall above them shook as a chunk of lava stone exploded above them.

Stunned, Ouderling gaped at the enraged goliath. If they didn't do something fast, they would have to find a way to escape the path of the next stone the creature lifted from the ground beside it.

Dragon Sect

Severing the Serpent's Head

Balewynd waited impatiently for Pecklyn to work his magic. As stealthy as they were, she didn't fool herself. It would only be a matter of time before their presence in the keep at Orphic Den was discovered. A scenario that on any other occasion would make their life difficult, but with the political climate that had besieged the land, being found out now would mean certain death. If Headmaster Sagora had anything to do with it, their demise would undoubtedly be one of slow suffering.

Pecklyn nodded and she scampered free of the stairwell, down a wide hallway on the fourth level toward a set of closed, double doors at its far end. The Wizards' Assembly Hall was as good a place as any to start their search for the headmaster, but if the empty halls were any indication, she didn't think Sagora would be holding court at this late hour.

Crouching low, she placed an ear against one of the doors. Satisfied, she nodded for Pecklyn to join her.

Pecklyn settled in against the second door, pressing long fingers against its oaken surface in concentration. He glanced up with a look Balewynd knew well. There was someone within the chamber.

He rose to his feet and pulled his saber free, positioning himself to rush in as Balewynd unsheathed her dagger and eased the door open.

Thankful for well-oiled hinges, she opened the door wide enough to reveal two elven guards sitting on the bottom step of a wide dais on the opposite side of a dimly lit chamber. Polearms propped on the steps, the guards conversed in hushed tones.

Pecklyn adjusted his sword, poised to charge, but Balewynd held a staying hand between them and turned her head to listen.

"It's not a good sign, if you ask me," the elf on the left muttered.

"They won't attack," his companion answered. "Not with Orlythe's troops holding the far end of the pass."

"Why not? If they're as outnumbered as I hear, they'll have little choice. The queen's not going to stand by and wait to be slaughtered."

"Surely she must know the power the guild wields."

"True, but if she gets wind of the headmaster's condition, she might risk it."

The elf on the right shrugged. "Maybe. If she has spies here, she might."

"Oh, you can be certain the daughter of the War Dragon has spies everywhere. I wouldn't be surprised if one watches us now."

Balewynd pulled the door shut and held her breath as the guards searched the chamber with their eyes. Though hard to tell, it didn't sound as if the guards had gotten up. Raising eyebrows at Pecklyn, she leaned into the door enough to expose the steps again. The guards hadn't moved.

Dragon Sect

The guard on the left stared at something Balewynd couldn't see in the front corner of the chamber. "You think the high wizard had anything to do with it?"

His companion shrugged. "I wouldn't put it past the cretin." His head swiveled, taking in the hall as he lowered his voice, "Although it could've been that lich."

The other elf's eyes widened. "Come on. We best finish our rounds."

Balewynd eased the door closed and tilted her head for Pecklyn to follow her back to the stairwell. Ducking inside, she peered out in time to watch the two guards exit the hall and walk toward them. She was about to warn Pecklyn to descend the stairs when the guards turned down a side hallway and were lost to sight.

Crouched beside her hip, Pecklyn peered out. "What did they say?"

"Hard to say. I think something's happened to Headmaster Sagora."

Pecklyn frowned.

She shrugged. "He might be sick."

A slow smile crossed Pecklyn's face. "If that's the case, he'll be in his sleeping chambers."

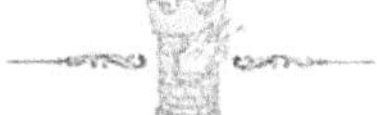

Darting into an alcove stuffed with statues of wizards and various creatures, Balewynd scanned their surroundings as Pecklyn focused on the solitary door across from them. Sagora's private chamber.

Pecklyn nodded. "There's definitely a strong magical presence on the other side of that door."

"That'll be the headmaster." Balewynd regripped her dagger. It was time to use it. She made to step into the hallway, but Pecklyn grabbed her upper arm to prevent her from doing so.

"I've never detected magic this strong."

Balewynd turned a puzzled gaze on him.

"Not even from Master Aelfwynne."

"You think there's a dragon in there?"

Pecklyn concentrated on the door a moment longer. He shook his head. "Definitely not dragon magic. I can't put a name to it. If anything, I would say it's closer to earth blood than anything living."

Balewynd frowned.

He shrugged. "It's *not* earth blood, but I have no idea where the magic stems from. We may be walking into something beyond our comprehension."

Balewynd's mood darkened. They were here on the king's order. Queen Khae had fallen victim to something Hammas considered otherworldly. Her eyes widened at the revelation.

She pulled free of Pecklyn's grasp and hissed, "The Dragon Witch Wraith!"

Pecklyn shrugged again. "Could be. If that's the case, we might want to reconsider what we came here to do."

Balewynd ignored him. Nothing would prevent her from confronting the one responsible for killing her father. She had never forgiven herself for not standing up to it at Castle Grim. Making sure the hallway was clear, she padded across and put an ear to the door. Nothing.

At her signal, Pecklyn joined her and placed his hand against the wood. He withdrew his touch almost immediately. "Whatever it is, it's definitely in there. You sure about this?"

Balewynd stared him in the eye, her angular nose giving her demeanour a malicious appearance. Without a word, she waited long enough for him to ready his saber before grabbing the bronze door latch and opening the door wide.

Dragon Sect

In practiced unison, Pecklyn's blade led him across the threshold into the room beyond as Balewynd stepped behind him to appear on his other side—her dagger ready to engage.

Not sure what she expected to find, the startled looks of a haggard, elderly chamberlain and a meek servant elf staring up from where they knelt on either side of Headmaster Sagora's bed gave her pause. The bulk of the great wizard of Orphic Den lay beneath crimson sheets; thick hands folded atop his ample stomach. Rushlight glinted off the many baubles adorning the headmaster's fingers—a wealth of unknown power.

The elderly chamberlain jumped to his feet from the far side of Sagora's bedside. Moving faster than his frail appearance suggested him capable of, he yelled, "Assassins!" and bolted through a hidden recess in a side wall.

Balewynd fought the urge to chase him. They were here for Sagora's head. Nothing else mattered.

The female servant raised her hands before her, shaking her head. "P-please, spare me. I've done nothing. I'm j-just a minor ch-chamberlain."

Pecklyn advanced across the room, his saber poised to strike.

Ever ready, her companion's movement elicited a grim smile on Balewynd's scarred face. Should something happen to Pecklyn, she would never find anyone as remotely capable or compatible as the white-haired elf.

"Please," the servant begged, dropping to her knees.

Balewynd ignored her and stepped around Pecklyn to approach the head of the large bed. "What's wrong with him?"

"He was struck by lightning."

"Lightning?" Balewynd scanned the headmaster. Other than long, disheveled grey hair splayed across his pillow, it looked as if there was nothing wrong with him.

"Magical lightning," the servant added with a knowing nod.

Balewynd glanced at Pecklyn. He shook his head in ignorance.

Balewynd turned back to the servant, her mind reeling with the implications. She couldn't rid her mind of the ghastly image of the wraith. "Did he do battle with another wizard?"

The frightened servant shook her head. "I don't know, m'lady. It came from the sky. The healers claim he's under a spell." She attempted to back around the bed, but Pecklyn stayed her with the tip of his blade.

Conscious of being in the heart of Orphic Den, Balewynd steeled herself to the gruesome task the king had charged them with. She reached out with both hands—one to hold the wizard by the hair and the other bearing her jagged-edged dagger, intent on severing the serpent's head.

"Bale! Wait!" Pecklyn shouted.

Pecklyn's empty hand hovered over Sagora, a stunned look transforming his features. "The magic I sensed is coming from him."

"That's impossible. He may be a powerful wizard, but there's no way he possesses the magic you speak of."

The servant girl forgotten, Pecklyn held both hands over the prone leader of the wizards' guild, divining his malaise. "It's not Sagora who possesses the magic," he whispered in awe. "It's the magic that possesses Sagora."

"We need to take his head," Balewynd snarled.

At the mention of what they planned to do with Sagora, the servant girl cried out and dropped trembling to the floor at the foot of the bed.

Dragon Sect

Pecklyn shook his head. "I'm thinking that won't end well for us."

Balewynd glared. "We have no choice. If we're caught…" she trailed off, her gaze flicking to the open door behind them.

Standing in the hallway, surrounded by six wizards, the stoop-shouldered chamberlain pointed a bony finger their way. "There they are! Seize them!"

Dragon Sect

Diary of a Dead Witch

Stunned, Scale gaped at the door. Without having to check, he knew it would do him little good to try to open it, and yet, he had to know.

He was right.

Zorain's roar sounded a long way off, though the pounding and scratching on the door bespoke otherwise.

"It's okay. I'm not hurt." He searched the dark interior for signs of anything unusual in the chamber. Aside from the wet footprints he had left in the dust, nothing disturbed the serene tower. If the fine hairs on his skin standing on end were any testament to the predicament he found himself in, being alone in the mystic tower promised not to end well.

The pounding on the door stopped. Moments later, Zorain's screech sounded on the far side of the tower.

"Zorain! Check the top of the tower for a way out," he yelled at the outer wall. Looking up he had no idea how he would reach the roof should the dragon find one.

For some reason, Zorain never spoke—an unusual happenstance given the dragon's chatty nature when it was just the two of them. He swallowed his misgivings. Not as knowledgeable as he would like to be regarding the subtle nuances of magic, it was as if the strong presence they had sensed was responsible for severing the intimate bond they shared as dragon and rider.

A sudden, deep loss gripped him—the emotion so raw it was like he had lost his best friend. Reflecting on it, Zorain was that friend.

He shook his head at the futility of feeling sorry for himself. Aelfwynne's voice sounded in his mind, berating him for his weakness like only the grumpy, old goblin could. The high wizard would be angry if Aelfwynne was to find out how much the crisis he faced had incapacitated him.

"Think Scale, think," he said aloud, spinning a slow circle across the floor. "The tower is infused with magic…Why?" He cupped his chin. "Why go to all the trouble to protect an empty tower? Unless…" Comprehension lit up his face. "It's not empty!"

The staggering revelation left him dumbstruck. As a fledgling wizard, he should know these things. Powerful magic-users had the ability to hide things in plain sight. If that was the case, there must also be a logical reason behind an entire castle being built in the middle of nowhere—in what he suspected was nothing more than wasteland north of the realms of man. It made sense considering the extreme temperature change and the fleeting glimpse he'd had of the landscape when they had touched down in the lake.

The problem facing him was how a novice apprentice like himself would be able to find a way to see beyond the optical illusion someone had painstakingly enacted to deter creatures like himself.

'Search for trigger points,' Aelfwynne's teachings echoed in his head. *'Mind the wards, for they will create a calamity*

of grand proportion. Once sprung, not even the worthiest of wizards is adept enough to defend against them.'

He pulled his wet clothing tighter around him in a futile effort to ward off the chill as he searched the empty chamber. Where to start? Other than the exit door, the interior of the tower was nondescript. The walls were carved from a single piece of rock—its smooth surface well-polished.

He stared at the door. It had slammed shut and locked itself, but how? Bewildered at what forces might be involved in facilitating such an act without a spellcaster nearby sent shivers up his spine. If there was another magic-user inside the tower with him, he would be helpless to defend against them.

"Zorain? Can you hear me?"

No response.

"Arg!" He shouted his frustration. If Aelfwynne were to hear of his incompetence, he would likely exile him from Highcliff.

He studied the plain door and muttered, "What would you do, Master Aelfwynne? What would you look for?"

The wood felt no different than any other he might run his hands along. Its oak surface was weathered with age, but a quick probe confirmed it was nothing but wood.

Defeated, he let his forehead thump against the unforgiving barrier. Perhaps that was the whole purpose behind the tower. To trap hapless victims. To keep them contained until…what? Until they died? And then what?

He thumped the door with a clenched fist and turned to stare at the chamber—letting his back slump against the stone.

Faint light filtered through random window slits; airborne silt visible in the muted rays. His eyes adjusted to the gloomy atmosphere; he could just make out the top of the tower. There did not appear to be another way out.

Zorain's roar sounded again, but from where, Scale could not guess. His dragon would be frantic with worry. He was surprised Zorain hadn't torn the roof off the tower.

Sighing, he had no idea what Aelfwynne would do in a situation like this. Perhaps he should have paid more attention to the high wizard's ramblings.

He spit out a laugh. Who was he kidding? Even if he survived this impossible quest Aelfwynne had sent him on, he doubted he would ever be able to concentrate long enough to get the most out of one of the high wizard's monotonous lessons.

Nodding, he imagined what his father's reaction would be should he see him now. The captain of the Home Guard would fold his arms across his broad chest and look down his nose at him—mocking him for trying to become something he was not.

The wand!

He reached into the little pouch he stored the short length of metal in and studied it. What could he do with the wand of destiny? If ever he needed to discover the wand's namesake, now would be the time, but the cold steel offered no insight into how he might employ it.

Discouraged, he lowered his gaze to the ground before him, absently tracing the wet footsteps his passage had left in the thick layer of dust. His path had meandered around the interior of the tower with no real purpose to a point beyond the centre of the chamber.

His gaze followed the confusion of footprints where he had turned lazy circles, his passage arcing near the far wall and starting back toward where he had first entered the tower, the paths joining near the doorway.

He blinked in consternation as he scanned the ground. Halfway across the floor it appeared as if he had jumped clear of the centre of the chamber—his passage around the tower evidenced in the dust, was missing several footprints.

Pushing off the wall, he walked toward the middle of the chamber. As his viewing angle changed, so did the footsteps he was able to see. The closer he got to the centre, the less the stretch of footprints were concealed. Something lay hidden in plain sight in the centre of the tower floor.

The more he thought about it, the stranger the discovery became. He had walked straight through the spot where he perceived the deception was hidden. If something did occupy the spot, why hadn't he bumped into it?

Kneeling where he thought the hidden object lay, he felt at the air before him and rubbed the flagstones at his feet. Airborne particles swirled about in the wake of his movement, eliciting a racking cough so intense that his eyes watered to the point he could no longer see.

He stood up and stumbled backward to escape the small eddy. Hacking to clear his throat, he chanted, "Osteno revalara," in hopes of clearing his vision, and immediately fell backward over an old wooden table that sat between two, high-backed settees—spilling the table's contents and himself to the ground.

Shocked, he jumped to his feet—wild eyes searching every which way at once. Unable to believe his blurred vision, a fully furnished chamber greeted him, complete with large rugs running between four sitting areas and a fair-sized fountain set off to one side. An arched fire mantle comprised much of the wall opposite the doorway, its hearth bursting to life with flames that lapped at great logs set on cast iron cradles.

Dragon Sect

Wand forgotten, he pulled his dagger free, fully expecting an attack, but after a few hair-raising moments of panic, he realized he was still alone.

He struggled to calm his hammering heart and regain a semblance of normality to his breathing as he surveyed the lavishly appointed room—one that would complement the fancy chambers of Borreraig Palace. Gold and silver glinted in the light of flaming sconces that suddenly flared to life along the exterior wall.

The entire chamber was decorated in such a fashion that all the aisles and sitting areas commanded a view of a tiny, marble stand in the centre of the chamber. A long spear, much taller than himself, stood behind a little lectern, held within an iron ring attached to the stand. On the lectern's tilted tabletop sat a small book.

Unable to believe what he was seeing, nor that he was the only one in the chamber, he carefully scanned the room. Aside from the hearty crackle and pop coming from the hearth, nothing disturbed the tranquility of the room. Other than the insistence of the book demanding his attention.

The magical presence he and Zorain had sensed bombarded his senses. Positive the overall essence resonated from everything in the chamber, he was drawn to the pedestal and its contents. The long spear looked to be a weapon that might best be utilized from the back of a dragon, but it was the book that drew his attention.

He slid his dagger into its sheath and was about to put away his wand but stopped—its blackened tip was exuding a faint, crimson glow.

He frowned. His magic, whenever it had shown itself, had always been limned in white light. Taking a deep breath, he stepped up to the pedestal, surprised by the text written along the book's spine—'Diary.' Realizing the word was written as a rune jarred his common sense. Of the belief that only elves utilized the ancient language, the appearance of the rune this far away from South March gave him pause.

But it wasn't the text that intrigued him most. It was the aura the diary gave off. Like it possessed a life force of its own. Invested with a magic unlike anything Scale had experienced before—even that of the wood sprite Dithreab. It was as if the book hummed with power. Afraid to touch what could only be an ancient relic, he reached out with the end of his wand—cringing with the expectation of a backlash as he flipped the cover open.

Half expecting a similar reaction to the one he had experienced in Crag's Forge when he had freed Aelfwynne, he was relieved when nothing untoward happened.

Curious as to what he might find written on the pages of the diary, he was shocked to see his name clearly written several times on the first few pages, the words also written in the ancient language of what he had been told belonged to the gods.

Scale! What happened?
Scale? Where are you?
I can't open the door. It's magically warded.
Can you hear me?
Scale?

Not sure what he was looking at, he flipped the page.

I'm going to look for another way in.
Don't worry. I'll never leave you.
If you can hear me…what the?
What's happening?
The magic is stronger.

Dragon Sect

Scale! Are you alright? Scale!

The text ended halfway down the third page. Scale's jaw dropped as comprehension set in. The words were Zorain's.

He swallowed in horror and stared harder at the pages. Had the strange magic claimed Zorain and placed him inside the book?

Forgetting his misgivings, he used his free hand to flip through the diary, but the rest of the pages were blank. He turned back to the last page the text appeared on and shouted at the book, "Zorain? Are you in there?"

Not sure what to expect, he was shocked as his name etched itself across the page below the last line of text.

Scale?

"Zorain? It's me! Are you trapped in the book?"

Trapped in what book?

"The diary within the tower," he said, his voice dropping off as a third presence entered the conversation. Though he didn't know how, know he did. The voice in his head came from the diary.

"Take me and my rod. It's time we returned to the world of the living."

Scale gaped at the open book, his gaze flicking to the non-descript spear, but as much as he wanted to, he couldn't pull his hands away from the diary as more words wrote themselves across the top of the next page.

Dragon Sect

You're not making any sense. I'm standing by the door in the bailey. I can't break the door down. What's happening in there?

Scale spun to face the door, the diary in hand. As soon as the book left the pedestal, the floor trembled beneath him. Frightened, he searched the ground, but his eyes were drawn to the diary as more words etched themselves across the page.

"Take up my rod," the impelling voice directed.

His mind reeled. Doing as he was instructed, he lifted the spear clear of its bracket, marveling at how light it was. Consumed by everything going on around him, he couldn't escape the fact that there was something about the book that resonated with him, tickling the depths of his memory. He had heard of something like this. Recently, in fact.

Adjusting the spear in his grasp, he flipped to the next page of the journal and watched in stunned silence as more of the runic language appeared before his eyes.

Scale! What's happening in there? What did you do?

All at once, he was instilled with the wonder of what he held in his hands. Aelfwynne had spoken many times of a sacred journal that had been lost to the world when the Dragon Witch had died.

He swallowed hard. Could it be that he held within his white-knuckled fingers the diary of a dead witch?

Flustered, he responded to Zorain's question, "I didn't do anything!"

Well, someone did something! You have to get out of there now! The castle is falling!

Dragon Sect

Rock Troll!

'Snick.'

Ouderling and Jyllana spun at the sound in time to witness their escape route disappear beneath them—the steps in the stairwell tilting to create a steep slope, dumping them back onto the small platform.

Turning to face the creature intent on destroying them, they watched in disbelief as a stout dwarf, half the height of an elf, dropped over the lip of the stone dragon's head, landing on the platform and challenging the behemoth with a double-bladed great axe and shield. "Hey, beastie! Why don't ye pick on someone yer own size?"

The creature roared and swiped at the dwarf, its massive hand swatting the squat axe wielder.

The dwarf yelled in defiance, swinging his mighty weapon, but its blade merely clanged off the side of the creature's hand—a great spark marking the impact. A mournful wail accompanied the dwarf's demise as he tumbled into the abyss with arms and legs flailing in a futile attempt to grab onto something. His axe spun after him.

Dragon Sect

"Oi! Beastie!" Another cry echoed in the bottomless chamber—the deep shout taken up by more voices as several dwarfs spilled from the dragon's head bearing battleaxes and warhammers to confront the creature.

"Over here, stone troll!"

"Yer a poor excuse for a rock."

"Come 'n face me axe."

"Yer uglier than me mate 'ere." A dwarf, rounder than he was tall bellowed, indicating a taller, red-bearded dwarf who gave him a sour look.

The red beard turned to look across the chasm. "'ave no fear, lassies. Sarsen's finest are 'ere for ya. Get yerselfs up the ramp, afore it's too late."

Mesmerized by the brave dwarfs, Ouderling was loath to abandon them to their fate.

Jyllana grabbed her arm and shook it. "Your Highness! Climb the ramp! It can't harm us in the stairwell."

Ouderling swallowed her misgivings. Witnessing another dwarf tumble into the void, however, spurred her into action. She slung her bow over her shoulder and attacked the steep slope but found it almost impossible to find purchase on the smooth surface. She slid back to the ledge.

"Try again. I'll boost you." Jyllana said, her attention jumping between Ouderling and the scene unfolding across the chasm.

"I can't."

Jyllana shoved Ouderling against the slope, her hands wrapped in the princess' green cloak. "Yes. You. Can," she grunted as she physically lifted Ouderling into the stairwell.

Bolstered by Jyllana, Ouderling scrambled up the narrow shaft. Once inside its tight confines, she found that by pressing her thighs, knees, elbows, and back against the walls, she was able to keep from sliding back down, though it required every bit of strength she possessed.

Inside the stairwell, the battle sounds of the chaotic scene in the vast chamber fell away to a dull roar. Almost impossible to see below her, she screamed, "Come on, Jyllana! Grab my ankle and pull yourself up."

Her protector's fingers wrapped around the bottom of her boot, the sudden weight almost dislodging her. Desperate to hold on, she ignored the pain shooting through her straining limbs. If she were to slip, she would not only doom herself and Jyllana, but the courageous dwarfs distracting the…rock troll?

She blinked in confusion. She had never heard of such a creature before.

Her upper hand slipped. Then her opposite knee. Pressing her body against the confines of the stairwell with everything she had, she gritted her teeth against the screaming agony of her trembling muscles. A frantic look up the steep shaft wasn't one of her best ideas. Even with her acute dark vision, she was unable to see the top. Before she had a chance to give in to the despair that the realization instilled in her, a deep rumble shook the walls.

Jyllana's sudden scream jolted her senses. At first, she believed the rock troll had thrown another projectile across the chasm as Jyllana's fingers released their hold on her boot, and the redhead's voice dropped away, but the rumbling persisted. In the absence of Jyllana's weight pulling on her, Ouderling realized the truth.

A hidden slab of rock had slid into place at the base of the stairwell, extinguishing the faint light of the dragon's head chamber as surely as if it no longer existed.

Panic gripped her. Trapped within the stairwell, having no way of knowing whether Jyllana still lived or not, she pounded on the unforgiving stone with the sole of her boot and screamed, "Jyllana!"

The rough stone of the shaft scraped her skin through her clothing. Her hands wet with sweat, she slid down the shaft and came to rest with her legs crumpled beneath her.

The heat in the subterranean chamber was so oppressive, she feared she might pass out. Shrugging free of her leather surcoat, it fell around her feet.

Devastated, she cried out again—her voice cracking as it lost its fervor. Trapped at the bottom of the stairwell, appreciating how far into the mountain the steps had descended, and accompanied by the fear that Jyllana would soon be dead, Ouderling lost all will to save herself.

Dragon Sect

Go Ghost

𝕬 scream ripped free of Braen's throat, competing with the one Cassava had just finished emitting. Limned in light, his hands trembled violently, not sure what was about to attack them. Fighting hard to resist it, he quelled his inherent magic's urge to make itself known.

A crazed laughter came from the tunnel ahead, but not from where he would have expected. He pulled his rapier free, the weapon awkward in his hand.

Cassava's mischievous smile met his horrified gaze. "You scare easily, South March prince."

Braen's white-knuckled grip shook so hard he wouldn't have been capable of striking something if it stood right in front of him. His blade wavering between them, he frowned at the strange woman.

"Put that away before you stick yourself with it. I'm just playing with you."

Braen's jaw dropped. Unable to express his indignance at being fooled to the point of nearly wetting himself, all he could do was stare.

"Now come on. We're almost there. I apologize if my antics are unbecoming of a queen."

Not sure whether his trembling legs would respond, it took him several tries to sheath his blade—finding it almost impossible to slide the tip into the thin slot at his waist.

Cassava's grin widened but she said no more as she disappeared around the bend, taking the torchlight with her.

The narrow tunnel walls jarred his shoulders and scraped his elbows as he scrambled after the Queen of Aldebaran, not happy about being left in the dark beneath a graveyard. He spit out a laugh as he rounded the corner and caught sight of her silhouette in the distance. Chasing after a crazed, homicidal maniac from a land far away didn't exactly strike him as a great idea either, but what choice did he have?

He gulped as the woman turned another corner, leaving him to grope in the ensuing darkness. If not for his dark vision, his fear might have caused him to drop to the earthen floor and wail like a wee elfling.

The smell of burnt pitch should have warned him, but the sight of Cassava's penetrating brown eyes greeting him as soon when he rounded the corner made him yelp—the extinguished torch smoking on the ground at her feet.

Cassava slapped a large palm over his mouth. "Are you trying to get us killed?"

He shook his head as much as his captive face would allow—an ironbound, wooden door greeting him from over her shoulders.

Dropping her hand and wiping it on her tunic, she said, "This is the grave digger's secret entrance to the castle. A discreet way for ones of their persuasion to move about the castle grounds without being seen."

"How do you know that?"

She raised her eyebrows at him.

"Um…I don't want to know."

"Good choice," she said with a smile. Turning to the door, she pulled a rusty key from the front of her fancy armour and unlocked it.

Braen wanted to know where she had come by the key, but decided the less he knew, the better.

A short hallway ended at a second door. Cassava's key opened that as well.

Flickering light spilled into the dark entranceway as she eased the door open and stuck her head inside.

She whispered, "Clear," and stepped into a pungent smelling corridor lined with steel cages built into the walls—a few of them housing what looked like emancipated bodies lying in filth.

Braen followed Cassava through the dungeon level, unable to keep from staring at the unmoving forms inhabiting the cells. Moans sounded from the dank enclosures, but it was the sudden set of eyes that opened in the last cell he passed that made him jump—as if he hadn't expected the prisoners to be alive. Instinctively, he pulled his cowl over his head

Cassava glared at him from an open doorway at the end of the corridor. "If you get any slower, you'll become a permanent resident."

"Sorry, I was just…" He trailed off. The queen had already started to ascend a wide set of steps, the curving stairwell thick with black smoke from greasy brands embedded at regular intervals into the stone block walls.

He caught up to her at the head of the stairwell, her ear against a wooden door.

She placed a dagger tip to her lips in a shushing motion and stepped into a dimly lit hallway beyond. Checking both ways, Cassava seemed to hesitate, but after staring down the bare corridor, she turned left and padded silently away.

Braen cringed every time his soft suede boots slapped the flagstone, marvelling at how the woman moved without a sound. Forced to run fast, his cowl fell onto his shoulders.

Cassava darted into a side hallway, reaching back to drag him in behind her, and forced him into a crouch.

What happened next occurred so quickly that Braen couldn't give an accurate account if someone had asked. One moment he stared in scared expectation at an empty hallway, but as soon as he locked eyes with a startled man in leather armour and chainmail, Cassava exploded into motion.

Two castle guards had stepped into view, making no effort to be quiet. Before they could so much as breathe their next breath, the closest man held his hands to his punctured windpipe and dropped to his knees. The second guard stumbled backward against the opposite wall with the tip of Cassava's dagger drawing a drop of blood from the guard's stubble-covered neck—shock and fear in his terror-stricken stare.

"Where can I find the king?"

"Ask him about Alexis," Braen piped up, carefully stepping around the man writhing in the middle of the floor, his dying gurgles enough to turn Braen's stomach.

The pinned guard's eyes flicked from Cassava to Braen to his companion on the ground and back again.

"The king," Cassava snarled, her dagger dimpling the guard's neck.

"H-he's in his chambers," the guard sputtered.

Cassava stared into his eyes. "I don't believe you." She leaned her weight into the arm pressed against his chest. "Last chance. Where's the king?"

The guard's Adam's apple convulsed as the dagger's tip pressed in a bit harder.

Dragon Sect

"He's interrogating a prisoner," the guard gasped, his gaze jumping to Braen, focusing on his pointed ears. "Torturing the man *he* speaks of."

Braen's quick intake of breath was overpowered by the queen's snarl.

Growling like a feral cat, Cassava's eyes narrowed. With each distinct word she waggled the hilt of the dagger against his neck, threatening to push it through. "Where. Is. The. King?"

"In…In the throne room."

Cassava held his terrified gaze a moment longer.

The guard's eyes grew wider as her dagger slid into his neck—not stopping until it struck the wall. With a satisfied grunt, Cassava pulled the blade free and stepped back.

The man slid down the stone grasping at his mortal wound—a red smear on the wall behind him.

Braen watched in horror as the guard tried to staunch the flow of blood. Staring incredulously at Cassava, he asked, "Why'd you kill him? He told you what you wanted to know."

Cassava returned his hard gaze, the point of her bloody dagger waggling between his crossed eyes. "A dead guard is the only ally you'll find in an enemy's house. Bear that in mind if you wish to see the sunrise."

Braen swallowed, unable keep from staring at the dagger. He nodded slightly and the dagger fell away.

"Now," Cassava whispered, "we need to sneak into the throne room and finish our mission. It's time to go ghost."

Braen frowned at her odd turn of phrase. Not caring to know what she meant, he looked to the second guard already dead in the middle of the floor, and searched the shadows of the corridor stretching away to either side.

Dragon Sect

He wasn't on any mission. He had only come to inquire about what had happened to Prince Alexis. If the king was torturing him as the guard claimed, Braen wanted nothing to do with it. He couldn't help wondering what would befall his own fate should he be caught in the castle—especially after being a party to the one who had dispatched two of the king's men. Not to mention the fact that he was an elf.

He was about to suggest that they return to the passage beneath the graveyard and be gone from Nordicia Castle, but a strange sensation gripped him. His head snapped back to where Cassava had stood moments before.

Of the assassin queen, there was no sign.

Left alone in the corridor with two dead guards didn't bode well. Not with the sound of metal-shod footfalls ascending the stairwell in a hurry.

Not sure what to do, he ran in the opposite direction, but stopped after several steps and stared in dismay at the next junction in the hallway.

Looking none too pleased, a large guard dressed in boiled leather and pieces of accompanying scale armour stepped into the hallway, his dark glare taking in the grisly scene behind Braen.

The man's attention fell on the eleven prince's ears. Drawing his sword, he advanced.

Dragon Sect

Time to Visit the War Dragon

Khae Wys floated in what seemed like an alcohol-induced stupor, though drunk she certainly was not. Her essence trapped in a world not of her own, it was difficult to ascertain what was real and what was illusion.

Vaguely aware she had reached out to forces beyond her ken, she had utilized her natural gift in a way she had never dreamt of doing. If what she believed was happening was true, she had successfully left her mortal self and breached the world of the Fae—something High Wizard Aelfwynne had told her that only her late son was capable of. A bittersweet smile turned up a corner of her mouth. Ordyl had gotten his talent from her. The problem she faced now was how to get back.

The atmosphere around her appeared as nothing more than a veil of swirling mist on a field of impenetrable black. She mused that perhaps she had ascended into the night sky but on closer inspection, no sign of the stars or moon was evident. It was like the world had winked out of existence, leaving a vapourous black hole in its wake.

Dragon Sect

Drifting in a field of tranquil nothingness, she hadn't a care in the world. Unfettered from the trials of her previous life, she was free to simply drift. No more having to deal with unthankful elves. No more worrying if the crops would yield enough to feed the kingdom during the long, winter months. No more having to fret over Ouderling's welfare.

Her smile deepened, a pleasantness infusing her thoughts. Aelfwynne and Xantha would see to Ouderling's safety. No matter what happened, the princess was in the best of hands.

Even if they tired of Ouderling's presence, as she knew all too well how wearing her daughter could be, Hammas would never allow anything to happen to his Little Sprite.

The mist swirled violently around her, drawing her out of her complacent reverie. The sole reason she had dared to breach the barrier into the realm of the Fae was to rescue Hammas from the danger he faced.

Her husband and troops were entrenched in the Wizard's Walk facing annihilation unless something drastic was done to alter their fate. Unless she was wrong about Aelfwynne, the stubborn goblin would hold true to his belief that he needed to protect the Crystal Cavern at all costs. There would be no help coming from that front. His error in judgement last year had nearly cost them dearly. If the human wizard had been successful, not only would Ouderling have been killed, but the realm would have been taken to the brink of disaster.

Panic gripped her. The impending slaughter of the Royal Army would go a long way to sealing the kingdom's future, regardless of Aelfwynne's presence in Highcliff. A grim future she feared would come to pass anyway once her brother gained control of the Willow Throne. If she allowed that eventuality to come to pass, it would only be a matter of time before Highcliff fell, regardless of the Guardians.

Dragon Sect

How had things gotten so far out of hand so fast? A sinking feeling clouded her vision. The dim light emitted by the swirling mists was quelled by an evil pall of encroaching darkness. The Dragon Witch Wraith!

Though she didn't know how she knew, it was brutally apparent that once the darkness overtook the last of the fading mist, her fate would be sealed. She would never be able to find her way back to where her body lay in the royal pavilion. Her death would bring about the destruction of South March and the death of many of her subjects.

Angry with herself, she should have known better. She owed it to her people to be vigilant. Her brush with the phantasm beneath Borreraig Palace had been the harbinger of the calamitous events gripping the realm, and she had done nothing to prevent them from happening.

Her mother's presence facilitated through the intervention of the Dragon Witch and the Queen of the Fae had tried to warn her that this day would come, and yet she had still failed to act. Her faith in humanity had blinded her to the evil that flaunted itself in front of her very eyes.

Battered, and beaten into submission, the forces of goodness had been brought to heel—submitting to the strengthening current instead of swimming against it. By turning a blind eye to Orlythe's shortcomings, she had allowed the tide of darkness to sweep across the land.

So enrapt in the commiseration of her failure, she almost allowed the last wisp of mist to disperse. Her love for her husband prevented that from happening. As long as she retained the faintest of conscious thought, she would fight against the tyranny that threatened his life. If not for Hammas, then for all the unfortunate souls who had given their lives in service to her mother's vision of South March.

An ideal for a land to not only live in harmony with each other, but with nature itself.

In her mind, she gasped. The wisp of vapour had faded to a tiny eddy on the brink of winking out of existence.

"No!" She heard herself shout but couldn't be sure whether she had spoken at all.

Hammas needed her. The kingdom needed her. Her only living child depended upon her doing what she now knew was her only course of action. Firming her resolve, the eddy expanded, swirling around her and growing in intensity until it filled her vision. Remembering who she was and why she had risked her journey into the nether realm, she searched for the one being that would help her save the realm. Sagora.

Just the thought of the headmaster made her shudder in revulsion, but she knew beyond a doubt that he was the key to South March's salvation.

"Where are you, headmaster?" She reestablished her link with the Fae, the one that had been severed when she had been thrown from the top of Grim Watch Tower by the self-proclaimed leader of the Wizards' guild.

The mist condensed, its light increasing to the point that it caused her otherworldly vision to squint. Staring hard, she willed the scene to reveal in her mind's eye the location of where the headmaster's spirit had flown, for it had become abundantly clear that their spirits had clashed atop the warlock tower.

Considering she was still stuck in her out-of-body experience via her nature's essence, she hoped that Sagora also faced the same dilemma of finding his way back to his mortal self. If she could locate him before he did, she might still have a chance to help Hammas—if only to alleviate the threat posed by the wizards' guild. Whether her Royal Army would be strong enough to win free of the Wizard's Walk was another matter entirely, but that was out of her hands.

Her vision cleared, exposing a chaotic scene within what appeared to be a bedchamber.

Unseen to the elves in the chamber, Headmaster Sagora's spirit struggled to resurrect his corporeal body. Enshrouded in a magical essence that would undoubtedly prove deadly to anyone who tried to interfere with its otherworldly composition, it would only be a matter of time before his wizards figured out how to bring him back. An opportunity not open to her…Unless.

Concentrating hard, she called out to Aelfwynne, urging him to use his profound magic to come to her aid.

Just when she was about to give up, a stirring in the mist along the periphery of her vision informed her that the high wizard sensed her.

She delved deeper to extend her essence into his thoughts in an attempt to impart a message within his mind. Another presence had latched onto her probing magic, instilling her with a cold so deep she was sure her body back in the Wizard's Walk shivered. The same cold that had found her in the passageway beneath Borreraig Palace all those months ago.

All at once she realized that what she wished for would only expedite Highcliff's downfall. With a fleeting thought, she urged Aelfwynne *not* to respond to her dilemma in the north. Whether he received the message or not, she didn't dare linger long enough to find out—not relishing the idea of the wraith catching her in her present state.

Severing her tie with Aelfwynne, she had to be content in knowing that aid from Highcliff was not coming. If she insisted, she knew any response from Highcliff would precipitate the sacred community's downfall. It had become apparent to her that the Dragon Witch Wraith lay in wait for the Guardians to come to her aid in the Wizard's Sleeve.

Steeling herself to the fact that she was on her own, she concentrated on what was happening in the keep at Orphic Den. Though not actually able to see the scene within the headmaster's chamber, her nature's essence sensed two bodies that, although she wasn't very familiar with them, she knew without a doubt that they belonged to two of Aelfwynne's personal protectors.

She knew at once that neither soul was the ancient Guardian Xantha. That could only mean that Balewynd Tayn and Pecklyn Ors stood within the headmaster's chamber. What they were doing there, she could not fathom, but by the darker powers gathering around them, she was sure that their lives were in peril if she didn't act fast.

Not knowing either Guardian personally, she knew of them. Aelfwynne had spoken highly of his protectors on more than one occasion over the years. Though the goblin was a crotchety, seemingly unfeeling creature, it wasn't lost on her how dearly he cared for them. She owed it to Aelfwynne to deliver them from a fate they could not escape on their own.

Knowing how to go about it was another matter entirely. Just as despair flitted along the periphery of her mind, it was as if the universe had come to a standstill. Time ceased to exist as the elusive answer to all of her immediate troubles became perfectly clear.

By saving Aelfwynne's protectors, she would in turn save her husband from certain death. At least from the hands of the wizards' guild. It would be the Royal Army's duty to see that he survived the imminent clash with her brother's troops.

Dragon Sect

And yet, she hesitated. By doing what she knew had to be done, she was saddened by the fact she would never see her beautiful daughter again. Nor would she feel the love she shared with the one elf that meant more to her than life itself.

Hardening her resolve, that last thought settled it. In order for Hammas to survive and have a chance to make a difference, she must latch onto Sagora's soul and sever their link with the world of the living. If she trusted her instincts, her nature's essence—the magic that had blessed her many times over the years—would serve her well by using it to take her own life. A somber sense of elation filled her. By doing so, she would also take the headmaster with her.

Though she had talked tough during her reign as Queen of the Elves when the times had called for it, she had always been a gentle soul. Taking the life of an animal for food, or even that of an insect just because it disgusted her, had always left her feeling bad. In retrospect, her penchant for caring and forgiveness had proven her downfall.

It was time to atone for her shortcomings as queen. Being the leader of a great realm came with heavy responsibility. Her mother had known that. She nodded to herself. It was time to visit the War Dragon.

"Sagora?" She reached out with her nature's essence. Bolstered by unseen hands that she believed belonged to the White Witch, she beckoned, "Come to me if you dare."

The presence of the headmaster searched her out and filled her, threatening to smother her essence—a sense of victory in his confident manner.

A solitary tear rolled down her spiritual face as she enveloped the headmaster's soul and prepared to meet her destiny.

Dragon Sect

Taking a deep breath, she enveloped Sagora's essence in ethereal arms, and spirited them both beyond the threshold of the mortal veil. "It's time you answered to Nyxa."

Dragon Sect

No More

Queen Khae lay quietly on her pallet within the royal pavilion erected in the Wizard's Walk, hundreds of leagues from home.

Hammas clasped her clammy hand, fretting over her malaise. He should never have allowed her to attempt the unfounded journey she had proposed.

He took a deep breath, shaking his head. Who was he trying to fool? Once his headstrong wife made up her mind, there wasn't a creature alive that could dissuade her. As soft and caring as she appeared to her subjects, no one knew her as intimately as he did, besides perhaps, Ouderling. As much as Khae rarely displayed her more formidable side, she was every bit as strong as her mother had been. There was no doubt in Hammas' mind that his stubborn wife possessed the War Dragon's toughness.

However, that knowledge did little to console him now. He didn't dare think about a future without her, and yet, holding her hand, the fleeting warmth filled him with a knowledge he refused to accept. There was a good chance his soulmate had entered into a spell that had no return.

Dragon Sect

He swallowed, tears dripping off his chin. If Khae were to die as a result of Orlythe's treachery, he vowed to storm down the Wizard's Walk, fight his way through the Grim Guard, and tear the man's heart out with his bare hands.

The brazier popped behind him, bringing his attention back to his surroundings. Without having to look, he knew that Commander Keel, Captain Kall, and Captain Hondrick waited patiently on his command around the war table in the centre of the pavilion. As fierce as the queen's defenders were, they respected his need to be left alone at Khae's side.

He laid his head against the top of her hand hoping beyond hope that Pecklyn and Balewynd might be able to do something at Orphic Den. They had to. With two dragons at their command, they were his last hope.

"Come back to me Khae. We'll find a way out of this together," he whispered to the richly embroidered duvet draped over his wife's frail body. His shoulders shook. "Don't leave me. I can't do this alone. I need you."

As if she had heard him, Khae exhaled a contented moan.

Hammas looked up in hopeful expectation in time to see her face light up in one of her beautiful smiles. "He squeezed her hand. "Khae? Can you hear me?"

Aware that the murmurs of the commanders had fallen away, Hammas sensed their eyes on him, but he didn't care—his sole attention on his wife.

He straightened his back to see her better, wiping his eyes on the thick shoulders of his royal tunic, but cringed as a spasm shook her.

Khae gasped. "No!"

"Khae. It's okay. I'm here with you." He grabbed her shoulders and shook them gently. "It's me, Hammas."

As if she heard him, her head turned his way. Eyes closed, her lips parted, "Where are you, headmaster?"

Hammas blinked, taken aback. "No. It's me. Hammas. Your husband."

Her body tensed in his hands.

"Sagora?" Khae's head turned back to face the ceiling, her eyes opening and staring at something Hammas couldn't see. "Come to me if you dare."

"Khae?" Though her eyes were open, Hammas realized that her mind was elsewhere. Something deep inside informed him she was back at Orphic Den, confronting the Headmaster of the Wizards' guild.

He cupped her face. "Khae. Leave him. We'll deal with Sagora in due time. Come back to me so that we may face him together...Khae!"

The queen's body relaxed under him, a semblance of the former smile on her face. He shook his head. He knew her too well—the smugness of her smile informed him she was about to do something profound.

A single tear escaped her vacant stare, rolling down the side of her face to wet his finger.

He squeezed her face in his hands. "No! Don't you dare leave me!"

A long exhale escaped her lips, her sweet voice whispering, "It's time you answered to Nyxa."

Hammas stared in disbelief. Lowering his forehead against hers, his life had just slipped through his fingers.

The queen breathed no more.

Dragon Sect

There's a New Power in Town

Headmaster Sagora convulsed beneath the crimson cloth draped over his well-earned girth, his pudgy hands clasping an elaborately bejeweled dagger on his chest.

Pecklyn's sabre swung from where it pointed at the wizards standing in the corridor with spells ready, to the pallet in anticipation of having to fend off Sagora, but the leader of the wizards' guild remained unresponsive.

He could tell Balewynd struggled to refrain from cutting off Sagora's head—if not for the king, then for the shock the act would instill in those confronting them.

Pecklyn shook his head. "No, Bale! If you touch him, the spell he's under might kill you."

The way Balewynd regarded him didn't bode well. He knew that look. She was either going to ignore his warning or run at the wizards. Either way, things were about to get a lot worse for both of them. Once her eyes narrowed the way they had, there was no stopping her.

He side-stepped in front of the cowering servant to shield her from what was about to happen. Steeling himself, he assumed his fighting stance.

Dragon Sect

Balewynd's movements were unorthodox. A step one way, two steps another, a slight stutter-step and then a lunge toward the doorway, served to confuse the wizards.

Two spells were discharged, both missing Balewynd by the scantest of margins. One crackled off the floor near the head of Sagora's bed while the other sizzled dangerously close to where Pecklyn stood—the residual static tugging at his long tresses.

He instinctively ducked after the fact. Had the spell been aimed his way, he would have been hit. Crouched in front of the headmaster's pallet, he reached back with his free hand and pulled the servant in close. "When I move, get behind the bed."

Not waiting to see if she understood, he said, "Now," and made his own beeline toward the startled wizards.

Three spells were directed his way. All three hit.

The first glanced off his right shoulder knocking him into the path of the second that impacted his left hip. Off-balance, his attacking stance left open, he took the brunt of the third spell full in the chest, the force of the invisible casting lifting him from his feet.

Taking the breath from his lungs, the spell tossed him backward though the air. He feared he might land on Headmaster Sagora but fell short. Before his blasted body hit the ground, he caught sight of the black death descending upon Orphic Den's defenders—his companion a whirlwind of destruction in the midst of the magic-users.

He landed hard—his sabre clattering off the ground somewhere close by. White light flashed inside his head as his skull cracked against a flagstone.

Content that Balewynd had made it to the wizards, his world went black.

Dragon Sect

Absolute rage consumed her, but instead of dulling her senses, Balewynd had learned long ago how to channel her negative energy into a positive reaction. Focusing on a sole purpose, she mentally blocked out everything around her. The wizards meant them harm. Had done Pecklyn harm.

She covered the last bit of ground separating her from the nearest wizard and struck hard and fast. Pulling her dagger free of his crumpling body, the next spellcaster barely had time to gape before she dispatched him on her way toward the third wizard in line—Xantha's lessons flowing through her.

Without looking back, she sensed that Pecklyn had gone down. Had she not cared so much for the perpetually smiling elf, she might have disposed of every magic-user present, but her concern for her friend caused her to hesitate for the briefest of moments—a moment too long.

A magical force ripped into her as she stepped free of her third victim, the impact stopping her advance toward an older wizard with a white beard. She stumbled sideways, the use of her legs seemingly taken from her.

She reached out to the wall to keep from falling. With nothing to grab onto, she slid to the ground. Unable to keep her knees beneath her, she ended up on her side.

The white-beard stepped toward her but jumped back to avoid her slashing dagger. "Whoa, Balewynd Tayn. You're a feisty one for the daughter of a chamberlain."

Balewynd glared up at him, dragging her incapacitated legs behind her as she tried to get at him.

"I clearly see your father in you. He reacted much the same way when we cast him from the guild." The wizard nodded, keeping his distance. "Though I must say he lacked your gumption."

Dragon Sect

The wizard's words gave her pause. On closer scrutiny, she still couldn't place him.

"Oh, you don't know me. Well, you certainly wouldn't remember me. I was part of the coven that decreed that your father be ousted from the wizards' guild for the treachery he committed against the previous headmaster."

Balewynd frowned and grunted as she lunged deeper into the hallway to slash at his robed legs. "You're a liar!"

The wizard avoided her attack. "As much as I'd like to refute your assertion, you're correct. I've been known to lie on occasion when it suited the greater good."

"My father wasn't a wizard. Nor would he ever have anything to do with the likes of you."

"So sure, are you? Perhaps your father is a liar as well, hmm?"

Balewynd's eyes narrowed to mere slits as she tried to move her legs to get at the wizard taunting her.

"Oh, right," the wizard said. "*Was* a liar. The old fool's dead, isn't he?"

Balewynd threw her dagger—the throw not having its usual power due to her prone position.

The wizard easily sidestepped it.

She screamed in frustration and snarled through gritted teeth, "When I get up, you'll be joining him."

"The headmaster!" the old chamberlain cried, diverting their attention.

Movement on the bed drew everyone's attention.

The meek servant scurried from where she hid and scrambled farther into the chamber, tripping over herself in her haste to be away from Sagora's pallet.

Balewynd forgotten, the remaining wizards approached the bedside, stopping a respectable distance away. To an elf, they jumped when Sagora suddenly sat up and shouted, "Khae! No!"

And then it was as if someone had delivered the hardest of punches to the headmaster's stomach. He exhaled a long, gasping breath and fell back to the pallet, dead.

Aside from the scraping of Balewynd dragging her body into the chamber to get at the wizards, Headmaster Sagora's quarters became deathly still.

"What are you waiting for?" the chamberlain screamed. "Kill them!"

The remaining wizards frowned at each other in bewilderment, as if they had just awoken from a deep sleep. Shock twisted their faces as they took in the carnage in the hallway.

Grunting his dissatisfaction, the chamberlain wrested the ceremonial dagger from Sagora's hands and turned to deliver a killing blow to Pecklyn who lay motionless on the floor at his feet.

"Pecklyn!" Balewynd cried out. Pulling herself across the floor as fast as she could, she knew she would not reach him in time.

Spittle flew from the chamberlain's mouth as he straddled Pecklyn and crouched low. Cackling hysterically, he swung the dagger through the air—the polished blade glinting in the rushlight.

"No!" Balewynd screamed.

The dagger dove deep, eliciting the strangest of squeals from the chamberlain.

Balewynd slumped to the floor, gasping for breath.

The chamberlain stood up, blood dripping from where the dagger had taken *him* in the lower abdomen. He gaped at the elderly wizard with contempt, opening his mouth to speak, but fell to the ground and said no more.

Dragon Sect

Turning on Balewynd the wizard said, "Fear not, daughter of Bale. If I'm not mistaken, the evil pall that has blanketed the wizards' guild for decades has been lifted with Sagora's death. Rest assured there's a new power in town."

Not caring about whatever the wizard was talking about, Balewynd dragged her body to Pecklyn and lovingly removed strands of white hair from his face—the long locks splattered with blood and soaked with sweat.

Studying his paler than usual skin, she grimaced at the pool of blood surrounding the back of his head.

"Bale's got you," she soothed. "Everything's going to be okay. Stay with me."

He didn't react.

Cupping his cheeks in her hands she pressed her forehead against his, tears flowing freely, fearing the worst.

"You can't leave me," her voice cracked. "You just can't."

The pain in his eyes as they opened were the happiest thing she thought she would ever see. The only elf that really mattered to her was alive.

She spit out a wet laugh at the sight of the slow smile creasing his haggard complexion and held her face against his.

Dragon Sect

Inexplicable Sense of Loss

Aelfwynne bumbled around his wizard's lair, aware of the fact that he was grumpier than usual. Unable to concentrate long enough to perform the most rudimentary of spells served to darken his mood. The kingdom was coming unraveled, and he was helpless to do anything about it.

Stuck in Highcliff, with no viable means of assisting Queen Khae, made him sick at heart. After everything they had been through together—and survived while in Nyxa's service—he could not in good conscience intervene. With the return of the Dragon Witch Wraith, it would be irresponsible for him to leave the Crystal Cavern unguarded again.

He stopped before the smoked glass window overlooking Crystal Lake and stared absently at the distant volcanic peaks—thoughts of his apprentice never far from his thoughts. Knowing the big galoop, he'd probably gotten himself and Zorain in a heap of trouble. Nor did the white dragon have a lick of common sense in his head. Between the two of them, he doubted they could find their way out of closet without the aid of a map, and yet, he had seen fit to send them chasing after the errant son of a dead witch.

He shook his head. What had he been thinking? Thumping the window with the heel of his palm, he ambled to the central pedestal to gaze at the bronze vessel he had had the smiths fashion to replace the previous scrying bowl. As much as Scale's suggestion to forge a magical vessel ingrained with its own inherent magic had been a brilliant idea, Aelfwynne was afraid to utilize the Focal Stone in such a capacity with the shard in its present state.

He ran a claw along the eight-sided vessel, appreciating the beautifully etched runes adorning the bowl's many surfaces. Someday the new scrying bowl would become much more than just a viewing device. The possibilities were endless if he could find a way to enhance the vessel's properties without destroying the Crystal Cavern.

He sighed, his mind drifting to his many other troubles. If the queen died, Ouderling would be the last stumbling block in Orlythe's path. He shuddered, his spasm not entirely due to his worsening condition. For all he knew, the princess might already be dead.

The shiver wracked him again, his hands trembling for a few moments more before the worst of the shakes abated. Growing old was maddening—his deteriorating condition only made matters worse. He couldn't afford to die of natural causes. Not when there was so much at stake.

His only consolation came from the fact that Pecklyn and Balewynd wouldn't fail him. He imagined they had reached the queen by now. That fact alone kept him from doing something he wasn't sure he had the heart to do—even if it meant keeping the Crystal Cavern out of the wraith's control.

With any luck, his faithful protectors would be on their way back with the king and queen in their company. If South

March were to survive Orlythe's offensive, Khae must not fall.

Thoughts of dear Nyxa's daughter brought a bittersweet smile to his face. As long as the prodigy of the War Dragon drew breath, there would always be hope for the land.

A deep frown creased his forehead. Visions of a distraught Khae filled his consciousness. Unsure why, he had a fleeting awareness that she was trying to reach out to him. He puzzled at the odd sensation, putting it down to the effects of the duress he had been under lately. Unless Khae had already arrived at Highcliff, which he knew she had not, there was no way that she should be able to infiltrate his thoughts. Not even a dragon possessed the magic required to project their voices much beyond the cliffs surrounding the southern aerie.

And yet, he had experienced so many wondrous and inexplicable things during his lifetime that he couldn't dismiss the notion outright—Dithreab's bauble had been the latest. Khae was a powerful magic-user—of that there was no doubt, but to reach across hundreds of leagues?

He wandered back to the window and searched the patches of low hanging clouds. "What're you trying to tell me?"

He knew the answer without having to hear it spoken. Against his better judgement, he knew what he had to do. By the tone of Khae's distress, Balewynd and Pecklyn had been unsuccessful in winning her free. If he didn't act at once, there was a very real chance that she would perish in the Wizard's Walk without his assistance.

He gnashed his pointed teeth. Although he knew it was the worst thing he could do, his loyalty to Nyxa would not allow him to do otherwise. He would risk it all if it meant saving the daughter of the War Dragon, and in turn, Nyxa's granddaughter.

Dragon Sect

He turned to leave the lair to go in search of Kingstone but stopped short. Another distant thought, more insistent than the previous one left him reeling. It was as if Khae had changed her mind and was now pleading with him to ignore her last request.

Unsure how he knew, there was no doubt in his mind it was indeed Khae that spoke to him. The strong feeling didn't elaborate on what was happening in the north, but it was clear that she now implored him to remain at Highcliff.

Staggered by the implications of the otherworldly message, he barely made it back to the central pedestal. Leaning on the edge of the stone, he found it difficult to catch his breath.

He concentrated on putting aside his conflicting emotions, forcing himself to breathe deeply—the same way he had trained Scale and Ouderling over the better part of the last year—and extended the limited reach of his magic, attempting to sense what was happening far to the north.

As an aged wizard, he had read a few accounts of exceptional magic-users utilizing their profound gift to communicate across great distances, much like the scrying bowls facilitated proficient wizards to see things in faraway places.

Never having attempted such a feat, his beady eyes narrowed for a moment before snapping open as the reality of what was happening dropped him to his knees.

An inexplicable sense of loss incapacitated him to the point that he shook uncontrollably in the wake of the earth-shattering revelation of his probing gift.

The crown had fallen.

Dragon Sect

Castle Fall

Scale stared in horror at the locked door. Propping the spear against the wall, his gaze returned to the runic text writing itself on the pages of the small journal in his hands.

Well, someone did something! You have to get out of there now! The castle's falling apart!

Zorain's warning gave him the chills. Even though he didn't want to think about it, the trembling of the flagstones beneath his feet left him with little choice.

Finding it difficult to think straight, panic gripped him. He was a low-level magic-user at best+—or, as his father and friends used to say, a wannabe wizard. As such, he should be able to win his way free of the tower. He had figured out a way to reveal what was in the tower, albeit unwittingly, but if that was any indicator, he should also possess the knowledge to extricate himself as well. All he had to do was discover how.

Dragon Sect

Something deep inside urged him to recall his lessons, but in his frantic state, nothing came to him. At least nothing noteworthy.

Hurry! The rear corner towers are crumbling!

The runic warning wrote itself on the page—the urgency of Zorain's plea causing the book to shake in his grasp. If he didn't figure out a way to escape soon, his failure might very well spell the death of his dragon too.

"Leave me!" He shouted at the door. "Save yourself!"

He had no sooner spoken than a series of runes appeared in the book. He flipped to the next page to read the entire message—fearing his shaking hand would tear the paper from the journal.

You know I can't do that.
We're bonded.
We're life mates. I am honour bound to face the danger
with you until the end.

"No! I release you from your obligation. Fly away fast!"

I will not. Now think. What would Aelfwynne do?
Appearances can be deceiving.

Despairing the danger his dragon was in because of him, he blinked at the text in awe—Scale's message instilling a profound sense of having experienced a similar scenario within him. He swallowed, staring at the forgotten wand cradled in his hand. It was as if he was reliving the scene beneath the cathedral at Castle Grim with a snarling goblin wizard glaring in disgust at him for being such an incompetent magic-user.

Forgotten until now, Aelfwynne's words resonated in his mind, *'Appearances are best left at that. The second rule you need to take to heart is this: misconstrue someone, or something, based on your limited perception of them at your peril. It's the surest way to end up dead.'*

Certain that Aelfwynne's lesson also pertained to what they were experiencing now, he struggled to come to terms with how it might assist him in unlocking the door.

He stared at the wand, its tip protruding from beyond the top of the journal. Thinking hard, more of Aelfwynne's advice came to him. *'Magic is something few individuals are born with. Some call it a gift but I say nonsense. It's what you make it. A gift. A curse. A non-entity. It's up to you how you wish to behold it. Just like a bird can fly, or a fish draws breath underwater, it's who you are. A bird cannot fly unless it flaps its wings. Magic can't respond if you don't embrace its presence and truly believe. Do you think the fish doubts its ability to draw air? Until you come to terms with the simple truths, your magic will be lost to you.'*

The message made sense. Until he fully believed in himself, his magic would inevitably falter. He lifted his chin with resolve. Though not sure where they had ended up, he took solace in the fact that he alone had unraveled the secret to successfully summoning a dragon *and* its rider—without the aid of Eolande, the high wizard, or the enhanced magic of the Crystal Cavern. He, Scale Wood, son of a captain in the queen's guard, had done something no other wizard had. Now if he could only live to tell about it.

The knowledge of his triumph should have bolstered his confidence, but staring at the obstinate doorway, the barrier did little to make him feel worthy.

Dragon Sect

Scale! The ramparts around the tower you're in are starting to crack!

He gulped, his heart hammering and his breathing coming in short, rapid gasps. Swallowing his mounting fear, he focused on Aelfwynne's most rudimentary lesson. He needed to calm his body and ease his mind into a level of clarity to think straight or he was finished. He knew this, and yet, it felt like an impossible thing to do.

"Slow and steady, Scale," he said out loud. Holding his hands out before him, the journal in his left hand and his wand in his right. He was dismayed by how much they shook. Forcing a deep breath, he whispered, "You can do this."

Realizing that reading any more of Zorain's words would only serve to aggravate his anxiety, he closed the diary and placed it inside his tunic.

The floor trembled, matching the groaning and creaking of the stone walls—eddies of dust sifting from the heights above.

If only the door would shake loose of its hinges, he absently hoped.

That was it! That was how he might breach the obstacle barring his exit. Remove its hinges.

He started to put his wand away in order to employ his dagger, but a nagging voice made him rethink his decision— the voice uncannily imitating that of the high wizard. Since he was trapped inside an enchanted tower, it stood to reason the hinges on the door would in turn be magically infused.

Aelfwynne's lessons came rushing back to him. '*Check for traps.*' Extending his arm, he channeled his inherent magic through the wand of destiny and probed the door. At once he sensed the strong magic instilled in the tower's construction. Its energy exuded from the walls, almost overpowering the aura that hid the minor nuances that lay underneath. Not sure of what he was about to do, Scale latched onto the faint anomalies.

To his wonder, he perceived a ward deep inside the two great hinges that secured the door to the stone frame. He knew at once he did not want to find out what would happen to anyone who disturbed them. He almost fainted realizing he had pushed open the door on the way in without bothering to check it first. Why the wards had not reacted then, he had no idea.

Panic seized him for a moment—fearing he had forgotten Aelfwynne's lessons on disabling wards. According to the high wizard, most wards, no matter how complex, were easily disabled—momentarily, at least. But, should someone err in their magical intrusion, they would set them off as surely as if they had unwittingly sprung them.

The ground continued to tremble, at times lurching beneath him. He resisted the urge to pull the diary from his tunic and read Zorain's updates. Whatever was happening outside must be catastrophic.

He fought to still his fear. If he wanted to save himself, and in turn, his life companion, he needed to win free of the tower, and fast.

He concentrated on what he had been taught. To his surprise, his magic flowed freely into his wand, coalescing into a tiny pinprick of brilliant white light at its tip. A gentle nudge was all it required to leap from the wand into the upper hinge to confront the ward.

He cringed as the two forces made contact, almost losing control of the focused power at his command. Steeling himself for whatever may come of his interference, he used his magic to manipulate the ward like Master Aelfwynne had instructed.

Though there wasn't a definitive sign left behind that he had disabled the protective charm, he had to be content that his manipulation had temporarily bypassed the ward. Fairly confident in his ability, he made quick work of the lower hinge and moved onto the locking mechanism securing the door.

Drawing on his experience when he had sprung the lock on the floor hatch in Castle Grim's cathedral, it wasn't difficult to discover how to turn the tumblers and release the latch.

He held his breath as the door swung back to reveal the chaotic scene awaiting him. Thick fog, basked in a reddish glow, swirled around the bailey—the eerie phenomenon accompanied by the continuous roar of rock crashing to the ground. For the briefest of moments, he dreaded he had taken too long, but a cry from above directed his gaze to where Zorain's bulk appeared through the mist—the dragon landing hard in front of him.

"Scale! You did it!" Zorain exclaimed, his attention on the ramparts behind the tower.

Scale stepped in beside Zorain and spun to look beyond the bulk of the mystical spire, his eyes growing wide. The massive corner tower that had been there not long ago was nothing more than a squat pile of rubble, as was the section of the high wall on either side of the debris.

Great chunks of stone toppled from the ramparts between where the corner tower had stood and the mid-tower he had just won free of. Through all of the bedlam, Scale sensed that the peculiar mist appeared to be coalescing into something more substantial. Something malign.

Dragon Sect

Zorain crouched low, his intense gaze searching the encroaching vapour. *"Get on! We've got to get out of here! The mist is alive!"*

Scale didn't need to be told twice. He sheathed his dagger and was about to climb onto Zorain, but something impelled him to retrieve the long spear that had fallen to the ground inside the doorway. Scrambling up Zorain's side, he had barely swung his leg over the dragon's shoulder before Zorain leapt into the air and flew toward the front gates.

Not believing what was happening, Scale looked back at the crumbling ramparts—their destruction sending up clouds of dust to coalesce with the reddish mist. The bank of fog expanded to envelop the remaining walls, that for the moment, had remained intact. "Fly faster!"

"I can't! Something's pulling on me!"

Scale searched Zorain, but aside from the advancing mist he couldn't see anything else around them. They had barely cleared one of the corner towers attached to the gatehouse wall when Scale discerned the malevolent presence in the expanding bank of fog grow more intense.

Dragon Sect

A bone-chilling cold accompanied the mist as it crept across his back.

Zorain's forward momentum slowed to a stop despite the dragon's wings beating furiously at the air. He roared, a great belch of flames accentuating his distress. *"I can't break free!"*

Doing the only thing that came to mind, Scale allowed the incantation he had recently created to pass by his lips. Should he err in the casting of any part of the complicated chant, he would kill Zorain as surely as if he drove his spear through the dragon's heart. Panic clouding his thinking, he feared he couldn't remember all the words.

He paused mid-spell and cringed, but nothing untoward happened. Sensing they didn't have much time, he pleaded, "Help me with the spell!"

His limbs trembling in the bitter cold, he did his best to intone the summoning spell. The words flowed more easily than he dared hope as Zorain's magic merged with his own.

Involuntarily lapping at a sweet wetness that coated his lips, he feared he was losing control of the powerful spell.

Zorain's frantic wingbeats were futile against whatever held them in its grip. They were being pulled back to the castle by whatever lurked in the fog.

Scale faltered. A gust of wind threatened to tear him from Zorain's back. Blinking rapidly to protect his eyes from a sudden rainstorm that lashed at his face, he screamed the last of the words—his voice lost to a thunderous detonation that vibrated through him.

Unable to breathe, the world went blank.

Dragon Sect

The Wings of an Angel

Crushing despair consumed Ouderling's dark thoughts. Trapped in a shaft within a volcano hundreds of leagues from home, any chance of saving her mother had been taken from her when the stairwell had sealed her in a world of darkness—her exceptional night vision barely able to discern the rough-hewn stone of her prison.

The rock wall against her back and the hatch beneath her crumpled legs shook. A muted roar reached her. She cringed, hoping that Jyllana's death would be quick.

Unable to keep her limbs from trembling in sheer terror at what had happened, she could not catch her breath. What a foolish decision it had been to think she could convince the mighty Grimclaw to change his mind.

With the exception of High Wizard Aelfwynne and the old Crystal Cavern caretaker, Eolande, the infamous dragon was older than any creature she knew. It would take a lot more than the words of an eighteen-year-old elfling to convince the ancient dragon that his view of the greater world left much to be desired.

𝔇ragon 𝔖ect

The rock shook again, followed by another muted roar—the sensation making her flinch as if whatever had been thrown might breach the stairwell and crush her. She almost relished the thought.

A distant screech, different than anything she had heard within the volcano, caught her attention. It sounded like a dragon!

She swallowed and looked around her prison. What was a dragon doing in the temple? She imagined they were able to fly into the volcano, but they were much too large to be of any help where she and Jyllana had gone.

The dragon cry sounded again, closer.

At first, she didn't recognize who it belonged to, thinking it must have come from one of the dragons in Grimclaw's colony as it certainly wasn't the roar of Miragan or Dagomar.

It came again, sounding right on top of her—the mournful screech hurting her ears as it reverberated within the stairwell.

Shocked, she glanced upward into the blackness. "Keaf?"

She covered her ears as an answering screech thundered in the stairwell.

"Keaf! It me! Ouderling! I'm down here!"

"Princess. I sensed you were in trouble. Come to me."

"I'm trapped. I can't get out of here."

A long silence ensued. Just when Ouderling feared Keaf had left her, the stone beneath her knees and forearms shuddered. Rock grated together. The smooth slope bit into her limbs as the sharp edges of stone steps materialized beneath her.

"Did that do anything?"

Incredulous, Ouderling jumped to her feet, not quite believing what she knew to be true. The steps had reappeared, their steep path ascending into the darkness. "Yes!"

Uncaring that she left her surcoat behind, she attacked the steps as fast as her legs would carry her, thankful for the torturous training Balewynd had put her through over the greater part of the past year. Even so, her thighs were screaming and she was out of breath before reaching the top. Cresting the last step and bursting into the light of the volcanic crater, she ran into the green dragon. Without hesitation, she hugged his neck in appreciation. "Keaf, you're amazing! What did you do?"

"I'm a dragon. This is a dragon temple," he said, as if that explained everything.

"Where's Jyllana?" Dagomar asked.

Ouderling searched the vast crater. The red dragon rose into the air from the encircling ledge on the far side of the cavern.

Before she could answer, movement to his left exposed Miragan lifting off from a ledge higher up the wall. *"Pretty lady. You're alive!"*

Ouderling stepped back from Keaf and looked around as the ground vibrated under a distant impact. The fact that the rock troll was still shaking the cavern with its attacks boded well for Jyllana. "We have to save Jyllana!"

"We have to get you out of here," Dagomar said, crossing the centre of the lava lake.

She spun on the red dragon. "I'm not going anywhere without her."

Dagomar tried to land on the ledge next to them, but his bulk wouldn't allow it. Hovering beside the drop-off, he said, *"You're the heir to the Willow Throne. You must be preserved at all costs. If things are as bad back home as we are led to believe, you may soon be queen."*

Dragon Sect

Ouderling swallowed.

"Dagomar speaks wisely, pretty lady," Miragan said with an air of compassion that was absent in the larger dragon's voice. *"Jyllana's sole duty is to keep you safe. She wouldn't want you risking your life to save hers."*

Unable to comprehend their lack of empathy for their mutual friend, Ouderling shook her head. "I can't just leave her to die."

"You must, Your Majesty. She may be dead already. Sacrificing yourself to find out is not a decision a wise ruler would make," Dagomar argued. *"Get on Miragan and let's be gone from this place."*

"I promised Grimclaw I would rid him of the rock troll."

"Rock troll?" Dagomar's voice boomed. *"The old dragon's lost his mind sending you against a creature as dangerous as that. It would take many dragons to defeat such a beast."*

Ouderling stamped her foot in frustration. The last thing she wanted to do was encounter that atrocity again, but she knew in her heart that if she fled without knowing whether Jyllana still lived, she would never be able to live with herself.

She pulled her bow free of her shoulder and used it to point at the stairwell behind her. "There's a cave at the bottom of that tunnel. A wondrous chamber large enough to accommodate many dragons in flight. Jyllana isn't the only one in danger. There's a bunch of dwarfs down there as well. We have to find another way to reach the cave."

"We have to extract you from harm's way. That is our primary objective," Dagomar objected.

"You forget, I'm the princess."

A throaty laugh escaped the hovering dragon. *"It is you who forgets, Your Highness. I'm a dragon. I don't answer to anyone I don't want to. And right now, I choose to answer to High Wizard Aelfwynne. Your safety is my only concern."*

Ouderling stepped to the brink, red eyes glaring defiance at Dagomar.

"I'll pick you up and carry you with my claws if I must," Dagomar said, undeterred by her displeasure.

A deep growl escaped Miragan, the wyvern looking none too pleased with the dragon's attitude. *"Easy, Dagomar."*

Dagomar adjusted his position in the air to face the wyvern. *"Don't even think about it, granddaughter of Perch."*

Miragan turned to confront him. *"You wouldn't dare treat the princess that way."*

"If it means she lives another day, I'm prepared to deal with the consequences of my actions. Under no circumstances will I allow her to place her life in peril. Is that understood?"

"Is that a threat?"

"I don't threaten. I...Hey!" Dagomar's voice rose in pitch.

Far below the two wyrms arguing about her safety, Ouderling clung to Keaf's thin neck as they plunged into the crater. If Jyllana was alive, she meant to do everything possible to save her.

"Are you sure you can carry me?" she asked.

Keaf laughed. *"A little late to worry about that now."*

Ouderling couldn't find her voice as they descended toward the churning lava lake. Swallowing her fear, she managed to croak, "How do you know where you're going?"

"I don't. But the sounds I heard from the stairwell you were trapped in match the sounds I noticed before I found you. They were coming from a shaft near the fire lake's surface."

Dragon Sect

Ouderling was certain they were about to die as the lava bed rose up to meet them, gurgling spouts of liquid rock spurting into the air around them and falling back with great splashes of magma. An involuntary scream ripped free of her throat as the heat threatened to singe her hair and melt her skin.

"Pretty lady!"

Miragan's voice sounded a long way off.

Snatching a quick look over her shoulder, the wyvern and Dagomar had dove into the crater after them. Unable to maintain her backward stare, she leaned forward and clung to Keaf's neck, closing her eyes in fear of their impending impact with the surface of the fiery lake.

At the last possible moment, Keaf altered his trajectory and folded his wings tight against his body as they slipped into the mouth of a yawning hole in the crater's wall close to the surface of the roiling lava.

Ouderling ducked her head beside Keaf's, her wildly flailing hair brushing the tunnel's entrance. With the realization that they hadn't hit the lake, she opened her eyes. Before her vision could adapt to the darkness, light from the far end of the chute they had fallen into rushed toward them, blinding her.

She took a large gulp of air and winced. They were plunging toward pool of lava at the bottom of the narrow shaft. Closing her eyes again, she gasped as her stomach lurched under a sudden change in momentum.

Bursting from the end of the narrow rock tube, the wings of an angel lifted her free from a horrific death.

Keaf's furious wingbeats carried them up the side of a wide, cylindrical shaft, away from the oozing magma at its bottom.

Dragon Sect

Hanging onto Keaf's neck lest she plunge to her death, Ouderling stared at a place high above where the sound of stone crunching stone was coming from—the limbs of the rock troll visible beyond the lip of a ledge they flew toward.

Dragon Sect

His Mother's Magic

Courage was not an attribute Braen ascribed to. His reaction to the approach of the tough looking castle guard testified to the fact that he was by no means a fighter.

Hands in the air before him, he stepped backward, shaking his head, bemoaning the fact he hadn't pulled his cowl back over his head. "I-I didn't do this."

The large man raised the business end of a sword in Braen's face. "I find that hard to believe, *elf*."

Braen's attention solely on the advancing guard, he bumped into the wall and tried to press through the unforgiving surface at his back.

The sword tip came to rest on Braen's breastbone. "Where are the rest of your people?"

A genuine frown creased Braen's forehead. "There's no one else. I came alone."

As the booted footsteps climbing the steps drew closer, Braen looked to the open stairwell. Though he had no delusions that he could not win free of the man holding him at sword point, once the second person arrived, his fate would surely be sealed.

Dragon Sect

An older, grey-haired guard stepped into the corridor from the stairwell, stopping to take in the scene—his face darkening as his attention came to rest on Braen and his captor. "What's going on here? Who's this."

"Appears we have a pointy-eared assassin in our midst, captain," the man holding Braen said.

The captain stopped to inspect the two slain guards before stepping in front of Braen—his gaze taking in Braen's ears. Disgust twisted his expression, followed by a puzzled look that transformed into one of shock.

Before the captain had a chance to draw his sword, Cassava released her grip on the larger guard and introduced him to her efficient daggers.

Her rapid upward strike under his chest armour lifted the captain to his toes momentarily—his unbelieving expression on the large guard who was dead before he had hit the floor.

Thrusting her three-bladed dagger deeper and twisting, Cassava rode the captain to the ground, catching herself deftly on one knee and sprang back to her feet—the captain writhing between her legs.

Not sparing attention for the grey-haired guard, she stepped clear and glared at Braen. "What is it with you? Keep up."

Braen swallowed, fearing he might yet end up on the end of the assassin queen's blades.

Without a sound, Cassava slipped down the corridor and turned into a narrow stairwell set behind a statue.

Braen stared hard at the hidden passageway. Had he not witnessed Cassava disappear, he would never have known the access existed.

Breathing hard by the time he reached the top, he found Cassava crouched at the head of the steps appearing as if she hadn't exerted herself at all. Though he didn't know much about man castles, he couldn't help himself from whispering as he crouched in behind her, "Wouldn't a throne room be on one of the lower floors?"

Not looking back, Cassava purred, "It is. We go this way to avoid the rabble."

Braen nodded, despite the fact he had no idea what she was talking about.

"Quickly," she said, and sprinted down the next corridor—this one more confined than the one below.

Had he not been watching her, he would never have seen her disappear again. The floor to ceiling tapestry barely wavered as she slipped behind it and held the bottom corner aside for him to follow her down a steep flight of narrow steps built within the walls.

He barely had the wherewithal to keep himself from yelping as she stopped suddenly in front of him and held up a dagger to stave off any questions.

It wasn't until she tilted her head to indicate he follow that he heard a latch 'snick' somewhere below. He expected to hear someone ascending the stairs, but she answered his unspoken query.

"A servant," was all she said before wasting no time descending the last leg of steps.

Though he had no way of knowing, he was sure they had descended more than one floor in the close confines of the sparsely lit passageway. A plain, wooden, round-topped door blocked the bottom of the stairwell.

Cassava whispered, "Wait," and pushed the door open.

Braen didn't dare disobey but he didn't have to wait long.

Two thumps preceded Cassava popping her head back into the stairwell. "Clear."

Stepping through the door, Braen's senses were inundated with the smell of baking bread and spices—a wave of warmth enveloping him as he stepped into the back of what appeared to be a large kitchen.

A man and a woman in aprons lay sprawled on the flagstone floor—a basket of round loaves splayed across the ground.

Despite his fear of the assassin queen, Braen frowned at her victims, on the verge of protesting, but Cassava shook her head.

"I'm not totally barbaric, but they'll have a headache when they come around."

Braen swallowed, not sure if he believed her, but took solace in the fact that he couldn't see blood pooling around their prone bodies. Fearful of what he might discover if he checked, he decided he had better just take her word for it.

"Let's go," Cassava snarled, already standing at a doorway opposite from where they had entered.

The castle halls were quiet in the dead of night—the only sound coming from Braen's amateurish attempt at being stealthy. Pulling his cowl over his head, he wanted to ask Cassava how she knew where she was going, but again decided he was better off not knowing. All he wanted was to be free of the castle and the land of man—his initial curiosity about the northern kingdoms had lost its glamour. After speaking with the snarly baker in Apexceal, his run-in with the sea-hands on the *Coastal Cutter*, and the animosity he had experienced whenever someone laid eyes on his ears, he wanted nothing more to do with the barbaric northern folk.

True, Alexis and his father had treated him with kindness, but it had become glaringly apparent that the two men's actions were out of character for the inhabitants of the five kingdoms of man—six, if he counted Cassava's island nation of Aldebaran. He stared at the back of the woman's head, unsure how he felt about her.

She hadn't killed *him* yet. There was that. He found himself smiling as a strange thought entered his head. It would be interesting if he were to bring her into his uncle's court. He nodded at the idea. Orlythe had openly entertained a human wizard.

The thought of Afara Maral darkened his mood. Perhaps introducing Cassava to the Duke of Grim wasn't such a great idea after all. If she were to align herself with the elf, who knew what mischief he would get her into?

Caught up in his idle musings, he almost ran into Cassava's upheld dagger—her intense eyes glaring promised death.

He stopped and backed up a step, afraid to speak.

Cassava stood with her back against the wall next to a wide doorway. She placed the tip of her second dagger against her lips in a shushing motion and turned her attention to whatever was happening inside the chamber beyond.

Now that he was paying attention, Braen heard muted voices. Angry words were being spoken.

Cassava bent forward for a moment and then drew back. She motioned for Braen to lean in so that she could speak quietly to him.

Apprehensive about getting too close to the exotic woman, he forced himself to do as she directed.

"There's two guards inside the doors. One on each side," she whispered. "I'll take the far one. As soon as I make my move, you take the near guard as he's sure to come at my backside. You got that?"

Braen stared wide-eyed. Managing the tiniest of nods for her benefit, he knew at once that killing a man was the last thing he was capable of doing.

Cassava held his scared look. "Don't fail me, elven prince. We're both dead if you do."

He swallowed and nodded.

Her gaze hardened. "Your dagger."

Braen's trembling hand pulled his blade free.

"Make sure you stick *them*, not me," Cassava snarled.

It seemed like they stood glaring at each other for a long time, but when Cassava finally returned her attention to the doorway, Braen thought for sure his legs were about to give out. He wasn't a killer. Heck, he didn't even like to argue.

One moment Cassava was leaning against the wall, and the next, she was halfway across the threshold before either of the guards were aware of her presence. In the time it took the guard on the far side of the doorway to reach for the hilt of his sword with one hand and raise his other arm to fend off her attack, Cassava had already stabbed him twice in the forearm and was moving beyond his block to finish him.

The nearest guard to Braen cried out, "Hey!" His sword jumped into his hand as he started across the doorway.

Braen stepped in behind him, but couldn't bring himself to stab the innocent man.

"Braen! Now!" Cassava screamed, engaged with the second guard—the man not allowing her killing blades to land, though it was obvious by the amount of blood soaking his tunic that she had seriously injured him.

"Take the elf sympathizer to the hole. Move!" A large, black-bearded man shouted at two guardsmen in chainmail and leather holding onto a thinner man with flowing, golden locks farther into the room.

"Alexis?" Braen's voice came out as a croak.

The guardsmen lifted the Prince of Carillon off his feet and dragged him toward a side wall—Alexis' head lolling on his limp neck.

The northern prince opened a bloodshot eye, looking at Braen through swollen, purple welts—pain twisting his battered features.

Dragon Sect

So enrapt with Alexis' plight, Braen staggered and tripped over his clumsy feet. In a wild attempt to catch himself, he flailed his arms, inadvertently burying his dagger into the base of the neck of the guard Cassava had expected him to deal with. The man dropped to the ground, taking Braen down with him.

An agonized cry sounded above Braen as the other guard's body hit the flagstone floor—the man's head creating an awful noise as it bounced right in front of him.

Terrified, Braen stared into the man's lifeless eyes.

"Nice one," Cassava's receding voice reached through his paralysis. "Come on. They went this way. There's no time to admire your handiwork."

Braen blinked in confusion, trying to come to terms with what he had just done. He looked up in time to see Cassava duck beneath a large tapestry behind the throne and disappear.

He sat up and looked around. Two dead guards were sprawled on either side of him—one with multiple stab wounds, the other lying in an expanding pool of blood where his dagger still protruded from his victim's neck.

"Down here! The king's in the throne room!" A deep voice reached him from the corridor they had vacated moments before. More guards were coming.

Afraid to be caught, his adrenaline surged. He pulled his dagger free, cringing as the blade slid free of the man's flesh, and raced across the throne room. Lifting the edge of the tapestry, he stepped onto a narrow landing fronting the top of a steep stairwell. A flight of narrow steps carved into the bedrock dropped away into darkness.

It was deathly quiet at the bottom of the stairwell beneath the throne room. Not sure what he was walking into, Braen held his breath and inched his way to the end of the connecting tunnel. A large cavern opened up before his eyes, its damp, natural wall flickering in the sparse light of sconces scattered around its perimeter.

He stopped and leaned into the cavern to listen—the lack of sound most peculiar considering there didn't appear at first glance to be any exit tunnels along the walls. A pool of dark water comprised much of the middle of the floor, but he doubted that would provide anyone a means of escape, though the stagnant water certainly contributed to the putrid smell of death accosting his nostrils.

He briefly considered climbing back up to the throne room to get as far away from the danger his senses told him lurked beneath the earth. If not for the fact that more guards were likely already searching the throne room, he would have.

Against his better judgement, he stepped free of the stairwell alcove to study his surroundings. Larger than it had first appeared, the cavern's walls were lined with chains attached to manacles and shackles. He grimaced. Some still held rotting remains.

If he bothered to dwell on it, the creepiness of the eerie grotto instilled in him the same terror he had experienced beneath the graveyard. Trembling from more than just the cold of the cavern, he wished the nightmare journey he had gotten himself into would come to an end. He pulled his cowl over his head, swallowing his unease; sensing his dilemma was about to get much worse before it got better.

A loud clang sounded from the top of the stairwell. The racket of many booted feet descended the stone steps—metal armour scaping and clanging against the stone walls.

Alarmed, Braen's latent magic stirred, stronger than it had beneath the graveyard. So afraid it was on the verge of surfacing, he jumped as a flurry of bats dropped from the heights behind him.

The runic symbols embroidered along the hems of his cloak sprang to life—something his mother had told him would happen should he ever change his mind and pursue his gift. A course of action he had never wished to entertain.

A scream from somewhere in the gloom along the edge of the cavern jarred his senses. His gaze fell on the remains of the victims hanging from the walls, thinking they were either not quite dead yet—which seemed impossible given their state—or had been resurrected.

A fireball materialized in his hand, as much a shock to him as it was to the Nordician guardsmen exiting the bottom of the stairwell.

Six men-at-arms clattered into the cavern, spreading out in a semi-circle, wary of the flames roiling in his hand.

A boisterous laugh resonated off the dank walls, drawing everyone's attention. From behind the guardsmen, the two throne room guards stepped out of an unseen alcove farther along the wall—a dark-skinned female struggling violently in their grasp. Holding Cassava as best they could, they made way for their black-bearded companion who stepped past them and thrust Alexis forward. "Let me demonstrate what happens to pointy-eared scum when they show their insolent faces in Nordicia."

Alexis staggered a couple of steps before dropping to his knees, barely able to keep from falling to his face. Through the pain etched on his scrunched-up features, he snarled, "Your day's coming, Drannor. When my father finds out, he'll—oof!"

King Drannor kicked Alexis in the spine, dropping him to the ground. "He'll meet the same fate as his elf-loving son."

Dragon Sect

Something snapped inside Braen's head. Cupping the fireball in both hands, it was time he embraced his mother's legacy and became the reluctant warlock his uncle had proclaimed.

Dragon Sect

A Dragon's Love

Keaf's laboured flight was anything but reassuring. For every few feet of height he gained he appeared to lose half that between frantic wingbeats—his flight so erratic that Ouderling found it hard not to strangle him to keep from being tossed from his shoulders.

"I'm too heavy!" she yelled, afraid to look down to see how far they would fall if his stamina gave out.

"Nonsense. I've got you," Keaf's laboured voice sounded in her head. *"We'll show the creature who it's messing with."*

Ouderling sucked in a great breath as Keaf pitched sideways and his wingtip brushed the wall. He leaned back into the middle of the chasm, dropping quickly until he managed to stabilize his flight.

Daring to breathe again, Ouderling looked up. She could just make out the underside of the platform she believed housed the carved dragon head. A glimpse of the insubstantial rope bridge spanning the gap confirmed it, but of Jyllana, there was no sign.

Dragon Sect

A great roar echoed throughout the wide shaft, accentuated by rock shattering overhead.

Ouderling screamed and tucked into the side of Keaf's neck to avoid the aftermath of debris tumbling from the small ledge at the base of the stairwell. Fearing the pieces of broken stone would knock Keaf out of the air, she took comfort in the fact that if the rock troll was throwing rocks across the chasm, there was a good chance her protector still lived.

"Faster Keaf, faster! We have to save Jyllana!" But even as she said it, she knew there was no way her dragonling would be able to carry both of them.

A long, drawn-out cry of a male in distress marked the fall of another dwarf—his squat body tumbling past Keaf and Ouderling on one side while his spinning battle-axe came close to biting Keaf's opposite wing.

It was difficult to tell if Keaf's erratic flying was responsible for them not being hit by the brave soul that had done battle with the gargantuan nightmare awaiting them. Unable to take her eyes from the unfortunate dwarf, she winced—the unknown hero was soon to meet a horrific fate in the lava flow far below.

"Faster, Keaf! They're dying up there!"

The dragonling's eyes narrowed, his body tensing beneath her. Somehow his small wings lifted them toward the platform to where she knew the monstrosity rampaged.

She marvelled at Keaf's determination in the face of imminent danger, her emotions filling her with an alien sensation. Gooseflesh prickled her skin. The thought of being bonded to a dragon flushed her with a warmth she had never known before.

Drawing a deep breath to calm her jittery nerves, her whirling thoughts reflected on the one creature whose appearance and snarly attitude made her shiver to this day. As she envisioned the goblin high wizard, the monotonous lessons he had droned on about forever came to mind. The tedious instruction hit home now that her life, and the lives of the two beings she cared deeply about, were in danger.

That thought gave her pause.

She understood her feelings for Jyllana. They had been together for a few years now, and had become closer due to the recent events they had endured, but the reality of how much she cared for the wild dragon that had taken it upon himself to fly her toward certain death shocked her senses. She barely knew Keaf. And yet, something magical had occurred during their foray into the lands of Grimclaw— binding them as surely as a wedding circlet confirmed the mutual love between partners. Perhaps more so. Staring at the back of Keaf's head as he fought with everything he had to rise up the shaft, she knew without a doubt that she would rather die than let anything to happen to the unruly dragon.

Another roar reverberated in the cavernous chamber. A chunk of rock as big as Keaf spun overhead. It fell short, impacting the wall beneath the small ledge where Jyllana cowered.

Thankful the projectile had missed its mark, she blinked in confusion. Several squat creatures raced across the shabby bridge, its deck undulating under their frenzied steps— braving the uncertain span to reach Jyllana's side.

Two more rocks arced overhead. The first impacted the wall beside the ledge and careened into the chasm. The second flew true. It crunched into the front of the small ledge, tumbling into the dwarfs who huddled around Jyllana and were trying to avoid the stone without falling off the edge.

Dragon Sect

Ouderling's breath caught but her attention was diverted as Keaf's wingbeats intensified and they rose above the stone dragon head, coming up behind the rock troll.

The beast bent over to smash his fist into the side of the dragon head to break another chunk of lava stone free, but stopped, suddenly aware of their presence.

Fancy bow in shaking hands, Ouderling struggled to nock an arrow, though she doubted it would be effective against a creature comprised of stone.

Keaf shrieked in rage. Hovering out of reach of the troll's gangly arms, a puff of black smoke escaped his mouth.

The rock troll lunged, its great step forcing Keaf to retreat into an alcove behind the stone dragon head—the space's unfinished walls and ceiling supported by seven, masterfully carved pillars arranged on a platform near the cavern wall. It swiped at Keaf—its unorthodox gait causing it to step sideways to get beyond the back of the dragon head.

Keaf's wings beat furiously, angling at the last moment to spirit them away from the rock troll's reach.

Ouderling flinched, the tip of her arrow threatening to fall from where she supported it in the middle of the bow.

The beast roared so loud she feared she would never hear properly again should they find a way to survive.

And then the strangest thing occurred. The rock troll covered its face with its forearms to protect it from a thin spout of flames that Keaf spewed forth.

As odd as it seemed that a creature made of rock would be deterred by flames, it struck Ouderling as even more bizarre that Keaf had the capacity to create fire at such a young age. No expert when it came to dragons, she had heard it said that most typically developing dragons' ability to create fire didn't happen until they were over a year old.

Dragon Sect

She smiled despite the peril they faced. Keaf was anything but typical. He possessed a trait that set him apart from his peers—a trait that made him seem unusual in people's eyes. Ouderling had been one of those who had wanted nothing to do with him at first because of his differences. She found it humbling to realize that his uniqueness actually made him special. Through his actions, Keaf had proven he was capable of a level of compassion and strength seriously lacking in many of the elves Ouderling had associated with during her short lifetime. She took a deep breath. They could all learn something from Keaf.

As soon as Keaf's fire sputtered, the rock troll dropped his arms to its sides and thrust its head toward them, its great mouth opening wide to bellow a feral shout of rage.

So afraid, Ouderling inadvertently loosed her arrow. It ricocheted off the troll's lower jaw and clattered to the ledge.

The troll's head snapped sideways momentarily, as if shrugging off a gnat, and glared hatred at her. Unable to break its stare, she noticed out of the corner of her eye that Jyllana led four dwarfs across the rickety bridge—running headlong toward the rock troll.

Keaf moved in closer, emitting a spout of flames that washed over the troll's exposed face.

The beast closed its eyes and turned its head, holding its arm up to deflect the fiery barrage, but if the flames had any real effect, Ouderling could see no evidence of it.

The troll's free arm swung around to swat at Keaf.

Time slowed for Ouderling. Hanging onto Keaf to keep from falling off as he flapped hard in reverse, the troll's hand impacted Keaf below his wing, knocking her from his back.

She flew against the nearest pillar and dropped to the ground. Dazed, she struggled to get to her knees—fighting to draw air while anxiously searching for Keaf. Catching sight of where the dragonling fought to rise back into the air, her blood ran cold.

The rock troll reached out, plucking Keaf from the floor— holding the dragonling at arm's length to prevent his snapping jaws and scratching talons from causing it much damage.

Keaf screeched in outrage, his one, free wing flapping furiously in a frantic effort to escape the troll's crushing grip.

A curious series of guttural cries rose in crescendo to fill the cavern, the din so close that Ouderling was at a loss as to where it originated.

"Trolls! Protect the lass!" a dwarf belted out, his urgent plea followed by a clash of weapons and agonized cries.

The dwarfs that had escorted Jyllana safely across the bridge rejoined their companions who were backing away from the dragon head statue, fending off a horde of hairy, mountain trolls that had entered the cavern through the tunnel within the dragon head's mouth.

Unconcerned by what was happening around it, the rock troll attempted to crush Keaf with its hand but the dragonling clamped its fangs onto its fingers and began to gnaw on its hard skin.

Infuriated, the rock troll slammed Keaf into the wall, the impact shaking the pillars and dislodging a thick, circular stone that dropped from the top of an incomplete column. The smooth stone hit the ground at the rock troll's feet— drawing its attention.

Bending over to grab the stone, the beast swung it against its other hand.

A spurt of flames spewing from Keaf's mouth was cut short as the stone impacted with the side of his neck—the dragonling twisting its neck to avoid the full brunt of the blow.

Dragon Sect

Unsure what she could do to help her dragonling, Ouderling spared a brief glance for the battle raging on the far side of the platform. Surrounded by hardened dwarfs no taller than her chest, Jyllana held her own amongst the savage trolls that had spilled onto the ledge.

The rock troll roared again and shook Keaf in its fist, preparing to hammer him with the stone a second time.

Helpless to intervene, Ouderling strung another arrow, fretting that she had nothing else to use as a weapon. Staring at the puny arrow, she again was besieged by Grimclaw's mocking words, *'An arrow will not save you.'*

Ignoring the elder dragon's message, the pain registered in Keaf's amber eyes made her cry out, "Stop!"

Not knowing how to save him hurt her more than any physical pain ever could. Now that she had experienced a dragon's love, if only briefly, nothing in the world would matter if Keaf were to die.

It took everything she had to resist a primal urge to run at the creature and beat it with her fists. If not for the training sessions with Balewynd, Pecklyn, and Aelfwynne, she would have, but their combined lessons had allowed her to find in herself an odd sense of calm amid the chaos that had erupted all around the platform deep within a volcanic shaft.

Staring at her pitiful arrow, she frowned. What could she hope to do with it? Never having heard of such a creature before, she deemed by its very nature that something must be keeping it alive. She doubted the beast was the product of a wizard's spell. If it truly was alive, it meant it could be killed. But how? Nothing she nor Keaf possessed in their arsenal had had an effect on it.

'You must rely on your magic,' the other half of Grimclaw's warning reached through her distress. The omen made no sense. She was a novice practitioner of nature's

essence at best. She had no real magical ability. Communicating with the Fae would be of little use against the monstrosity confronting them.

The rock troll smashed the stone on Keaf's exposed head.

Keaf ducked into the top of its hand to avoid the worst of the killing stroke.

The troll pounded the top of its hand repeatedly, but every time it lifted the stone free to inspect the damage it had inflicted, Keaf popped his head up and spit fire at it.

The rock troll leaned in close, ignoring the flames, and roared his displeasure—spittle flying in all directions.

Keaf screeched back, attempting to snap at its face.

Spittle? Ouderling's red eyes grew wide. The rock troll *was* alive!

She took a deep breath. And then another. And finally, a third—doing her best to ignore the pandemonium. Delving into the untapped recesses of her mind, she called upon nature's essence, urging the magic to breach the veil separating her world from that of the mystical Fae that lay just beyond elven comprehension. Unaided by an amplifier like the Focal Stone or whatever haunted Grim Watch Tower, she wasn't sure she had the strength to do what she intended.

A sorrow threatened to consume her, the malaise arising from a time not long ago, and yet it felt as if years had passed since Perch had died defending the Crystal Cavern. It seemed strange to suddenly dwell on the ancient wyvern, but his memory infused in her a deeper sense of calm.

From out of her sadness, words he had spoken in the Crystal Cavern pushed away her lingering doubts. *"Release your reservations...Flush your mind...Close your eyes... Concentrate only on what you hear...At this moment in time, nothing else matters."*

She shuddered. It was like the magnificent wyvern stood by her side, providing her with the strength so desperately needed. He had believed in her when she had not. She looked around, hoping beyond hope, to see the old wyrm one last time.

She shook her head at her foolishness. All around her, dwarfs and trolls were dying. Her friends Jyllana and Keaf fought for their lives while she wasted time dreaming of something that could not come to pass.

Closing her eyes, she attempted to rid herself of the overlying terror gripping her. Keaf couldn't survive the rock troll's fury much longer. When it had disposed of the pesky dragonling, it wouldn't be long before the beast turned its attention on the dwarfs and Jyllana. When that happened, all would be lost.

The chill of the cavern raised gooseflesh on her exposed skin as she stared dumbly at the rock troll, but instead of listening to the chaotic scene, she concentrated on Perch's memory, his voice sounding in her head as if he were there, encouraging her.

"Release your worldly worries...Allow your essence to seep into you...Feel your connection to that which you have neglected for far too long."

Perch's faraway voice firmed her resolve.

"Now feel your connection...Hear it speak to you...Embrace its magic...You are Ouderling Wys...Heir to the Willow Throne...Through you, may we yet know salvation."

At first, she felt nothing but a void where her magic should be, but drawing on Perch's memory, an odd tingling crept up her neck and flowed down her arms. Pulling an arrow free of her quiver, she held her breath to help her nock it without fumbling.

Her late-night sessions alone in her sleeping chamber at Highcliff bolstered her confidence. Pushing everything else from her mind, her surroundings faded as she tapped into a higher level of consciousness.

Not visible at first to those on the platform deep within the bowels of the volcano, Ouderling sensed their presence. The Fae had responded.

Lifting her bow, she yelled at the rock troll, "Over here! It's time to end this!"

A pinprick of red light burst into life on the shaft of her arrow, followed quickly by many more. Growing up, she had associated white light with the faerie creatures, but somehow she knew the red flecks swirling around her arrow belonged to the Fae she had summoned—their combined light basking her in a red haze.

In Ouderling's mind, all the noise on the platform ceased to exist. If she had taken the time to study her surroundings, she would have noticed that the dwarfs and the mountain trolls had stopped fighting and were looking in her direction.

The rock troll stopped battering Keaf. Tilting its head to one side, it turned its focus on her.

The only one making noise was Keaf—his teeth gnashing on his captor's fingers, amidst short bursts of fire.

Aggravated by Keaf's relentless attack, the rock troll shook the dragon, but his attention remained on Ouderling. Dropping into a crouch, he bent at the waist and opened his mouth wide, roaring louder than ever as he brought the large stone overhead to crush her like a bug.

Ouderling was sure her hair blew back, but she didn't care. Nor was she concerned about the rock poised to smash her. Taking a deep breath, she concentrated on her nature's essence, putting her faith in the gift inherited from her mother. "Guide my arrow true."

Dragon Sect

The arrow leapt from her bow and dove into the rock troll's mouth, disappearing down its throat.

The creature straightened to its full height, its deafening shout echoing throughout the cavern. Clutching at its chest, it released its grip on Keaf and staggered backward.

Keaf fell to the ground forgotten at its feet, flapping his crumpled wings, but was unable to rise into the air. Spitting a pitiful bout of flames, he clamped his mouth around the rock troll's ankle and thrashed his head from side-to-side.

Ouderling nocked a third arrow, her sole concentration on the creature towering over her, but held her shot.

Aided by Keaf's insistent attack on its leg, the rock troll groaned and toppled backward. Felled like a tree, the rock troll's impact shook the platform.

Ouderling wasted no time. Arrow at the ready and the Fae surrounding her, she ran at the beast, prepared to launch another arrow into its mouth, but she need not have worried. The rock troll lay dead on its back, the stone it was about to kill her with still clutched within its fingers.

Adrenaline surging, she hopped onto the rock troll's splayed arm and ran to stand within his open palm, daring them to attack her.

The horde of mountain trolls surrounding Jyllana and the few dwarfs still alive stared at her in disbelief as Keaf fluttered briefly in the aura of the diminishing faerie light and landed behind her, screeching his support.

The yellow-eyed mountain trolls gaped at the sight, obviously shocked by what had just taken place. It wasn't long before they disappeared into the open-mouthed dragon statue—their grunts and cries of terror dying away as they fled into the volcanic tunnel.

A great shout arose from the remaining group of dirty and bloodied dwarfs. They thrust their battleaxes and warhammers over their heads, extolling Ouderling's triumph.

Humbled by the response, Ouderling almost fainted in relief at the sight of Jyllana stepping free of her newfound allies, a weak smile lighting up the weary face of the battered Home Guard.

Ouderling jumped from the rock troll's hand and embraced her friend.

"Thank you, Your Highness. You saved us," Jyllana said with her head pressed against Ouderling's. "I'll follow you to the edge of the world."

Six dwarfs, all that remained of the many who had battled to keep Jyllana from harm, stepped in behind the Home Guard. They doffed their crude helmets and nodded in agreement.

A lump formed in Ouderling's throat. Trying hard to keep the emotion of the moment from getting the better of her, she fought back tears as she drew strength from Jyllana's embrace.

Dragon Sect

'I knew you could do it,' Perch's voice sounded in her head. She looked over Jyllana's shoulder, searching the cavern in awe. Her wyvern friend was nowhere to be seen but his voice whispered on, *'That's why you'll always be my princess.'*

The scene around her blurred. Afraid her legs were about to give out, she let go of Jyllana and turned to wrap her arms around Keaf's neck. Holding her face against his rough scales, she allowed tears of happiness and exhaustion to flow unabashedly.

After a while, she stepped back and wiped her cheeks on her shoulders. Grasping Jyllana's blood-covered hands, she said, "Thank the gods you're alive."

Jyllana smiled.

She released Jyllana's hand and wrapped an arm around her protector's shoulders. With a smile of gratitude, she said to the dwarfs, "Thank you for saving this elf. She means more to me than anything in the world."

Keaf lifted his head high and screeched.

Ouderling rolled her eyes and spit out a wet laugh. "Yes. I love you too."

The largest of the dwarfs stepped forward. "Och, lassie. I'm thinkin' it's ye that 'ave saved our sorry hides. From what Miss Jyllana says, ye ain't t' be a normal elf."

Ouderling chuckled, conceding the point. She squeezed Jyllana hard. "Oh, she did, did she?"

Before she knew what was happening, the dwarf took a knee, his long, black beard brushing the ground as he bowed his head. "Sarsen's Rest is fore'er in yer debt, Your Highness. Ye can rest assured that should South March e'er find itself in need, our nation will be there for ya."

Dragon Sect

Ouderling was further taken aback when the remainder of the dwarfs followed his lead and dropped to a knee—bowing their heads and murmuring their agreement.

Stunned, she couldn't help thinking how prophetic their offer might become in the not-too-distant future. A lump in her throat, she said in a higher voice than usual, "You honour my people, good dwarf. Who do I have the pleasure of speaking with?"

The black-bearded dwarf looked up with bashful eyes. "Me kin call me Ohz the Neutral."

Ouderling smiled at him, curious as to the qualifier to his name, but now wasn't the time to ask about it. Clearing her throat with the hopes of sounding regal, she said, "I bid you all rise. It's time Grimclaw fulfilled his obligation to save the Queen of the Elves."

Dragon Sect

Strange Travelling Companion

Cassava struggled to break free of her captors. Grunting and screaming incoherently, she flung her head at them, stomping on their feet, and lurching back and forth in their grasp, but she was no match for the strength of the two men.

"Shut her up!" King Drannor said over his shoulder.

Braen couldn't help but notice what a ruckus his strange travelling companion was making. After seeing firsthand what she was capable of, he was amazed they had caught her in the first place. He pitied them if they were to lose their hold on her. From what he had witnessed, she was more than capable of killing everyone in the cave.

Movement directly in front of him made him tense. The six guardsmen that had followed them into the cavern fanned out to encircle him, their wary eyes never leaving the roiling ball of flames in his hands. It wouldn't be long before one of them made a move. He had to be ready.

The guard farthest along the line stepped sideways by the edge of the water and feigned an attack.

Startled, Braen thrust his hands forward, but hung onto the fireball, not quite sure how to use it.

Dragon Sect

The guard stepped back, a knowing sneer on his face. "Easy now. You don't want to do that."

Braen's eyes darted every which way at once. "Release my friends or else," he said, trying to sound brave, but winced as his voice came out as a squeak.

"Or else what?" the same guard asked, taking another step. It wouldn't be long before he could no longer keep an eye on all of them at once.

"Stop moving!" Braen yelled, nearly dropping the fireball. Sweat beaded on his forehead. The flaming orb was the only thing separating him from death. Once thrown, the guards would cut him to pieces.

Movement from the open stairwell drew his attention. Another guard entered the cavern. Taking stock of the situation, he pulled a crossbow from over his shoulder, put his boot in its stirrup to ratchet back the string, and inserted a forearm-length bolt that he produced from a small quiver hanging from his belt.

The crossbowman raised his weapon, pausing momentarily to look at the king.

King Drannor snarled, "Kill him."

"My pleasure, Your Majesty."

Braen stared hard at the death slinging machine pointed his way. He had watched enough of his mother's troops training with the cumbersome weapons to know there was no way he could hope to escape the quarrel's path.

A 'snick' was the only warning he received.

Having no time to think about it, he instinctively cowered, the action dislodging his fireball. Flinching despite the fact he hadn't been hit, he was vaguely aware that his fireball had incinerated the bolt on its way to its unintended target.

The crossbowman cried out in pain. His chest ablaze, the crossbow clattered at his feet—his hands slapping at the flames in a vain effort to extinguish the wizard's fire. Tormented screams reverberated throughout the cavern, following his stumbling passage toward the lake, but he never made it.

"Help him!" King Drannor shouted, stepping forward, but before anyone moved, the crossbowman dropped to his knees engulfed in flames. His blackening torso twisted one way and then another as he cried out in agony before dropping to the cave floor to never move again.

King Drannor's purple face was livid. He drew his sword and started toward Braen, but a foot shot out and struck his ankle, dropping him to the cavern floor.

Fully expecting to be attacked, Braen was as surprised as the Nordician guardsmen at the king's misfortune. Distracted, one of the men holding Cassava lost his grip on her arm.

As much as Braen detested violence, he couldn't help but admire the ruthless efficiency of the assassin queen. She moved so fast he didn't see the dagger she pulled from the guard's belt until it took the man in the side. The blade dove underneath the bottom of his leather chest armour and twisted.

The second guard shouted in surprise and attempted to throw her to the floor.

Her feet left the ground, but instead of resisting the guard's effort to subdue her, her momentum separated her from her captor. The man hung on as best he could. Her shoulders pivoted, followed by her hips. Deftly hitting the ground, she took advantage of the overbalanced man. Despite his superior size, a firm yank brought him staggering into an awaiting knee.

He bent over her thigh, avoiding the worst of the impact, but was helpless to prevent the dagger from plunging into the base of his spine.

Not bothering to finish him, Cassava tossed him aside and pounced on the king's back before he could regain his feet. Dagger against his throat, she stood him up and sneered at the Nordician guardsmen facing her.

Alexis groaned on the floor behind her.

"You must be Prince Alexis," she said to him, not taking her eyes from the men watching her. One hand firmly wrapped in the king's unruly hair, she held Drannor close and asked Alexis, "Can you get up?"

Without answering, Alexis rose on all fours, shaking his head as if to rid it of cobwebs. Stretching his neck from side to side, he stood.

"Grab a sword and make yourself useful," Cassava ordered. Her attention on the guardsmen, she pulled hard on the king's hair, keeping pressure on the confiscated blade. "Drop your weapons."

Alexis stepped up beside her, a sword in hand and nodded to the hesitant guards, his gaze inviting them to look over their shoulders. "I'd do as the lady asks."

A new fireball between his hands, Braen met the Nordician guards' confused stares and raised his eyebrows twice in quick succession.

Metal clanged off the cavern floor as they did what they were told.

"Move to the water's edge," Cassava directed. When they didn't comply fast enough, she tugged on Drannor's hair, the dagger drawing blood. "Now!"

"Do as she says, dammit!" King Drannor croaked.

Dragon Sect

The guardsmen held up their hands in compliance, backing away from Cassava and the king, clearly unhappy with how events were unfolding.

"You!" Cassava said to Alexis. "Grab my daggers."

Alexis returned to the alcove Braen had seen them emerge from earlier. He had no sooner disappeared than he popped back into view carrying Cassava's tri-bladed weapons.

Tugging on Drannor's hair, she growled, "Don't move."

In a movement so fast it defied description, she released the dead guard's dagger and snatched one of her own from Alexis. Positioning its long blade against the king's neck, she thrust out her hip and said to the Carillon prince, "Put the other one in its sheath."

Alexis slid the second dagger home on Cassava's belt and stepped back to keep an eye on the guardsmen.

Cassava dragged the king to the base of the steps, her gaze flicking from Braen to Alexis. "Go."

Alexis picked up the dagger Cassava had discarded and slipped past her into the stairwell.

Allowing his fireball to dissipate, Braen hurried after him, but stopped on the first step and looked back.

Cassava still held the king by the hair, her dagger dimpling the side of his neck. "Your tyranny ends here," she growled.

Braen gaped as her triple-bladed weapon cut into King Drannor's neck.

The king convulsed in her grasp, a wet gurgle escaping his blood-covered lips. He dropped quivering to the ground, his hands trying to stem the blood spewing from his mortal wound.

Cassava stomped on the side of his head and brandished her bloodied dagger at the astonished guardsmen. "That's what happens to those who despoil my kingdom."

Dragon Sect

Braen winced at the sound as she stomped the king's head a second time. Afraid to move, he stared in disbelief as she stepped past him like nothing had happened.

"You plan on staying down here?" she asked. Not waiting for an answer, she took the steps two at a time.

Braen swallowed his discomfort and started after her.

Of Alexis, there was no sign.

Braen hadn't exited the top of stairwell emptying into the throne room before the sound of pursuit from the cavern below reverberated after him.

Pushing through the tapestry, he searched the throne room for Cassava and Alexis. A ruckus in the corridor beyond brought him to the doorway. He stepped carefully over the slain guards, eyeing the man he had killed earlier—a twinge of guilt made him shudder. Stepping free of the grisly scene, he spotted the cause of the disturbance. The Prince of Carillon and the Queen of Aldebaran were engaged with several guards—a couple of which lay moaning or unmoving on the floor at their feet.

Braen's movement into the corridor distracted the remaining guardsmen for the briefest of moments. Judging by the way Alexis took advantage of his enemies' lapse in concentration, Braen would have sworn the man prince had shared the same trainer as the assassin queen.

Alexis stood over the last man he had impaled, a sword in one hand and a dagger in the other. They had dispatched of their attackers with a ruthless efficiency He nodded to Cassava who returned the gesture as she broke into a run.

"Nicely done back there," Alexis said to Braen before he chased after the deadly woman.

Not sure what Alexis was referring to, Braen followed. It didn't take him long to realize they were retracing their steps back to the graveyard tunnel. He hesitated, not sure his heart could take much more. Hurried footfalls from the opposite end of the corridor made up his mind for him.

"There's one!" A deep voice shouted.

Ducking into the secret stairwell they had used on their way to the throne room, Braen wasted no time ascending the narrow steps.

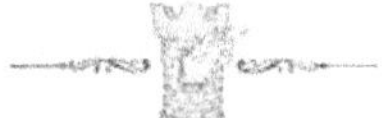

How they had gotten past the activity in the upper corridors and the corresponding byways that led to the kitchen, Braen did not know. Nor could he count how many Nordician guardsmen had joined the chase, but by the thunder of their boots and clanging armour, there were more than his accomplished companions could handle.

Several times he feared he had lost track of Alexis and Cassava, they were so far ahead, but Alexis' head would inevitably peek around a corner to set him right.

His companions had encountered resistance in the dungeon level, but by the time Braen stumbled onto the scene, they had already dealt with the opposition.

The tunnel below the graveyard seemed shorter on the way out. Bolstered by their need to escape and the absence of Cassava playing tricks on him, the creepy passageway was almost bearable.

He caught up to them at the tunnel's far end and stopped. Cassava fiddled with something on the underside of the sarcophagus' lid.

"What's the matter?" Braen's haunted gaze jumped from Alexis to the eerie tunnel stretching away behind them into darkness—the muted sound of pursuit telling him they didn't have much time.

"It's stuck!" Cassava grunted from the top of the short flight of steps.

Dragon Sect

Pounding the hilt of a dagger against something Braen couldn't see, the assassin queen screamed.

"That's not good," Braen whispered.

Alexis shook his head in agreement.

Creaking leather and pounding footfalls increased in volume—the dark tunnel lightening in the distance.

"Hurry!" Braen shouted. "They're almost on us!"

Alexis pushed past Braen and prepared to do battle.

Terrified, Braen's nerves jumped further as the semblance of a fireball formed in his hand without his knowledge. Staring in horror at the angered faces of bearded men visible behind rapidly approaching torchlight, he yelled at Cassava. "Let me try!"

Cassava took in the roiling fire cupped in his hands, flames dripping like water to the ground at his feet. She leapt free of the steps and joined Alexis, readying herself to meet the guardsmen.

Unsure of himself, Braen took a deep breath. Perhaps his fleeting idea hadn't been as great as he had first thought.

"Now Braen!" Cassava shouted.

A feral cry from one of the guardsmen prompted Braen to discharge his spell.

A resounding crack rocked the tunnel, shaking dirt loose from the ceiling. Shattered pieces of the sone lid clattered on the steps.

Though still dark outside, the hole Braen's fireball had created was illuminated by faint light. Daybreak had fallen.

"Come on!" Braen bolted up the steps.

The sound of weapons clanging made him pause to look back after jumping free of the coffin. Peering into the casket, he was nearly knocked from his feet as first Cassava and then Alexis charged up the steps and leapt clear of the tunnel.

Dragon Sect

Alexis' iron grip latched onto Braen's wrist, pulling him across the floor as they exited the mausoleum behind Cassava.

An immeasurable number of castle guard jumped free of the casket and gave chase.

Fleet of foot, and not as encumbered as the Nordician troops, Braen fled across the graveyard after his companions toward where they had tethered their horses. Running faster than ever before, he stumbled and fell more than once on the uneven ground. If they could make it to the horses, they might yet escape.

Shouts from the castle walls followed their harried flight across the field. An arrow shattered against a gravestone, followed by two others that thumped into the ground near their feet.

The flight of a spear whistled past Braen's head and stuck in the ground where Alexis' trailing foot had just vacated, its impact causing Braen to stagger sideways to avoid it. Catching his balance, he hazarded a look over his shoulder and almost fell again—disheartened by the number of guardsmen giving chase.

He broke into the forest and almost bumped into his companions. For some reason, Cassava and Alexis had come to a stop.

Waiting amongst the trees, their silhouettes outlined in the twilight of the new day, a line of bowmen on horseback held strung bows pointed their way.

With no where left to run, Braen's legs gave out.

Dragon Sect

Grimclaw's Own Admission

Grimclaw's yellow eyes opened to narrow slits, his massive body prone on the ground in front of the unfinished entrance of the Dragon Temple. Upon seeing who stepped free of the mountain tunnel, his eyes opened wide, surprise evident on his intimidating countenance.

"Ouderling Wys. What an unexpected pleasure. I didn't expect to see you again…so soon."

Ouderling didn't miss the dragon's slip. Dressed in her leather surcoat, she walked up to him, standing no taller than the top of his snout. "I don't suspect you did. But here I am. And I bring with me what's left of the Sarsens Rest contingent."

She directed her gaze to the dark tunnel where Ohz the Neutral led five dwarfs from the temple.

"And what of your friend?"

Ouderling knew he meant Jyllana, but she said, "Oh, you mean Dagomar and Miragan." She looked skyward, the dragon and wyvern responding to their names being called. "Here they come now. Unlike the dragons around here, they're not afraid to enter the volcano."

Dragon Sect

Grimclaw rose to a sitting position and watched as Dagomar and Miragan landed in the clearing, close to the wall with the arched tunnel passing through it.

Jyllana sat tall and defiant upon Dagomar's shoulder, her polearm held upright.

Before the flabbergasted Grimclaw could respond, Ouderling added, "Oh, and Jyllana is no worse for the nightmare you sent us against."

"But...but my dragons could not go where the rock troll attacked."

Ouderling gave him an 'oh really' look. "That's strange. My companion managed it with no problem."

"But she's an elf."

"My *dragon* companion," Ouderling asserted.

A high-pitched screech drew everyone's attention to the opposite side of the clearing. Keaf had landed beyond the wall and was now walking through the tall arch—a peculiar, white dragon watching his approach from the top of the wall.

"Your dragon companion?" Grimclaw asked in surprise.

"Grimclaw, meet Keaf. The only dragon brave enough to go where others would not."

Grimclaw scowled.

"Surely you have smaller dragons amongst your settlement, do you not? Could they not have been sent in to rescue these fine gentlemen?"

Ohz and his companions stared hard at Grimclaw, clearly unhappy.

"Well yes, but—" Flustered, Grimclaw observed the party of dwarven craftsmen. He frowned, turning his attention back to Ouderling. *"You have a dragon companion?"*

"Why wouldn't I? Because I'm a princess?"

"No, but—"

"Oh, you're surprised because you think I'm like my mother—which I am by the way." She held up a staying finger and continued, "No, neither of us is like my grandmother. There will never be another Nyxa. Just as there will there ever be another Khae."

At the mention of the queen, Grimclaw looked away.

His reaction struck her as odd. "What do you know?"

It took a few moments before Grimclaw returned his attention to her. *"Nothing, it seems."*

He sat straighter under her scrutiny and drew a deep breath. *"You've done well, princess. You may have what it takes to do Nyxa's memory proud."* His voice lowered to one of heartfelt compassion. *"I may have been wrong about you."*

"About a great many things, it would seem," Ouderling admonished. "Now, I believe you've an obligation to honour. My mother needs help and she doesn't have much time. The gods willing, we're not too late already."

Grimclaw's yellow eyes appeared to gloss over. He wouldn't meet Ouderling's gaze. *"Yes. We may be."*

Ouderling frowned at his odd choice of words. She wondered what he wasn't telling her, but let the suspicion pass. "Does that mean you'll accompany me to South March?"

"I am but one dragon."

Ouderling shook her head, her gaze taking in the array of dragons sitting around the clearing—her attention captivated by the glacier blue eyes of the white dragon sitting above the archway. The dragon appeared too young to have white scales, reminding her of Zorain.

Turning her attention back to Grimclaw, she said with calculated intention, "You have many dragons at your disposal. Are they not brave enough to join you?"

Dragon Sect

The assembled dragons muttered amongst themselves, their wings and tails twitching in aggravation at her harsh assessment.

"Of course they are." Grimclaw looked pointedly at Dagomar. *"Every dragon here is braver than those who remain loyal to Highcliff, I promise you that."*

Dagomar puffed his chest out and growled, a puff of black smoke escaping his nostrils.

"Easy, Dagomar. Now's not the time. You'll have your chance."

Grimclaw's eyes narrowed.

Unperturbed, Ouderling knew she had the mighty dragon where she wanted him. "If your dragons are as brave as you claim, they shouldn't fear doing battle with a bunch of rogue, elven troops. Or have the dragons that fled their responsibility to South March become soft hiding out here in the wilderness?"

Before Grimclaw could answer, she added, "A wilderness within the kingdoms of man. The same people who dealt grave harm on dragonkind not long ago. Or have you forgotten what Nyxa did for you?"

"I forget nothing!" Grimclaw's throaty growl reverberated between the wall and the steep slope of the mountain.

Ouderling worried she had gone too far.

Grimclaw lowered his head to stare at her with one eye. *"My dragons fear no one."*

Pulling away, the mighty dragon ruffled his wings and stretched his neck. He squatted momentarily, before leaping into the air—the great downthrust of wind generated by his wings blew Ouderling's hair around her face—ruffling her tunic and matching skirt.

She nodded to Jyllana astride Miragan. By Grimclaw's own admission, he had no choice but to act.

Dragon Sect

The Fate of a Kingdom

"**What** exactly did you use as a focal point this time?" Zorain asked as they drifted over dense forest. The sun breaking over the eastern horizon basked them in glorious warmth.

"Not so much, *what*. More like a feeling," Scale replied, trying to make sense of the terrain. Snow-capped peaks stretched away behind them from the east to the west, but they looked nothing like the Dark Mountains around Highcliff. Perhaps they had jumped too far south.

"A feeling? That sounds ominous. What does that mean?"

"Well, last time I envisioned mountains similar to the Steel Mountains, except in the north. Wherever we ended up, it certainly didn't seem like we were in the kingdoms of man anymore. So, to avoid that from happening again, not to mention we were about to get taken by whatever lurked within that evil mist, I decided to focus on something more tangible. I summoned us toward elven magic."

The ensuing silence informed Scale that Zorain wasn't impressed.

"What else could I do? I didn't want us to end up on the other side of the world." He wasn't convinced that they hadn't just escaped such a place.

"How do you know there aren't elves on the other side of the world?"

Zorain's question made him sit up straighter. He had never thought of that.

"There." Zorain tilted his wings. *"A castle."*

A cold wave of fear flushed Scale. Not another one.

Far below, south of their position, a large castle dominated the centre of a wide clearing.

"Something's going on down there."

Scale had no idea what Zorain was on about but as they drew closer, he saw people running across a graveyard beyond the castle's southern wall. "They're headed for the trees. Can you see anything in the forest?"

Time passed as they glided on wind currents. Angling his wing tips, Zorain swooped lower. *"There's a line of horsemen in the woods. I think a battle is about to take place."*

Scale squinted but couldn't see into the shadows of the forest. Having grown up the son of a well-known captain in the Royal Guard, he knew a little about warfare tactics. "That doesn't make sense. Look how scattered the runners are. No commander would allow his troops to attack in such a disorganized manner."

"Perhaps they're fleeing the castle."

Scale thought about that. On closer inspection, organized units of defenders stood along the castle's ramparts, unconcerned about anything happening within the walls.

An odd feeling tickled Scale's senses. Peering into the gloom at the edge of the clearing his eyes widened in shock.

Dragon Sect

Hunkering against Zorain's neck, he said, "Take us in for a closer look."

Braen groveled in the underbrush, his attention divided between the archers holding Cassava and Alexis at bay and the raucous cries of the castle guard charging across the open field.

He thought of crawling through the thickets, hoping beyond hope to avoid the notice of the horsemen, but froze as a voice rang out.

"You there. On the ground. Come out at once and identify yourself." The voice was that of a male—his tone deep and full of authority.

Conscious that he'd wet himself, Braen swallowed, his limbs visibly shaking.

"Now!" the voice bellowed.

Somehow Braen found the strength to get to his feet. He stumbled around Alexis, mindful not to stick himself on the bloody dagger the man prince held at the ready.

The speaker became apparent. Sitting astride a tall, black charger, the well-dressed man was the only one not holding a bow. He regarded Braen with a finger curled around his chin. "So, it's true. The elves have crossed the border."

"N-no. I come alone," Braen squeaked.

The Nordician leader stroked his blonde goatee. "I don't believe you."

"Believe what you will, commander," Cassava growled, her daggers poised to strike. "The elf speaks true. If you know what's good for you, you'll let us pass before your rabble arrive."

Braen glared at the maniacal woman and looked over his shoulder. Terrified of being killed, he wanted nothing more than to shut her up.

Dragon Sect

Movement through the trees drew his attention skyward. A great shadow passed over the edge of the clearing—an ear-piercing shriek dominating the frenzied shouts of the chasing guardsmen.

Dragon Sect

In the dim twilight, the field burst into flame—the subsequent cries of men in agony causing Braen to shudder.

Oblivious to the dragon creating havoc in the field behind her, Cassava advanced on the commander.

Alexis moved in unison with the assassin queen and shouted, "Zephyr Knight!"

Braen cringed, expecting to be cut down, but the arrows never came.

Twigs snapped and branches broke. Mounted men fought to control their panicked horses. The frightened animals reared and stamped wildly before bolting deeper into the woods to escape the chaos the dragon had created as it let forth another swath of deadly fire along the treeline.

Cassava started after the commander but his horse moved too quickly for her to follow. She turned to scan the underbrush. Not detecting a threat, she stared through the edge of the trees at the fiery grasses.

Alexis stepped in beside her. "Who do you suppose that is?"

Cassava didn't answer. Instead, she turned her gaze on Braen.

Braen balked at the sudden attention. "How would I know?"

"You're an elf," Cassava stated as if that should be explanation enough.

Braen chuckled nervously, his attention divided between the intense woman and the underbrush, expecting a Nordician guardsman to leap out at him. He half-walked, half-stumbled to stand between his companions, putting a hand on Alexis' forearm and squeezing as the white dragon dropped from the sky to settle on the edge of the woods.

Dragon Sect

A dragon rider clad all in black and carrying a long spear slid from the dragon's back. He propped the spear against the nearest tree. "Prince Wys?"

Braen almost fainted. How did the long-haired elf dressed in Grim Guard livery know his name? "D-did my uncle send you?"

The dragon rider scrunched up his face, but dropped to a knee. "Not unless your uncle is a goblin, Your Highness."

Braen frowned. "I don't understand."

"My name is Scale Wood. I was sent by High Wizard Aelfwynne to find you, though I must admit, I'm as surprised by your appearance as you are of mine."

Braen frowned deeper.

"Never mind. I'll explain it to you on the way."

"On the way where?" Braen's gaze fell on the white dragon stalking the edge of the flames along the treeline.

"To Highcliff."

"And just how are we getting there?"

Still kneeling, Scale looked over his shoulder. "On dragonback, of course."

It took all of Braen's strength to remain on his feet. After everything he had gone through, there was no way he could even contemplate climbing onto a fire-breathing beast and taking to the skies. "Um…That won't be happening."

"Master Aelfwynne commands it."

The dragon rider's tone irked Braen. Gathering a semblance of dignity, he said, "As the Prince of Urdanya, I don't take orders from a wizard. Now, arise Scale Wood."

Scale obeyed, wiping the dirt from his knee. "Time is of the utmost importance, Your Highness. The future of the kingdom may depend on it."

"Have things gotten that bad?"

Scale didn't answer at first, his attention on Alexis and Cassava. "Let's just say your presence is required back home."

Braen followed his gaze. "Its okay. You may speak freely. I assure you, they bear no allegiance to the kingdom of Nordicia. Allow me to introduce you to Cassava, the Queen of Aldebaran."

Cassava's emotionless stare held Scale's.

Scale dipped his head, touching his knee to the ground momentarily. "Well met Queen Cassava."

"And this," Braen continued, "is Prince Alexis of Carillon."

Scale knelt momentarily again, accepting Alexis' handshake as the man prince pulled him back to his feet.

"Prince Alexis is a Zephyr Knight," Braen said, looking for a reaction, but didn't receive one. "You may speak freely. What news is there out of South March?"

Scale hesitated, but seeing Braen raise his eyebrows in anticipation, he said, "Master Aelfwynne requires your attendance at Highcliff to assist him with a very important matter regarding the Crystal Cavern."

That puzzled Braen. He had never been sought after by the dragon colony or the high wizard before. He could not imagine what Aelfwynne would need him for. "And what would that be?"

Scale appeared to mull over his answer. "Let's just say it's important that you attend Highcliff at once."

"What of the queen?" Braen recalled the rumours of unrest while on the road north out of South March.

"You haven't heard?"

"No, pray tell."

"The duke's forces have taken Urdanya and are harrying the Royal Army. Last I heard, Duke Orlythe had the queen's forces trapped in the Wizard's Walk. That's another reason we must make haste."

Braen wanted to inquire how the duke had gathered an army big enough to do what Scale claimed, but lacked the nerve. Inwardly chastising himself, he knew the answer. He felt the need to say something profound. Something to justify his decision to leave Urdanya's forces in the hands of the Duke of Grim, but there was nothing he could say to refute his mistake.

The thought of standing up to his uncle almost made him laugh out loud. He held no authority over the duke. Taking a deep breath to steady his frayed nerves, he said, "I'll not leave Seafoam." He observed Seafoam pulling at his tether to escape the dragon's presence. "Nor will I climb aboard that…that…thing."

Scale appeared on the verge of protesting, but Braen's scowl stopped him. Scale bowed his head. "Very well, Your Majesty. I'll return to Highcliff with news of your imminent arrival."

The dragon growled, drawing everyone's attention to where it waited.

"Zorain says the castle troops are regrouping," Scale explained the dragon's unrest. "We'd best be away from here."

Scale started toward the treeline but stopped. "Just exactly where are we?"

Incredulous, Braen asked, "You mean you don't know?"

"I'm afraid not, Your Majesty."

"We're in Nordicia." Braen pointed at the castle. "That's Nordicia Castle."

Scale bowed his head. "Of course, Your Majesty. I'll anticipate your arrival in the south."

Dragon Sect

With that said, the elf in the Grim Guard uniform walked away. Moments later, the grass fires burning close to the forest's edge jumped and crackled in the aftermath of the dragon's departure.

Alexis watched the dragon soar out of sight before holding out a hand to Braen. "Well met, Prince Wys. Thank you for not giving up on me."

Braen accepted the handshake, wincing as Alexis' grip crushed his hand. He nodded toward Cassava who had moved to the edge of the forest to watch the castle. "It was all her, believe me. If she hadn't have come along, I would've been long gone by now."

Alexis' smile dropped. He held Braen's stare for the longest of moments and nodded faintly. "That may be so, but you accompanied her nonetheless. That's what's important."

Braen swallowed, feeling sheepish. "What will you do now? Will you come with me to Highcliff? It sounds like South March is in need of fighters."

Alexis released Braen's hand and untethered Char. Mounting the black warhorse, he said, "I've learned all I need to know. I must return to Carillon to inform my father that we have a battle to prepare for. Tell your queen the Knights of the Wind will rally to her banner."

Before Braen could respond, Alexis clicked his tongue and gently pulled on Char's reins.

The black charger lifted his front hooves sideways and started through the trees, circumventing the clearing—their diminishing form soon swallowed by the forest.

"They're coming, elven prince. We must be away." Cassava joined him beside Seafoam.

Braen searched the woods. "Where's your horse?"

Dragon Sect

Cassava scowled as if the question were ludicrous. "I'm the Queen of Aldebaran. I have no need to ride a beast." She slapped her thighs. "I have these to carry me."

A shout came from the direction of the castle, answered by several others. The Nordician Guard had regrouped.

Braen swallowed. "Ya, well your legs may not be enough to outrun a squad of horses."

Cassava leaned forward to squint at something Braen couldn't see. She turned back to him. "You may be right."

Braen mounted Seafoam and held out a hand to assist the Aldebaran queen in settling in behind him.

Conscious of her body pressed against his, he said with as much authority as he could muster. "Hang on."

Seafoam lifted his head high and whinnied. A gentle prod from Braen's heels spurred him into motion. Hanging onto the reins, he barely managed to avoid being dislodged from his mount's back as he ducked time and again to avoid low hanging branches until they broke onto the roadway and galloped down what he now knew was called Redfire Path— the main roadway connecting the kingdoms of man from north to south.

Standing beside Seafoam as he drank from a small stream crossing the roadway, Braen stretched his back, deathly conscious of how red his cheeks likely appeared at having had the exotic woman cling to him for the better part of the morning.

He bent down upstream from Seafoam and filled his waterskin—almost yelping as the shapely woman stepped up beside him.

Without preamble, Cassava purred, "There's something different about you."

He swallowed, not daring to meet her gaze. "How so?"

Dragon Sect

"I don't know. Not that I'm an expert on elves, mind you, but something about you tells me there's more to you than you let on."

"Ya," he muttered. There was no sense trying to pretend to be something he wasn't. The assassin queen was no fool. "I'm a coward."

Cassava nodded, not disagreeing with him. Her legs turned so that she faced the way they had come. "Perhaps there's truth in that, but that's not what I mean. You did yourself proud back there."

Goosebumps flushed Braen's skin. He put the stopper in the waterskin and straightened to his full height, following her gaze up Redfire Path. He half expected to see a troop of Nordician Guard appear over a distant rise.

Cassava placed a finger to her chin in thought. "You're an enigma, Braen Wys. One that I plan to unravel."

Braen couldn't prevent his jaw from dropping at her ominous statement, unable to bring himself to explain to the intimidating woman that his bravado back at the castle had come about purely by accident.

"I believe we're free of our pursuers," Cassava said casually, and gazed into his eyes.

Totally out of character, Braen heard himself ask, "Why don't you come with me to South March. I'll find you passage to Aldebaran from there."

Cassava laughed for the first time. "Are you kidding? Elves are more arrogant than men."

He didn't know what to make of that, so he let it go. Her smile affecting him more than he was willing to admit, he blurted, "But you'll be hunted in Nordicia."

Cassava shrugged and walked to the middle of Redfire Path. "Let's hope we reach Ember Breath before news of the king's death breaks."

Dragon Sect

Braen took hold of Seafoam and walked him onto the roadway, recalling the maps he'd studied of the region. "But Ember Breath can't be more than a day's hard ride from here."

The assassin took a couple of steps in the direction of Nordicia Castle, the sun overhead glinting off the sheen on her skin. She looked over her shoulder and winked. "A lot can happen in that time, elven prince. Look what transpired last night. The fate of a kingdom decided simply by my blade finding the king's heart."

The afternoon passed in blissful silence—the assassin queen's intimidating presence pressed against his back enough to keep Braen's heart hammering in his chest until long after the sun had set over southern Nordicia.

Dragon Sect

Nemesis

"Are you sure you want to do this?" Kingstone asked, lifting off from the promontory fronting Highcliff.

"I'm not sure of anything anymore," Aelfwynne grumbled.

Xantha squeezed Aelfwynne within her arms, the ancient Guardian holding him in place at the base of the great dragon's neck. "We don't have to do this."

Aelfwynne leaned his back against her. Flying off in a desperate act to save the king was totally out of character for him. He had preached for years that there was nothing more important than the security of the Crystal Cavern, but after his premonition about Khae's death—something he instinctively knew had come to pass—he had come to the startling revelation that perhaps he had been wrong. Something he had been guilty of more than once since Ouderling Wys had cursed his doorstep.

He sighed. It wasn't the princess' fault. In fact, if he allowed himself to see past his ancient beliefs, he might even come to appreciate the merit of some of the elfling's crazy ideas.

His body convulsed with strong shivers. He dreaded the day he had to tell the princess of her mother's passing. She would blame him.

"Are you alright?" Xantha bent over his shoulder, her long hair blowing wildly in the wind of dragonflight. "It's getting worse, isn't it?"

"Bah, my pet. 'Tis but the cold." Even as he said it, he knew she didn't believe him. The darned elf was too smart for his own good.

It had been two days since Khae's spirit had departed the mortal realm. Two days of Aelfwynne fretting over the state of the kingdom in her absence. For all he knew, King Hammas and what remained of the Royal Army were still alive in the Wizard's Walk. A circumstance he was certain would not last much longer once Duke Orlythe learned of the queen's passing.

With Hammas and those loyal to the crown out of the way, Ouderling Wys' life would be a moot point. She would inherit an empty throne. Without troops, she could not hope to survive an attack on Borreraig Palace. He sighed again, another habit he had acquired recently. He had no way of knowing whether the princess still lived.

Damn that fool Dagomar. He shuddered.

"There it is again," Xantha whispered into his ear. "Come on. Let's turn back before it's too late. Khae's gone. There's nothing you can do for her now. We must protect the Crystal Cavern. Just like we always have. If you wish to honour what she died for, don't abandon your beliefs now."

"My beliefs are wrong," Aelfwynne growled in a voice he had never used in Xantha's presence before. "What good are a bunch of rocks to a barren throne? All the magic in the world won't bring Khae back. If the line of Nyxa is eradicated, South March, and indeed the greater world, will fall under a shadow that I doubt even the War Dragon and the Dragon Witch could survive. I have failed the queen, and, if I'm not mistaken, everyone else in South March as well."

Xantha kissed his cheek. "Then let's hope your recent form continues and you *are* mistaken."

The elf's cheeky words angered him at first, but as Kingstone rose above the ridgeline of the Dark Mountains, the southland spread out before his deteriorating eyes. He took a deep breath and released a long exhalation. He was too old to continue in his capacity as High Wizard. If they survived the coming days, he would have to find someone to replace him. Someone other than his bumbling apprentice.

Kingstone's smooth flight missed a beat.

Aelfwynne sensed it too.

Always intuitive to her life mate, Xantha tensed. "What is it?"

Aelfwynne held up a staying claw, concentrating.

Kingstone's wings stopped flapping. Gliding over the northern slopes of the Dark Mountains, moonlight glinted off the bronze highlights of his green scales. *"The grotdraak?"*

That had been Aelfwynne's first thought as well, but he shook his head. "Too strong. Even for that ancient beast."

"It can't be the Crystal Cavern. I've never sensed it this far away. Besides, there's a malignance in its presence. A profound evil."

The truth of what he and Kingstone perceived emanating from somewhere below became perfectly clear. Aelfwynne's beady eyes opened wide in shock. "Kingstone, turn us around."

He felt Xantha lean back, the sound of her once, formidable sword sliding free of its baldric giving

Aelfwynne the chills. He had witnessed the carnage his mate had been responsible for in her younger years. To this day he had never encountered her equal, but her time of prominence was long gone. The mother of his only child had aged beyond the point of being a force to be reckoned with. As much as she would always retain the heart of a dragon, her body was no longer capable of withstanding the rigours of battle.

"No! Take us down!" Xantha declared. "It's the wraith, isn't it? Let's end this."

Aelfwynne cringed, his rough skin flushed in goosebumps at the authority in Xantha's tone. She sounded like the Xantha of old. Someone who took charge without being asked.

He, too, desired nothing more than to be rid of his troublesome nemesis once and for all, but he wasn't naïve. Xantha wasn't the only one no longer in their prime. Even with Kingstone and Xantha by his side, he wasn't a match for the creature that had plagued his existence. Drawing strength from the Staff of Reckoning clutched tightly in his right hand, he patted her thigh with his left—the lack of her former musculature not lost on him. "Easy, my pet. We dare not. At least not yet."

Ignoring him, Xantha raised her voice. "Kingstone. Do as I say. It's time the Soul faced the wrath of Nyxa's Demon Rogue."

Aelfwynne sensed Kingstone's hesitation—the dragon unsure who to listen to. He sighed. The only one more stubborn than himself was the fierce elf riding behind him. It wouldn't surprise him if she jumped from Kingstone's back, trusting in her ability to survive the fatal drop so that she might engage her enemy singlehanded. If he couldn't find a way to put her off, her senseless death would be on his hands as well.

"Allow me to reach out to it. Let me try to discover its intent," Aelfwynne pleaded.

"Its intent is obvious!" The indignance in Xantha's voice made Aelfwynne shudder, but this time she paid his ailment no mind. "Why else would it skulk around the Dark Mountains? Kingstone, take us down. Now!"

"No Kingstone." Aelfwynne's tone brooked no argument from the dragon. "I forbid it."

Xantha moved behind him. He feared for what she was about to do though he should have known better. Whenever danger was about, Xantha was the first to run toward it. He should have left her at home.

"Can you see it?" Aelfwynne asked, if only to distract Xantha until he could figure out a way to keep her from harm. Little Dithreab needed at least one parent alive as he grew up.

"I cannot. I sense where it is, but see it? No."

"There!" Xantha pointed at an outcropping of rock to their right.

Kingstone adjusted his flight, dropping closer to where she indicated. *"Yes. I see it now."*

The faces on the Staff of Reckoning came to life.

"Get away! Now!" Aelfwynne shouted, but his warning came too late.

A magical pulse shot up from the crag, the reddish-hued orb impacting Kingstone's wing—its energy crackling along the dragon's wing membranes.

Kingstone shrieked, his other wing flapping uselessly as they fell from the sky.

Dragon Sect

Dragon Witch Wraith

Aelfwynne's death had been a long time in coming. It was also satisfying to know he had taken down the Demon Rogue as well, not to mention the dragon left in charge of Highcliff since Grimclaw's fortunate departure.

Stepping out from the rock formation he had sheltered in many times over the years while keeping an eye on the comings and goings of Highcliff, the Soul made his way to where the green dragon had hit the mountainside. He wouldn't be satisfied until he saw the goblin's corpse. The cockroach had survived worse. His escape from Crag's Forge had proven once again that only a fool would underestimate the high wizard's resourcefulness.

But there comes a time for everyone…Well, everyone except the Dragon Witch Wraith. He chuckled at the title he had been labelled with from the time he had done battle with the Dragon Witch and the War Dragon. If not for the warlock's intervention, he would already be enjoying the power the Crystal Cavern had to offer.

With Sagora holding Khae's spirit hostage in the netherworld between the mortal realm and that of the Fae,

Dragon Sect

South March's resistance would falter long enough for him to discover a way to harness the elusive earth blood. All Orlythe had to do was to keep the queen and her forces bottled up in the Wizard's Sleeve until then.

There was also the matter of the upstart wizard, Ryedyn, but he still had a use for him. Him and the crystal shard he had somehow pilfered from the Crystal Cavern without anyone's knowledge. He snorted. Without anyone's knowledge but his own.

A feeling of contentment filled him like nothing he had known for many long centuries. The Soul. The name he had been given by the original Dragon Witch. The silly girl from the world beyond the horizon. It had been so long since they had left their former life that he couldn't recall his real name anymore. He stopped to scratch at the mottled skin covering his skull. The fact that he couldn't remember was disconcerting.

He sighed. It mattered not.

Cresting a ridge, the bulk of the dragon came into view—its body broken across a jagged tor. It had proven a masterstroke to allow his essence to be detected by the dragon. Of the Dragon Mage and the Demon Rogue, there was no sign.

The Soul stopped, sending out feelers. Startled, the strong magic of the dead dragon was still enough to overpower his senses, but he could tell at once that it was but residual. Whatever the dragon had done as it fell, it had left a taint on the air.

Honing his senses, he attempted to scan the area beyond the dragon's bulk, wary of his formidable foes. There was a reason they had lived so long. If anyone could survive a fall from the sky…

Dragon Sect

He jumped sideways, but his movement was hampered by the weight of the body that had fallen on him. The bite of steel pained him more than he would have thought possible. He believed he had moved beyond the mortal limitations of his corporeal body, but the debilitating blow left him reeling.

The pull of the blade's withdrawal from his side turned him to face his attacker. The Demon Rogue!

Angered by his carelessness, he staggered backward, his step impeded by what would have been a fatal wound centuries before.

The Demon Rogue's sword swung at his neck, the force behind the swing incredible for such a frail looking elf, but he was ready for her this time. Even though he was confident in his ability, he couldn't help flinching as the killing stroke whistled through the air.

The Demon Rogue's sword hit hard, the impact causing her arms to shudder as the blade came to a sudden stop. She screamed in rage and hacked again at the other side of the Soul's neck, her sword meeting the same resistance.

Turning his fiery eyes on her, the Soul said in its grating voice, "Your time has gone, protector of the War Dragon. You have failed once again. You weren't strong enough to save Nyxa then and you aren't strong enough to protect the Dragon Mage now."

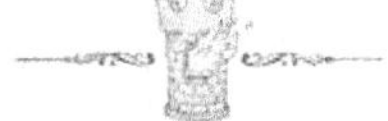

"Think again, wraith," Aelfwynne snarled from where he stepped beyond Kingstone's head and discharged his most powerful spell—its force aided by the writhing staff in his hand.

The concussion that lifted the wraith from its feet should have been enough to obliterate it, but for some reason the potent magic only tossed it through the air.

Dragon Sect

It hit the ground hard and rolled precariously close to the edge of a steep drop-off.

Xantha followed its progress, her boots sliding on the loose scree along the lip of the brink. Steadying herself, she stabbed at his exposed chest, but her sword deflected to the side, the clanging tip eliciting sparks from the rocky ground.

"Xantha! No!" Aelfwynne's hysterical plea echoed off the heights, but in typical Xantha fashion, the elder Guardian refused to listen.

Throwing her sword to the ground, she grabbed onto the wraith's ratty robes and lifted it into the air over her head.

A bone-chilling laugh escaped the ancient creature as Xantha threw it over the brink. "You can't kill me. I'll survive the fall. You've failed again, Demon Rogue…" Its voice trailed off into the darkness—the Dragon Witch Wraith disappearing from Aelfwynne's view.

Xantha's feral scream made Aelfwynne cringe in fear. Taking up her sword and holding it point downward in both hands, she leapt after the wraith.

"Xantha!" Aelfwynne's drawn-out cry followed the legendary warrior over the cliff's edge. The anguished faces carved into the Staff of Reckoning went still as it fell from his hand and clattered to the ground.

He staggered to the edge of the precipice and fell to his knees. Looking down, he was unable to see into the shadows at the base of the cliff.

Blinded by tears, he stared at the spot where the love of his life had left him. Trembling uncontrollably, his anguished cry reverberated off the heights.

It took Aelfwynne the better part of the day to navigate his way to the bottom of the steep slope. All the way down, his heart refused to believe what his brain told him to be true.

Dragon Sect

He shook his head. Xantha had survived worse over the centuries. Bigger than life, she was known to have defied the odds no matter how improbable they had seemed. A simple fall couldn't be how the infamous warrior's story ended. Numb with dread, he refused to believe she was dead.

Late afternoon sunshine glinted off Lake Grim—its calm surface far below the base of the cliff Aelfwynne descended toward. The sun would soon drop behind the brooding hulk of Faelyn's Nest in the west and blanket the land in twilight.

Physically exhausted and emotionally spent, Aelfwynne paused after slipping and falling on loose scree to where he landed at the bottom of the defile—the Staff of Reckoning providing him little support. Looking at the brink of the cliff where they had battled the Dragon Witch Wraith took his breath away.

He swallowed hard, trying to console himself with the knowledge that in the history of the elven lands, Nyxa's Demon Rogue had no equal when it came to resourcefulness. If anyone could survive such a fall, it would be Xantha. He pictured her angelic face waiting for him, grinning as if her tussle with the wraith had been no big deal.

Barely able to breathe, he steeled himself to the reality of what he was about to witness. Hobbling around the remnants of a long-ago rockslide, his life no longer held any meaning.

Lying on her back on a bare patch of rock, her ancient beauty undisturbed by the trauma her body had surely undergone, Xantha's empty stare met his approach.

"Xantha?" Aelfwynne's pathetic voice squeaked. He stopped to stare, clinging to the irrational belief that Xantha would sit up and hold her arms out to him.

Unable to bring himself to confirm the obvious, he remained in that spot, his life frozen in time, until well after the lengthening shadows melted into nightfall.

Dragon Sect

Clouds drifted over the bulk of the Dark Mountains. Oblivious to everything else going on in South March, forcing himself to stagger to her side was the hardest thing he had ever done in his life.

He struggled to breathe as he knelt beside the legendary warrior and touched her cheek with a trembling hand.

Her skin was cold.

The world was cold.

Shaking uncontrollably, he whispered, "Oh, my dear pet. You can't be gone. I need you."

Not caring to live another day, he lay across her chest and wept.

Alone in the wilderness, exposed to the elements and the predators that prowled the Dark Mountains, a gentle rain fell, sending shivers along his body.

He cared not.

He didn't think he would ever be warm again.

Dragon Sect

In Honour of a Lost Friend

Hammas welcomed the percussion echoing through the pass. The louder it grew, the faster his heart beat. It was time to face the one whose actions had precipitated the death of the most precious elf to have ever graced the land. Ignoring his commanders, he felt compelled to spearhead the Royal Army's attempt at breaking the Grim Guard blockade. If for no other reason than to expedite his reunion with Khae.

Aside from Ouderling's safety, his life no longer held meaning. The fact that she was in the capable hands of the Highcliff Guardians gave him the comfort he needed to do what he felt must be done. Something that should have been done many years ago.

After three days of little sleep since Khae's mysterious death, the thundering hooves of her troops kept his adrenaline surging. He looked over his shoulder, unable to see the cart laden with her body that trundled along at the rear of their procession. He owed it to her memory to break free of Orlythe's troops, if only to deliver her body to the Royal Tomb beneath Borreraig Palace. If fate was kind, he may even get a chance at ending the Grim Duke before he, himself, fell in battle.

Commander Keel's ominous gaze met his—the purple-plumed helm of the Royal Army's leader bounced rhythmically atop the powerfully built elf's head as his armour-plated warhorse kept pace on Hammas' right.

Hammas glanced at Captain Kall riding silently on his left, the captain's chin set hard. Being the elf in charge of Khae's personal safety, Kall had taken Khae's death harder than most.

Behind Hammas, Captain Hondrick headed the Queen's Shield—each member of the devout group eager to avenge their fallen monarch.

As the war drums advanced on their position, the only one King Hammas allowed to ride ahead was Khae's standard bearer. Resplendent beneath his white-plumed helm, the fact that he would be the first to fall did little to dampen his decorum. Chin high and shoulders back, he bore Nyxa's War Dragon banner with pride.

Hammas was grateful for the steadfast loyalty of his troops. As such, other than the standard bearer, he refused to allow anyone else to lead them into the coming fight.

He tensed in his saddle—the shadow of the advancing Grim Guard darkening the pass ahead was almost upon them. He swallowed hard, steeling himself for what was to come. It was a shame they were all about to die.

The canyon narrowed to what Commander Keel called a pinch point, prompting the standard bearer to lift a bone horn to his lips. A mournful note echoed up and down the pass— a harbinger of what was about to befall the thousands of elves who were caught up in the senselessness of it all.

The Royal Army files were reduced to three horses wide. As the canyon walls narrowed, the pennant bearer slowed his advance until he rode directly in front of the king. Behind them, the thin tail of the royal banner snapped in the wind that whistled through the gap.

A terrific shout arose from the lead ranks of Grim Guard.

Arrowshot filled the confined space, the missiles' flight issued from both sides.

The standard bearer took an arrow in the right shoulder, twisting him sideways. He lowered the horn, his face twisted in pain, but straightened as best he could and carried on. A second arrow buried itself in his left side. Struggling to remain in the saddle, he bent over in agony—and yet the War Dragon pennant never wavered.

Commander Keel expertly rode his horse against the king's, a wide tower shield held before him. Keel's arm bucked several times—the impacts inducing the king and the commander to wince with every hit, but their forward march never faltered.

Two arrows thumped into the standard bearer's horse, missing its armour plating, one right after the other. A third arrow took the brave elf in the throat.

King Hammas leaned out and snatched the banner from the dying elf's hand, barely able to remain in the saddle. The sudden extra weight of flagpole threatened to dismount him as the standard bearer and his mount dropped away.

Commander Keel expertly navigated his horse around that of the fallen standard bearer and grasped Hammas' flailing arm to steady the king until he regained his seat.

Affording the commander a quick look of appreciation, Hammas sat tall in the saddle and held the banner high for all to see as they forced their way between the pinch point and engaged the Grim Guard.

A roiling sea of black leather armour, and conscripted troops out of Urdanya, spread out before them as far as

Dragon Sect

Hammas could see—the offenders outnumbering the Royal Army by more than he cared to know. But it wasn't the sheer number of elves who had risen against the crown that surprised Hammas the most. Rank upon rank of Grim Guard marched in uniform files—the footfalls of the unmounted troops matching the cadence set by the drummers. Duke Orlythe's men were better disciplined than Hammas would have believed.

As the narrows widened, the Royal Army surged forward, two separate groups following Captain Kall and Captain Hondrick respectively to either side of the contingent behind the king and his commander.

Keel stood in his stirrups and lifted his sword high. "Avenge the queen!"

"Avenge the queen!" The canyon rumbled with the battle cry.

Uncaring of the archers ahead, Hammas manoeuvred his black charger beyond the protection of Commander Keel's shield. Rapier in one hand and the queen's standard the other, he urged Shadow into a gallop.

"Protect the king!" Commander Keel shouted—his plea answered by the thunder of hoofbeats.

The Royal Army charged forward—quickly swallowed by a black sea of death.

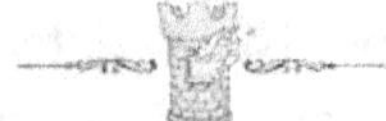

"There!" Jyllana pointed with the tip of her polearm.

Ouderling leaned forward, her jaw dropping as the reality of what she witnessed hit home.

Flying across the Wizard's Sleeve, they had passed by Gullveig at the base of the Wizard's Walk and had turned eastward toward Orphic Den.

Dagomar and Miragan had insisted on flying at the head of the dragon wing that had flown from what Ouderling had taken to calling, Dragon Home, but as soon as Jyllana drew their attention to the chaotic scene unfolding in the canyon, Grimclaw's great wings carried him into the lead.

"In honour of a lost friend!" Grimclaw's voice rang in Ouderling's head with a menacing growl.

The sentiment of the old dragon joining battle in the memory of her grandmother tugged at Ouderling's heart.

Desperate to spot where her parents rode within the roiling mass of green clad bodies mixed amongst the black livery of her uncle, she couldn't help but admire Grimclaw's flight. It was incredible how quickly he outdistanced Dagomar and Miragan. Before the rest of the dragons had a chance to tighten their formation, the blue dragon had fallen upon the rear lines of the Grim Guard.

Engrossed with the advance of the Royal Army, Duke Orlythe's troops had no idea what was about to hit them until Grimclaw shrieked. Not giving them time to respond, his head recoiled momentarily on his thick neck and stretched forward, disgorging a path of dragon fire so wide that it charred elves four files wide.

If the carnage of Grimclaw's attack wasn't terrifying enough for the surprised legions in black, a dozen more dragons swooped in Grimclaw's wake, their shrieks unbearable in the confines of the pass.

The bulk of the Grim Guard turned to face the oncoming threat—many with raised shields, while others took up a position behind them and lifted bows. As the reality of the danger they were in transformed their faces to one of shock, the remainder of Orlythe's troops squatted and raised forearms in front of their faces in a futile attempt to thwart the unforgiving firestorm that swept up the pass.

Miragan followed on Dagomar's tail. *"Get low against me, pretty lady. Watch for arrow flight."* The fearless wyvern tucked her wings in and dove toward the battlefield like a peregrine falcon dropping on its prey.

Ouderling held on tight, cringing as they rushed toward the grisly scene below.

Unable to discriminate Grim Guard from Royal troops where the armies had come together, Ouderling looked on in horror as black leather and green surcoats were caught in the rain of fire—their writhing bodies quickly reduced to ash. Just when Ouderling thought they would collide with the converging canyon walls, Miragan spread her wings wide, tilting them to catch a wind current, and vaulted into the sky.

Ouderling's eyes watered in the wind created by their swift flight as she looked around in panic. It took a moment before she spotted Jyllana safe upon Dagomar off to her left—the red dragon preparing for another pass.

"Look for my parents!" Ouderling shouted over the rushing wind.

Miragan had made to follow Dagomar, but on Ouderling's instruction, the wyvern slowed her flight and turned to fly over the rear of the Royal Army that pressed toward the battle from the far side of the narrows.

Dragon shrieks, accompanied by the cries of their victims, echoed up and down the battlefield from beyond the narrows as she leaned out to inspect the mass of bodies below. Unable to spot the Queen of the Elves, she directed Miragan to fly her back to where the armies were engaged in battle.

She gasped as she spotted the War Dragon banner fluttering above a knot of troops who were fighting hard to keep a crush of Grim Guard from reaching the standard bearer.

Commander Keel's purple plume was instantly recognizable, but it was the long, black hair of the standard bearer that gave her pause.

Dragon Sect

"Father?"

Miragan's head moved slowly from side to side. *"Where is he?"*

Ouderling didn't answer. Something was dreadfully wrong. Her mother would never allow the king to enter battle without her by his side. And why was he carrying her pennant?

She swallowed, her tears having little to do with the wind. She leaned on the back of Miragan's neck, her hand extended past the wyvern's right eye. "Look to the long pennant there. That's the king. Do you see my mother?"

Several wingbeats later, Miragan's voice was full of compassion, *"I do not, pretty lady. They may have been separated."*

"We have to find her!" Ouderling cried. "Take us lower."

A horrendous shriek rose above the bedlam, drawing their attention to an orange dragon falling out of the sky with what appeared to be a small tree trunk piercing her hide.

"They have ballistae!" A dragon's voice Ouderling didn't recognize warned.

The threat had no sooner registered than a blue dragon cried out—its wings crumpled. It, too, dropped from the sky.

Below them and off to the side, Dagomar laid down another line of fire—a green dragonling doing likewise by his left side.

"Keaf! Get out of there!" Ouderling screamed.

Grimclaw's command diverted her gaze from her dragon. *"Concentrate all fire on the dragon killers!"* Grimclaw ordered.

Ouderling searched the canyon floor, locating the ancient dragon flying low over the rear lines of the Grim Guard.

All around them elves and dragons died. Arrows filled the skies, aimed at stopping those who rained death from above.

Most bounced harmlessly off dragon scales, but Ouderling could see that a couple of the Dragon Home dragons had arrows lodged between their protective plates. Although they remained aloft, she could only imagine the hurt the arrows caused.

Surveying the battlefield, she was appalled to see where another dragon had fallen. Surrounded by a sea of Grim Guard, it fought valiantly from its side, its exposed wing mangled beyond repair. It wasn't long before it was overwhelmed by the merciless hacking and slashing of Grim Guard blades.

Unable to concentrate on where her mother might be, she flinched. The tell-tale cry of another dragon made her shudder. Locating a green dragon in distress, her first thought was that she was relieved it wasn't Keaf.

The injured dragon fought to keep aloft—its wings beating inconsistently. It didn't appear to have been hit by a ballista bolt, but on closer inspection, it became apparent how many arrows had lodged into its body. Hovering close to the spot she had last seen her father, it slowly lost height as arrow after arrow found their mark.

"Take that ballista out!" Grimclaw roared.

Ouderling searched for the launcher in question.

"I'm on it!" Dagomar's voice replied.

It took a moment for Ouderling to find where Jyllana and the red dragon had gone, but their fast descent drew her gaze to where they fell upon a wooden war machine being operated from the back of a large wagon.

Dagomar's wings expanded moments before he levelled out, bathing the ballista in deadly fire, but not before the crew launched the killing bolt.

Wide throws leaped forward, and the wagon bucked under the force of the released bolt. Barely missing Dagomar, the sharpened tree trunk flew true. The struggling green dragon took the killing bolt square in the chest, the force of the impact knocking it from the sky to where it fell on a group of troops fighting below.

Dagomar reared in the air above the ballista, keeping a steady stream of fire on the offending apparatus. The war machine burst into flames, along with its handlers and others in the general vicinity—all incinerated where they stood.

Hard to tell from such a distance, Ouderling feared Jyllana might have taken an arrow, but as Dagomar winged into the air, her faithful protector remained on his shoulders, the redhead's polearm held aloft.

Ouderling breathed a sigh of relief but felt a pang of guilt for being thankful it had been another dragon that had died instead of Keaf.

She took a deep breath and surveyed the battle. Although the dragon attacks had bought the Royal Army a reprieve, it was obvious from her vantage point that her mother's troops would not live to see another day. The duke's forces were too many and they were dealing with the dragon threat.

She shook her head, not wanting to believe what the Chronicler had taught her at an early age. Even with the aid of dragons, her grandmother's army had suffered great losses while repelling the human invaders centuries before.

Even though the Chronicler had said as much, she had never put much stock into the horrific accounts of the majestic creatures who had been reportedly decimated by the armies of man. In her mind, such an outcome was inconceivable. Witnessing it firsthand, however, gave her a better understanding of the difficulty they faced. A wing of dragons constituted a feral attack force, but they, too, were merely mortal.

Dragon Sect

Ouderling returned her attention to where the War Dragon banner still fluttered—the number of green surcoats surrounding the king diminishing at an alarming rate. "We have to find my mother!"

"I cannot sense her anywhere." Miragan altered her flight to take them away from the king and risked flying lower.

Ouderling stared at the back of Miragan's head. "What do you mean you can't sense her?"

"Don't be alarmed, pretty lady. It may be nothing, but I can sense the magic in you. I always have. Just like granddaddy."

"You and Perch can sense magic?"

"Kind of." Miragan banked hard to avoid the flight of two arrows. Straightening out, she said, *"Not any kind of magic, mind you, but for some reason we're in tune with the magic you share with the queen. Granddaddy was more so than me, so that's probably why I can't sense her now."*

Ouderling couldn't help imagining the worst-case scenario. Scanning the canyon, its floor littered with maimed and contorted bodies for as far as she could see, she feared her mother lay dying somewhere within the morass of bodies, unable to defend herself.

She was about to demand that Miragan set her down close to her father, but a detonation within the ranks of the Grim Guard made her hesitate.

It was unclear whether the billowing plume of smoke rising above an obliterated ballista was where the explosion had originated, but from the corner of her eye she caught sight of another war machine bursting into flame. Large pieces of blasted wood twirled away from a blackened circle on the ground.

"Wizards!" Miragan exclaimed. *"Dawnbreaker and Mirage have come bearing wizards!"*

Dragon Sect

From out of the sunshine in the east, the squat bulk of Dawnbreaker flew above the narrows with Mirage winging along beside her. Sitting behind Pecklyn and Balewynd respectively were two, dark robed figures—the wizards launching magic into the bulk of the Grim Guard, taking out the last of the ballista launchers.

A great shout arose from the beleaguered Royal Army.

"In honour of a lost friend, let's finish this!" Grimclaw growled.

Forming into an organized wing behind the ancient beast, the dragons of Highcliff joined with those who remained of Dragon Home.

Without the aid of the dragon killers, it wasn't long before the Grim Guard came to realize their fate.

Dragon Sect

A Time Between Times

Miragan landed beside Dawnbreaker and Mirage beyond the canyon narrows. The Queen's Shield stepped away from where they had defended King Hammas against impossible odds. Injured and dying elves lay twisted and moaning on the bloodstained ground between the dragons and the King of South March—the wounded being tended by those who hadn't been seriously maimed.

Dagomar settled in next to Miragan to allow Jyllana to leap to the ground and assist a distraught Ouderling from the wyvern's shoulders. She attempted to embrace the princess, but Ouderling only had eyes for the king.

Hammas spoke in earnest with Commander Keel and Captain Hondrick, but catching sight of his daughter, he stopped in mid-sentence and met her halfway.

Ouderling's skin tingled with cold. Her father's haunted face informed her that her fear had been justified. Barely able to see, she stared numbly at the emotion transforming her father's expression from a hard-nosed leader to that of a heartbroken husband. She fell into his embrace.

Dragon Sect

"Oh daddy. No." She leaned back in his arms and cupped his tear-streaked cheeks. Looking around, she said through her pain, "Where is she? I have to see her."

Hammas held her stare, his grief unbearable, making it difficult for him to speak. He shook his head. "She's…at peace, my child. She died…three days ago."

Ouderling swallowed, shaking her head in denial. "But…but that's impossible. I got here as soon as I could." She glanced at the dragons on the ground and looked to the sky. "I brought the dragons with me to save her…She can't be gone."

Hammas took a deep breath and nodded ever so slightly.

"Oh, daddy! I was too late."

Hammas hugged her close as she collapsed in his arms. Resting his chin on the top of her head, unable to see through his own tears, his voice came out as little more than a croak. "It's okay, Little Sprite. Daddy's got you."

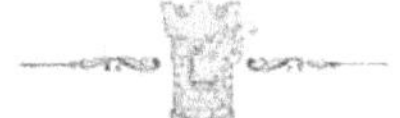

Grimclaw growled at the wizard speaking to those assembled in the cobblestoned town square of Orphic Den.

With the dark keep of the wizards' guild at his back, the old elf gave the great dragon a nervous smile. "Alright, alright. They can stay here until we figure out what to do next."

King Hammas and Commander Keel stood shoulder-to-shoulder beside the wizard as they conferred with the great, blue dragon.

Sitting on a stone bench, against the base of the keep with Jyllana trying to comfort her, Ouderling barely heard a word they were saying. Nor did she care. Her mother was dead. Although her uncle was ultimately responsible for Khae's death, Ouderling couldn't shake the guilt that she had failed to convince Grimclaw to act sooner.

Dragon Sect

Keaf sat next to the bench, the irascible dragonling unusually quiet. Every now and then he would glance at her with downcast eyes.

So many thoughts clamored for space inside Ouderling's head that they jumbled together into incoherent gibberish. In light of her mother's death, so many things needed to be done. There was so much that required an explanation. Most of what had occurred recently defied reason. Without her mother to guide her, she was lost.

She reflected on the battle in the canyon. If not for Balewynd finally convincing the wizards' guild to send help once Pecklyn had recovered enough to fly, it might have ended much differently.

In the end, her father had called off the dragons who had wanted to chase after Orlythe's retreating troops. As treasonous as the Grim Guard's actions had been, the king had maintained the wherewithal to realize that the bulk of the duke's army had merely been following the orders of one of the royal family—as bizarre as it must have seemed for them to be waging an assault against the crown.

It was hard to appreciate the level of restraint her father had shown after what had happened to the queen, but Hammas had always been the one to do the right thing. Nor would he change his ways going forward, even if it led to the cause of his own death.

Perhaps what unsettled Ouderling the most was the fact that the spineless duke had not been present with the Grim Guard forces who had attacked her mother's army. The last real account they had of the Grim Duke's whereabouts placed him back at Urdanya Castle with his wizard, though rumours had recently filtered into Orphic Den that Duke Orlythe had sailed up the Ors Spill with an armada of troop laden boats.

Dragon Sect

She shuddered. There could only be one destination in her uncle's mind. The seat of South March was about to be usurped and there was nothing she or her father could do to prevent it. Everything her mother had believed in and fought for was about to have been for naught. Once the Grim Duke sat his carcass on the Willow Throne, the kingdom would undergo a drastic upheaval. Changes that would not favour the average elf.

Grimclaw growled, looking none too pleased. *"You should have allowed my dragons to destroy the Grim Guard."*

Hammas met the intimidating dragon's glare head-on. "To what end? Kill more innocent elves. The queen would have been appalled."

"The queen is dead because of her unwillingness to do what needed to be done."

Ouderling looked up at the dragon's harsh assessment, but in her heart, she knew he spoke the truth. She need not have feared her father's reaction. Hammas was no fool. He knew better than anyone that the duke should have been dealt with a long time ago. Still, to openly speak badly of the queen was uncalled for—especially since they hadn't buried her yet.

Jyllana patted Ouderling's hands in an effort to mollify her. She didn't doubt her protector had taken notice of her reddening eyes.

To Hammas' credit, he kept his voice calm. "Khae was an elf of impeccable standards. No matter how badly her subjects behaved, she always found a way to get the best out of them."

"Her kindness was her downfall. A leader must be decisive if they wish to maintain the respect of their followers. Ruthless even, when the time calls for it. I was saddened when I perceived her downfall three days ago, though I wasn't surprised. Nyxa would never have—"

Dragon Sect

"You what?" Ouderling snapped, recalling her conversation with Grimclaw outside of the Dragon Temple after she had slain the rock troll. She remembered saying to him, *'The gods willing, we're not too late already.'*

Grimclaw hadn't been able to meet her gaze when he had answered, *'Yes. We may be.'*

Jyllana jumped to her feet and followed as Ouderling stormed up to Grimclaw, pointing a finger at him. "You knew all along! Didn't you?"

Grimclaw pulled his head back as if confused.

"You knew my mother had died and you didn't tell me," Ouderling elaborated.

A long silence settled over the town square—a gentle breeze toying with Ouderling's hair as she dared Grimclaw to refute her accusation.

His yellow eyes narrowed. Lowering his head to the ground to look straight at her, he said, *"I sensed that she no longer lived."*

The frankness of the dragon's admission shocked Ouderling. Taken aback by his honesty, she wanted to scream at him for not confiding in her. Her breathing came in short, heavy gasps. "Why didn't you tell me?"

"Two reasons, princess. The first being that I didn't know for certain. This may be difficult to understand, but through the bond I once shared with your grandmother, I find I've been attuned to everyone directly descended through her bloodline."

Ouderling frowned.

"Yes. That means you, too," Grimclaw answered her unspoken question. *"I felt your brother's passing, just like I sensed your birth a couple of years later. As long as Nyxa's line exists in the world I will be forever cursed with their wellbeing."*

Dragon Sect

Accepting what he told her to be true, she muttered, "And the other reason?"

"Telling you of your mother's death at that time served no purpose."

"Served no purpose? I'm the heir to the Willow Throne. Did you not think that...?" She trailed off as the reality of what her mother's death meant to her station in life hit her. Her eyes widened, their red hue fading to orange.

"That's right. With your mother's passing, you've become the Queen of the Elves. A title that brings with it grave responsibility. If your predecessors' lives bespeak to the legacy of the crown, I'm afraid it will bring you little joy."

Ouderling gaped. Searching the faces around the town square, every elf bowed their heads as her gaze fell on them. If not for Jyllana's steadying hand, Ouderling believed she would have fallen to the cobblestones.

Grimclaw's voice commanded her attention, *"Your mother's death came at a time between times. You had just rescued the dwarven stonemasons from a creature I could not deal with, while the forces loyal to the queen were penned in the canyon with no means of escape. To inform you of your mother's death while you were hundreds of leagues away served no purpose."*

Ouderling was so incensed at the callousness of Grimclaw's statement that she found she couldn't speak.

"Whether or not you agree with my reasoning is but a moot point. Through your actions, you have convinced me that even at your young age, you're a most capable descendent of Nyxa. Thus, you're someone I feel I can put my trust in. A happenstance I did not foresee happening again in my lifetime."

Dragon Sect

Ouderling struggled to think beyond her fury and make sense of Grimclaw's cryptic response. "So, you will help us stop my uncle?"

Grimclaw sighed. *"I cannot."*

"But you just said…"

"I brought a dozen dragons with me from Dragon Home. Only seven will return to their family. This is the very reason we left South March all those years ago."

On another occasion, Ouderling would have smiled at Grimclaw adapting her name for Dragon Home, but not today. "Without your aid, my uncle will take the palace uncontested."

Grimclaw merely nodded.

Ouderling sensed, rather than saw, King Hammas step up behind her. He put a hand on her shoulder. "Grimclaw speaks wisely. This is not his fight."

She spun on her father. "But…What will we do? Where will we go? Uncle Orlythe isn't going to sit back if you and I still live."

Hammas presented her with a sad smile. "No, he most certainly will not. But, with the aid of Orphic Den," he nodded at the old wizard with a grey goatee, "who have graciously agreed to house us and what remains of the Royal Army, we'll find our way forward." He glanced at Pecklyn and Balewynd standing quietly beside their respective dragons. "When the time is right, I'm sure your friends from Highcliff will prove instrumental in reclaiming our rightful place, you'll see."

Pecklyn and Balewynd stepped up and took a knee.

Bowing his head, Pecklyn said solemnly, "Highcliff will forever be at your disposal, my queen."

Goosebumps riddled Ouderling's skin. She *was* the Queen of the Elves.

Dragon Sect

Clandestine Order

Grimclaw and his dragon contingent remained until Queen Khae was interred the following day. Her burial was a solemn occasion, attended by Hammas, Ouderling, Commander Keel and Captain Hondrick, along with the two Highcliff Guardians and the new Headmaster of Orphic Den.

Captain Kall, the steadfast elf who was always seen at Queen Khae's side, was buried next to her—a fitting end for the elf who had forever watched over her.

The irony of Khae being granted a place of honour in the garden of the wizards who had openly defied her call for assistance wasn't lost on Ouderling, but Sagora's role in the disobedience of the guild's members helped smooth relations between King Hammas and Orphic Den.

Well after the last words were spoken, Ouderling remained behind to stare at the mound that marked her mother's last resting place. She shivered. What a cold place to spend the remainder of eternity in.

Vaguely aware that not everyone had left the graveyard, she sighed as a familiar hand gripped her shoulder. Not trusting herself to speak without crying, she forced a grateful smile in appreciation of her father's company.

"I have something for you," Hammas reached inside his tunic and pulled out a small bundle covered in a familiar rag. The stained cloth smelled of her mother's perfume.

She frowned.

"Open it," Hammas said.

The pain in her father's eyes was heartbreaking. Swallowing the lump in her throat, she knew without having to look, that the gift was going to make her cry all over again. Taking a deep breath, she pulled back the folds.

Sure enough, her eyes blurred. Her hands shook so hard she feared she might drop her mother's old, bone comb. The one Khae had so meticulously pulled through her hair every morning and night for as long as Ouderling could remember.

Her father cupped her hands in his to keep the comb from falling to the ground. Without saying a word, he held her close.

"Don't worry, Your Majesty. I'll stay with her for as long as she wishes," Jyllana's voice reached through Ouderling's numbness.

"Thank you, Jyllana. I want you to know that Khae appointed you personally. After what you two have been through recently, I understand why she placed so much faith in you."

"Thank you, Your Highness." Jyllana bowed her head and spoke to the ground, "She was a great queen."

Hammas' footsteps informed Ouderling that she was alone in the graveyard with Jyllana and the lengthening shadows. It would soon be dark in the Wizard's Sleeve. With the night came the cold in the upper reaches of the mountains.

Dragon Sect

Her body had trembled uncontrollably ever since the burial ceremony had begun in the mid-afternoon. Worrying about Jyllana, it was time to leave her mother to the ages.

Just when she thought she had cried herself out, her eyes misted again. "Good-bye, mommy. I love you."

She turned and stared into Jyllana's teary eyes.

Jyllana embraced her for a moment. Placing a consoling arm over Ouderling's shoulder, she whispered, "Come on, my friend. Let's get you out of the cold."

"Ouderling Wys!"

A deep voice rang through Ouderling's head. She looked up in time to witness Grimclaw drop out of the sky and land gracefully on the edge of the graveyard.

Clearing her throat, Ouderling said, "I thought you had left."

"We'll be leaving shortly. I waited out of respect for your privacy until I could have a brief word with you."

Ouderling tilted her head, wondering what would make the ancient dragon wait on her. He must have been watching the graveyard from afar. "Of course. You saved my people."

Grimclaw dipped his head in acknowledgement. *"That's true. But at what cost is still to be seen."*

"The sacrifice of your dragons will not be forgotten."

Grimclaw dipped his head. *"That is appreciated. It's because of that sentiment that I'm here, Your Majesty."*

Ouderling could only imagine how shocked she looked at the mention of the honorific. She doubted the infamous dragon felt subservient to any creature.

Exhausted and drained, both mentally and physically, all Ouderling wanted to do was find a place to curl up and be alone. "What did you want to talk about?"

"I've been doing a lot of thinking about that day you found Dragon Home."

Dragon Sect

"I'm glad you like the name I gave your new warrens."

"New to you, perhaps. We've been there for over a century."

Ouderling tried to smile, but it wouldn't come. "What about it?"

"I don't say this lightly, but perhaps I was wrong about our role in the world." He paused, as if what he had just imparted had taken a great deal of effort. Looking around, he lowered his voice, *"You mentioned forming a clandestine order of dragons and riders."*

Ouderling blinked several times, not sure she heard him correctly. "You mean my idea for a Dragon Sect?"

"Yes! That's the term you used."

"But I thought you hated the idea. You said I was no better than…" her voice lowered to one of disgust, "Orlythe."

Grimclaw cleared his throat as if embarrassed. *"I did, didn't I?"*

Ouderling crossed her arms and nodded.

"Well, again, I may have been a little hasty in my assessment. In all honesty, I didn't think you had what it takes to follow in your grandmother's footsteps."

Ouderling didn't respond. She stared him in the eye, waiting for him to continue.

"Okay. Make me say it. I was wrong," he growled. *"That being said, given what has transpired recently, I'm inclined to think that a discreet alliance with a certain number of elves may be beneficial to both our peoples."*

Ouderling fought to keep the incredulousness from her face. In the end, she didn't think she was successful. "I agree. We've got a lot of things to put in place, but with the help of Aelfwynne—"

Grimclaw's grunt of annoyance interrupted her thoughts.

Dragon Sect

"What? I agree the high wizard is a hard one to like, but his heart's in the right place. If we're to make this work, we have no choice but to include Highcliff. It only makes sense, seeing that Highcliff's the only place in South March that *has* dragons. Besides, he and a couple of others at Highcliff are working on something I think might prove beneficial to all if they can pull it off."

"Oh? And what would that be?"

Ouderling sighed. If only they had perfected it before her mother had died. "Let's just say, that if they get it to work, the Dragon Sect will be able to move between the kingdoms much quicker than dragons can fly at the moment."

"Interesting."

Grimclaw held her gaze for a long moment as a biting wind cut through Ouderling's clothing. He appeared to be on the verge of saying something more, but in the end, he ruffled his wings and stretched his neck.

"Well, I should be off. You'll be safe until we figure out a way to defeat your uncle and the foul creature he has aligned himself with. As long as you remain in Orphic Den, that is."

Ouderling chuckled, a mischievous glint in her blue eyes. She winked at Jyllana. "Like that's going to happen."

Jyllana rolled her eyes—the poor elf shivering uncontrollably.

Ouderling pulled her protector into a one-armed hug as they watched the blue dragon jump into the sky without so much as a good-bye.

"Do you think we'll ever see him again?" Jyllana asked as they walked toward the imposing wizard's keep.

Ouderling stopped. It took her a moment to catch sight of the wing of dragons high over the Wizard's Sleeve. She glanced back to where Dagomar, Dawnbreaker, Mirage,

Miragan, and Keaf huddled on the far edge of the graveyard, watching them.

She waved at the dragons and hugged Jyllana tight. "He wouldn't dare disappoint four dragons, a wyvern, and a fierce elf protector."

Jyllana laughed through chattering teeth, leaning her head against Ouderling's shoulder as they left the graveyard. "I'll say. He'd be crazy if he thinks he can hide from the Queen of the Elves."

Dragon Sect

We Must Believe in Ourselves

Their flight home seemed to take longer than Scale thought it should. Cutting eastward across the forestland of Nordicia, the land gave way to a vast swampland along its eastern border. From there they had turned south, following the Steel Mountains down the length of South March.

He had been tempted to invoke the summoning spell to expedite their progress, but Zorain had talked him out of it. Seeing they knew where they were, it didn't make sense to risk ending up somewhere unsavory.

Scale had acceded to the merit of Zorain's reservation. Going forward, it would be best to wait until they had a better handle on how to choose their destination.

With the sun rising over the snow-capped peaks on their left, Scale recognized where they were. A brooding castle sat on the north shore of an immense lake abutting a line of dark mountains. Just the sight of Castle Grim gave Scale the willies.

Zorain's casual flight turned westward toward the castle.

Alarmed, Scale sat up straighter. "What're you doing?"

"Going in for a closer look."

"Do you think that's wise?"

Zorain chuckled, *"Please. When has anyone equated wisdom with either one of us?"*

Scale couldn't argue with that.

"Besides. Last we heard, the duke was in Urdanya."

"What about his wizard?"

Zorain shrugged.

Scale felt the movement. "Just make sure you stay out of ballista range."

"Aw. You really do care."

"Let's just say I'd rather not have to swim back. Nor do I relish getting eaten by the cave dragon prowling about the Passage of Dolor."

"That's understandable. You're apt to give the creature indigestion and send it on a wild rampage. Try explaining that to Master Aelfwynne."

Scale smiled. He didn't know what he had done in life to deserve his fate, but he would be forever grateful for whatever had conspired to bring him and Zorain together. He couldn't imagine life without his best friend.

Gliding low across the Bascule Plains, staying far east of the black walls, Zorain concentrated on the castle.

"Sense anything?"

"Nothing. If the wizard remained behind, he isn't active."

"What about the duke?"

"I don't think I could sense him if I wanted to. I can only detect strong magic. And that's usually only when it's being employed."

"So, we've just risked exposure for nothing. There's bound to be many eyes on us."

"Who cares? They don't know what we're about. Let them spread rumours that aren't true."

Dragon Sect

Zorain flapped his wings and rose higher—the calm waters of Lake Grim slipping beneath them. The more altitude they gained, the colder it became.

Scale welcomed the strange comfort the bare hallways and chambers at Highcliff would bring. It would be good to be home.

His smile grew wider. Never in his wildest dreams would he have believed last year that he would consider a dragon colony overseen by a crotchety goblin wizard as home.

The familiar slopes of the Dark Mountains towered overhead. In typical Zorain fashion, they would barely crest the lowest peak on their way to Highcliff. The dragon's penchant for testing his flying abilities had always made Scale nervous, but there was nothing to be done about it. Aside from clipping the edge of the odd tor, his dragon's antics had never caused them harm.

The ominous, black door barring the entrance to the Passage of Dolor passed beneath them. Every time Scale had seen that door since the day the contingent from Borreraig Palace had perished, he couldn't help but shiver. If his father hadn't decided to punish him for his negligence in safeguarding Princess Ouderling, he wouldn't be alive today.

Zorain's rhythmic wingbeats faltered.

In tune with his dragon, he asked, "What is it?"

"There's a strong magical presence coming from somewhere over there."

Scale followed Zorain's westward gaze, his guard up. Slope after cliff after jagged tor were all he could see. Clenching his spear tighter, he asked, "The grotdraak?"

Zorain glided on the currents, wings angled to fly them along the steep edge of the mountainside. *"No. It's strange. It feels malign, but it doesn't strike me as evil."*

Dragon Sect

Scale swallowed. "That makes no sense."

"I know."

If Zorain feared whatever it was he searched for, Scale couldn't tell. His dragon's earlier words mocked him. *'When has anyone equated wisdom with either one of us?'*

"Um, I have a bad feeling about this."

"Me too," Zorain agreed, but instead of flying away from the perceived danger, he swooped in closer, his flight taking them toward the base of a cliff halfway up the mountain.

"Oh no."

Scale's eyes widened. He didn't have to ask what Zorain was talking about. Unable to believe his eyes, Kingstone's broken body lay sprawled across a sharp ridge.

"Master Aelfwynne?"

Scale was sure his heart skipped a beat. Practically unseating himself to get a better view, he asked, "Where?"

Zorain didn't answer. He dropped at a dizzying speed toward a rockfall at the base of a wide cliff.

Scale closed his eyes and hung on tight, not able to breathe.

At the last possible moment, Zorain back-flapped and reared close to the rock face, his talons crunching into the rocky ground.

The scene unfolded eerily before Scale's eyes. Zorain had landed next to Aelfwynne's Staff of Reckoning—its disfigured faces seemingly alive. That made sense. The staff's magic would have been what Zorain had detected. He wondered if the staff had summoned them.

He jumped free of Zorain. "Do you see him?"

Zorain stretched his neck. *"There!"*

Scale ran in the direction of Zorain's gaze, his disbelieving eyes focusing on the hunched, green body of the High Wizard of South March as he came into view.

Dragon Sect

Not sure whether Aelfwynne still lived, the sight of what lay beneath the goblin brought Scale up short.

Legs splayed at an unnatural angle, Scale knew at once who they belonged to. High Wizard Aelfwynne lay draped across the legendary warrior, Xantha.

Trying to fathom what had happened, gooseflesh rippled his skin. He scanned the immediate area for danger as Zorain crunched up behind him.

"Is he dead?"

Scale swallowed. He was afraid to check.

Taking slow, deliberate steps, he approached the motionless bodies. Looking back at Zorain, as if seeking permission, he waited for the dragon to nod before he put a hand on Aelfwynne's back. "Master Aelfwynne?"

At first nothing happened, but as Scale moved in for a closer look, Aelfwynne turned a beady glare on him.

"Leave me alone," the goblin snarled, his face a mess of grime, tears, spit, and snot.

Scale jumped back, hands in the air. "What happened?"

By the evil look he received, Scale feared the high wizard might incinerate him. Unable to help himself, he persisted, "Who did this?"

"The Dragon Witch Wraith," Zorain answered for Aelfwynne. *"I sense its stain."*

Scale pulled his dagger free. "Where is it?"

"Gone," Aelfwynne snarled.

Scale frowned and turned back to Aelfwynne who had sat up beside Xantha. "Did you kill it?"

Ignoring the question, Aelfwynne's grief-stricken gaze focused on Scale's blade. "What have I told you about that damned knife? You're a wizard, not a butcher."

Scale felt his cheeks redden. Putting the dagger away, he wasn't sure whether it was a blessing the snarly goblin lived or not.

He immediately admonished himself for thinking that. Not sure what to do, he recalled Kingstone's body higher up the mountain. Perhaps the dragon had been killed in the air and crash landed, throwing Xantha and Aelfwynne over the edge of the cliff. Whatever the case, the high wizard appeared frailer than ever before. Almost like he was about to die. "Come on. We need to get you off the mountain."

Aelfwynne's hard glare was accentuated by the venom in his voice. "I'm not leaving her."

"No Master, we wouldn't dream of leaving her by herself. Zorain will carry her," Scale said solemnly.

Against his better judgement, Scale stepped around Xantha and knelt by her side. He stared at her peaceful face—ruggedly beautiful even in death. Caring little for the tears streaking his dirty cheeks, he pulled a strand of her hair from in front of her eyes and tucked it behind her ear. In a soft voice, he said, "She was a lovely soul, Master Aelfwynne. The world will never see the likes of her again."

Aelfwynne glared at Scale's fingers stroking the side of his soulmate's head, but instead of slinging one of his nasty comments, his expression softened. "It's a good thing for our enemies that it won't."

Aelfwynne turned a loving gaze on Xantha and smiled—a rare sight during the best of times. "I'm going to miss you, Demon Rogue. You were the best thing to ever happen to this slovenly fool. Fly well, my pet. I'll see you soon."

Scale reached across Xantha's body and grasped one of the goblin's hands. He squeezed Aelfwynne's rough-skinned claws and stared him in the eyes with a compassionate smile.

Dragon Sect

Tears dripped off Aelfwynne's chin, but he didn't look away. Taking a deep breath, he nodded. It was time to go.

Scale assisted him to his feet. "Fear not, Master Aelfwynne. We shall avenge Xantha and everyone else the Grim Duke and the Dragon Witch Wraith have affected, you'll see."

Aelfwynne's gaze lingered on the love of his life. Lowering his head in acceptance, he stepped toward Zorain.

Scale placed a hand on his shoulder, ready to catch him if he stumbled. "Just like you said to me that day beneath the cathedral, we must believe in ourselves."

Aelfwynne stopped to look up at him.

"It's true, Master Aelfwynne. If we don't, our world is already lost."

The End

...is but the means to a new beginning.

I hope you enjoyed **Dragon Sect.**

If you would be kind enough to leave a review on Amazon, or wherever you purchased the book, it would be greatly appreciated. Thanking you in advance.

~ Richard ~

Coming late spring 2022

Windwalker, book 3 in the Highcliff Guardians

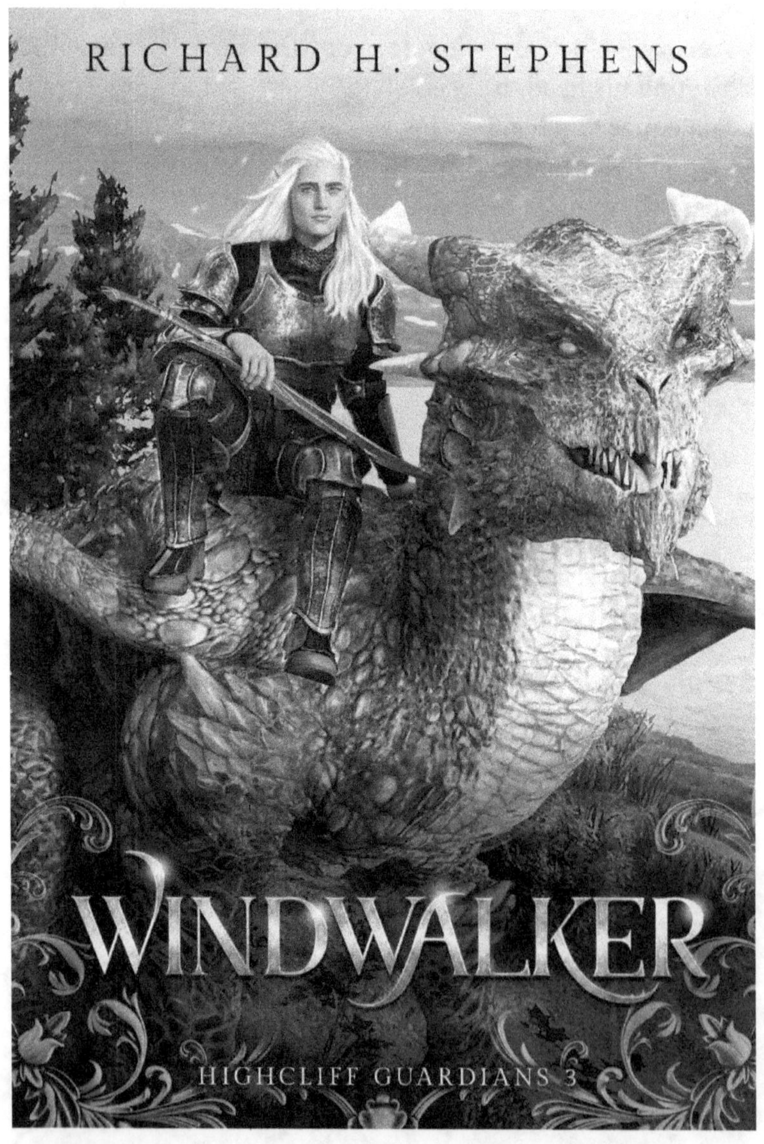

I offer personalized, signed, paperback copies,
complete with bling!

A discount is offered on the purchase of a trilogy.

If you wish to order, please contact me at
r i c h a r d h s t e p h e n s 1 @ g m a i l . c o m

(Don't forget the 'h' and '1' in the email address.)

To keep up with everything going on in the Soul
Forge Universe, please visit my website at:
richardhstephens.com

All books are written within the
Soul Forge Universe.

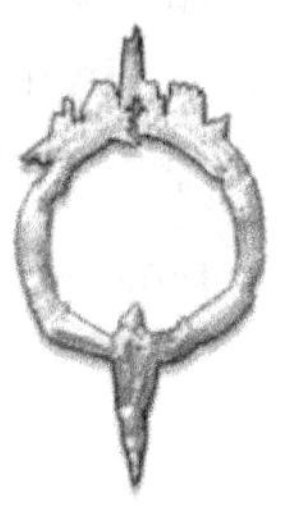

Books by Richard H. Stephens
in Chronological Reading Order

Highcliff Guardians

Keeper of the Jewel – Book 1

The Queen of the Elves is bothered by a disturbance in nature's essence. One she believes will lead to the death of her only living child.

Daring to visit the haunted tower on Grim Ward Island, Queen Khae's worst nightmare is revealed.

In a desperate attempt to save the heir to the Willow Throne, the princess is exiled to the only place capable of protecting her. Highcliff. The home of the coveted Crystal Cavern and the dragons that watch over it.

The Grim duke has other plans.

Dragon Sect – Book 2

The Dragon Witch Wraith has returned.

With the Grim Duke in his place, and a tentative pact with the wizard's guild, the Queen of the Elves' only real concern is for her rebellious daughter. Or so she is led to believe.

Buoyed by the news of unrest in the land's largest city of Urdanya, Duke Orlythe's new wizard attempts to convince him that a path to the coveted Willow Throne lies within reach of someone bold enough to seize the opportunity.

The return of the Dragon Witch Wraith prompts the ailing high wizard to find a way to thwart his arch nemesis before everything South March has fought for is lost.

Oblivious to the dangers of the world, Princess Ouderling sets out on a quest to locate an ancient dragon, in a desperate attempt to save her mother from an inevitable fate.

Should she fail, the Grim Duke will ascend the throne.

Coming in 2022

Windwalker – Book 3 in the Highcliff Guardians

When Legends Rise – Book 4 in the Highcliff Guardians

The appalling mannerisms of those entrusted to protect the kingdom are shocking.

Braving the perils of a cutthroat city isn't what Reecah envisioned when she sought out a better place. Can a ruthless giant equip her with the skills she needs to confront the king, or will his unorthodox ways end up being the death of her dreams?

Is an alliance with a murderous elf and a sly dwarf the best way to avert the plight of the dragons? And what is this *Gift* everyone seems to know about? Everyone, except Reecah.

Find out how the machinations of the evil prince and a traitorous wizard turn Reecah's quest on its head in this epic, second installment of the Legends of the Lurker.

Reecah's Legacy – Book 3

The culmination of the Legends of the Lurker trilogy.
Reecah Windwalker comes into her own as she finds peace with her past and bravely sets out to fulfill her legacy.

Keeping a promise to a dead witch, Reecah seeks those who can help her learn the ways of her dragon magic as she embarks on a desperate journey to save the last of the dragons from the dark heir.

The races come together, but their combined strength may not be enough to prevent the high king's dragon slayers from eradicating the beauty from the land.

Of Trolls and Evil Things

The (standalone) prequel to the Soul Forge Saga series!

Travel down an ever-darkening path where two orphans battle to survive a perilous mountainside, evading predators and prowlers that prey upon its slopes, and within its catacombs.

When danger forces them from their mountain home, they wander the cutthroat streets of Cliff Face in an effort to survive.

Strange circumstances spin their lives out of control, forcing them onto the nefarious slopes of Mt. Gloom to escape the unpleasant reality looming over them—only to discover their worst nightmare awaits them with open arms.

The Royal Tournament

(A standalone story from the Soul Forge Universe)

The Royal Tournament has at long last come to the village of Millsford.

For Javen Milford, a local farm boy, the news couldn't be better. Finally, Javen can perform his chores on the homestead and partake in the biggest military games in the Kingdom, hoping that just maybe, he might catch the eye of the king.

Javen enters the kingdom's flagship tournament only to discover that in order to win, one must be prepared to die.

The Banebridge Companion Novels

Larina – Book 1

Growing up on the streets of Storms End, Larina knows the only way to survive is to take matters into her own hands.

Skulking about the seedy alleyways and taverns of a great city fallen from grace, survival has become a game of steal and lie, or die.

Larina uses her ill-begotten abilities to help the vulnerable, less fortunate souls abandoned by life. An act that fills her with a sense of purpose and pride.

That all changes when the man with the black warhammer comes to town. Now the Storms End Lightning Bolt must decide whether those she has fought so hard to protect will be better off if she ends up dead.

Sadyra – Book 2

Living in the shadows to avoid the brutality of parents harbouring a dark secret, Sadyra must force a violent confrontation if she is to keep her younger sisters from harm's way.

Begrudgingly accepted to work alongside a hardened group of sailors, Sadyra learns how to survive in a ruthless world.

To save her sisters from a fate worse than death, Sadyra goes against everything she feels is right, and life as she knows it will never be the same.

Pollard – Book 3

Called together to prepare for the defense of the kingdom's most sacred resource, the son of Thoril Half-Hand sets out to train the realm's most promising fighters.

To keep the recruits performing as a cohesive unit, Pollard is unprepared to deal with the eclectic personalities of those entrusted to oversee the future defence of Zephyr.

A dark secret assails the band of warriors and their very existence is threatened by creatures they are sworn to protect.

Soul Forge Saga

Soul Forge – Book 1

Haunted by the murder of his family, a forgotten hero embarks upon a perilous quest fraught with demons both real and imagined.

Silurian Mintaka only wants another drink, but when the people of Zephyr need someone to save them from an evil sorcerer, he agrees to put aside his bitterness and wreak his revenge.

Deception, betrayal, and fantastic beasts stand in his way. With the fate of the kingdom in the hands of a homicidal lunatic, the only thing left to do is pray.

Wizard of the North – Book 2

What do you get when you disturb a 500-year-old spirit who is in charge of protecting an ancient magic? A death-defying flight to the heart of a serpent's nest.

If pulling a man through the flames wasn't enough, the highest wizard in the land detonates a thousand years of magical lore.

Not sure whether the king survived the firestorm, the people are left with little choice but to place their trust in a corrupt bishop.

A beast is unleashed and the kingdom's future lies in the hands of an eclectic band of companions who have lost their way.

Can an upstart mage, who isn't what they appear, stand against the evil sweeping the realm?

Into the Madness – Book 3

The epic conclusion of the Soul Forge Saga.

How do you survive a confrontation with a wyrm bent on destroying the world? Walk into its gaping maw and fight it from within.

A ragtag group of assassins set out to end the land's suffering only to discover death awaiting them with open arms.

A carefully hidden truth is revealed—the key to the kingdom's salvation if the Wizard of the North and her unstable companion can live long enough to unlock its secret.

Waylaid by an eccentric necromancer, and suffering a tragic loss that threatens to ruin their poorly laid plan, the companions stagger toward a fate no one ever envisioned.

An obsidian nightmare is summoned, and Zephyr will never be the same.

Born in Simcoe, Ontario, in 1965, I began writing circa 1974; a bored child looking for something to while away the long, summertime days. My penchant for reading The Hardy Boys led to an inspiration one sweltering summer afternoon when my best friend and I thought, 'We could write one of those.' And so, I did.

As my reading horizons broadened, so did my writing. Star Wars inspired a 600-page novel about outer space that caught the attention of a special teacher who encouraged me to keep writing.

A trip to a local bookstore saw the proprietor introduce me to Stephen R. Donaldson and Terry Brooks. My writing life was forever changed.

At 17, I left high school to join the working world to support my first son. For the next twenty-two years I worked as a shipper at a local bakery. At the age of 36, I went back to high school to complete my education. After graduating with honours at the age of thirty-nine, I became a member of our local Police Service, and worked for 12 years in the provincial court system.

In early 2017, I retired from the Police Service to pursue my love of writing full-time. With the help and support of my lovely wife Caroline and our five children, I have now realized my boyhood dream.

If you wish to keep up to date on new releases, promotions and giveaways, please subscribe to my newsletter by checking out the contact tab on my website.

richardhstephens.com

Facebook: **@richardhughstephens**
Twitter: **@RHStephens1**
Instagram: **@richard_h_stephens**
YouTube: **bit.ly/2NKpOhn**

 Born in Simcoe, Ontario, in 1965, I began writing circa 1974; a bored child looking for something to while away the long, summertime days. My penchant for reading The Hardy Boys led to an inspiration one sweltering summer afternoon when my best friend and I thought, 'We could write one of those.' And so, I did.

As my reading horizons broadened, so did my writing. Star Wars inspired a 600-page novel about outer space that caught the attention of a special teacher who encouraged me to keep writing.

A trip to a local bookstore saw the proprietor introduce me to Stephen R. Donaldson and Terry Brooks. My writing life was forever changed.

At 17, I left high school to join the working world to support my first son. For the next twenty-two years I worked as a shipper at a local bakery. At the age of 36, I went back to high school to complete my education. After graduating with honours at the age of thirty-nine, I became a member of our local Police Service, and worked for 12 years in the provincial court system.

In early 2017, I retired from the Police Service to pursue my love of writing full-time. With the help and support of my lovely wife Caroline and our five children, I have now realized my boyhood dream.

If you wish to keep up to date on new releases, promotions and giveaways, please subscribe to my newsletter by checking out the contact tab on my website.

richardhstephens.com

Facebook: @richardhughstephens
Twitter: @RHStephens1
Instagram: @richard_h_stephens
YouTube: bit.ly/2NKpOhn

www.ingramcontent.com/pod-product-compliance
Lightning Source LLC
Chambersburg PA
CBHW071955190726
48293CB00001B/39